Emma Guilia Sacatti
(And Family)

A Novel

By Charles (Buddy) Hurley

Copyright © 2025 Charles Hurley
Cover by Michael Hurley, Whittier, Calif.

All rights reserved. No part of this publication may be reproduced, distributed, or transmitted in any form or by any means, including photocopying, recording, or other electronic or mechanical methods, without the prior written consent of the publisher, except in the case of brief quotations embodied in critical reviews and specific other noncommercial uses permitted by copyright law. For permission requests, write to the publisher, addressed "Attention: Permissions Coordinator," at the address below.

ISBN: 9798312680942 (Paperback)

This book is purely a work of fiction. Any references to events, real people, or real places are used fictitiously. Names, characters, and locations are products of the author's imagination.

First edition, first print
May 11th, 2025
Emerson Publications
1350 Ave. of the Americas
New York, New York 10019

To my good friend,
Father Victor Ruvalcaba.
Rest in God's Peace!

"You're never alone when there's a book nearby," my mother used to say. "Never ever."

Other books by Charles (Buddy) Hurley:

KITE (A Love Not Given Only Lent)
Who'd Want to Kiss Her?
Eddie
Blaise (Bright Jewels and Watches on East Pattern Way)
Always You (The storied Life of Orville Garey)
Maisie
William Benson- Clocksmith (A Fairy Tale)

EMMA GUILIA SACATTI

(AND FAMILY)

Charles (Buddy) Hurley

Prologue

Emma's mind raced from deadly mind delirium to the reality of what sat before the world. A mystic blend of fever and God's revelation to the young teen. She could not separate the anxiety nor the horror found in her dream.

Every Sunday, the Sacatti family returned to their Craftsman home after attending mass at St. Cyprian's church. Built-in 1910, the Sears pre-fab house purchased through the company's catalog provided a comfortable and loving home for Emma, Mia, Dario, and their parents Eugenio and Palmira.

The Sacatti's neighborhood, founded in a rural section of Lakewood Village, never quite changed in fifty years. Private neighborhood homeowners preferred the rustic, country atmosphere over the crowded and condensed suburbs swallowing any remnant of Lakewood's bucolic history.

Across the unpaved street of the Sacatti's home, a community college exited. Originally a teachers' college in the late 1800's population grew until 1942 when the state authorized a more liberal campus focused on general education and medical instruction for much-needed nurses aiding the war effort and growing population of California.

Built on twenty-five donated acres, Richard Harvey envisioned professionalizing the teaching field for those individuals who chose to enter the classroom.

A series of a thousand Fremont cottonwoods, Coast live oak, and Laurel sumac surrounded the school's perimeter. During the summer of 1950, a cement based sidewalk was laid surrounding the entire campus. Village citizens, however, voted to keep the college campus continuto represent the beauty of the late nineteenth and early twentieth-century atmosphere.

With his remaining two hundred acres Harvey spurred a breathtaking village filled with one and two-story homes carefully constructed to last over a century. Small stores and markets dotted the neighborhood, providing the neighbors with a complete self-sustaining rustic environment. From banking to grocery essentials, the village thrived over the decades. The old stores still stood and prospered while village homeowners rejected outside burgeoning name-brand, 'BIG BOX' markets. Lakewood Village homeowners supported their mom-and-pop businesses instead.

In the private community village, owners continued to vote down so-called improvements. Paving their roadways with asphalt was out of the question, choosing to impact many of the streets with cobblestone or gorgeous rounded river rock.

Eugenio, through veteran financing, purchased his home during the aftermath of World War II for ten thousand dollars. His mortgage of 50.00 dollars per month, however, placed a crimp on the day-to-day family budget. Nevertheless, he welcomed the rural neighborhood while working outside of it in a typical pet food plant.

His wife worked for Dr. Howard Bishop, an eighty-two-year-old physician tied into the community since the early days of the village's existence. A medical secretary, she often assisted with nursing duties during emergencies.

The couple's children, respectable students at the local parochial school, brought well-earned smiles to their educators. The cost proved challenging, though, to the Sacatti family, cost, which could usurp the financial well-being of their lives.

Chapter One
May 1960

Blessed with her grandmother's thick Italian hair, Emma Guilia Sacatti brushed her silky locks one hundred times every evening and again every morning before she set off to school.

Only ten years old, most of the boys at school centered on her natural beauty. Only a few boys would admit how attractive they were to Emma's flawless skin, her perfect body structure, and, of course, the hair that drifted below her back.

Each year, it grew longer before her mother suggested Emma donate ten inches to a children's charity focusing on girls like Emma who told they needed chemotherapy, robbing many of them of their natural curls.

Emma did better than that; she told the hairdresser at her mother's beauty salon to cut her hair down to the length of most boys in her class. Alarmed, her mother, Palmira Sacatti, forbid reducing such thick natural hair to a 'boys' short length. "Remember your grandmother, Emma, your wonderful long tresses are from none other than her. No one else in our family has been blessed with such long curls and beauty as you."

"Momma, I don't care to be beautiful. I want people to like me because of who I am."

"I don't understand you, honey. You do well at school and are popular with all your friends and the teachers have told me since you first entered school that you are bright and contribute to all your classes."

"Mother, a few of the boys stare at me too much and one of them has already asked me to go steady with him."

"What are you talking about? You're only in fifth grade."

"Times have changed, Mom, but I agree with you; I'm only ten years old and don't need to have some boy treat me like a high schooler."

"I'll talk to your teacher. What's the boy's name."

"Don't do that, Mother; I can handle him myself."

"Honey, God has given you many gifts, one of which is your beauty. Please understand that as you grow up, there will be many boys who are attracted to you, and someday, you will select a wonderful man, one who will make you happy."

"I don't think I want to marry Mom. Sister Eberle talked to all of us about a vocation to religious life. Some of the boys laughed and were asked to stand in the hall. I pray that's where God will lead me."

"That's wonderful, sweetheart. Have you mentioned this to your father?"

"Yes, Momma, I did, and out of respect, I'll keep my hair long to honor Grandma Caterina."

"So only ten inches, Mrs. Sacatti?" asked the hairdresser.

"Yes, just ten."

Emma, now a sixth grader, couldn't understand her fifth-grade younger sister's obsession with boys. A complete turn-around since fourth grade, or so Emma thought.

"One of the boys told me my name is beautiful. Another boy standing next to him told me I was more beautiful no matter what he thought of my name. I think I like the boy who likes my name more, but do you think he thinks I'm pretty? I'm trying to figure out if I should ask him."

Emma knew answering longer than two words would keep her up all night, encouraging Mia to drone on about this boy and that. She answered with an emphatic, "No!" and told MIA to go to sleep or she would tell Mother.

"Go ahead, Emma, I don't care. I already asked her, and she left it up to me. I'm going to ask because he's cute and one of the smartest boys in the classroom. If he tells me 'yes,' he'll probably want to go steady."

Emma got up, grabbed two balls of cotton from the bathroom drawer, and tuned out Mia for the rest of the deep evening, not wanting to listen to her sister's buzz about the 'mysterious' Gregory.

On Tuesday morning, the girls, expected to rise no later than 7:30 a.m., found one of them, Emma, out of bed fifteen minutes early. By 7:45, the sixth grader was forced to drag her sister out of bed if needed.

Groggy, Mia opened her puffy eyes, her sister reminding her that she was not supposed to ask the 'mystery' boy whether he liked her sister or not.

"Oh, God! What time is it!"

"Enough time to throw on your uniform and brush your teeth. I wouldn't bother to try and get rid of the bulbous swelling under your eyelids. You must have not gotten enough sleep last night."

Emma could hear her sister scream through the restroom walls. She next found her mother storming through the hallway.

"What happened, Emma? Where's your sister?"

"She's in the restroom crying."

"Did you check on her!"

"No, I didn't. Why?"

"Oh dear God, what am I going to do with you girls?"

Palmira opened the bathroom door only to find her daughter, Mia, crying on the seat of the toilet, her hands covering her face. "What is it, sweetheart? Your mother is here." Mrs. Sacatti reached out and embraced her daughter.

"Momma, my face is deformed!" Tears poured down her cheeks while Mia revealed her face.

"Why honey, you look beautiful! God's angels always blessed your face. How many times have I told you that? You and Emma are two of the most beautiful girls at St. Cyprian's."

"No, I'm not, Mom; look under my eyes. I look like I'm thirty years old. I can't go to school today."

"You look perfectly fine, like an adorable fifth grader. Now get ready; you have five minutes and brush your teeth."

Mia did as she was told and later sat in the back of their 1956 Plymouth station wagon and brooded.

Mia's day went well, considering her puffy eyes that seemed to disappear as the morning moved to the early afternoon. At lunch, she shared with her girlfriends that Gregory wanted to know if she was okay; her eyes were puffy.

"Why, what happened, Mia," asked Cameron. Mia's third bestfriend.

"Tell her, Jennie!" Frustrated having to defer to her best friend Jennifer, Mia rolled her eyes.

"Cameron, Mia Sacatti, walked into school this morning, sad. Didn't you notice how her eyes drooped like an old woman? By the way, your eyes now look perfect, Mia. She wanted to go home, but her mother wanted her at school. Of all days, Mia was supposed to ask Gregory if he liked her."

"Oh my goodness, Mia, what did he say?"

"Mia's asking tomorrow. It's Hot Dog Day, and she hopes Gregory will be in a better mood. Anyway, bloated eyelids or not, Gregory sensed Mia was sad when not even the teacher noticed; he asked her if she felt okay."

"You mean your eye bags they look normal. Sister Eberle would never notice anything like that," said Cameron.

Mia fumed, "Eberle would have noticed if she knew my pristine sister was anywhere half as sad. Sister Eberle doesn't care about any girl interested in boys."

Cameron looked at the two girls and said, "You're probably right," and left the lunch table.

Looking to her left Mia felt she was forced to say, "What in the hell is wrong with Cameron? I'm moving her down on my best friend list."

On Thursday, May 15th, Mia cornered Gregory away from other students and asked him a question pertinent to the fifth grader. "Gregory, do you think I'm pretty? I mean, like the prettiest girl in the whole fifth grade, including Miss Davis's 5th grade classroom."

"I thought you knew that, Mia. Yes, I believe you're the prettiest girl in the entire 5th grade."

"Well, Mr. Gregory, I think you're the most handsome boy in the whole school. So does that mean...well, you know."

"I'm sorry, Mia. Do I know what?"

"Don't be ashamed, Gregory. It's something only the most mature 5th graders have done at our school for a long time, and my answer is yes."

"Whatever you want, Mia, it's fine with me."

"You've made me so happy, Gregory. Did you lose any sleep over this...oh you don't have to answer; you're a boy, and I know boys like girls to think you're as tough as nails. But we need to seal it with a kiss."

"A kiss?"

"You do want to kiss me, don't you?"

"We are alone, aren't we?"

Mia nodded. Gregory leaned in and pressed his lips against hers, the first 'real' kiss of his young delicate life.

Mia absorbed the kiss, noticing Gregory never hesitated. He even tilted his head like Mia was told to do in TEEN MAGAZINE she borrowed from her friend Cameron. Let's kiss tomorrow, Gregory, and every day at school right here. If you want, we could hold hands after the teachers go back to the convent or go home."

Gregory nodded and leaned in again, brushing another sensual kiss. This time, Mia timed it. *Five seconds is just enough time to wake the butterflies in our stomachs. Tomorrow, he'll bury his hand in my hair just like Rock Hudson with Doris Day.*

Intoxicated by Gregory's kiss, it exploded the absolute passion in Mia's heart. His lips soft, almost silken, pillowy against her own. Mia remembered clearly the soft tickle of Gregory's breath under the tip of her nose his fingers carding through her hair. He indeed was a pro, Rudolph Valentino dressed in salt and pepper slacks with a crisp white shirt buttoned to the top.

Mia floated for the rest of the day, keeping the two kisses a forbidden secret. *I tell, and the next thing it will get back to boy hating Eberle, and I'll be forced to confess it to pervert Father Gibson.*

Gregory found the idea of kissing a girl as pretty as Mia Sacatti exciting right up there with baseball cards and Little League. Although he wanted to, he had no time to hold hands after school football practice began at 3:30 p.m. sharp, and besides, he knew Mia walked home with Emma and her brother Dario at 4:15 p.m. after his sister's volleyball practice.

Although she was dying to get her secret out, Mia, unlike herself, held in her passionate episode with her newest boyfriend. Emma knew something was up but failed to pry, giving up on her sister's crazy obsession with boys. She hoped, instead, wishing Mia's antics would dissipate at least during her years at St. Cyprian.

And prayers didn't seem to work any for her sister. By the time Mia Sacatti would reach eighth grade Mother Killian would be forced to suspend the girl twice and place a set of boys on school probation. Mia appeared to resemble a tricky house fly moral leaders could not swat.

Eighth grade brought Emma close to her teacher, Sister Bridget. St. Cyprian's good sister did not, however, push vocations.

"My dear I understand thoughts have been put in your head to attend the pre-noviciate in Woodland Hills. I don't recommend it. Your calling may be real, but give yourself a chance to experience high school to rub elbows with new girlfriends and, more importantly, to experience a chance at love possibly dating a few boys.

"You're a beautiful girl, Emma; many of the high school young men will set their eyes on you, just like the boys do here. If you find a kind young man, you'll find yourself attracted to see how much he cares for you, too. You never know.

"Vocations are plentiful. Marriage, single or religious life are just a few. What counts the most is your dedication to your career, to make a difference while God has you walk this earth. You might change the world or at least have a profound effect on those you encounter. Being a nun may or may not satisfy your aspirations.

"Emma, I know many nuns who are not happy. Many of them, they felt, were paraded into the convent under cheering parents and parishioners. Many of these nuns never attended a typical high school, while those who did were encouraged into a life of empty prayers. I don't think they would know how to love a man, get married, and have children. Most of them, if they leave the convent, only seem to relate to girls similar to their former religious background."

"So you suggest I attend Saint Anthony or St. Pius X; they're coed, and both have a terrific sports program. I could try out for the volleyball and basketball teams and then attend the football games in the Fall. I understand boys and girls at St. Anthony meet after the games at a designated pizza place.

"As you said, I have a career to shape, and these schools are two of the top academic institutions in California. I won't let a boy get in the way of my studies. Who knows, though, maybe I'll connect with a real nerd."

"I don't think you'll ever falter, my dear. Whatever you do, put your whole heart into it, and don't rush. You're young, and you have plenty of time. Who knows, you might be our first female President of the United States. I know you visit the church often after lunchtime to pray on what we talked about."

Thursdays were, by amount spent, the boys' favorite day. Most of the children left their lunches at home and attended school with a quarter and nickel.

The women's club, Daughters of the Blessed Sacrament, sponsored a hot dog lunch with chili, corn nuts, Fritos, fudgecicles, and whatever they placed on the lunch counter. Some of the wealthier students brought as much as fifty cents and delved into whatever the menu offered, including occasional homemade cupcakes topped with loads of tasty icing.

Emma, Mia, and their little third-grade brother Dario brought to school thirty cents. A hot dog was fifteen cents, and with chili, it came to twenty cents. A bag of corn nuts or Fritos costs five cents, and white milk also costs a nickel. Each of Palmira's children bought what they pleased. Little Dario, noticing the older boys like to throw corn nuts at each other, picked them off the ground, washed the corn nuts off, and ate them. He never purchased the chili hot dog combo. A hot dog and a separate bowl of chili were more plentiful and the same price as a combo. He also bought a bag of Fritos, saving a nickel by navigating away from the cost of corn nuts and purchasing a pack of Topps baseball cards after school instead. Someday, if his stomach held up, Emma promised her brother he would make a good businessman when he refused to take his sister's nickel and purchase his own cards, at least on occasional Thursdays.

After lunch Emma slipped into the church, kneeling in the pew located in the rear of the church. This week, she found three of her eighth-grade students kneeling on the altar rail when, all at once, two girls and one boy let out a scream, running out of the side of the church.

Emma could hear the boy yell on the playground, "We saw the Virgin, we saw the Virgin!" It was reported the girls ran to the school office crying and wanting to call their mothers.

In the meantime, a thought trickled through Emma's head: *Why would the Virgin Mary appear to Patrick Caravan? He's never been anything but trouble. And those two girls, how many times did they ditch school?*

Hmmm? Maybe Mary appears to those less deserving of her divine presence.

Emma lifted from the kneeler and walked up to the space; before the rise to the altar, she noticed drops of wax on the carpet. Stepping up, she approached the wax drippings, ready to touch one of them when pastor Father Gibson walked through the sacristy.

"WHAT ARE YOU DOING GET OFF THE ALTAR, AND WHERE'S THE COVERING ON YOUR HEAD. GET OUT OF HERE!"

Sister Bridget arrived simultaneously. "You get this girl out now! She committed two serious sins." Gibson grabbed Emma by the arm and threw her toward Bridget, almost knocking down the elderly nun.

Sister Bridget rushed Emma, now in tears, to the privacy of her classroom.

"What happened, sweetheart?"

"Never mind what happened, Sister; Father Gibson can't do that! He's, he's out of his mind!"

"Probably, but he is our pastor. Did you see those kids?"

Emma, trying to calm down, reported she did. "They were kneeling at the altar, and an instant later started screaming."

"They all reported they saw the Virgin Mary. Did you see her?"

"No, Sister, I did not."

"It's probably nothing more than a crock of nonsense.

I noticed wax on the altar. Did you see the girls or Patrick with candles? No sister, I didn't see them rush out with any candles."

"We searched them and couldn't find any such thing."

Into the late afternoon and night 'pious' individuals, mostly mothers bored at home, poured into the church trying to collect what was left of the "miraculous" wax. Father Gibson conveniently set up a donation table inside a row of pews with a theft-convenient slot to place their money. He encouraged those who donated could approach the foot of the altar with his consent and place a fraction of the wax on a holy card of the Virgin Mary, also sold next to the donation box.

By Saturday, Bishop Joseph called St. Cyprian and encouraged Father Gibson to end the show.

On Monday, the school's custodian discovered three wax candles located in a trash canister located on the right side of the church.

Although cashing in on the delinquency of three eighth-grade students, Father Gibson was forced to suspend them and hear their confessions.

A few weeks later, Emma Sacatti graduated from a school filled with mixed teen emotions and the wisdom of Sister Mary Bridget.

Chapter Two

November, 1960

Kennedy, through the first televised speech in October, brushed past Nixon in the November election. "Sister Bridget, within her eighth-grade class, commented on the election, stating the positive attributes of both men. "First, you boys and girls need not criticize Father Gibson because he supported Nixon."

Ignatius 'Iggie' Fontaine threw up his hand. "Sister, he doesn't care about Nixon. He only voted for him because the big contributors to the church are Republicans."

"Iggie, Nixon is a Californian who grew up nearby and helped run his father's grocery store in Whittier. He attended Whittier's high school and college before graduating again from law school at Duke University in North Carolina. He's a good man married to a good wife and would have led our country well.

"Now Kennedy is young and vibrant, an excellent speaker and will lead our country for years to come, and as you know, is a good Catholic the first ever elected."

"Who did you vote for, Sister?" shouted half the classroom as Mia sat there bored out of her mind.

"Never any of you mind who I voted for; it's no one's business."

High school at Saint Anthony of Long Beach proved challenging. Emma worked toward honors in her newest subjects, including algebra and biology. World history also proved stimulating as her teacher required multiple projects besides what she found she had to study in her six-hundred-page detailed history book.

Since Emma played volleyball, she was exempt from Physical Education, only to replace that class with Home Economics.

Preparing meals and desserts in her household was a give. Since she was ten, Emma prepared dinner on occasion, alleviating the workload on her mother, Palmira who worked as a medical secretary five days a week. Her father, Eugenio, worked at Skippy Can Dog Food, making minimum wage, and together, Emma's parents put enough income to ink out a respectable but meager living.

She shined in her home economics class, preparing a few of her mother's favorite Italian dishes, placing a bright smile on her classmates and a wider smile on Mrs. Regina Holden, her instructor.

After school, with a four-year background in competitive volleyball, she was selected to the varsity team. Already an expert Emma managed to include a wicked curve to her serve. An expert at digging, she dug out almost every serve and spiked ball coming her way.

Emma's coach and Home Economics teacher, Mrs. Holden, watched the young freshmen time and again setting up a volleyball for an invariable attack by the taller players on her team. Because of her shorter stature, Emma found blocking a vicious spike hard to perform. At 5'6" tall, she did hold her own. By season's end, the girls found themselves extending into the 3rd round of the Division One C.I.F. championships before dropping to the powerhouse and eventual champion Hermosa Beach.

After school practice, she took the bus and arrived home no later than five, carrying every Thursday night an Italian dinner made at school and kept fresh in the classroom refrigerator. Mrs. Regina Holden was a dear teacher and never wasted an ounce of food.

On Friday nights, one would think Emma would find her way into the stands of her home football games. With nine games on the schedule and only four played at home, the freshman created the time to attend only one with her father, Eugenio.

Eugenio found he loved the game of American football and attended all four home games while Emma locked herself at her desk and prepared for Monday's classes.

Considering that the St. Anthony football team only managed a 4-6 record, Emma figured not much was lost, pretty much ignoring the season.

———

Sister Bridget gently asked Dario to wait outside her classroom after school while she discussed with Mia her responsibility to her brother.

Sister gave the boy a picture book to keep him occupied. She kept the door ajar to periodically check on Dario.

"Mia, you will not send your brother to the convent after school. The sisters refuse to run a babysitting service while you ignore your protective responsibility to Dario."

"Sister Bridget, I talked to Emma last night, and she agreed to pick up Dario after her basketball practice. As you are aware, she's quite the athlete and student..."

"MIA, STOP! What in the hell does Emma have to do with picking up Dario in the convent? Like I said we are not a babysitting service. Did you tell Emma we would be happy to watch over your brother?"

"As a matter of fact, I did. Caring for Dario can't be any harder than putting up with Father Gibson's nonsense."

"What are you talking about!"

"It's no secret Emma came home crying last year. She told me Father Gibson shoved her into you and that he almost knocked you down. Besides I see how Father bosses the teachers and especially Mother Killian. He shouldn't be a priest."

"You're very good at manipulating the conversation, Mia. You parade around this school as if you're nothing more than a buffed-up wooden nickel, Miss Sacatti. I'm going to warn you, dear, you fail to walk your brother home, and I will be forced to recommend to Mother Killian to have you suspended.

"One more thing before I let you go. What are you doing when you leave Dario on our doorstep?"

Mia began to chatter and screech like a chimp.

"Dear God, what are you doing, Mia!"

"I'm sorry. I thought we were making meaningless noises."

"Answer my question: what do you do when you leave Dario at the convent's doorstep?"

"I spend time at the city library. I like to read."

"What you like to do is spend time with Clifford Maury. Several of our students told me you're kissing him behind the bleacher seats on the football field."

"So why are you asking what I'm doing if you seem to know the answer."

"Never mind that! Clifford Maury is a troubled delinquent at our local public middle school. Mother Killian called Principal Russell Newman, and he warned us to keep that boy off our campus.

"He's trouble, Mia. I'm going to notify your parents to make sure you stay away from him. Do you understand!"

"I imagine I don't have a choice."

"Good! Now take your brother and head on home."

Picking up her books, she headed outside, took Dario's hand, and led him to the church. "Sister Bridget recommended you pray inside the church for an hour. Do you see the clock? It says 3:30; you are to pray until 4:30, then head to the convent. Emma is taking you home today."

"Where are you going, Mia? With that boy?"

"You're a confused snooper, Dario. I'm headed to the library to read."

"Why can't I go? I like reading more than praying."

"We shouldn't disobey Sister Bridget. Now I'm late, so I have to go."

―――――

You waited, Maury...we gotta move out of here. Evidently, Sister Bridget has got her spies out here watching us, those perverts."

"Boys or girls?"

"I'm sure they're girls. Sister Bridget can hate boys as much as Eberle."

"Hell, that's good news. Those spies, as you say, should all join us. When your lips wear out, I got another girl who can step in."

"Oh my god, you're a lousy delinquent, just like your principal said."

"You talking about Newman he hates girls. He's gotta be a genuine fagboy. And yeah, I'm his favorite villian, probably why he likes me."

"We gotta move, Cliff. I'm already in a world of trouble. The school is going to suspend me tomorrow, and I know I'll be forced to walk home."

"Both your parents work, don't they?"

"Yeah, both of them."

"So will have the whole house to ourselves, and I got protection with me now."

"In my house, no, no way, Clifford. Let's move outta here; I think I know a place."

Near an abandoned chicken ranch, Mia Sacatti lost her virginity in a foul-smelling abandoned chicken coup outside of old Lakewood Village where no spy for Bridget or Eberle would venture forth.

―――――――

Playing basketball for the legendary coach, Tanya Errion could make a dream come true for freshman Emma Guilia Sacatti if, for some miraculous dream, she could make the team.

Errion, winner of eight league titles in ten years and the recipient of a Division One C.I.F championship in 1957, 1958, and 1960, pursued excellence year after year. She never possessed any favorites; all of her players dedicated their entire season to each other, and never did a player appear mentally removed from a single game.

Arriving at Saint Anthony High School with four years of quality basketball and a love of the game, Emma, standing no taller than 5'6", knew being picked, whether a persistent bench warmer or not, as a guard held the hardest challenge.

Her elementary school coach, Bobbi Walker, insisted every player establish the toughest skills required on a varsity high school court; she was also friends with Tanya Errion. Dribbling confidently with both hands was an imperative first lesson. Next, landing the basketball through the legs at full stride came next. Players were requested to shoot the ball over their heads, developing a natural jump shot coming off an expected pace and stopping on a dime.

Practice sometimes went overtime when the coach asked the players to triple up at separate baskets. When each station player achieved twenty out of twenty-five made free throw shots, practice was over. If one player missed their individual goal, the entire team started over. Players were not allowed to ridicule each other, yet were required to practice at home all summer. By the Fall of Emma's seventh-grade year, she was invited to one of the strongest teams in the three-hundred and twenty massive C.Y.O. multiple leagues, and twice St. Cyprian's moved to the colossal championship game, overcoming dozens of equally talented teams.

She took the tryouts with confidence, pacing the court like Jordan later would in Chicago. *If I make it, I will thank God for all he provided for me, including a terrific and inspired elementary school coach who never gave up on us.*

Errion expected her latest freshmen to display her best moves on the court. She was a Bobbi Walker protégé who shared the same philosophy with Saints coach Tanya Errion.

Emma astounded the coach, never known for any kind of surprise; she expected the best basketball players to often gain peak performances by their junior year. This young lady was phenomenal. In practice, Emma could change speed and direction, throwing the best defensive player on the St. Anthony team on her talented rear end.

Her footwork was perfect as she stayed low. Hands active, she swiped up, keeping her shoulders lower than the girl she guarded. Whether playing zone or man-to-man, Emma was always ready to strike, turning a defense instantly into an offense by stealing the ball.

Emma demonstrated uncanny court vision reading defensive and detecting weakness among her opponents. One of the youngest girls ever to make a St. Anthony Varsity team, she quietly led and demurred to no one. The seniors admired her and were happy she was included on the varsity squad. Humble Emma personified the culture of a championship team.

Throughout the season, she juggled her games, often attending the varsity boys' play, too.

A starting guard, she noticed a few varsity boys attended a couple of her games. "It's always two games a year when their practice is dismissed so they can cheer for us," said Cindy Marquez, captain of the girls.

"You see that boy with curly blond hair? That's my boyfriend, Ryan Finch. He's 6'7" and can leap."

"Can he dunk? He's got long arms," wondered Emma out loud, beginning to take more than an interest in a few of the boys on campus.

"Sure he can; he's got the reach of almost a seven-footer. You've been to a couple of games. Haven't you seen him slam the ball in the hoop?"

"No, I haven't, at least not yet."

"Well, wait, you'll see him dunk against Mater Dei; they're one team that gives our boys trouble every year. You got to go!"

Tanya Errion looked over, "Quiet girls until the game ends, then you can chat your heads off." Saint Anthony's girls led in the fourth quarter 52-18, and Coach Errion decided to give her bench plenty of playing time.

Cindy leaned into Emma and whispered, "You see the boy sitting next to Ryan?"

Emma stared, then said in the lowest tone she could manage, "Two boys are sitting next to your boyfriend."

"The boy to our right!"

"What about him? He looks cute."

"That boy likes you."

"He does?"

"Yes, he told my boyfriend, you're smart and got more talent than him."

"Hmm, I know I've seen him before outside of basketball, and he sounds as if he might exaggerate."

Chapter Three
Bancroft Middle School, January, 1961

I hope a suspension helped you think, but my good sense tells me otherwise. I'm told I need to check your backpack, Mia. If you refuse, I'll call your father at Skippy's and have him go through it."

"Check it. What do I care?" Mia walked to her school desk and placed the backpack in Sister Bridget's hands. "Have fun!"

Without rummaging for more than fifteen seconds before Sister Bridget came across three condoms. "Plan on seeing Clifford Maury anytime soon?"

"What do you think?"

"We find out you're involved in sexual activity with that man, and we won't have any choice but to expel you. I'm confiscating your condoms, now seven of them, I see, more than a week's worth. Did he make you buy them?"

"Of course not. A girl can't be too careful, you know. Well, maybe you don't know that aspect of it, do you?"

"They're going to a wastebasket of my choosing, Mia. You won't have to worry about being too careful. I got you covered."

"Okay, whatever, may I go now?" asked Mia, ready to meet with Cliff in her newest 'secret' location.

"If it weren't for Emma and your brother, I'd give up on you. Don't do anything that will harm your future.

"I made arrangements with your mother; Emma will pick up your brother at 5:30 p.m. Your so-called generosity seems to have created a sitting service in our convent."

"Can I go? I need to work on my homework at the library."

Bridget threw up her hands, saying, "I'm praying somehow the Holy Spirit will enlighten you. You may go."

Mia sashayed from her classroom, practicing her moves for the boy while she crisscrossed a rural path. Clifford hid behind an old chicken coup.

Ten minutes later, she met him, embracing him and waiting to lay on her wintertime blanket removed from her home closet as typically Clifford wasted no time.

February 1961

Cravings appeared to obsess the eighth grader, adding fifteen pounds to her once-alluring frame. *Damn, where in the hell did Maury go! Two-timing prick! It's like he disappeared off the face of the earth. No, he would have told me if his family moved.*

Late that evening, she vomited in the toilet. *All this junk food. I got to stop. If Cliff saw me now, what would he* say, 'Mia, you look like a tub of shit,' and he would be right. I can't look like this.

The second time, she never made it to the girls' restroom at school. Mia vomited at her classroom's doorstep. Sister Bridget called for the custodian to clean up the mess while sending Mia to the nurse's office.

"Mia, you don't have a temperature. What's troubling you," asked St. Cyprian's nurse Pamela Slauson.

"Too much junk food. I'm eating it day and night. I gotta stop before I swell up. I already put on twenty pounds since the start of school."

"You need to cut down on the goodies and maybe start exercising a bit. Your sister was always an athlete…"

"Never mind about Emma, I know what to do."

Mia stormed out of the office and returned to the classroom.

After school, she walked passed the abandoned farm, always peaking to see if Clifford was there, and multiple amounts of times, she was disappointed again.

Why did he stop seeing me? We were intimate. He said he loved me, whatever that meant, and then he didn't show up for over two months.

Determined, she beelined toward Bancroft Junior High School. Approaching the school office, Mia concocted a story. "Hello, my name is Emma Sacatti from St. Anthony High School. I need to see Clifford Maury. My grandfather passed away, and they were close."

"Honey, I'm sorry you lost your grandfather, but sadly, Clifford doesn't attend Bancroft anymore."

"Did his family move?" *That might explain why he was missing from their favorite spot.*

"No, his family still lives on Ademoor Ave."

"He wasn't expelled, was he? We knew he could be a bad boy, and my grandfather seemed to be the only man who could try and get through to him, sort of calm the anger inside of Clifford."

"Again, I'm so sorry you lost your grandfather, but understand, honey, we're not allowed to share personal information. I could give you his parents' address, though."

"That would be a godsend, ma'am. Maury knowing about my grandfather would relieve my family. Grandpa asked how Maury was doing before he died."

Mia left, now finding out where the "son of a bitch" lived. *Where in the hell is Ademoor?* She thought.

Inside the middle school office, Suzanne Collins turned her head, thinking about the poor girl and addressing her assistant secretary, Trudy Fields, "I really hope her family finds peace."

"Yeah, I do, too," said Trudy. "Clifford was no better than a snake. Her grandpa had to have a world of patience."

I'll look at my father's Thomas Road Guide tonight. I'm going to find that damn moron this week, thought Mia.

———

Moving to her now claimed seat in Biology, Emma sat in seat number one, front row, and to her farthest left near the refreshing air of the open windows.

Teacher Monica McCarthy enjoyed calling on Emma from time to time. Today was no different. "Where do we get the majority of our oxygen?"

Hands shot up. Miss McCarthy instead called on honor sophomore student Lisa Mercedes. "Trees, Miss McCarthy. We're concerned about the destruction of forests in the Amazon. South America contains the largest forest in the world, and for the sake of economic growth, they're cutting down thousands of acres of precious woodland daily."

"Sounds like you did quite a bit of research, Lisa."

"Unlike most of the world, I'm concerned about our environment," replied the honor student.

"Let's hope more of the world joins you. So raise your hand if you agree with Lisa. Hands flew up row after row, except for the freshman Emma, who appeared to hesitate."

"You're not disagreeing, are you, Emma."

"Not entirely, Miss McCarthy. Lisa is entirely correct about our rainforest. Stripping the Amazon of its trees affects all of us. We might want to contact our political leaders to put pressure on a few of our South American countries, especially Brazil.

"To answer your question, though land trees aren't the biggest contributor of oxygen on earth, it's the ocean. But Lisa does have a valid point. However, oxygen also comes from marine plants and plant-like organisms such as phytoplankton. When it clumps together, it looks like green slime."

"Emma, you are correct; however, as Lisa said, our world is under a serious threat. If oxygen decreases, our earth will warm up enough to cause life-ending droughts, forest fires, and the decay of human and animal life.

"Class, I'm impressed by these two girls. Don't forget their information; it will be included in your next test. I'll see all of you tomorrow in the lab."

Emma rose from her desk, turned, and noticed the tall boy waiting in the back of the room.

"Hi Emma, my name is Ted Accenti. You sure come up with the right answers. I understand you're only a freshman; I always figured I attended a sophomore biology class."

"I can't disagree with you, Ted. I just looked at my schedule in September and found the school placed me in Miss Trujillo's science class."

"My captain on our team told me you're a genius, and we both agree that includes the basketball court."

"I saw you play twice, a sophomore guard on a man's basketball team and one of the best in C.I.F. I'm impressed."

"You too, Emma, a freshman varsity basketball player. Never happens here as good as we are.

"I'd like to ask you, do you have a boyfriend?"

"Who me? No, not at all. I'm too young."

"How old are you?"

"I'll be fifteen in two months."

"Fifteen, that's not too young. Could I ask you out, Emma?"

"No, not at all, Ted. Thank you, though."

She left out the classroom door, ready for her French course and eager to sit down with her teammates for lunch after class. Today was Thursday.

She borrowed Emma's bike letting her mom know the nurse said Mia needed to exercise. Palmira and her husband, Eugenio, noticed their daughter put on a noticeable amount of weight. "Diet and exercise are a good combination; Mia, stick with it," said Eugenio.

On Thursday morning, Mia hopped on her sister's Schwinn Varsity, wobbled a bit, gained her balance, and set off to school, cutting across a wooded path.

To Palmira's relief, she noticed Mia pulling into the bike racks at St. Cyprian's. "Your sister is beginning to take on some responsibility, Dario."

"Is God listening to my prayers, Mama? Emma told me I should pray for her."

"Yes, your sister is right. God always listens to our prayers."

After throwing Sister Bridget a few spiteful grins during the day, Mia loaded her backpack and feigned another day at the library which lately she made an actual habit of attending.

"Mia, hold on, I'll be brief," said her eighth-grade teacher. Miss Sacatti, you stepped up your studies since late November. You scored exceptionally high on the Iowa Test last month, one of the best in the class. I'm going to place you on the honor roll if you can maintain good behavior. Can you do that, especially for your parents?"

"Yeah, I could do that," said Mia. "Can I go? I rode my bike today to try and lose weight."

"Yes, and keep up the good work, Mia."

She approached the bike rack and took off in the opposite direction of the library four miles east on paved Del Amo Blvd. and left off the street after crossing Bellflower Blvd. "Where is Ademoor?"

She biked another block before giving up and turning left on Hardwick. "There it is! Ademoor doesn't extend through to Del Amo."

Mia made another quick left when she noticed Sharon Tilden, who recently exited a bus on Bellflower adjacent to Hardwick. A student also attending St. Cyprian's, Sharon, placed in Mother Killian's other eighth-grade classroom, was familiar with Sister Bridget's student.

"Hi Mia, nice to see you on my side of town. You got a new bike, I see."

"Sharon? You live around here?"

"Five homes up on the left. Don't ride your bike to the end of the street, Ademoor dead ends. We're always getting traffic up our street, and then they're forced to make a U-turn when they find the road ends.

"You live closer to St. Cyprian's than I do. What are you doing here?"

"Trying to lose weight. I'm extending my bike ride and had to deliver a message from my grandfather, who counseled Clifford Maury. Do you know what happened to him?" Mia slightly changed her story.

"I sure do! His dad sent Cliff to Indiana to live with his uncle."

"Why?"

"He got kicked out of Bancroft for decking his Shop teacher, but that was only a minor infraction compared to what else he did. Cliff got two girls pregnant. One of them is only twelve and lives a street up on Bellflower. The other girl was an eighth grader at Bancroft."

"That son of a bitch!"

"Your grandfather isn't going to like hearing this with all of his counseling going to waste."

"How pregnant are they?"

"That was over three months ago so they got to be at least showing.

"I found his uncle is mean and will use his fist if Maury doesn't straighten out."

"That's awful! His fist? I don't think I'll deliver the message. It might be better to tell my grandfather Clifford moved.

"It was nice seeing you, Sharon. I'll see you tomorrow at school. I better hurry along; it's getting late."

"Okay, Mia, see you tomorrow." Sharon waved and walked in the direction of her home.

Mia lifted on her sister's bike pedals but not before looking back at Cliff Maury's home, her heart broken.

My God, two girls are pregnant. If he weren't a minor, they would have thrown him away in jail. OH MY GOD! That was the time Sister Bridget took my condoms. That son of a bitch was filthy ripe and probably got me pregnant!

I need to stop at a pharmacy and buy a pregnancy test. I only got a dollar, though. I'll have to steal it, and I know just how I'll do it!

She parked her sister's bike against the wall of the pharmacy, walked in, found the boxed pregnancy test, threw it into her backpack, and quickly walked toward the greeting cards placed two aisles over. Walking up to the sales counter, she first grabbed two packs of nickel baseball cards and indicated to the cashier Mia looked forward to Dario's birthday.

"That's sweet honey. What school do you attend?"

"I'm an eighth grader at St. Cyprian's. My brother is a third grader and loves baseball. He's a starter on his little league team."

"St. Cyprian's is a wonderful school; my niece attends there.

"Sweetheart, is that someone near your bike?"

"WHAT!" Mia darted toward the exit while the cashier and pharmacist, Harriet Slauson, phoned the police.

"Get away from my bike, you bastard."

"What kind of language is that from a young girl? No way is this your bike."

An obvious thief, he mounted the bike, lifted off the seat, and started to pedal, but not before Mia flew into the air and tackled the crook, flying him off the bike. The two wrestled until the young man lifted and started to run, just as the police pulled up.

Dr. Slauson had tossed Mia's backpack behind the counter, protecting Mia's valuables. A pregnancy test box flew out of the girl's book bag, and she knew this poor child was in trouble. "God help this girl today and every day after," Dr. Slauson said to herself.

One of the officers continued to ask if Mia was okay and checked the bike for damage. "Nothing but a scratch officer on my knee, and thank goodness my sister's Schwinn is fine."

"Good to hear. We're going to write the thief up for theft and assault. He'll have to answer in court."

"Will I have to appear as a witness? I'm an honor student and don't want to miss school."

"No, you stay in school, dear; my partner and I saw enough when we pulled up."

Mia thanked both officers and slipped the finger to the thief in the back seat. When Mia turned around, she noticed Dr. Slauson standing under the threshold.

"I guess the policeman did his job, ma'am. I suppose we could finish our business."

"I suppose we could do that. How's your hand? It looks as if you might have lost control of your largest finger."

Chapter Four
Del Amo Pharmacy- Dr. Harriet Sloane

Wednesday evening, the night before, Eugenio Sacatti arrived home to two letters from separate schools. "St. Cyprian's and Saint Anthony said we're behind on tuition payments. Four months. Haven't you paid those schools, Palmira?"

"Eugenio, our two salaries combined can't make ends meet. Between the mortgage, utilities, gas, and food, we don't have what's left but a half-pocket full of pennies."

"How'd we pay them in the past?"

"I made an unwritten agreement with Mother Killian at St. Cyprian not to get too far behind, or the Pastor, Father Gibson, would catch wind of it."

"How about St. Anthony?"

"Emma said she'd work off the cost of tuition at school, but if she didn't pick up Dario, I'd be forced to give up an hour of pay. Emma's now, as of late, bringing home two dinners a week, Eugenio. It started off as one. She's worth more to us than a job at the high school."

"I'll talk to Father Gibson on Sunday. We'll work this out."

"Not with Father Gibson, you won't. Oh, sure, he'll treat you fine until he brushes you off with the nuns. He treats all men with a notion of respect, especially the big shots who pad the collection baskets. He plays golf with a few of those men every Tuesday."

"Who told you that?"

"Our daughters' teacher for the last two years, Sister Bridget."

Mia turned and saw Pharmacist Harriet Slauson standing under the doorway. "Mrs. Slauson, I hope you'll forgive me for what I just did."

"What did you do, honey?"

"Something vile against what my parents taught me. I gave that thief the finger, something I've seen a few of the boys do at school. I was crushed with anger and flew into a nasty web."

"You're forgiven, dear. Come back in and bring your bike along with you."

Mia walked her sister's Schwinn toward the sales counter, noticing her backpack was missing.

"Don't fret, sweetheart. I took it off the counter, suspecting that man may have wanted to rob us. Threw it right down here, and guess what popped out? This here testing box was lying on the pharmacy floor.

"Were you planning on paying for it? I might be able to help you, young lady, and cut you a deal. This pregnancy test is relatively new, and we were lucky to get a few. I could show you how to use it accurately so there's no mistake."

"You won't have me arrested, Mrs. Sloane?"

"You're in trouble, aren't you, dear?"

"Yes, ma'am, I think I am."

"Let me close the place for ten minutes. I'll take you to the restroom and show you how to use it. When you're done, come to the front and stand to the side, away from public eyes, and I'll help you read it."

Harriet placed a close sign out front, locked the doors, and escorted Mia to the restroom in the rear of the pharmacy. Reading the pregnancy test directions together, the young girl was told that she was going to test what was called the human chorionic gonadotropin (HCG) in her urine.

"Let me know when you're finished urinating. I need to get back to the counter." She reopened her store pharmacy.

Sure enough, an older woman had turned away before Slauson called her back in to fill a prescription. Within a few minutes, Harriet satisfied the order, turned back toward the register and saw Mia waiting patiently with a urine specimen in her hand.

Sweat beaded down the young girl's forehead; her hand shook as she handed the small jar to the Pharmacist. Harriet placed one of the two test strips into the jar.

After two long minutes Sloane asked Mia when was the last time she had her period.

"I don't really remember. I don't bleed heavy like some of the girls in my class, but I guess I haven't had a period in about three, maybe even four months."

"Are you under severe stress?"

"Well, kind of like trying to figure out if I'm pregnant or not."

"You gain some weight?"

"More than usual, I can't seem to quit eating junk food. That's why I'm bike riding and laying off the sweets."

"Keep up the exercise and stay away from food that's not good for you. Mia, I need to tell you there's a 99% chance you're pregnant.

"Do you know the father?"

"Yes, I do. Cliff is fifteen years old and was forced to move to Indiana to live with his uncle. Mrs. Sloane, he got two other girls pregnant."

"His uncle might be smart to get that kid fixed. Three separate girls...all of us are pregnant. It's criminal."

"He didn't rape you, did he?"

"No, he's too smooth. Captured other girls like me. We all threw away our decent values for a so-called secret rendezvous. In my case, a broken down old chicken ranch, lying on a blanket stolen from my home."

"Should I call your parents? It's getting dark."

"My sister's bike has a light for the evening. I'll make it home, and Mrs. Sloane, I promise to pay you back. Could you give me a week?"

"I'll do that. Let me charge you for the birthday and baseball cards. I see you have a dollar. That will be .63 cents. Your kit was $1.98, no tax. Save up."

Pressing the Schwinn bike generator against her sister's front tire, she waved to the saintly Del Amo pharmacist. Immediately, the lamp lit up, casting a path across the dark streets.

Arriving home just before her father, Eugenio pulled into the driveway, she was told her dad planned a family meeting tonight.

Said to round up her brother and sister, the four of the Sacattis waited on the front couch of the living room. Emma already had set the table, and Casio E Pepe, an Italian dish warmed in the oven, waited for Mama Sacatti to arrive home.

A football and basketball fan, Eugenio asked Emma how her basketball play was coming along.

"I lead the team in points; as of now, we're playing Bishop Conaty at home tomorrow after school, Papa. They're are toughest opponent so far this year, and we expect a big crowd."

"I wish I could watch you. I haven't ever seen you play. I'm so sorry, pumpkin, my work and…"

"Say no more, Papa. I understand, and I always think of you when I'm playing."

Putting up a basket on the garage roof in the backyard as a fifth-grade birthday gift paid off. Many of the taller boys in the neighborhood often visited, many basketball stars in middle and high school in the area. Emma found all the competition she needed to hone her skills.

Since the Sacatti garage was pushed far hack into the driveway, basketball play was safe. Besides the fresh cotton net hanging from the rim and the wide early nineteen hundreds lot it attracted the basketball players. At St. Cyprian's, the M.V.P. at every girls' basketball game was allowed to take home a net. Over the years at the elementary school, Emma took home twelve of them.

Mother pulled into the long grass driveway adorned with used brick in the center and was met at the door with

Dario providing his mother with a warm hug. "Mama, Daddy wants a family meeting. We were waiting."

Palmira brushed her son's hair, bent down, and kissed his cheek. "It won't be long, my big boy, when I'll have to stand on my toes to kiss you."

Walking over, she kissed her husband and placed a loving peck on Mia's and Emma's cheeks. When she sat down on the matching sofa chair, she leaned forward and addressed the kids. Eugenio sat back patiently, listening to his wife.

Since Emma was born and following the next two children, Palmira took over the discipline and finances of the Sacatti home. Where most of the children's friends sometimes told scary stories involving their father, the Sacatti kids found themselves blessed with a mild manner daddy dedicated to his family.

"Last night, your Papa and I discussed our finances. He received a letter from the two schools you kids are attending. I am behind four months on our payments to both St. Cyprian's and St. Anthony.

"Emma made arrangements to spend an hour after practice working at St. Anthony. She won't arrive home until I do. She starts tomorrow, so that means Mia, you're going to have to walk your little brother home. No more of your brother staying at the convent until Emma picks him up. If you want, you can take Dario to the library. I understand you must have spent many hours there as Sister Bridget shared with your sister your homework and especially your first-semester test scores picked up. I'm told your test scores are one of the highest in the entire school."

Dario added, "Sister told me, Mama, that Mia is the smartest girl in the school, and she's going to get an orange sir ti fa..."

"An orange honor certificate, Mother," said Emma.

"Is that true, Mia?" asked her father, proud of his daughter.

"If I keep up the work is what Sister Bridget told me."

Palmira followed with, "I realize concentrating in school was always a problem for you, and you needed that quiet privacy in the library, but honey, your father and I don't make enough to send all of you to a private school. Picking up Dario would certainly help and…"

Mia flew up a hand, stopping her mother, "I'll care for Dario, Mama, and take him to the library. I think I got better concentration."

"Thank God, Mia. That would mean a lot to your daddy and me. Your papa is going to talk to Father Gibson after Mass this Sunday and let him know we're trying."

Bishop Conaty's reputation as a dominant girl's team proved more than accurate. Their halftime score of 22-18 opened the eyes of Saint Anthony's reputation for the last five years.

Tanya Errion, her voice hoarse, trying to direct her team over the shouting from the sold-out crowd, enlightened her team with a halftime speech, "We're going to enter the second half loosened up. Forget about any so-called status Conaty's brought to our gym. I've watched those girls; they're playing way over their heads. You're a far superior team, the best Saints team to take the court in all my years.

"I want you all to believe what I'm saying, girls. Let this Conaty team know basketball has two halves. Let's take this one, Saints!"

Emma Sacatti scored five points in the second half yet initiated fourteen assists, feeding the ball to center Cindy Marquez and corner forward Kathleen Joseph. Both girls couldn't seem to miss as the Saint Anthony Saint's pulled away in the fourth quarter with 4:02 seconds left in the contest.

Tanya watched how the Conaty girls stumbled under pressure. Wildcat's 6'2" center hands appeared as ten thumbs as she stumbled through the second half, permitting Coach Errion to empty her entire bench, providing the crucial experience for next year's team. Emma, now standing in front of the team bench with Marquez and Joseph, looked up and applauded the final five seconds. Saints 52, Conaty 34.

Home by 6:10 p.m., Emma prepared dinner with her mother while Mia set the table. Mrs. Sacatti noticed how quiet her youngest daughter was acting and made it a point to talk to her privately after dinner in the front room.

After grace, Eugenio noticed his son's enormous appetite, "I hope we have enough for you, Dario. You're putting away enough food for a football player."

"I'm really hungry, Papa; I read my eyeballs out in the library." That created a boisterous laugh from Dario's father, along with Palmira and Emma. Mia broke a small smile. Emma looked over a noticed her sister was deeply troubled.

Emma cleared the table, carrying the dirty plates to the sink. Afterward, she started washing the plates, utensils, and casserole dishes. She asked Dario to finish the leftovers, which he happily consented to.

Wanting to join her mother in the front room, Emma honored her mother's request for privacy. Even her father remained at the dinner table, lighting up a smoke while talking to his son.

Palmira sat down with her daughter and asked if Dario bothered her at the library.

"No, mother, he was a saint. I took him to the young children's section, and he found a few of the books that might interest him. He pulled out a few of the 'Betsy' books and settled on two of them, then grabbed a CAM JANSEN- The Mystery of the Babe Ruth Baseball. I don't know if the words Baseball, Babe Ruth, or Mystery captured his interest. He checked out two books because he finished one of the Betsy books sitting next to me in the library."

"That's good to hear, so tell me, sweetheart, what's on your mind. You sound like Dario wasn't any trouble."

"I'll be fine, Mother. I think my hormones are overcharged; that's what Sister Bridget tells the class all the time."

Palmira leaned into her daughter, kissing Mia's forehead. "Relax for a few minutes with your brother and father and send in Emma. Do that for me, Dear."

Emma walked into the front room as her mother padded the sofa seat next to her. "Sweetheart, something is troubling your sister. Try and find out before you go to sleep tonight. She always has worried me, now even lately, when she seems to be doing well."

"I'll talk to her, Mother, don't you worry."

"Send the family in; we'll all watch television together, tonight's Candid Camera, and when it gets late, we'll put Dario to sleep and watch Gunsmoke."

Laughter filled the living room as Fanny Flagg teamed up to fool a hapless messenger sent to pick up mail when he found himself face to face with a bearded female secretary. Out of the corner of her eye, Palmira found Mia joining in with her family on the hilarity of Allen Funk's clever comedy.

Mia excused herself before 9:00 p.m., claiming she found herself exhausted. Emma followed her sister fifteen minutes later. "Today's game took out a lot in me, Mama, and Papa." She kissed both their cheeks and trailed her sister to her bedroom.

Emma found her sister sobbing on her pillow. "Mama told me something was troubling you, Mia, so I need to ask you what is it. If you don't want our parents to know, tell me, and I'll keep it to myself."

Mia's sobs turned into uninterrupted wailing not heard in the front room. Dario, however, found himself checking in on his sister. "Are you alright, Mia? Mommy thinks you're sad."

"I`m not really sad. I don't have any money for your birthday on Tuesday."

"That's okay, Mia, you don't have to buy me a present."

"Come here and give me a hug, little brother; you're perfect!"

Dario left the room beaming. Tonight, he would dream of playing baseball with the 'Babe.' He finished the book before he fell asleep.

Mia looked over at her sister. *When was the last time I told her I loved her? Maybe when I stopped loving myself.* "Emma, I got something to tell you."

"What is it, Mia? I'm listening."

"Emma...I always loved you. I hope in the future, I can turn it around."

"I've always loved you too, Mia. We're sisters bonded together forever. No matter what you did or will ever do, nothing will stop me from loving you."

Mia started to cry and told her sister, "You never raised your voice; you helped lower my obsessive temperature. And, Emma, you never held a grudge against me; instead, you were the one to unlock my potential. As good as you are in school and sports, not once did you show off. You just showed up."

"I don't think Mia, I deserve all those wor..."

"Emma, I'm pregnant!" Tears flooded her soaked pillow.

Emma crawled out of bed and hugged her sister. Not a word was shed until morning.

Gunsmoke

Chapter Five
God Knows

"She's fine. Mother, Dario will tell you why she was upset," Emma told her mother while preparing breakfast.

"Dario, come here, sweetheart. What did your sister tell you," asked Mrs. Sacatti.

"She was sad because she didn't have any money to buy me my birthday present in three days."

"What got into that girl? Do I need to talk to Sister Bridget, Emma?"

"No, Mom, not at all. Its what Sister used to tell the eighth grade our hormones are crawling out of our ears."

Palmira smiled, "That's exactly what your sister told me."

After breakfast and the girls' house chores, Emma asked if Mia could pace her on the Schwinn. "I plan on a five-mile road run, Mom. I got a little too winded in yesterday's game. Don't worry; I'll take it slow."

"Just be careful and watch the cars."

"We will. Mia suggested it, wanting to lose a couple of pounds herself."

Before either of the girls showered that morning, Emma was told of the pregnancy test at the pharmacy. She let her sister know she had five dollars and would even the account.

"She didn't actually give it to me on credit. Mrs. Sloane caught me stealing that pregnancy kit but showed me kindness and remorse."

"Are you talking about Dr. Harriet Sloane?"

"She's a doctor! No wonder she knew what she was doing."

"No, not truly a medical doctor. Dr. Sloane actually received a PhD in Pharmacy. They give them what's called a

PharmD. She'll tell you she's a pharmacist, so customers won't think she's an actual M.D.

"In any case, she's a wonderful woman. And Mia, don't pay me back. I found that $5.00 tucked in a bus seat, so we'll get you all paid up."

Finally reaching Del Amo Blvd. Emma suggested Mia ride her bike on the parkway. "Cars don't drive as fast, and there's not as many. I can run on the grass strip. It'll go easier on my legs."

"I appreciate you are helping me, Emma, but I'll find a way to pay you back."

"I believe that $5.00 was a gift from above. What I thought about last night was how to tell Mom and Dad about your condition."

"You'll come up with the best idea. I trust you," said Mia as she pedaled toward the pharmacy.

"When Mom and Dad talk with Father Gibson, you and I will visit Sister Bridget in the Church Hall. She sells religious artifacts with Mrs. Holmes and attracts the parishioners to buy donuts, milk, and coffee."

"Do you think Bridget will help me?"

"It's what God called her for, Mia. She'll be our peaceful bridge."

Mia found out Emma had a lock and key and used it to secure the Schwinn in the store's small bike rack. Walking into a busy Pharmacy, the sisters waited until they could get the Pharmacist's attention.

"Emma and Mia, I'm so happy to see you both," said Doctor Sloane.

"I'm sorry, Dr. Sloane, I addressed you as Mrs. Sloane. Emma told me how hard you must have worked toward your doctorate."

"Mia, I am married, so Mrs. was appropriate. You can call me Mrs. or Doctor any time, although, in the pharmacy, we prefer Pharmacist. Some people might confuse me with a medical doctor, so the word pharmacist has always helped."

"Dr. Sloane, Mia is here to satisfy her bill for the pregnancy kit. What was the total?"

"I recall it came to $1.98. How are you feeling, Mia?"

"Right now, I'm fine, Doctor Sloane. We haven't told my parents yet."

"Do you need some help? I know your mother, Palmira; she fills your father's prescriptions here. I could talk to her if you want and your father too, that's fine. Whatever you decide, Mia, you need to get in and see a doctor. Let me know your decision. Your pregnancy is important to your health and the health of your child."

Mia looked over at her sister, and she let Emma make the decision. "Mia, Dr. Sloane, as Sister Bridget, is blessed with a similar vocation, helping people."

Dr. Sloane, away from filling a prescription, was far enough away not to overhear Emma's words.

"I trust her professional approach; if we need to talk to Sister Bridget on Sunday, we can always do that."

Ten minutes later, the store died down to two customers shopping for odds and ends. "Dr. Sloane, when can you meet with my parents?"

"Tonight after I close at 5:00 p.m. We're closed on Sunday, and we both have Mass and family, so try and get your parents down here. We'll meet in the back. Mia, you have got to meet with a doctor as soon as possible.

"Tell your parents I'm having a problem with Eugenio's prescription, which is half-true. Tell them I need to see them right away and that I'm waiting in the store."

Mia sobbed, overwhelmed by her horrible secret. "I'd rather die, Dr. Sloane. My parents will be crushed. I've disappointed everyone, and I'll never recover."

Dr. Sloane, like a dear mother, enfolded the twelve-year-old in her arms.

"You recover, dear. Pray that soon you will turn your sorrow into God's joy, that one day you'll dance as if no one is watching. And like your sister Emma, you'll love again and never be hurt; you'll sing even when nobody is listening. Live honey like it's heaven on earth, and never give up on hope."

Dr. Sloane kissed the child on the forehead and sent the sisters on their way.

Emma picked up her pace on the way home, pushing Mia on her bike when she needed to. "Let me talk to Mom about the prescription. I often come with her to the pharmacy to pick up his medication."

Out of breath, even with the occasional shove of the back of the Schwinn, Mia managed to say, "God...God bless you, Emma."

Eugenio and his son were working prepping the porch rails for painting when the girls rounded the corner. Dario, now allowed to use the paintbrush, worked his way along the perimeter base of the lower rails, looked up, and waved at his sisters.

His father finished applying a white primer with his son and took the hedge clippers, clearing the jacarandas away from the base of the porch. He stopped and watched the perspiration soaking through his daughters' tee shirts. "Looks like you two had a good workout."

Wiping their brows, the two sisters couldn't disagree with their father. "I need to lie down, Emma. I'm exhausted."

"You pushed hard today, Mia. I'll talk to Mother while you're napping." Mia parked the Schwinn in the old garage, walked through the back door, and immediately retreated to her shared bedroom.

On this clear early afternoon, Eugenio asked his son to take a break. Both of them admired nature's majestic wonder in the faraway snowy mountains. "They look close enough to touch Dario."

"Could we go up there someday, Papa?"

"Sounds like a good idea. I'll talk to your mother."

Emma convinced her mother, Dr. Sloane, needed to see her and her father, Eugenio, personally. "Some minor issue, Mother. She wants to see Daddy, too. Could we go along? Mia and I want to look at the school supplies. Mia must get the right notebook. She's edging in on honors."

"Well, who'll take care of Dario? Can't one of you stay behind?"

"I need to show where Mia can find the correct stack. They all look alike."

"I don't understand, but okay. Are you sure Dr. Sloane wants to see your daddy?"

"She looked pretty adamant."

"Maybe I can stay here and watch over Dario."

"Mother, you know how Papa is forgetting his medication. You better go."

"Alright, this is so unusual. Where's your sister anyway?"

"She felt tired and had to lay down. I think I forced her to pedal too hard."

"What! You're the one that ran five miles; your sister was on a bike. That girl needs to exercise more."

All five Sacatti's piled into their mother's '56 Plymouth at 4:55 p.m. Shadows found their way up and down the streets, choking out the sunlight as each second passed.

When Eugenio pulled into the pharmacy parking lot, thousands of stars appeared in the winter sky. On a brisk evening, Palmira told her children to button up their jackets. "No colds in this family."

Dr. Sloane met the family at the pharmacy door.

While Dario and Emma browsed the store shelves Mia was invited to the pharmacy backroom with her parents. "Mr. Sacatti, for years after your mild heart attack, you've been ingesting Beta-Blockers for three years now. The dose is high. How have you felt during that time."

"Fine, I imagine."

"I recommend you see your doctor and check if such a high dose is necessary. If, after three years, you feel fine, your doctor may recommend cutting the dose in half. It's cheaper and most likely safer."

"Thank you, Dr. Sloane. I'll set up an appointment for my husband," said Palmira.

"My second comment is vital for you to hear. I recommend both of you exercise compassion. As a pharmacist, I've seen many girls experience this problem. Those girls from loving families suffer the least and go on to successful lives."

"Is anything wrong, Dr. Sloane? My husband and I are more than willing to help."

"I'm happy to hear that Palmira. I have always known you and your husband to be both patient and compassionate. Mr. and Mrs. Sacatti, your daughter Mia is pregnant."

Anticipating the reaction of the parents and daughter, Harriet Sloane had secured a box of tissues within reach. She took hold of the Kleenex and handed the tissues to Palmira while pulling a few more and giving them to Mia.

Eugenio, taken aback, was the first to speak. "You're pregnant, Mia. How do you know?"

"I gave your daughter a pregnancy test. She came to me alone and alarmed. There's a 99% chance she's with child."

Palmira leaned to her right, choking on her tears, and hugged Mia. "My little darling, I love you. Mama and Papa are here for you."

Tears crowded the floor of the pharmacy back room as mother and daughter wept. Eugenio got up and joined his wife. *Unconditional love. It's what Sister Bridget talked about in September. Why couldn't I see it? Why was I so blind?*

"Oh, Mama, Papa, I'm so sorry I hurt you!"

Eugenio leaned in and gently asked his daughter, "Do you know who the father is, Mia?"

"I do daddy. I'm the 3rd girl he got pregnant. His school expelled him, and I found out his father sent him to his uncle, a disciplinarian, in Indiana."

Eugenio asked, " What's his name?"

Emma stood near the entrance of the supply room, leaving her brother safely tucked away, looking at the packs of leftover baseball cards on the counter, "His name is Clifford, Papa, Clifford Maury." Mia nodded her head in agreement. "He's hurt too many young girls."

"Do you want me to talk to his father, Mia?" Eugenio's anger was beginning to build.

"No, please, Papa, I don't want them to know," cried Mia.

"She's right, Momma and Daddy. Save all of us the heartache. Only you two deserve to be the baby's grandparents," pleaded Emma, entering the back room.

Dr. Sloane spoke softly, "Her care is of the utmost importance. Take her with you to a physician. What your daughter has told me is that she's over four months pregnant. Mia should start showing within a few weeks."

"St. Cyprian's will never allow her to stay if they see that our Mia is with child."

"No, they won't, and neither will a typical public school. If Mia wants to continue to pursue her education, send her to St. Agnes. It's a large convent dedicated to assisting unwed mothers, and there's no cost. They're outstanding educators, nurses, and counselors. Your daughter will be in good hands."

"My husband and I want to thank you for helping Mia in her crisis. God bless you, Dr. Sloane," said Palmira, wiping the tears from her eyes and adding, "Will get my daughter to a doctor right away and Eugenio, too. I'll also let you know what we decide about giving Mia a chance to board at St. Agnes. We'll look into it."

"All of you know I'm always here. I'll keep you in my prayers, Mia, and wish you the best, sweetheart."

On their way out of the back storage room, Emma slipped her sister a quarter and asked her to buy a few packs of baseball cards for Dario. "His birthday is this Tuesday."

Mia didn't want to tell her sister she had already purchased two previous packs. "Dario, step up to the counter and pick out five packs of baseball cards."

"REALLY!" he said. Never was Dario ever able to purchase more than two packs of Topps cards.

"Don't be shy; go ahead and pick out what you want," Emma said, still consoling her mother and sister.

Dario had already practiced fumbling around through the box while his family talked in the back. He immediately pulled out five packs from the bottom of the Topps box and handed his quarter to Dr. Sloane. "Well, thank you, young man. Who do you hope to find?"

"My teacher told me to say a prayer every night that someday I'll find a Sandy Koufax card."

"Any luck so far?" asked the pharmacist.

"Not one yet, and I got over two hundred cards."

"I'll tell you a secret. You might want to remind your son of this, Mr. Sacatti. Topps sends out cards in six series. One before the season begins in April, number two in May, three in June, and four in August. Next, they send out series number five in September at the end of the season and number six in October when the regular season ends. This is when Topps includes quite some of the superstars like Sandy Koufax. They call series six the high number cards and that's where you might find someone like Koufax if you never found him during the baseball season.

"Most of the kids, Mr. Sacatti and the little fella, quit collecting baseball cards in September when school and football start. That's why I still have a few boxes of baseball cards left. Think about what I said for next season."

"Sounds like you sure know your baseball cards, Dr. Sloane," said Mrs. Sacatti, beginning to recover.

"My nephew is a baseball card collector. He filled me in on the secret."

"Well, again, we'd like to thank you, and Dario will make a smarter collector next year, won't you, Son."

"I sure will! Thank you, ma'am."

"You're welcome, young man. Hope to see you again," Dr. Sloane said, smiling at the entire Sacatti family as they left.

Quiet appeared to swell in the 1956 yellow Plymouth station wagon until Dario broke the silence. "Mama, can I open up the baseball cards?"

"Maybe just one pack; save the rest for your birthday on Tuesday night."

"Could I chew the gum inside?"

"No, Dario, it's too late. Put it away in the wrapper, and you can have it perhaps tomorrow after lunch.

Dario opened the Topps pack, placed the gum in the wrapper, and then placed it in his filthy jeans pocket layered with grass stains and ground-in dirt on the knees.

At home, Palmira turned toward Dario and told him to hand over the four packs of baseball cards until Tuesday. "That way, you won't be tempted to open them before your birthday." Her son handed her the packs without a complaint. "Dario! Would you look at yourself? What did you do, crawl through the mud today? Hand me those jeans, and I'll throw them in the wash."

Stripping down to his underwear, he handed the filthy denim jeans to his mother, and she tossed them into the wash, the gum still tucked into his front pocket. "Now, take a bath and get ready for bed."

Mia and Emma, having showered before they attended the pharmacy, were happy to go to bed early. Emma's pregnant sister appeared relieved. *Round one,* she thought.

"Emma, are we going to talk to Sister Bridget tomorrow?"

"I think it would be a good idea. What do you think?"

"I think so. Sister might be able to tell us more about St. Agnes. Emma, going there scares me, though."

"Sister Bridget will give us the pros and cons. If there is anything that's negative, it's probably what you just said: girls arrive there scared."

"Dr. Sloane said they don't charge. That will make it easier on Mom and Dad, but how will Dario get home?"

"Will talk to Sister Bridget about that."

"Maybe talking to her will amount to too much stress on her. Maybe I could stay there for a couple more weeks and walk my brother to the library and then home. That would be long enough for her to consider me for honors, and it would make Mama and Papa happy. It's the least I could do after my horrible behavior."

Chapter Six

His voice was like a quiet melody.

Each of the sisters prayed hard that night, asking Our Lord to intervene tomorrow. Within a few minutes, a shadow drifted over the girls, sending Mia and Emma into a deep, restful sleep. Without their knowledge, they encountered the same dream, and each of them smiled.

Sunday morning, the Sacatti family, as they did every week, dressed in their finest to help celebrate the holy sacrifice of the Mass walked to church less than a mile away from home.. Celebrant Father Gibson sailed through the Mass in record time, looking forward to the delicious morning spread greeting his hungry stomach on the rectory dining table. Sunday morning brunch always included prime rib with accompanying horseradish.

Walking out of the sacristy, Father Gibson ran into Mr. and Mrs. Sacatti. "Father, could I have a moment of your time?"

"What is it? I need to be heading to the rectory as soon as possible. The bishop is expected to call me on the phone."

"I'll let you know right away, Father. My wife received

an invoice from the rectory stating we're four months behind on my children's tuition. My wife included an extra hour in her work day, and we promise to pay back every penny by June plus our monthly cost."

"You'll have to discuss that with the good sisters; they handle all of the business collecting tuition."

"Yes, Father, we're sorry we took up your time." Eugenio turned and headed toward the parish hall, expecting his wife to follow him. She held back as her daughters and Dario approached their mother after chatting briefly with their school friends and the girls' eighth-grade teacher.

"Wait for a second, Father; that invoice came from your rectory, specifically from your personal accountant. The nuns don't handle the tuition; you do, and you, Father, threatened to dismiss my children from the school if we didn't come up with the money."

"Listen, Mrs. Sacatti, a woman who drops an envelope of fifty cents into the collection basket every week has no business questioning what I do or don't do. If every parishioner were as cheap as you, we'd have to shut down. Your pittance of a donation doesn't even cover the communion wafers, so be off and quit annoying me."

He turned and took two steps toward the rectory when Emma's voice reversed his walk. "You have no right to talk to my mother that way. What is wrong with you!"

"Oh! So it's you, Emma, little miss heretic, trudging up on the altar and without anything covering your hair. I don't recall you ever had the decency to confess your sin, and still, you insist on parading your indecency, nudging your way to the altar rail."

"I'm a sinner! You grabbed my arm and threw me into Sister Bridget, almost knocking her down. You have no sense of humility, no sense of decency."

"Find another parish! All of you!" Father Gibson threw up his hand and marched toward the rectory; his appetite was lost in the commotion.

What in the hell is wrong with them? I'm calling Mother Killian and telling her to throw them out of school.

Emma and Mia skipped talking further to Sister Bridget, encouraging their mother and father to go home instead.

Once at home, Emma shared with her mother that the sisters planned to wait a few weeks before pulling Mia away from St. Cyprian's and into the single mother's convent of St. Agnes. They hoped Palmira would agree.

"Honey, it sounds as if our pastor might have the nuns order us out. We may have to reenroll Mia and Dario in a public school."

"Mother, I know Sister Bridget would fight the dismissal of my brother and sister tooth and nail. She'd take it to Bishop Jerome if she needed to. I think if worse came to worse, she wouldn't mine being forced to transfer. Although perfectly patient and humble, she'll stick to what is morally right."

"You're probably correct, but would you want the children to lose such a beautiful nun as Sister Bridget? It appears to me that priest is more than powerful."

"His power comes from his inflated ego. If he ever experienced genuine sorrow for his actions, I would be surprised."

"Call your sister in here." Emma walked to her bedroom and let Mia know Mom wanted to talk to her.

"Yes, mother?" asked Mia as she walked into the kitchen.

"Tomorrow, I'm going to drop Dario off at school and then will head to Dr. Miller in the city. I'll let the school know you'll be back by noon. How are you feeling, honey?"

"I feel okay, Mama. Thank you for asking."

"You look tired; why don't you take a nap after breakfast? I'm starting on it now."

The following day, Palmira dropped her son off at school with a note to hand into the office. She then headed to the doctor, her nerves matching Mia's.

Checking into the medical clinic, Palmira filled out a short form and five minutes later walked into one of a few medical waiting rooms. A nurse asked Mia the purpose of her visit. "It's a female issue," replied Mrs. Sacatti, offering no more information.

Told Dr. Miller would only be a few minutes. Mia began to wring her hands. Palmira moved next to her daughter, providing a lifeline embrace. "Dr. Miller is here for you, sweetheart. He'll oversee your health and well-being. He's a devoted member of the parish, so don't worry."

A sudden knock on the closed door and Dr. Miller walked in, shaking Mrs. Sacatti's hand while greeting her daughter. He sat down, looked at the nurse's notes, and asked, "A female issue? Enlighten me, ladies."

Tears lifted in Mia's eyes. Dr. Miller, sensitive, immediately grabbed a few tissues behind him. He looked over at the mother and understood.

"Mia, are you pregnant? Nod if you are."

With a tissue, Mia stopped the phlegm spilling from her nose and nodded 'yes.'

Mrs. Sacatti told Dr. Miller, "Yes, our Pharmacist tested Mia and felt she is pregnant."

"Okay, Mia, I'm happy you came to see me. What I'll do is check your blood and urine. Have you experienced any fevers?"

"No fevers, Dr. Miller," responded Mia.

57

"Excellent," said the doctor. "Do you feel more tired than usual?"

"Yes, almost every day."

"You have a better chance of becoming anemic because your red blood cells are reduced, causing you to feel weak and, of course, tired. We'll give you a few vitamins to give you a lift.

"Mia, teenage pregnancy can lead to what we call PIH (pregnancy-induced hypertension), premature births, and cephalopelvic disproportion. That's when the baby's head is wider than the pelvic region.

"Prenatal care can solve these problems. You're in good hands, dear. I'll need to see you every two weeks, and don't you worry sweetheart, you're not the first pre-teen or teen I've seen.

"Mrs. Sacatti, I need to perform a few tests and check on the health of the baby. We won't take more than an hour. I'm going to permit our technicians to perform something around for only a few years. It's called ultrasound or sonogram to detect the baby's development. Mia, the ultrasound department is next door, so I'll walk you over."

"I'll wait in the outer office in case you need me, doctor," said Mrs. Sacatti, hugging Mia before she exited the medical room.

What would I do if my job didn't offer insurance? She teared up when, out of nowhere, a tall, young woman approached her, "Are you alright, miss? I assure you Mia will make it through the pregnancy. How are you, though? May I help you?"

"I'm sorry, I'll be alright. I guess I was counting my blessings. I'm lucky to have insurance; otherwise, my daughter might be in serious trouble. God bless you for your concern."

"God bless you too; I'm Dorothy Marquez."

"Nice to meet you, Dorothy. My name is Palmira Sacatti."

"Sacatti! You're not related to Emma Sacatti, are you?"

"She's my daughter."

"Wonderful! Your daughter is on the same basketball team as my daughter Cindy."

"Small world. I'm so happy I met you. Isn't your daughter captain of the team? My daughter idolizes a Cindy on her team."

"Yes, Cindy is the senior captain. My husband and I have watched your child play. Our Saint Anthony girls are drawing hundreds of fans. Every one of our home games is sold out. Your daughter is astonishing. Saint Anthony labeled your daughter the 'Freshman Sensation.' A true miracle on the court.

"She's alright, isn't she?"

"Emma? Oh yes, she's fine. It's my other daughter experiencing some discomfort."

"I hope she gets better. I'll pray for her. I got to go now, it was nice meeting you, Mrs. Sacatti. Maybe we could sit together at the next home game."

"Yes, thank you; perhaps we could do that."

A half-hour passed when Dorothy Marquez exited the medical office. "Mrs. Sacatti, you have a pleasant day." She left the building, and as Palmira looked out the window, she saw the young lady open the door to a 1960 pink Cadillac.

What a beautiful car. Never could she understand my family's financial disaster. "Mrs. Sacatti!" the medical secretary called her to the window. "You haven't paid your two-dollar deductible yet."

"I'm sorry, it's my fault." She reached into her purse, and her mouth flew open. The two dollars were missing. "My dear God, where did it go."

Stopped before a red signal light, Dorothy Marquez found two dollars sitting on her dashboard. She slapped her forehead, saying, "How could I forget!"

Mr. Sacatti rummaging through her purse, came across a wad of paper crammed into a lonely corner of her purse. Palmira pulled it out to throw it away. "Could you toss this for me," Palmira asked the secretary, Sarah Lucas.

Mrs. Sacatti handed across the window the bunched-up scrunch of paper. Miss Lucas, ready to toss the paper, noticed embedded security fibers and undid the gob of paper.

"Palmira, this is a twenty-dollar bill. Let me get your change."

"Excuse me, Sarah?"

"You must have lost this in your purse. I caught the embedded fibers in the paper; you're one lucky gal."

The distraught mother was handed eighteen dollars in change. Tears reached Palmira's eyes. "Sarah, of all the time in my life, this is a miracle, a puzzling wonder. And now eighteen dollars in my hand."

"I'm sure you could use it, Mrs. Sacatti. Your daughter should be out in a few minutes. Her sonogram is complete."

A nurse called Palmira back to the medical room, where she found Mia and the doctor discussing the result of the ultrasound's 2d view of the baby.

"Mrs. Sacatti! Come on in," said Dr. Miller. "Your daughter's baby is healthy. A little girl, from what we could tell. We estimate Mia is in her fifth month. Your extra weight, sweetheart is more than likely your baby and the extra fluid in your body. Neither of you has anything to worry about.

"Now Mia mentioned she might transfer over to St. Agnes in Los Angeles. I've made some personal calls visiting the convent, the sisters do more than an excellent job. Mia would be happy there if she attended. I recommend the facility."

Mia and her mother thanked the doctor for his help and especially for understanding the girl's startling pregnancy. *Doctor Miller must live off a healthy salary. He probably donates fifty times what Mother can afford in Gibson's collection box, enough to mellow the old priest. Enough for Father to appear 'Christ-like.'*

I wonder if Mama knows that?

"When you were getting your sonogram, I met this beautiful young lady. Her name is Dorothy, and she told me her daughter, Cindy, a senior, played basketball with Emma at Saint Anthony. How old is a high school senior, seventeen, eighteen?" Her mother looked no older than thirty to thirty-five tops. She must have experienced a teen pregnancy no more than whatever her daughter's age is now.

"I've seen that woman or at least read about her somewhere. I think Mia, Dorothy must be rich. She drives a brand new Cadillac, a pink one."

As Palmira and Mia headed toward their Plymouth, they left behind the Dorothy Marquez clinic. A cornerstone read:

Dorothy Marquez M.D.
Philanthropist, Associate, and Friend
May you rest in peace.

Palmira pulled her '56 yellow Plymouth into the parking lot at St. Cyprian, dropped Mia off at school then walked over to the school office.

"I'm here to pay my back tuition for almost all of the four months." She reached into her purse and pulled out her wallet. Reaching in, she took out the entire amount of cash, a ten, a five, and one, two, three...four? Five?.

Sitting in my wallet the entire time. HOW? Thank you, St. Anthony. "I'm sorry, Mrs. Carpenter, it looks like I can pay off the entire bill." She handed the secretary the cash just as Father Gibson walked through the door.

"Came up with the money, I see, how convenient, only a day. It appears my conversation must have held a little weight. Your money can't change my mind." He addressed the secretary, "Where's Mother Killian?"

"She's probably in the convent eating lunch," said Mrs. Carpenter.

"Mother is not there I checked."

"I'm here in my office, Father Gibson," said Mother Killian, opening a half-closed door.

"You playing tricks on me, Carpenter. I ought to have you dismissed," fired a heated Gibson to the school's alarmed secretary.

"Father, she didn't see me coming in as Nancy was escorting a new student to the 2nd grade."

"The attorney's son, Paul?"

Nancy Carpenter, still shaken up, said, "Yes, Father, Mr. Dementer's little boy."

Gibson turned to Mrs. Sacatti and pointed, "He pays his tuition and donates his fair share at church. This school needs to lose families such as yours, Mrs. Sacatti."

"I'm sorry you feel the way you do, Father Gibson; I need to get back to work. I've lost half a day's pay." Palmira stormed out of the office with her purse and receipt in hand.

Gibson walked angrily into Mother Killian's office. "I want that woman and her kids gone tomorrow. Get rid of them, or I'll have the Bishop transfer you to the hottest place on this earth."

"I can't let them go, Father. The Sacattis are paid up, and besides, her daughter Emma was a year-to-year honor student and a tremendous athlete. And I understand Mia, her sister, is about to make honors."

"You have no business being a principal of any school. You're not led by what is right; your damn emotions lead you. Do what I say, or I'll be on the phone with the Bishop."

"First of all, Father, emotions do not lead me. I always do what I think is right. I'm sixty-two years old, and if the bishop wants to transfer me to Death Valley, he'll have to do it through Mother General. Now, I want your sorry ass out of my office, or I will have Nancy call the police on you for abuse and harassment! My entire convent will back me up, too."

Father Gibson left the office and headed toward the rectory, somewhat hesitant to bother the bishop at this time.

> Forgive us our sins as we forgive
> those who sin against us.

Chapter Seven

Dr. Dorothy Marquez

Mia walked into her classroom at the same time the students stood to recite the Angelus, followed by the grace before meals. Five minutes later, Sister Bridget exited the students row by row.

Mia's row called last. Sister Bridget asked if she might stay for a minute or two. "Where's your lunch, sweetheart."

"My mother and I ate in the car along the way." In truth, with all the early morning commotion, Mia and her mother forgot to eat breakfast and even lunch. She realized that couldn't be good for the child she was carrying. She'd make it up and head directly home after school with her brother Dario.

"Mia, I understand Father Gibson raised his voice to your mother yesterday. Is that true?"

"How do you know, Sister?"

"An altar server cleaning up the sacristy looked out the window and saw Father screaming at your mother. When Father Gibson left, the boy ran to tell me in the parish hall."

"Yes, sister, Father hollered at my mother and sister. He threatened to throw us out of school and told my mother to save her 'lousy' fifty-cent donation in the weekly envelopes and clear out of the parish.

"Sister, please understand my parents struggle week to week. She now has to work an hour extra every day to pay for tuition here at St. Cyprian and Saint Anthony. Emma also works an hour after practice to help cut down on the cost. My parents and Emma are really trying."

"I'm so sorry dear, between you and I, that man is a beast. I've talked to Mother Killian, and she's fed up, too. She wanted to contact the bishop, but I told her a lot of luck that would do. Father Gibson and the bishop are golf buddies.

"I suggested she ask Mother General to visit the convent. All of the nuns are together on this issue with that complaint with Father."

"Sister, I don't want to hold you back on your lunch. May I have permission to leave?"

"Of course, dear, I'm sorry I held you up. Please keep what I said to yourself."

"I will, Sister. You have my word. Sister Bridget, if you don't mind who was that altar server?"

"Know I don't mind; he's a fine boy...Gregory."

Classes went well at St. Anthony. Emma met with her team in the girls' locker room and isolated her discussion with Cindy Marquez. "St. Pius X canceled their home game with us and agreed to play us here. An extra home game and at night."

"Yeah, something about Pius renovating their gymnasium for the boys' big game with us."

"I'm excited about a night game my mom and dad can attend. I can't wait to tell them. How about your parents? Don't they attend most of the games anyway?"

"You got that mostly right, my dad and his sister, my

Auntie Grace."

"How about your mother?" asked Emma.

"I was born with my twin brother Carlos, and soon after, my mother died. Complications of the heart, my dad told me. I found out she bled to death. Her platelets were low."

"I'm sorry to hear that. I'll pray for your mom and you."

"Thank you, Emma. My mother, Dorothy, was a physician, out of residence for a mere two years. She wouldn't marry my dad until she completed her residential probation at the hospital she was assigned to.

"Afterward, through my dad's help, she purchased her very own clinic. My father, Michael, is a successful stockbroker. He paid cash for the thirty-eight hundred square foot office and, with the help of two other doctors, created the first medical clinic that accepted patients without insurance. It was my mother's idea, and they still thrive today.

"My father had a plaque made honoring my mom. It's located against the wall on the left as you enter the clinic."

"Your mother sounds like a wonderful woman. You and your brother take after her."

"Thanks again, Emma."

"How's your brother, Carlos doing? I rarely see him on campus."

"He's fine. U.S.C. recruited him. He'll be attending there in September. Right tackle position, I hear. He's certainly big enough."

"Southern Cal. Contacted me, too. A full scholarship, imagine the first brother/sister twins recruited to the university."

"Let's move it, girls. On the court now!" shouted Coach Errion into the girls' locker room.

Primary level dismissal occurred at 2:40, twenty minutes before the 4th through 8th grade exited their classrooms closing the day. "Thank you for waiting outside my room, Dario. You're such a good boy."

No longer would Mia force her brother to pray in the church before he shifted to the convent. "We're going directly home, Dario; I didn't eat today."

Mia's brother opened up his lunchbox. "I couldn't finish all my carrots today. You can have these then we could go to the library. I finished my BETSY book."

"Thank you, little brother, but I don't believe a few carrot slices will help me. She chewed on the small orange vegetables before missing her footing. We need to stop Dario; I think I'm going to…"

Mia managed to kneel on the grass of a remote side road when she, to Dario's alarm, collapsed on the old Lakewood Village cobblestone lane. Dario knelt over her sister when a Cadillac stopped. Running toward the boy and his sister, the woman knelt over Mia.

"Your sister, Dario, is low on sugar. Crawl inside my back seat, and I'll place Mia's head on your lap."

A stranger to Dario, perhaps Mia knew the young lady; she seemed to know both of their names. *Maybe she's a teacher at our school.*

Sitting in the driver's seat, she reached into the glovebox and pulled out a Milky Way candy bar. "Dario, wake your sister and give this to her."

Within a few minutes, the Cadillac pulled into the driveway of the Sacatti home. The woman escorted Mia inside as Dario, now entrusted with the keys, opened the front door.

"Your baby needs something more nutritious than a candy bar. Fruit? Peanut butter on a few more carrots; your baby is crying for nutrition, Mia."

"How do you know?" asked Mia as she took down the store-brand creamy peanut butter.

"I see and know more than you think."

Leaving through the front door, Mia and Dario, siblings who shared a close bond, watched the woman climb into her Cadillac and drive off. "I neglected to thank her, little brother," Mia said, feeling a pang of guilt.

"I thanked her because she gave me an extra candy for helping you," said Dario.

"You did! Dario, did the lady tell you her name?"

"The lady sort of told me her name. She said, 'I'm Dorothy, and Dario, tell your mother I said hello.' I'm going to tell Mama when she gets home tonight. I don't know her last name, so I didn't know how to talk to her. She was a strange lady, but she seemed to know us," Dario explained, his brow furrowed in confusion.

Mia paused, then said, "You didn't know her, did you? I sure never met her."

"How come she knew both our names?"

"I don't know, Dario, and"...*how did she know I was carrying a child?* That thought troubled the eighth-grade girl. "Dario, I made you a peanut butter sandwich too. We'll eat it and finish with an orange. Our Dorothy was right: my blood sugar it's too low."

"Could you put some jelly on my sandwich, Mia? I like peanut butter with jelly."

"I can do that. Let's go back to the kitchen."

———

Arriving home before her mother and father, Emma was a bit surprised to see her sister completing her homework in their bedroom. "Not able to visit the library today, Mia?"

Dario, overhearing his sister, ran into the girls' bedroom and said, "No, Mia fainted when we walked home."

"Oh, dear Lord. Are you okay?" said the concerned older sister.

"I'm fine. Mom and I had so much on our minds this morning we forgot to eat breakfast, and I also forgot my lunch. My blood sugar fell, and I guess I collapsed. Dario offered me leftover carrot sticks from his lunchbox, but evidently, it wasn't enough."

"And then a lady got out of her Cadilla…"

Mia looked right through her brother, glaring at him. "Dario, you know our rule. If your homework is not done by the time Mom gets home, I'm going to share your candy bar with Emma."

"Okay, I'm almost finished," and he darted back into his bedroom.

"What was that all about," asked Emma.

"I'll tell you before we go to sleep. By the way, how did you get home so early?"

"Ryan drove me home. He's Cindy's boyfriend."

"Cindy's boyfriend? Are you sure? Emma, have you lately looked at yourself in the mirror? You're gorgeous, and you share an interest in the same sport."

"Hold on, Mia. Ryan's committed to Cindy, at least for now. He's mature, and his eyes don't roam. Besides, his basketball buddy Ted Accenti was with him in the car."

"Ted, his name is coming up again. Isn't he the boy who asked you for a date?"

"Yes, he did, and I gave him an emphatic no. I'm too young to date Mia. Anyway, their coach kept them late preparing for a game against St. Pius X. It's in the school's renovated gymnasium. Ryan saw me walk out of the girl's locker room and offered me a lift home."

"Emma, how'd Ted work his way into Ryan's car?"

"Ryan gives Ted a ride after every practice. They both live within four blocks of each other near Long Beach State College."

"That's at least a few miles from here. Does Ryan and his friend plan on taking you home every night?"

"I don't think the coach wants the boys home no later than five p.m. Coach Dye places a high premium on academic performance. Ryan and Ted told me the average G.P.A. of the team is 3.4.

"I wanted to get home as soon as possible. My home economics class prepared stuffed bell peppers. I was allowed to take home six of them, two for Papa. I need to heat them before our parents arrive home."

"I'll set the table, Emma," replied Mia.

Sitting down to dinner, Emma was the first to update her day when Dario jumped in and mentioned Mia fainted on her way home. Alarm overcame Palmira's face as she looked toward her pregnant teen. "Mia, what happened, dear!"

"Mother, Dario is exaggerating. I felt a little dizzy and sat down. Remember, we forgot breakfast, and I left my lunch in the refrigerator. My sugar must have dropped."

"You're a liar, Mia. You fell on the grass and weren't moving. Mama, she made me cry. I thought she died until a lady came and rescued her."

Eugenio spoke up, "Dario, never call your sister a liar!"

"But Papa, that's not what happened." Frustrated, Dario played with his bell pepper.

"Tell us what happened, Mia. Don't worry, sweetheart, we'll listen."

"He's right, Mama. I blacked out and came to in the lady's car after Dario woke me and fed me a Milky Way."

"Your dizziness pointed to low blood sugar. Who was this woman who helped you?"

"She never told me; I did, however, thank her for her help."

"Mama, the lady told me her name, but not to Mia. She said, 'Tell your mother I said hello. My name is Dorothy.'"

"Did Dorothy drive a big pink car?"

"Uh-huh. A really big one for rich people. She was smart and knew both of our names and told Mia she needed more natrition."

Palmira corrected her son, "You mean nutrition, Dario. I do know her; she must be a nurse or doctor. I saw her walk out of the medical office clinic, and she introduced herself. A doctor? That might explain why she drives a Cadillac. I never mentioned your names, though, especially Dario's. Did she ask you?"

"No, Mama, she acted as if she knew us forever," said Dario.

Eugenio intervened, "I'm happy you're better, Mia. We need to settle back to dinner. Emma, these peppers are delicious. Is this your mother's recipe?" Mr. Sacatti asked his oldest daughter.

"It sure is Papa. I wrote out the recipe for extra credit, and my teacher made copies for the class."

"You did a great job, honey, so if no one minds, I'll eat the last one."

"Mom and Dad, I hope I have a surprise for all of us. St. Pius X girls' team canceled their home game and rescheduled it at Saint Anthony for next Wednesday. The good news is it's my first game in the evening!"

Eugenio, the first to respond, exclaimed, "Four years and I've never seen you play. A night game, this is good news!"

"Maybe you should just take Dario. Mia and I can stay home," said Palmira.

"Four tickets is something we could afford. We'll somehow manage. We may never see Emma play again. Football was only seventy-five cents for adults and a quarter for kids, and of course, Emma doesn't have to pay. That's two dollars for all of us. We'll go as one family."

After brushing his teeth and washing his face, Dario knelt at the side of his bed, closed his eyes, and pointed his fingers toward heaven. He whispered, "God bless Mama, Papa, Emma, Mia, and all my friends. Teach me to be a good boy and not get in fights. Amen."

Dario eagerly crawled into bed, reached beneath his feathered pillow and pulled out the Milky Way hidden underneath since he arrived home in the back seat of the Cadillac. Unwrapping the treat, he savored his first bite and decided to save the rest for lunch.

On Tuesday morning, Dario pulled the candy bar from under his pillow and snuck it into his Sheriff John lunch box. At school Dario was compelled to tell his friend Lonny Price about the treat he slipped into his lunch pail. "Don't tell anyone, Lonny, and I might give you a small bite."

"A Milky Way! That's my favorite. We got a secret, huh, Dario."

"A top secret, bigger than World War II and the Dodgers."

"I won't tell anyone, I swear."

"Swear to Buddha, and it won't be a sin."

Lonny raised his right hand and swore to Buddha.

By recess, Lonny shared the secret with Stevie Walker, who shared it with Roger Connor, the 3rd-grade Dion Francis

DiMucci, who shared it with half the girls in Mrs. Holmes's 3rd-grade classroom."

Dario began staring at the clock by 11:30, counting down the seconds a minute at a time. Fatigued from recess kickball, his stomach began to growl by 11:55. Tears formed in his eyes.

I'm so hungry I can hardly see. Dario knew today was the best lunch day ever. His mother made him a peanut butter and jelly sandwich with three cookies wrapped in wax paper and a juicy apple, all of it including his CANDY BAR.

By noon, Mrs. Holmes asked the students to stand for the Angelus and the Catholic prayer before meals. *We should have already said our prayers. Why is she waiting so long? They ought to fire her!*

After what seemed like a half hour, the teacher called each well-behaved row to get their lunch and move to the lunch tables. Why is my row last? Damn it! Dario knew he'd have to confess that one, but why? He heard Father Gibson use that word often, even worse words. The nuns reminded the kids that the sisters and priests were higher up in heaven than regular people, so maybe that was it.

Finally relaxed at the lunch table minus two minutes of forbidden lunch table kickball, Dario opened his lunch box only to find his Milky Way was missing. "SOMEONE STOLE IT!" He said in a rage. Only Lonny knew of Dario's secret.

"Where is he?" Lonny sat two tables behind him. "You bastard! You're the only one who knew." Two cuss words and one of them in public. There was no way he'd get away with it. He found Lonny, however, who swore he didn't have it.

"You're no good, Lonny. You're a rotten liar; you ate it!" (Only his Papa didn't allow the 'liar' word).

"No, I didn't!" Lonny foolishly raised his fist, creating an invitation for Dario to strike. Sacatti's fist flew forward, landing square on the nose of the defiant 'ex-friend' who should have known better.

Thank goodness only a drop of blood appeared. Lonny, however, chose to find his teacher sitting at her desk in his classroom, exaggerating unpleasant bawling as he walked inside. "What happened, Lonny," asked Mrs. Holmes, not hardly masking the bored look on her face as she bit into an orange slice.

"Dario socked me for something I didn't do?"

"What did he say?"

"He said I ate his candy bar and said a cuss word. Then he punched me in the nose. I think it's broken. You know I I didn't eat his Milky Way."

"No, you didn't, Lonny," Mrs. Holmes said, covering her mouth with a napkin. "You go get him, and I'll punish him. Now wash your nose. I think you have a drop of blood."

Lonny rushed out of the classroom, choosing to leave what he perceived as an "enormous" amount of blood streaming from his nose, believing it was a badge of honor.

In the meantime, his teacher burst out in laughter, tears welling in her eyes. *Good for you, Dario; that little brat has gotten away with too much for too long.*

Lonny found Dario playing kickball and swore to the boy Mrs. Holmes was going to kill him. "You're going to get kicked out of school, Dario," Lonny said as he covered his nose, holding it back in the air.

Dario walked into the classroom with his head down. "Lonny, wait outside and close the door," said his teacher.

"You step forward, Dario. Lonny never ate your candy. I have It right here."

She drew it out of her desk to the boy's alarm. "I caught your so-called friend stealing it out of your lunch box at recess. I returned early after running off quiz papers and saw him getting into your lunch and pulling out your candy bar. He never saw me until it was too late.

"I understand you hit him."

"I'm sorry I didn't mean to."

"Oh, I'm sure you did." *You saved me the trouble I've always wanted to take a belt to that kid.* "You used a cuss word too?"

"Yes, Mrs. Holmes, I did."

"Anyone else hear it?"

"I think most of the kids did."

"What was it?"

"I said the word bas...bastard."

"I wouldn't worry about it; Father Gibson uses that word regularly. What you're going to do is apologize to Lonny, tell him you're truly sorry, and then offer him a bite of your candy bar. Here, take it, and I expect you'll be friends after school. Remember, candy is forbidden at St. Cyprian. We don't even sell it on hot dog day. Now go!"

Dario left, and the 3rd-grade teacher breathed a sigh of relief. *You never met a bastard until you met Lonny's mother.* She asked God to forgive her for thinking that way; however, getting back burner nerves off her shoulders gave the older woman a push for another semester.

I got to make it past Friday and relax in the parish hall on Sunday, chatting with my students and warm, friendly parents while selling with Sister Bridget religious articles.

Mrs. Holmes

Chapter Eight

THE INCOMPARABLE EMMA SACATTI

Dario survived the rest of the week, holding back the anger he felt for Lonny Price. God paid for his patience when Mia cashed in two miraculous curbside soda bottles, purchasing two Nestle Crunch candy bars at the Sad Sack resale store on Woodruff Avenue.

"Two of them, Dario, and I'll remind you not to take either one to school. You can sneak one on Friday night and one on Saturday. Is that a deal?"

"It's a deal, Mia, and you're the best sister in the whole world."

By Friday afternoon, the St. Cyprian's brother and sister headed to the city library. Dario checked out the last of the BETSY series and one HENRY HUGGINS baseball book for a quiet weekend of reading mixed in with the neighborhood game of baseball across the street on the Long Beach Community College front grass field.

Late Friday afternoon also greeted the exhausted but satisfied Saint Anthony basketball team. "In less than a week, girls will be taking this court to a sold-out crowd, a potential league championship, and a yearbook in June listing you as one of the greatest girls' basketball teams ever to take the court at Saint Anthony. It's up to you.

"St. Pius X sacrificed their home court in favor of their boys' team. Sexism seems to dominate sports over there, so their girls probably will be sky high to not only win this game but throw it in the school's face. Be gentle with them.

"Practice tomorrow at 8:00 a.m. That should be early enough so you young ladies can get back and finish your weekend chores." Coach Tanya Errion expected only the finest effort from her handpicked players.

By the end of the weekend, Emma's nerves walked on edge. "Not just Papa, Mama too," she shared with her sister before she retired.

"Papa knows his basketball. He's watched quite a bit on television. Wait 'til he sees you move up and down the court."

Emma drifted off to sleep, watching her father stand and cheer for her in the home stands. She never took her eye off him as she, too, watched the magnificent guard fly through the past five defenders and slam the ball through the hoop. *"Ladies and gentlemen, the incomparable Emma Sacatti."* She smiled into her pillow.

Up in the stands next to her Papa stood Ted Accenti shouting, *"I've always loved you, Emma, love me back!"*

"You heard Saint Anthony's fabulous sophomore guard, folks. He loves Emma and wants her to love him back!"

Why was she so nervous? Was it her family's parents attending her first game, or did she hold a secret thirst for a sophomore varsity player?

On Monday, the school campus joined together, welcoming all the players in and out of the hallways. Cindy Marquez busied herself handing out autographs, and Emma ducked into her classes, trying to avoid the rush of fans until lunchbreak when students swarmed the entire team.

Saint Anthony's student section sold out the day after when Coach Errion announced to the principal the girls were playing their first night game at home against the top contending team in California on Wednesday, January 29th, 1961. "We'll offer more tickets if they're playing here!"

Countering, St. Pius X sold out their allotted tickets in the same twenty-four-hour period. Parents of the players on both teams were asked to purchase a ticket just as the public.

Eugenio, a devoted Laker fan, chewed through his nails by Wednesday morning. The Elgin Baylor and Jerry West Lakers ate away at Eugenio Sacatti's basketball heart so far into the season.

They needed a center, maybe someone like Wilt Chamberlain. The father of three children reversed his allegiance to his daughter, Emma, to one crucial game. And again, Emma and the Saint Anthony girl's basketball team sparked his interest.

"Honey, you need to take your nails away from your mouth before they bleed. Eugenio I appreciate your love of the game, and also, this is the first time we'll both see our daughter play the sport she also loves, but I'm worried about you, Eugenio. You suffered a mild heart attack eight years ago. I won't let you work toward another, God forbid..." Palmira bent her head down, sniffling, holding back a cold.

Emma left that morning with her father, dropping her off at the 6:30 a.m. bus stop. She calmed him down, reassuring him it was only another game and there would be plenty more within the next three years. He smiled, kissed her cheek, and headed in the opposite direction to work.

Arriving an hour early before school began, Emma chose to ask her first-period teacher, Mary Pierce, if she could sit quietly in her classroom.

Emma knew her Algebra teacher chose to prepare for school each morning well before the initial bell of the first period.

"Avoiding the crowd, I see. Your big game is tonight, so I'll tell you what we'll do. You have my permission to leave Algebra five minutes before the rest of the students. That should leave you enough time to slip into 2nd period. I recommend you plead with your next teacher to let you out early."

By the fifth period, Emma comfortably sat in her Home Economic class, avoiding the crowded hallways and the cloud of stimulated students greeting the players.

"Why don't you stay inside the classroom and sidestep the cafeteria crowd? We made blueberry muffins today I'm sure you'll enjoy them."

Cindy Marquez understood Emma Sacatti feared large crowds surrounding the girl. "Emma does not savor attention.

She goes about her play, ignoring the typical roar of the crowd and zeroing in on her teammates."

Not particularly frozen shy, Emma thrived in the classroom, calling no particular attention to herself but rather responding to knowledge attained or delivered. Academic success was accepted on the one hand by the staff and, far on the other end, despised by less than adequate students whose limited vision only saw Emma as a showoff.

Darkness found Mia and her brother sitting on their porch, waiting for their parents to arrive home. Eugenio pulled his truck into the driveway first, followed almost soon after by Palmira driving her station wagon behind her husband's truck.

Mia leaped up with the popcorn she was told to make, two bags for the entire family. Mrs. Sacatti scooted over on the bench seat while her husband, who had showered and changed clothes at work, sat behind the wheel. Mia and Dario climbed into the back seat.

"We're off!" exclaimed Eugenio. "Twenty minutes should get us there, and we should be sitting in our seats, no later than seven, enough time to watch the girls warm up."

At 6:50 p.m., the Sacatti's could not find parking. "I'll drop off all of you in front of the gymnasium and look for parking on the street down the road." Eugenio handed his wife $4.00.

When he returned, he noticed a glum look on his wife's face standing near the ticket booth. "What's wrong?" She pointed. "Two dollars for adults and a dollar for children. That's more than a football game!"

"Even worse," said a disappointed Palmira. "Look lower." Her husband dipped his gaze; a small placard read, SOLD-OUT!

Heartbroken, he could only remember his daughter's words, *"There will be plenty more in the next few years."*

"I'll go get the car. All of you wait here." Eugenio turned and bumped into a young lady. "I'm sorry, ma'am, my apologies."

"MR. SACATTI! I'm so happy you brought your entire family. This game is billed as the game of the year, and there won't be another like this for a long time, especially for my Cindy, who's graduating in June."

"Mrs. Dorothy!" shouted Dario. He ran up and hugged her.

"I'm sorry, ma'am. Do I know you?"

"Probably not, but I know you. Hello Mia, and of course, Mrs. Sacatti over at the medical clinic."

"Yes, you drive that pink Cadillac. Our daughters are on the basketball court tonight; it's so wonderful to see you."

"I'm so happy to see all of you. I have a surprise for you, Mr. Sacatti. I know how much you like Laker basketball, but this one will top Los Angeles's entire season. FOUR TICKETS paid for in advance. I purchased them the day before they sold out." She handed Eugenio the tickets.

"I only have four dollars to give you, ma'am."

"Oh nonsense, my husband and I are wealthy, and Eugenio, do me a favor, call me Dorothy." She handed over the precious tickets and told the family to save her a seat. "I need to winky/tink you do understand. I haven't gone all day."

"That's not a bad idea. Mia and Dario, do you need to use the restroom?"

"Not me, Mama. I went just before we left the house," said Dario.

"I'll go with you ladies," Mia shared with the women.

"Let me give you the tickets," said the father. "I'll save five bleacher seats."

Two minutes later, Mrs. Sacatti left the ladies' room, followed by a pale-looking Mia. "Are you okay, sweetheart? Let me help you to your seat." Mia, her color beginning to return, hung on to her mother's arm without a word.

Mother and daughter slowly climbed the wrung of stairs, sitting at the very top looking down at the court. "My goodness, Palmira, that woman wasn't kidding. When's she coming back? The gymnasium's filling up."

"Mama, she left the restroom. I saw her; she walked through the door."

"Okay, then where is she?"

"Mama, she was in front of me, and the door was closed. She walked through it like a ghost."

Palmira's hand went to her daughter's forehead. "You don't have a fever."

"She's telling the truth, Mama. I saw Dorothy walk right through the ticket taker." I think she's standing on the court whispering in her daughter's ear. Do you see her?"

Palmira focused. Dorothy came into view. "Honey, can you see Dorothy?" said his wife, brushing her husband's arm."

"Yeah, what's she doing on the court? St. Anthony is going to get a team technical if she doesn't get off. What's she doing talking to her daughter? She could be her sister."

"They look alike, don't they daddy," Dario added.

Dorothy waved at the Sacatti's and darted up the steps. Mia reached into her father's arms.

Ten minutes before the national anthem, Cindy leaned over the basketball court barrier and introduced Emma to her dad and auntie. Too far to shake hands, Emma waved instead. Her head circled the crowd, finally spying her family up at the far top.

"That's my family up there!" said Emma loud enough for Mr. Marquez and his sister to turn toward Emma's pointing finger.

"Come on down and sit with us!" Marquez shouted. "We have plenty of room down here!" Michael Marquez had given up on his brother and family attending the game. He'd gladly hand over the choice seats to Emma's family."

"Let's get up, gang. We're asked to sit in the middle of the court down below. This night's getting better."

Eugenio gently guided his pregnant daughter down the bleacher seats. "Sit next to me, Papa, with Dario on my other side."

Once directly behind the Marquez's, Palmira turned and asked where Dorothy went. "Mr. Marquez, have you seen your wife."

His sister Connie grabbed her brother's forearm. Michael turned and asked, "You saw her!"

"I did. Dorothy provided us with tickets and was sitting next to us upstairs. Now I see you here. I can't understand why she wasn't sitting next to you." Palmira noticed tears flowing from her daughter's eyes.

Connie turned around and helped Palmira calm Mia. "Sweetheart, my sister-in-law will leave you alone if you just ask. You're not the only one who has seen her."

"Listen to Connie, my wife was unique and refused to move on. She achieved her doctorate in medicine and helped me pick the right Dow stocks before she gave her life to the twins. Her whole life was spent giving. She made us rich, as well as my clients. I still ask for her help at times.

"I asked Dorothy to keep her distance and not show herself, and she honors my request."

"Mama and Papa, Dorothy is gone. I can't see her no more."

Mrs. Sacatti leaned over and consoled Mia. "Like Mr. Marquez, ask Dorothy only to help you in your thoughts. She'll work with you."

"I can see Dorothy; I like her," said Dario.

"What's she doing?" asked Dario's mother.

"PLEASE STAND FOR THE PLAYING OF THE NATIONAL ANTHEM."

Dario leaned into his mother's ear, whispering, "She's standing next to her daughter with her hand over her heart."

"I heard you, Dario. You shouldn't wish to see a ghost," said Mia, reaching the ears of those around her.

"She's not a ghost; she's a human who died, kinda like Caspar."

"WILL YOU TWO BE QUIET AND SHOW SOME RESPECT!" Eugenio whispered as loud as his voice would carry.

Emma blew her family a kiss, which seemed to calm down her brother and sister.

Ten minutes later, Eugenio was standing with the crowd as his daughter stole the ball from All-League guard Stephenie Myers of St. Pius. Five dribbles down the court, and Emma layed it in the hoop. The score, now tied, ensured the intense rivalry of the game. No television broadcast of Eugenio's Lakers could match this competition. Both teams played with fierce hearts.

Halftime found the Pius X Warriors ahead by a single point. "I've sent up enough prayers, Eugenio; you've got to relax." Palmira was alarmed, her husband's blood pressure unfurling before her eyes.

Dario took his daddy's hand, "I prayed to Dorothy, Papa. You shouldn't worry; we're going to win."

Eugenio grabbed his son's shoulders, "You need to undo that wish. Jerry West and Elgin Baylor just need a center. These girls got to play with what they got. Take back your prayer and tell Dorothy for our girls to play their best. You got that."

Michael Marquez gently took hold of Eugenio's arm, "It's no more than a game, buddy; listen to your wife and enjoy the play. Let me get you all a coke."

When Emma and the Saint Anthony team returned for the second half, she blew her family another kiss. Sitting ten rows above her father sat Ryan Finch, Cindy Marquez's boyfriend with Ted Accenti, *like in my dream. Don't stand up and shout anything, Ted. I got a game. No distractions, please.*

Marquez won the center jump, tapping it to Virginia Coughlin, who in turn fed the ball to the team's star guard. Emma placed the ball on her hip, vying for a brief second. She rocked her hips up, making her defender rise in the air. Her body move allowed Emma to put the ball on the floor and attack the basket. Within ten seconds, the Saints retook the lead.

Warrior guard Evelyn Prather threw Emma a 'rocker' step. She stepped forward as though she was ready to blow past Emma, rocked back, and failed to drive forward. Sacatti anticipated the move, positioned herself, and took an obvious charge. "Always worked in the past, Emma; your footwork is damn quick," shouted her former St. Cyprian coach Bobbi Walker.

Virginia imbounded the ball, throwing it in high to Cindy Marquez, playing the low post. She turned around to the Warrior's shorter center and swished the ball through the hoop. Saints by three as Michael, Cindy's father, stood and threw his arms in the air. "That's my girl!" he shouted.

By the end of the third quarter, the St. Pius X 5'11" center, Kirsten Miller, drew away from the basket and began to throw in prayers from twenty feet in the corner. An expert at shooting a high arching shot, Cindy Marquez couldn't seem to contain the girl's prolific scoring. On a rare occasion when Kirsten missed, the Warriors' taller forwards were snagging offensive rebounds and putting in two points. Downey's #4 in the nation-ranked team moved ahead by four points.

Coach Tanya Errion asked Emma to cover the center and stop her from shooting. "Kirsten's ball-handling skills are something to be desired, and she's not near as quick as you are, Emma. She may have four or five inches on you, but I noticed she couldn't leap, not as near as you anyway. Cindy, stay low and neutralize their forwards. I don't want them making sloppy points. Hands together: One, two, three."

"GO SAINTS!" the St. Anthony girls shouted, reigniting the home crowd, including Eugenio Sacatti and, ten flights up, Ted Accenti.

Dario, content to hoard the two bags of popcorn, began to rub his stomach. "I have to go number two, Papa."

"Now! You can't wait?"

"I'll take him, honey. Mia, keep an eye on your father. Calm him if you have to," said Palmira.

Calm! How about me? Thought Mia.

Crossing crowded seats, they made their way to the far end of the gym bleachers, furthest from fourth-quarter play.

"Mama, you can wait outside when I go."

"Well, of course, you're a big boy now."

"That's what Dorothy told me for taking care of Mia in the back seat of her Cadillac. She gave me a candy bar to help my sister and then gave me another one for being what she called me, 'A big man.'"

"Okay, hurry up, 'big men' don't go in their pants."

Dario laughed while rushing into the empty restroom, did his business, and rushed out to his mother.

"Son, I don't want you bringing up your friend Dorothy's name anymore. I agree she's a lovely lady, but she scared the daylights out of your sister and me, too."

Dario's eyes shifted to the side. Dorothy was crying, and it broke the young boy's heart.

My goodness, Honey, your daughter just made four of the team's last five shots. You should see the way she reacts to the defender's feet and positioning, and this is their third girl trying to guard her.

"They shifted Cindy down low, taking out their forwards while Emma transferred to the corner defense, covering Kirsten Miller, their center. Miller's only made one shot and has been picked off twice."

"I noticed, walking back to our seats we're now ahead by three. That's a huge shift," said Palmira

Michael turned toward the Sacatti couple and said, "It's Tanya Errion. A genius at adjusting play. Notice my daughter playing low post on defense and your daughter taking away Miller's shots. My sister and I are going to miss Cindy's high school play next year. Enjoy Emma's next three years with that terrific coach."

High schools in at least Southern California's girls'

basketball circle ended without too much drama, with the St. Anthony team outscoring the hapless fourth-quarter Warriors 15-4, the final score ending Saints 47 and Warriors 40. Nationally ranked at number four, St. Pius X would most likely fall in the rankings and learn the hard way you never surrender a home team advantage. Basketball was too important on campuses across America, even in the Pre-Title era of 1961.

Chapter Nine

We have an angel watching over us. She's our friend.

She labored for twelve hours, struggling in Methodist Community Hospital located in Long Beach, California. Her physician recommended she abort the twins. What did he know?

What Dr. Norman Walker knew was Dorothy Marquez was a successful medical doctor two years out of residency and now operating her self-funded medical clinic in newly unincorporated Lakewood California, currently and officially a part of Long Beach. Married to a prosperous stockbroker (some of her friends had a notion it was because of her ingenious ability to pick apart numbers and come up with winning stock picks), he pocketed thousands, sharing them with his clients.

Her husband, Michael Marquez, paid cash for the empty building located on a popular site near Del Amo and Bellflower, and upon leaving her three-year residency, she opened the clinic, welcoming the public.

Walker knew Dorothy's life was in serious jeopardy;

her largest twin was breeching, and she would be forced to have a C-section performed. Walker also knew Dorothy suffered from Thrombocytopenia. Her platelets were incredibly low, and she could die of blood loss.

"Go ahead with the births, Dr. Walker. I understand the chances I'm taking. I've convinced Michael, too. Our twins are precious to us. They deserve a chance to live more than I do."

"Dorothy, your husband, and especially your clinic..."

"Michael will live, and so will my clinic. Most importantly, my kids will grow up and lead a good life.

"I trust your expertise, doctor. There's always a chance I might live."

Did you talk to her, Dr. Walker? I can't imagine living without her...and bringing up two infants. Doctor, I gotta confess my life has never been as generous as hers. She insisted I donate 30% of what we made in the last two years to charity. Sure, it's good for tax purposes, but 30%! I live in a tract home! A nice neighborhood but still a tract house.

"She even came up with a monthly budget. We both drive Cadillacs; however, she still shops bargains and cuts out coupons. We're not allowed to spend more than one hundred dollars on each other at Christmas, yet we have donated a quarter million for the last two years to her favorite charities.

"I couldn't even fathom running my company without her advice. You have to save her!"

"And your twins? Derek, people like your wife don't often walk this earth, at least with her abilities and moral qualities. I'll do everything to save her, yet she insists I deliver the babies. Nothing seems to change her mind."

Dr. Norman Walker put Dr. Marquez under sedation. He knew one wrong move, and she would bleed to death. An expert pediatrician, he delivered thousands of babies in the last ten years, never losing a mother. Nationally recognized for a DOP award for excellence in lifetime achievement. He made three wrong yet minor moves, most likely under the twenty mistakes the typical pediatric physician might make.

Carlos and Cindy were delivered completely healthy and eventually presented to a troubled but anxious husband. He immediately called his sister, who was single and living alone in an apartment complex where noise disturbed her day and night.

Connie accepted her brother's offer. "Derek, I'll assist you in a heartbeat. As crazy as it sounds, trading in babies crying for that damn overheated bebop in my apartment complex may be what I need. Besides, they smile too; they'll warm our hearts and help you recover."

Only buried two weeks ago, Connie loved her sister-in-law, and the thought of never seeing her again crushed her. *I have to be strong for Michael. Dorothy, please help me to do that.*

Placed on earth to spread and ignite goodness and faith, she embraced her mission. Early Monday morning Michael woke to inspirations fitting his business leadership. He juggled the numbers while eating breakfast and found Xerox and Boeing would soar in the next few years. The numbers worked, and Michael set off to work, confident his clients would follow his lead.

Dorothy whispered gently into her twin babies' ears; the newborns slept through the night, allowing Connie and her brother a well-deserved rest.

At 6:00 a.m., Carlos was the first to belt out his demand for a bottle. A half-hour later, Cindy followed suit. Michael, almost finished, held his milk bottle as Connie switched her attention to the other twin. "Michael, you have to see this; your son is holding his bottle."

Mr. Marquez bent down and cooed at his son, "One of these days, you're going to change the world, little guy, you and your sister." Carlos removed the bottle from his mouth and held his hands up.

"My little boy wants a hug. WHEW! You're a big guy, football material, Connie. How much did the doctor tell you he weighed."

"Less than two months, and he's surpassed sixteen pounds. Doctor Walker told me he's going through a growth surge. Not exactly his own words. Let me think; he said your son is going through a *massive* growth spurt. You're right about football, Carlos. He certainly will have the size."

Cindy looked up at her Auntie and smiled, placing her tiny hand over Connie's finger. "Your children are a blessing, Michael. Dorothy gave her life so these two might bring joy to us." A well of happiness filled the Marquez household as Dorothy stood nearby, proud of her divine assignment.

Soon, the children grew, each child highlighting their academic success and creating an unusual legacy on the Pop Warner football field and Junior A.A.U. basketball team. Cindy sprouted, growing taller than her 5'11" heavenly mother by eighth grade. Carlos continued his growth spurt well into high school, towering over 6'6", two inches taller than his father. And thanks to Carlos's affinity for muscle-building iron, he expanded his weight and strength by thirty pounds, surpassing his father. Both father and son appreciated the lean amount of fat casing their stature from head to toe.

Dorothy, bold enough to make her appearance when her family most needed her, was told to stop unless she was asked. "Dorothy, you no longer should appear physically.

Please, not now. I'm happy to listen to your comforting words and your advice. It's not right to frighten us by popping up."

Her guiding angel advised her. "Only when they call for you, Dorothy, and speak to them only in prayer."

"Popping up! I'm still Dorothy. You would think my family and friends would be happy to see me."

She continued to direct her husband, Michael, leading him into one of the highest cliques of the nation's top stock brokers. He declined any executive position in wealth management firms. *Go alone, Dear; avoid the sloppiness of the world's richest investors. Keep your picks simple for those who might only afford a few dollars, and don't forget your promise to charities.*

Millions poured into charitable trusts, including the Holy Land Christian Mission, beginning in 1948, eventually helping to stamp out worldwide polio.

The November 24th and 25th Great Appalachian Storm of 1950 affected over one hundred million people. Michael's million-dollar donation to the Red Cross helped save thousands of lives. An extratropical cyclone blew across as far West as the Appalachian mountains and as far East along the coastal seaboard. Temperatures dropped to all-time lows.

During the height of the cyclone in West Virginia, snow fell 56 inches. People trapped in homes with no electricity froze to death, claiming 160 lives. Red Cross, with the aid of the State and National Guard, poured through the driven snow with four-wheel snowplows, food trucks, and trucks carrying millions of supplies, bringing life back to the struggling small hollows dotting the great mountain state.

Michael would not accept any credit for his philanthropic endeavors; instead, a small plaque was placed on the outside wall of his wife's medical clinic, bestowing humble gratitude for her generosity.

By 1961, the Marquez family still resided in the 1940's tract home. Gifts not exceeding $100.00 were still respected in the household. Carlos mowed the lawn and pruned the henches with his father. Cindy helped Auntie Connie with household chores in the four-bedroom two, two-bath, 2500-square-foot corner home in Lakewood Village. By the time Derek's children reached sixteen, they were asked to obtain a limited part-time job of no more than ten hours per week to cover their spending costs among their friends.

After many rejections by her family members, Dorothy found a lovely friend in young Dario Sacatti. Not completely understanding the cultural taboo of welcoming someone from the spirit world, the young 3rd-grade boy welcomed Dorothy anytime, night or day, *"As long as you don't creep up on me. My friend Lonny likes to do that, and it scares me, so I sometimes sock him. I would never want to sock you, Mrs. Dorothy."*

Such an endearing boy, never crossed by ridiculous social offensives to God's people and angels. "No, you would never sock me, little Dario. God has saved a special place for you in heaven. We'll be best friends forever.

"Tell your mother Papa has a surprise for you tonight. Your daddy is the perfect fit, hardworking, patient, and kind. His boss just figured that out and is congratulating himself at this very minute. God bless him. Goodbye for now, my friend."

She disappeared without a trace, passing through Mrs. Holmes as the teacher told the students to stand for the Angelus and the prayer before meals. *Lunchtime already! Two peanut butter and jelly again because Mama says I'm getting big, and three Oreos!* Dario licked his lips halfway through the notoriously long prayer with three Hail Marys and the cavalcade of words in between. The lunchtime thank you prayer was affably short.

"Mr. Sacatti, your row first. All of you prayed with your fingers pointing to heaven." *And we are probably all starving.* It was turning out to be a gracious afternoon for the third grader and the kids sitting behind Dario. *You got anything to do with this, Mrs. Dorothy?*

When Eugenio arrived home, he walked with a high step. Smiling, he greeted Mia and his boy. "I got great news for the family. No more worry about tuition costs at either school. I'm going to wait until your mother and Emma arrive home. I'll announce it at dinner."

"Two surprises!" said Mia. "I'll save it for dinner, too."

"I remember I was supposed to tell Mama that you have a surprise for her," said Dario.

"How did you find out?" asked Mia.

Dario clammed up. He wasn't supposed to bring up the ghost in front of Mia. *She's too sensitive!* Papa and Mama would especially send him to bed if he said the word Dorothy. He would have to tell his momma about the 'surprise' in private when she drove up into the driveway.

A few minutes later, he thought he heard Palmira's car, only to see Emma crawling out of a coupe with two boys in the front bench seat. "That's your boyfriend, huh, Emma."

"No, Dario, they're just friends from school offering me a ride. They're both gentlemen." Dario waved back to the boys as the car exited the Sacatti home.

"I'm waiting for Mama to come home. Dorothy wanted me to tell our mama that Papa has a surprise."

"Don't mention Dorothy's name in front of Mia, Dario. She's going to deliver a baby in a few months, and revealing your friend would upset her."

I won't upset Mia, Emma. Never would I scare her. I told Dorothy not ever to sneak up on me and scare me. She said she would never do what my friend Lonny likes to do sometimes."

"When was the last time you saw Mrs. Marquez?"

"I saw her just before lunchtime prayers. She was standing next to my teacher."

"And you talked to her."

"No, I thought to her. She can hear me."

Palmira pulled the yellow Plymouth into the driveway and got out of her car as Dario folded his arms around her. "What a nice surprise; you must have had a nice day."

"Not as good as the one you're going to have."

"What is it, Sweetheart."

"I don't know Papa said he'll tell us at dinner time."

"Hello Emma, how was your day?"

"Fine, Mother, our team qualified for the top spot in C.I.F. playoffs. We're playing Palos Verde at home this Wednesday afternoon. We're not to worry, but I told you about our coach. She wants us to expect the best."

"Good advice. You've always been lucky with your teachers and coaches."

Dario, snarky while speaking out of turn, said, "Mama, Emma's lucky to have a boyfriend. He gets his friend to give her a ride home more than once."

"Mother, his name is Ted, and his friend is Ryan, Cindy's boyfriend. Ryan and Ted don't live too far from here, and they gave me a lift-saving extra day on bus fare."

"Well, that sounds like two well-behaved gentlemen. They both play on the boys' basketball team, don't they."

"Yes, they do. Ryan is the senior captain."

"You hear that, Dario. Mind your own business, and someday you might play on the basketball team in high school."

"I'm going to play baseball too, like Sandy Koufax. I still don't have his baseball card, though."

Palmira walked inside with her two children to the smell of baked chicken. "Mia, dinner smells good. Let me help you set the table."

Dario and I did that an hour ago. We got home half an hour early from the library. Neither of us had much homework, and I got something to show you. I'll wait until dinner."

Palmira kissed her husband, saying, "Eugenio, you look happy. Have a pleasant day?"

"More than happy, Palmira. I'm thrilled. Let's sit down and eat."

Baked chicken peppered with garlic savored on Dario's tongue as he dug into a drumstick. Eugenio played with his food, too nervous to eat.

"Palmira, my boss, said a blanket of divine inspiration overcame him today. I told you Jimmy Byrnes is retiring on Friday of next week; he worked for the canning plant for 32 years. So, five minutes before the end of my shift, my boss called *me* to his office and mentioned five of our men who'd make good supervisors, all of them with twenty-five years or more experience, and then he told me something steered him to pick me. I wasn't even on his list!

"His assistant checked me out. With only two sick days in nineteen years, I proved one hundred percent proficient in production and never complained. I never thought I was different from anyone else, except he thought my work ethic was proof I was a leader all along. In short, I'm not only the new supervisor..."

"You're a true leader! We always knew that, Eugenio."

"Not enough to ever be elected President of the company, but enough to pay me fifty cents more an hour! That's four dollars per day, twenty dollars per week, and eighty dollars over one month.

"No more worries about tuition, no more uncertainties about filling up on gas, and Emma, you don't have to work after practice anymore."

"I don't mind Papa, I've gotten used to it. We could use the extra money around the house."

"And Emma could use a free ride home every night," said Dario, again out of turn.

"What did I tell you, young man? You mind your own business." Palmira gave her son the classic, "Don't play with me with that stare."

When Palmira glanced over to her daughter, she noticed Mia holding up an orange piece of paper, a coveted honor roll certificate. Tears flooded Palmira's eyes as she got up and embraced her daughter. "Now, the day certainly is perfect, Eugenio."

Except for Emma, the Sacattis sat down to the Dick Van Dyke show, followed by Andy Griffith and finally Bonanza before settling down to showers, teeth, prayers, and bed.

Mia's pregnancy took a bit of notice. Sister Bridget spotted it first and agreed with Mrs. Sacatti to provide for a smooth transition to St. Agnes Home. "I understand, Mia; they perform a remarkable role for every girl needing assistance. No one here will ever know, including, of course, our friend Father Gibson. He finds out you're no longer attending St. Cyprian should make him feel comfy."

Hiding her pregnancy became problematic; however, once Mia walked through the doors, her anxiety disappeared in the heavenly mist of Sister Barbara O'Keefe. "Welcome home, Mia. We are here to serve you and to carry you in God's graces toward the birth of your child. Boy or a girl?"

"I understand I'll be giving birth to a little girl. I received a sonogram at our medical clinic, and they told me my baby appeared healthy.

"Wonderful Mia. Let me add, dear, that our sisters are all qualified L.V.N.s or RNs, and Doctors McCarthy and your Doctor Miller rotates their visits once per week. They're the best devoted to their profession and their faith. You'll look forward to talking with them. Your baby will be fine."

Sister Barbara O'Keefe

Chapter Ten

She needed to talk to a nine-year-old
to understand people again.

Your papa said we'd be able to afford both of you girls at St. Anthony next year."

"Mama, if you work, who will take care of the baby," asked Emma.

"Oh goodness, why didn't Eugenio and I think of that? Child care is expensive, far beyond what we make."

Dorothy stirred in the background, careful not to reveal herself.

"Do you think Mother, Mia will put the child up for adoption?"

"No, no, we discussed that. I'm only thirty-six still young enough to have a child. Mia wants me to identify as the mother until the baby is mature enough to know otherwise, if ever."

Why is money always a hindrance to decent decisions? Of course, Mia won't lose her baby to adoption; you're the perfect family. Mrs. Sacatti, your love brims up and over the lid. Pour over your newest child-like Holy Water at Baptism.

Why am I reduced to talking to a nine-year-old boy, as wonderful as he is, a boy of great faith and still filled with a child's innocence? Dario, you and I need to talk.

Dario walked in from neighborhood baseball across the street. "Sweetheart, I got off the phone this morning with Mrs. Gould; she said she would talk to Roger, who'll walk home with you after school."

"He's in the fifth grade, Mama. I don't think he's allowed to like me."

"Where do you pick up these crazy ideas."

"Sometimes, when I play baseball across the street, the big boys won't let me play."

"Was Roger a part of that? I want to know; otherwise, I'll find someone else."

"Well...no, he tried to tell them I was pretty good, but they wouldn't listen. The older boys got their rules, and I think Roger has to obey them."

Emma squeezed in her opinion of the fifth grader, "Mother, Roger is a good boy. I played basketball with his older sister at St. Cyprian and he always showed me and his sister respect when we walked home late after practice. You walked with us, Dario. You and Roger got along fine."

Palmira, who knew Roger lived in the same village, looked at her son and said, "Then it's settled. You will wait for Roger in front of his classroom and walk home with him."

"What if he has altar boy practice? He's a fifth grader."

"Then you'll wait Dario, you could start on your homework. Remember what I said: you're not allowed to walk home alone."

On Monday, ten minutes before lunch, Dorothy made her (what Dario referred to as) safe appearance, standing next to the sixty-plus teacher smiling down at her friend. *"So pleasant to see you, young man. I'm here to give you a message that will relieve your mother of her nervousness."*

"Mama's not nervous; she knows I'm going to walk home with Roger after school."

"I realize that, little man, I overheard her. What I want you to do is have your mother write a resume and turn it into my health center. They'll be looking for a medical secretary within a week. She needs to come to my clinic before the end of this week. She can take a half day it will be worth her while.

"Better yet, bounce it off Emma first. We pay more than your mother is making, and we include medical, dental, and child care. You got all that?"

"I think so?"

"You think what, Mr. Sacatti? You appeared to be centering on what I said, why don't you share it with the children."

"Tell your teacher the latitude lines go like this." Dorothy raised her hand and brushed a horizontal line in front of her. *"Show her."*

"Well, first, there's the latitude lines that go like this." Dario swept his hand horizontally.

"And next, there's the vertical or meridian lines that go like this. Dorothy drew her hand up and down.

"Next, Mrs. Holmes is the vertical line or the meridian that goes like this." He drew his hand up and down.

"Now do them both together like the sign of the cross. Tell her that's how you remember."

"This is how I remember." And young Dario made the sign of the cross.

Mrs. Holmes's mouth flew south. "Yes, of course, the sign of the cross. Brilliant young man."

Dorothy realized this teacher had a kind soul, as Father Gibson would have interpreted the boy's demonstration as nothing more than a grievous heretical gesture.

"You're on a roll, Dario. Tell your teacher Meridians are used to help us tell time. There's 24 of them."

"Meridian's help us tell time. There are twenty-four of them. Each is one hour."

"Not bad, little fellow!"

"I learned them when I went to the library."

"I'm so proud of you, Dario, mesmerized with me that way. You heard every word I said. I'm going to allow your row to go first again today." A chorus of eight, "Thank you, Mrs Holmes," rang out in unison.

"We'll skip the Angelus today and just recite the prayer before meals. Fingers pointed to heaven, children."

———

Dario sat outside in front of Room 12 of the 5th grade. He hoped the older kids wouldn't make fun of Roger. The bell rang for the upper grades, and students exited the classroom.

"Hey, what are you doing here, squirt? Mommy forgot to pick you up?"

A voice appeared from behind, "Leave him alone, Carl. I'm walking him home. You got a problem with that?" said Roger Gould.

"No, no, not at all. I just thought maybe the kid was lost or something."

"Sure you did; now you need to get lost."

"Sorry about that, Dario. Carl's the real squirt. He feels picking on the younger kids makes him feel tough. If Carl ever bothers you in the future, raise your fist and rock your foot forward. He'll run."

"I'll walk you home right after my bell until Thursday. On Friday, you're going to have to wait until four o'clock. I got altar boy practice. If you don't have homework, your mother asked if we could go to the library. You like the library, don't you?"

"I like it a lot. Mia used to take me there after school."

"Well, good, visiting the library will do me good. We're told to read a book a month, and although Miss Davis encourages us to read, our school library does not seem to offer much. I need to stop faking book reports."

Dario showed Roger his favorite section in the library. The fifth grader surprised the Sacatti boy by also taking an interest in the BETSY series. "I like baseball books too, Roger."

"I bet you do. I've seen you play. You're a good baseball player yourself."

"Thank you. Maybe someday the big kids will let me play with them."

"I'll tell you what I'm going to convince the guys to work you in. Hey! They got Hardy Boys books here. I've read a few. They're good. I think we should both check them out."

"Are the Hardy Boys books hard?" asked Dario, hoping he could keep up.

"For a kid like you, Dario. You'll be fine. I'll tell you, what do you like, adventure?"

"I guess so, whatever adventure means."

"You'll find out soon enough. You're going to read this one: *The Missing Chums,* and I'll read *The Secret of the Old Mill*. After you can tell me if you like the book and I'll do the same for you. We gotta a deal?"

"We gotta deal."

Dario thanked Roger when he eventually walked him home. Alone the boy started in on his homework. His mother wouldn't be home until nightfall. He decided to turn on the lamps and lock the doors before it got dark.

After he finished his assignments, he lay down on his bed and read his book. To his relief, an hour later, Emma arrived home first. Dario looked outside his bedroom window and noticed she had received another ride from those two boys. He wouldn't kid her. If it weren't for her two friends, Dario would have to wait by himself longer.

"You okay, Dario? Staying alone inside our house must have felt different?"

"I got a little bit scared."

"You weren't scared of Dorothy, were you?"

"No, she only talks to me in my classroom next to my teacher, usually around lunchtime.

"Dorothy wants me to tell you something Mama must do."

"What is that, Dario?"

"She wants Mama to make a recipe and take it to the doctor's office where she used to take Mia."

A recipe! Why would they need a recipe?"

"Because they'll pay her more and stuff."

"You must be talking about a resume."

"Yeah, that's it, a resume. Dorothy told me three things Mama needed to know. They need a person what Mama does; they pay more and something else."

"That's a job connected with the union. Of course, they pay more and would offer health care. I wonder...?

"What book are you reading?"

"A Hardy Boys book, *The Missing Chums*. So far, I'm on page twenty. I don't know if I'm supposed to finish it by Friday. I need to ask Roger because we have a deal. He reads a Hardy Boys, and I read another one, then we tell each other if we liked the story."

"You like Roger, don't you, Dario."

"I sure do. Roger has a lot of good ideas and said he's going to get the Big Boys to let me play baseball with them across the street."

Father drove into the driveway while almost simultaneously, Palmira pulled in behind her husband. The couple embraced each other with a quick peck on each other's cheeks. Walking into the house, Dario ran up to his parents, announcing Emma had good news.

"Mother and Papa, what I heard, Mama, you need to type a resume and present it at the medical clinic where you took Mia. I can help you."

"How is that good news? I already am employed with Dr. Bishop at his medical facility."

"I remember now!" said Dario, leaping into the air. "I think they will take care of me after school. I got a little bit scared today."

Palmira bent down and hugged her son. "You were scared. Let me talk to Mrs. Gould and see if you could stay at Roger's. We could pay him something."

Emma informed her mother she thought Dario might have been referring to a childcare provision with the medical clinic's pay schedule. "I think they also offer dental as well as Medical. The Marquez Medical Clinic is associated with a union operation. Mother and father child care would solve our dilemma with your grandchild."

"Who told you this!" insisted Eugenio.

Dario hung his head, ashamed to reveal the magical lady that appeared in his classroom almost daily.

Emma defended her brother, "Mother and Papa, Dorothy revealed a message to my brother in his classroom. It couldn't hurt to check."

Confident his sister supported him, Dario said, "This week Mama. Dorothy said right away and during the daytime."

"What do you think, Eugenio?"

"Sit down and type out your resume, take off part of your day, and look into it. It's worth a try."

Unlike Sunday morning Mass, the female residents of St. Agnes were not forced to attend morning prayers in the chapel. A few of the pregnant girls were ordered to rest in bed and not exert themselves. Protecting the young girl and her unborn child was paramount to the good sisters running the home. Mia felt fine and was bored lying in bed. She dressed and headed down to the large chapel located on the convent's far west end.

Morning prayers included a novena to Our Lady of Perpetual Help today to pray for the proposed passing of the 23rd Amendment, giving the citizens who lived in Washington, D.C., a chance to vote. "Depriving them for so long has been unjust," stated Sister Barbara. The nuns followed with the Joyful Mysteries, all five decades, rejoicing in God's intervention in eliminating the neglect of citizens in our nation's capitol.

Caroline, a seventeen-year-old experiencing the final triage of her pregnancy, leaned into Mia and whispered, "The nuns here are extremely socially conscious. We sent cards to South Africa last week protesting apartheid. You'll get used to it. They never force us to get involved in their political agenda, but they're for a good cause, so what the hell." A finger crossed the lips of a young sister, and Caroline quieted down.

The majority of girls were asked to volunteer for different responsibilities that ensure the success of a well-run home, as well as providing the girls with a 'buy-in' into the home's daily operation. Mia volunteered for kitchen duty involving breakfast and lunch. She was relieved of duties in the evening and on weekends.

On Tuesday, March 4th, Mia sat with Caroline and Betty, who was not yet assigned to her kitchen obligation. Betty looked over at the newest resident and asked, "So, how'd it happen?"

"Excuse me, how did what happen?" Mia said.

"How'd you get knocked up?" replied an audacious Betty.

Tired of the repulsive questions, Mia responded, "Well, it appears I must have had sex."

Caroline intervened, "Mia, I believe Betty is trying to ask whether you were impregnated through a boyfriend, cousin or you were raped. We're open around here and will offer you help if you need it."

"My so-called boyfriend 'knocked me up,' as you say. He also impregnated two other teens. His middle school reacted to complaints from the girl's parents and threw him out of school. His father sent him back east to live with his uncle."

"Does your friend know you're pregnant?" asked Caroline.

"No! And he never will. It's better for me and my child."

Betty agreed, "That kind of person will never measure up to fatherhood. They all talk and command their brains to only operate below the waist.

"I take it you're not going to adopt out your child."

"I plan on keeping my baby," stated Mia.

Betty, relieved, told Mia she had decided not to give the child away, "Up to two weeks ago, I was tossing and turning, hoping my child would find a good home. I couldn't sleep until I figured if I were determined enough, my child's best home would be with me.

" I live with my single mother, and I plan on taking care of my baby when mom's at work, then continuing G.E.D. classes at home when she comes home. I agree with you, Mia. I'll never let that bastard know he knocked me up. The hell with him, and good riddance."

Mia looked to her left and asked Caroline, "How about you."

"When my father found out I was pregnant, he was ready to throw me out into the street. Mother begged Sister Barbara O'Keefe to take me in. Sister didn't need much coaxing. This place has twenty-five bedrooms, with two girls in a room. Right now, there are only twelve of us; that's no reason why we don't get our own room. Hell, we're girls we'll keep them clean.

"Anyway, when I deliver my baby, I hope my dad changes his mind. He does have a good heart but a bad temper when he gets started on anything that he doesn't agree with. If he throws a shit fit, I don't know what I'll do."

"Excuse me, girls. I don't mean to interrupt your conversation, but Sister O'Keefe would like to speak with Mia when all of you are finished with breakfast."

Mia, since you have to get up early during the week, I'm going to move you and Betty to our only bedroom downstairs, down the hall from the kitchen. It's closer to your job and much larger. Are you okay with the change?"

"Yes, Sister, I understand. Moving down here won't be a problem."

"Good. I'm sure you're aware of our G.E.D. program we could get you started today if you're up to it. We just started the 2nd semester two weeks ago. How are you at Language and Mathematics?"

"I excelled in language; I never found it too challenging. Math, however, I needed to stay on top of it, otherwise it wasn't a problem."

"That's good to hear. Right now, two of our girls are enrolled in English and beginning Algebra. Sister Monica Dawkins will catch you up on what you missed. Class begins at 9:00 a.m., fifteen minutes from now. You, of course, would eliminate your lunchtime responsibility. G.E.D. class ends at noon. After lunch you need to nap and study when you get up. Are you ready?"

"Yes, Sister, I'll do my best."

"Wonderful, let me walk you to Sister Monica's class. She expects you."

Around three that morning, Mia detected a whiff of smoke in the upstairs room. Within a few seconds, she woke Betty, and both were driven from their room. Blooms of smoke hurdled their way down the staircase. Down the hall and out the door, the girls ran, drawing in fresh air while collapsing on the grass lawn. Looking over her shoulder Mia witnessed flames shooting out the upper floor windows. Biting their hands, the two girls sobbed as sirens approached the home.

Nuns rushed out of the adjoining convent, a few driven back by the intense heat violently hammering out the girls ' 2nd and 3rd story resident. Four of the pregnant girls exited down the stairs, collapsing near Mia and Betty, choking on the inhalation of smoke and wailing with dried tears. Suddenly, another girl appeared at the upper floor window and leaped, the fall knocking her unconscious.

Firefighters flew from their trucks dressed in fireproof gear and wearing masks to thwart off any smoke. Up the staircase, three rescue men ran as two of the firemen checked on the fallen girl. Paramedics provided oxygen to Mia and the four escaped young teens.

No girls were found on the second level. The rescue team fought their way through the flames, rushing up a near-collapsing third floor. There, they found six girls in separate rooms, four of them unconscious and not breathing. One of them caught in the flames, completely burning in her room as she ceased to exist, her body leaping with fire, engulfing the dead teen. In the room next to the deceased girl, a body moved low to the ground, her fingers drumming up and down as if to say, "I'm still alive."

Unable to carry the girls down the near-collapsed stairwell, the four firefighters worked their way toward a window gushing with water as fire gave way to smoke. Leaning out the window, they saw firefighters had set up multiple ladders against the structure, handing the girls down two at a time. Fire now leaped completely, immersing the hallway and surging back into the bedrooms. Rescue workers handed down the last teen, trying to avoid the intense heat creeping toward them. They hooked their boots into the rung of three separate ladders, heading down to safety as the fire consumed the second and third floors.

All of the girls were rushed to Cedars Sinai Hospital nearby. Three of the girls on the third floor succumbed to smoke inhalation, taking with them their unborn child. One of the unconscious girls survived but was told in the early pre-dawn morning that her unborn child didn't make it.

Running east on Beverly Blvd. toward his vehicle, police apprehended a suspicious young man. Searched, the large pocket inside his jacket contained lighter fluid. Inside the man's blue jeans, officers found a dozen wooden matches. His hands smelled of the combustible fluid. Taken to the police station, he was questioned.

Not willing to talk, he was escorted behind bars at 7:00 a.m., determined to see a lawyer. His prints and photos were taken to determine the suspected criminal's identity.

Detectives passed around copies of the young man's photo to all of the sisters at the connecting convent. "Anyone recognize this young man?"

Each of the nuns nodded their head "no."

By late Wednesday morning, the devastating tally of dead teen residents amounted to four. The surviving eight found three of them lost their unborn children.

Detective Pierce Langley, debriefing his assistants, said, "She landed on her back and fractured her spine. Deliberately turning her body during the fall probably saved her baby. Her name is Wondee Sinh age sixteen, an immigrant and alone in the U.S.A. She was raped two weeks after she slipped into the country by her Chinese runner. She was one of hundreds of young immigrants enslaved on this side of the border.

"Wondee chose to keep the baby."

"My God, what an unbelievable girl. Sacrificed that fall to save her child and a victim of a brutal rape. What shape is she in?"

"Critical, but she and the baby will survive. I don't think her rapist is connected with the fire. He's locked up, and I understand he was a nobody. They put him away in a Level 4 prison in Washington.

"I've targeted two girls who both survived pretty much unscathed. Interesting interviews I conducted with both Mia Sacatti and Betty Russo. Each of them is resentful of who impregnated them, and both harbor deep grudges. I showed Sacatti and Russo the picture of the man we apprehended. Russo's hand went to her mouth. She started to shake and nearly passed out."

"So our suspect is the fire starter?" wondered Vernon Munson, a new recruit to the detective bureau.

"One and the same, although he denies it. His name, according to Miss Russo, is Allen Hever.

"Betty told me he wanted to marry her and change her life for the better. Her mother is single and struggles. So she told Allen to go to hell and get out of her life. When, according to her, he found out she was pregnant, Betty told Allen it was another guy. I imagine enough for him to want to kill her."

"So why didn't he kill her? He certainly had the chance," wondered Paul Ortiz, a five-year detective and twenty-five-year veteran of L.A.P.D.

"I don't think Allen could find her."

"Hell, Pierce, how would he know what room she was in and the upper floors? Someone had to tell him. You think it was her?"

"Betty swore she never told him a damn thing. Why in the hell would she do that? Only her mother knows what room she stayed in. We called Betty's house, and there was no answer. That upset the girl. She told me her mother had two phones, and one was next to her bed. Betty told us her mother would always answer on the first or second ring. We sent the police out to her home in Hawthorne. We haven't heard back from the Hawthorne police as of yet."

Caroline's worry about whether her dad would accept her again was over. Her charred body found on the 3rd floor would trouble the father for the rest of his life, eventually leading to a major stroke and death at age forty-three. Caroline's mother, two years younger than her husband, would never marry again.

A call came in from the Hawthorne Police Department. Betty's mother, Carmela, was found unconscious when police forced their way inside. Her face was badly bruised, and she was transported to the local hospital. The emergency medical team found three of her ribs were broken, and she suffered a severe concussion.

"We got that son of a bitch as soon as she comes to," shouted Detective Langley. "I'm recommended the death penalty to the D.A. for that bastard."

Betty would not be told of her mother's condition until she was taken to the convent with the other three girls. Wondee remained critical in the hospital, and three of the girls who lost their babies received psychological help before returning to their families.

Chapter Eleven
Never drive faster than
your angel can fly.

Saturday morning, the Sacatti family gathered in the '56 Plymouth and drove to the St. Agnes Home and Convent. After a thirty-five-minute drive along the five-freeway, Dario rolled down his back seat window and placed his hand out, moving it up and down as he imagined it a plane cutting through the wind turbulence.

"Mama, how come Mia can't go to my school? I miss her."

"Your sister was lucky enough to live inside a convent and receive the attention she deserves," said Palmira, not too sure if her answer was adequate.

"I don't get it. Mia liked Sister Bridget and got that smart girl orange paper. Sister sure is going to miss her."

Emma tried to explain to her brother why Mia found a temporary home at St. Agnes. "Dario, when you get older, you'll understand why some people want to visit another home for a while. Don't you remember when Mother and Father dropped us off at Uncle Sal and Auntie Patsy for a week, and you cried? A week later, you didn't want to go home. You wanted to stay and cried because it was only the seventh day. You couldn't understand ten days wasn't a week."

"I still don't understand why a week is only seven days. It should be ten days because it's easier to count 10, 20, 30..."

Dario's mother intervened, "Alright enough, Dario. Besides sweetheart, the first day of the week is Sunday, God's day, and then there is Monday, Tuesday, Wednesday, Thursday, Friday, and Saturday. That's seven days. If we had three more, we'd have to invent new names."

"That would be fun. I could think of a million names like SANDY, number eight; KOUFAX, number nine; and DODGERS, number ten."

Eugenio smiled, saying, "Girls, I believe Dario has come up with an excellent answer for the confusing seven-day week.

"It looks as though we're here. Now, Dario, I want you to be quiet and not ask the nuns or your sister any questions."

Palmira's hand covered her mouth as her eyes glistened. "How awful Eugenio, the deaths, this God-awful tragedy."

He held his wife up as her face paled, thinking of just how close Mia came to facing a nightmarish death. Emma helped her father to the porch of the convent, where Sister Barbara O'Keefe recognized the grief that overcame the mother of three. "Take her to the couch. I'll get a glass of water."

Mia appeared in the living room doorway and ran to her mother. "Don't cry, Mama, I'm so sorry. I'm so God awful, sorry!"

"I thank God every day my children are safe, honey."

"Then why did God allow this, Mama," Mia said with tears inundating her cheeks.

"What did Sister Bridget teach us, Mia? You have to believe it to calm your soul," pleaded Emma, worried about Mia's unborn child.

"He gave us free will like that beast who murdered the girls and their babies. That's reality, Emma. Thinking God never takes and that he only receives doesn't work for me at this moment!"

Dario hugged close to his mother, saying, "Whose babies, Mama, not Mia's."

"No, not hers," Palmira reassured her frightened son.

"Mama and Papa, I want to get Betty," Mia said.

Sister Barbara brushed Mia's arm, saying, "Let me get her up. You stay here with your family. I'll be right back."

"Daddy, could you take Dario outside to the grotto? It's in the back," asked Mia.

"Why do we have to go outside, Papa?" said Dario as his father led him out the door.

"Sometimes girls need to talk among themselves. Someday, you'll understand."

"Mama and Mia, Betty's ex-boyfriend, Allen, is the suspect in the fire and murders. Please don't bring up what happened. Also, Allen attacked her mother, and she is in the hospital in bad shape."

Moments later, Sister Barbara appeared in the front room with a red-eyed Betty by her side. "Betty, the Sacattis; Mrs. Palmira Sacatti; and her daughter Emma. I don't see Mr. Sacatti and little Dario?"

Mia answered, "My Papa and brother went outside to look at Mary's grotto. They'll be back in a few minutes.

"Are you okay, Betty?"

Sister Barbara handed the pregnant teen a tissue as Betty walked to a cushioned single couch and sat down. "It's my fault, all my fault!" Betty cried without acknowledging Palmira or Emma. Her grief was so tormented she grasped for help, any guidance to ease her pain. "I missed the bus after school and ran to try and stop it. The bus kept going when a young man pulled his car to the side of the road, offering me a ride. Like a fool, I got in. A beautiful newer car, a sports car. He was perfectly nice and interesting and took me directly home. His name was Allen, and he wanted to know if he could see me again. I couldn't say no, he was so handsome. We went out three times when he forced himself on me, and you can see the result."

"He raped you!" asked Emma incredulously, startled by what this girl had just said. "Did you file a police report?"

Mia grabbed her sister's arm. *No more questions, Emma. She's pregnant!* Mia appeared alarmed.

"We're waiting for Father Hennesy to loan us his car to take Betty to the hospital to visit her mother. He, however, is visiting an elderly woman in her home. Her daughter requested the last rites before she passed on. Father then has an evening Confirmation he's attending in Pomona. It's his niece. He won't be back until late tonight. He promised us his car, however, for Sunday. He'll be around saying Mass all day."

Eugenio walked through the front door, Dario standing behind him, "All clear? Whoops!"

"Come in, honey, bring our son. I want to introduce two very fine individuals." He presided forward, Dario traipsing behind his father.

"Betty and Sister Barbara, this is my husband, Eugenio, and my son, Dario," said Palmira relieving Mia of the introduction.

"My son and I are happy to meet both of you," replied Eugenio.

"Sweetheart, Betty and Sister Barbara are experiencing a minor setback; they can't find transportation today to the hospital to visit Betty's mother."

Betty interposed, "My mother suffered a severe concussion and is in serious condition. Mr. Sacatti, I don't want to intrude; however, time for me personally is of the essence."

"Well then, what are we waiting for? My car could take us to…"

"To Hawthorne Hospital, Mr. Sacatti. Thank you for helping me. You're a dear man." Betty rushed with Mia to their room to grab warm sweaters.

Betty sat in the back seat with Mia and Dario sitting on Emma's lap. In the front, Eugenio sat behind the wheel with his wife next to him and Sister Barbara O'Keefe to Palmira's right.

Arriving at Hawthorne Hospital, Mrs. Sacatti asked for permission to visit Mrs. Julia Russo, the nurses station guided them to room 374 on the 3rd floor. "Since you're family, Betty you may enter the room along with Sister Barbara. Because she remains in serious condition, the rest of you need to wait in the hallway."

All seven rode the elevator up, with Dario quietly asking his father if he could press the buttons. The doors opened to what looked like a busy day. Again, Palmira approached the nurses' desk. We want to see our friend Julia Russo, her daughter, and Sister Barbara O'Keefe are with us."

"Of course, she's down the hall in room 302. We just took her out of critical care and placed her in a serious but stable room. She came out of a coma three hours ago and is doing much better. We notified the police immediately, as requested, and she identified her attacker. Thank God I hear he's locked up."

"Are we all allowed to visit her? We were told only family which we understand if she still is not doing well."

"We'll let her daughter decide once she walks in."

Nurse Theresa Masotto called Sister Barbara to the desk, whispering, "Hello, Sister. I understand you've experienced a hellish week. I'll keep you in my prayers."

"Thank you, Theresa. Did a Catholic priest from St. Joseph give Mrs. Russo Extreme Unction?"

"He sure did; a young priest, Father William Baxter, came in and gave her the last rites just in case. It sure did work. Mrs. Russo was much better the next day. They should change the Catholic rite to the sacrament of healing."

"Good idea I'll put in a word to Pope John." Both Sister and Theresa held back a melancholy grin.

"She's been moved to room 302. Her daughter must be anxious."

Betty walked into the single bedroom to find her mother vastly asleep. Nurse Lily Parker looked at the sad-faced pregnant young lady and said, "We gave her a sedative early this morning. She should be coming around. Go ahead and pull up a chair next to her."

"Mom, it's me, Betty. I miss you, mother, and love you so much."

Her eyelids fluttered, and a strained murmuring escaped her lips. "Betty, is that you?"

"I'm here, Mama, your Betty Boop." She grasped her mother's hand, hoping to stir Julia Russo wide awake.

"Betty Boop Poop Poop A Doop."

Betty's eyes filled with tears. "Julia Anna, she eats the banana."

I'm astonished witnessing the poetic display of loving fellowship between mother and daughter, thought Sister Barbara.

"Are you okay, sweetheart? I heard there was a fire."

"I'm fine, Mother, me and your grandchild. In fact, my roommate saved my life."

"Oh dear, saved your life how? Who is she?"

"Her name is Mia. She's right outside. Would you like to see her and her family?"

"Of course, send them all in."

When Mia first appeared, the pregnant girl's natural beauty took Julia aback. "Such a heavenly creature. Are you the girl who saved my daughter's life?"

"Maybe more like Sister Barbara, who moved Betty downstairs. We both work in the kitchen just down the hallway."

Sister Barbara smiled and said, "Your daughter was having difficulty waking up in the morning, and moving closer to the kitchen with a roommate would solve that niggle."

"Well, struggling to get up in the morning, that sounds like my little one, Sister Barbara.

"And who is this other beautiful girl, your sister Mia? You look so much alike."

"Yes, this is my sister, Emma. She's a tremendous varsity basketball player at Saint Anthony High."

"And I take it this is your mother, father, and little brother."

Emma spoke, introducing her parents, Eugenio and Palmira Sacatti and little Dario.

"I see a beautiful Italian family just like Betty and myself. Her birth name is Betina; however I was such a fan of Betty Boop I gradually changed her name to the English pronunciation of BETTY.

"Anyway, I'm so pleased to meet you, Mr. and Mrs. Sacatti."

Palmira and her daughters all bent down and hugged the heavily head-bandaged young mother of Betty Rizzo. "Thank you so much. I want you all to know how much I struggled. Falling into a coma was so confusing. I was ready to give my life when an angel appeared in my dreams, telling me to live on for my daughter and little grandchild. She was so beautiful and vibrant."

"It was my friend," said Dario.

"Your friend?" questioned Julia Rizzo.

"Go ahead and tell her," said Mia.

"I saw her yesterday in class, and she told me she would save a life. She must have meant you."

"Your 'angel,' what is her name?"

He looked again at his sister and then his mother who nodded approval. "Her name is Dorothy. She likes yellow dresses."

"Yellow?" uttered a mystified Julia.

"Yes, and she drives a pink Cadillac."

"She drives a pink Cadillac and appears in my sleep. You certainly do have quite an imagination, young fellow."

"It's not his imagination; Dario was taught never to lie or even stretch the truth. Was your apparition clothed in a yellow dress?" queried Mia.

"As a matter of fact, she wore a bright yellow dress, almost like staring at the sun. And her smile was just as radiant with deep blue eyes. She must have looked no more than..."

"No more than thirty years of age," interceded Mia.

Julia stared at the striking young teen and said, "You've seen her?"

"Yes, all of us except Emma. She currently appears to Dario because he doesn't fear her as much."

"Well, Dario, I want to thank your Dorothy. She's the second person who saved a Russo life.

"Thank all of you for visiting me. I don't think I could ever return to my house. The brutal assault because of Allen is something I could never get out of my head." She placed her hands over her face and broke down as Betty squeezed her mother tight, absorbing the hurt.

"We can move, Momma. I don't mind," Betty reassured her mother.

"Our elderly neighbors, Mr. and Mrs. Crawford, visited me this morning. They were lucky; the first visitors not being family allowed in my room."

Betty, holding her mother's hand, responded, "That was so kind of them, Mother. Mrs. Crawford hasn't been well herself."

"Yes, it was; however, I told them honestly that I didn't think I could ever step into my home again. They seemed to understand.

"Mr. Crawford said he knew of a fine realtor and that I should call him unless I changed my mind, though I don't know where we would move?"

Emma spoke first, "We have two houses for sale up and down our block. We have a wonderful neighborhood and a college across the street. The perfect location for you and Betty. Your daughter wouldn't have to walk far for her continued education."

Betty asked, "But who would take care of my baby?"

Palmira questioned Mrs. Russo, "Julia, where you work, are they unionized?"

"Oh yes, I've worked at DOUGLAS AIRCRAFT since the big war. Employed since 1942 as one of the original 'Rosie Riveters.' I met my husband just after he returned from the war with Japan. He signed in for a job and was hired. Douglas was kind enough to keep me signed on."

"Let me ask you a question, Mrs. Russo: does your work include child care?"

"They sure do. One of the first in the country. They cared for Betty long ago."

"Betty is part of your family; they could care for your grandchild while Betty attends school," revealed Palmira.

"That could work, Betty. It worked back when, especially after your father was killed in Korea, and especially when you were born."

"Oh, we're sorry, Julia, we didn't know your husband lost his life," said Emma, tears beginning to crowd her eyes.

"My Ben was a real hero. He served in two wars and was drafted to Korea as a reserve. Ben could have turned the draft down as little Betina was with us, but he felt his country needed him. Our Ben defended his bunker with five other men and took a grenade, saving three of his buddies' lives. I was presented with the silver medal at his burial. Betty remembers, don't you."

Her daughter nodded with her head down, not able to relive the sorrow. "I'm sorry, dear. You were so young. I thought the pain of losing daddy tempered."

"Daddy used to sing me to sleep every night when I was a toddler and young child. I still remember one song.

Somewhere over the rainbow
Skies are blue
And the dreams that you dare to dream
Really do come true.

Her eyes glistened as she remembered the soft voice of her daddy. "Go on honey, one more verse," said her mother as she, too, remembered the strong anchor of a man whose heart guided his soul. Tears circled the hospital room.

Someday, I'll wish upon a star.
And wake up where the clouds are far behind me
Where troubles melt like lemon drops
Away above the chimney tops
That's where you'll find me.

"I still wait for Daddy, Mommy." Her eyebrows lowered, pulling closer together. "He's forever with me." Betty felt her throat closing up.

Pain overshadowed the joy of the original visit. Dario, unknown to him, brought back the happy mood by retreating to the room 302 toilet, standing up, and letting it flow. The urine sound created a burst of embarrassing laughter followed by a blissful chorus of outright hilarity overshadowing the grievous losses at St. Agnes.

"Dario! You could have at least closed the door!" said Mr. Sacatti holding back a snicker.

"Sorry, Papa, I couldn't wait!" answered the little fellow. A reprise of bright smiles met Dario. "I just had to go to the bathroom real bad."

Somewhere over the rainbow skies are blue, and the dreams that you dare to dream really do come true.

Chapter Twelve

Whether you think you can or think you can't; you're probably right.

Monday found the Sacatti and Russo's pretty much facing lives more predictable nature, with no more fires and no more apprehension about whether mom Julia Russo would make it or not after the beating. Mia and Betty cradled in the arms of the good sisters at St. Agnes, felt again safe. And Emma faced her second round of C.I.F. playoffs in her home gym.

Dario, on Monday, didn't see his old friend standing next to Mrs. Holmes (Dorothy was said, according to upstairs rumors preparing for the second-round game against league champion East Torrance).

Eugenio, his day on his newest assignment not only felt comfortable, but he equally felt blessed. *Thank you for all you do, Lord. I will do my best to help the church.*

Palmira received a call that morning for her to report to her new job at the end of the week. She blessed herself after hanging up the phone. Her employer, Dr. Bishop, Palmira's eighty-two-year-old boss, would understand and wish her well.

By 4:00 p.m., a referee threw up a basketball in the

center circle. Cindy Marquez leaped and successfully tapped the ball to guard Emma Sacatti, and the onslaught of the East Torrance High School Tartars was underway. By halftime, the score stood at Saint Anthony 38 and East Torrance High 16.

Tanya Errion pulled her top players in the middle of the 3rd quarter. Saint Anthony led at the time by 28 now too late for the Torrance school to make any miraculous comebacks.

It appeared the astonishing play of the Saint Anthony Saints and the miserable play of the East Torrance Tartars had anything to do with Dorothy interfering with the game. However, their performances seem to indicate something fishy.

"I don't understand it; East Torrance's play wasn't at all what we studied in their films," Tanya Errion, confused, uttered East Torrance's misfortune to her assistants.

"It wasn't me!"

"Excuse me, who are you?"

"Never mind." And the lady dressed in yellow disappeared around the corner of the locker room.

"Who in the hell was that woman!"

"Get Emma in here!" Coach Errion asked one of her assistants.

Emma walked into the office dressed in her game uniform with a dust apron covering her. "You need to see me coach."

"Now, what's wrong with you? You look pale. Sit down. I'll get you a glass of water.

"Here, sip. Are you okay? You act as if you've seen a ghost."

"That makes five of us."

"Pardon me?"

"Four members of my family until now. I am the fifth.

A young lady dressed in yellow walked on the other side of the gym and disappeared through a solid wall."

"You said young and in yellow. My assistants and I saw her too. What's this about a ghost?"

"Coach this is something you should discuss with our center Cindy."

Saint Anthony's semi-final round would be played at the Los Angeles Sports Arena on Friday, March 21st. The maximum capacity for the four semi-final teams was 10,000 enough to facilitate every high school team.

Tickets sold at a typical level. The L.A. Arena did not predict a complete sellout. The first game feted C.I.F. #3 Notre Dame of Sherman Oaks against the #2 St. Pius X Warriors of Downey. Emma's Saint Anthony team ranked #1, would face the #4 team from St. Francis of La Canada.

"Mother I purchased three tickets with a student discount for seven dollars. I know how Papa wants to go if our team is playing a night game."

"Where did you find that kind of money?" asked Palmira.

"Coach asked the school to pay me since you caught up on tuition payments. I'm now paid $1.50 an hour. Five hours a week, and that's $7.50. So I still have a half-dollar until I get paid the following week."

When Eugenio arrived and was told of the tickets, he let out a 'WHOOP!' He talked of nothing but basketball at the dinner table. "So you put away those Torrance girls in the second round. That's our girl, Palmira, a genuine star.

"This #4 team, are they solid?"

"My coach and the team think so, but personally, I think we're a good match-up; we reviewed their performance on film."

Thursday flashed by, and Eugenio hurried home just in time to see Roger sitting on the front porch with Dario. Mr. Sacatti handed the young fifth grader two dollars for looking after his son for a week.

"Not a problem, Mr. Sacatti. Dario and I both recommended to each other the books we were sharing, the Hardy Boys. There must be a hundred of them, and so far, they're all good. Right, little pal?"

"Right, Roger. See you on Monday," and Dario waved goodbye.

"It would be best if you showered, son. We're leaving twenty minutes after your mother gets home. I'm going to make popcorn and maybe pack three bottles of soda. Hurry up and get in that shower."

Palmira arrived home to the smell of buttered popcorn. "I take it you don't want dinner?"

"No, you sent me to work with a huge lunch. I ate one of the chicken sandwiches on the way home. You're not hungry, are you?"

Not at all. I packed myself a big lunch, too, and told Dario to finish the chicken in the refrigerator with Roger when he got home. I made him a big salad, too."

"Good, the game before Emma's is St. Pius X. Remember them?"

"How could I forget."

"If they win tonight along with Saint Anthony, St. Pius is going to want revenge. We were their only loss this year. Now, if Notre Dame wins, our girls may have a tough time."

Eugenio lived all three major sports, including the European Soccer Championships, on television. His year didn't follow the typical calendar. Beginning in September was high school and college football, along with the World Series baseball games in October. His Los Angeles Lakers bled into November, and if his team made the playoffs, the final game would be played in June. Baseball rounded out his year of sports, baseball especially instilled in his son.

Public schools seriously complained about the unfair competition between a public school directed to only allow athletes from their immediate neighborhood to compete legally with Catholic schools that cast a wider net when finding eligibility to compete for the school. Reality often found, though, three or four Catholic High Schools competing against each other to recruit the best athletes from their Catholic parishes.

Tacking on tuition costs and mandatory academic testing to enter the school seemed to override any so-called complaint. However, reality did pose a clear argument in favor of the public schools as all finalists were Catholic institutions.

Eugenio wasn't interested in the ongoing grumbling between the two sides interpreting what schools possess the most powerful teams. He loved sports growing up as a child in his small hometown of Velletri a province of Lazio, Italy. He and his father, Alessio, played soccer once or twice per week year-round.

When Alessio, a staunch objector to the powerful dictatorship of Benito Mussolini, gathered his parents, family, and brothers and found their way from Italy to France and eventually to the New York shores of Ellis Island, he found blessed relief.

Alessio heard of the mild Mediterranean climate of California, and similar to many U.S. citizens, they migrated to the sunshine state and worked the orange groves in 1939.

By 1943, Eugenio was drafted into the United States Army. He served two years seeing both vicious combat with the Japanese and walking freely in the city of Tokyo, getting to know the defeated friendly Japanese citizens now living in extreme poverty.

In the spring of 1945 Eugenio was released from his conscription to the United States Army and obtained his citizenship by summer. During that time, studying for permanent American citizenship, he met Palmira, also vying for the same dream. Three months later, during the early fall, they united in a Catholic marriage, producing a child fifteen months later, a future basketball protégé lighting up the court at Saint Anthony.

And now the thirty-eight-year-old father of three sat comfortably sharing popcorn with his son in the Los Angeles Sports Arena.

Eight in the evening found the Downey High School Warriors leading at the beginning of the third quarter by eleven points. St. Pius X center dominated in the corner pocket all night long, throwing up two-pointers and when fouled even another point on the free throw line. Notre Dame made little to no adjustments, and at the end of the game, St. Pius dominated the court, winning by sixteen and crying for a rematch against the Long Beach Saints.

Eugenio knew a match-up could go either way. Still, first, his daughter would have to lead the team to victory over St. Francis, La Canada's team, a formidable line-up led by 6'2" center Kristen Bell and 5'10" power forward Rebecca Chase, both achieving All-C.I.F. first and second-team honors in the incredible powerful Almont-League. At 20-4, their record did not reflect a team that could easily lose.

St. Francis proved formidable for the undefeated Saints, the score ping-ponging back and forth. By halftime, the La Canada team led by a single basket. "This is where Coach Errion will excel," said Eugenio, leaning into his wife. "This gal knows how to make adjustments. But what can she adjust? St. Francis, under Coach Jackie Gunningham, plays perfect team ball."

Tanya didn't find adjusting the man-to-man defense would change anything. She stepped up her offense. Tanya's guards aggressively drove in on their star forward and center. She found a weakness. Both St. Francis girls would turn their bodies, afraid of a head-on collision, creating for themselves an automatic blocking call. Emma was perfect on the penalty line so far for the night, successfully sinking in ten out of ten free throws.

By the end of the 3rd quarter, both Kirsten Bell and Rebecca Chase were in trouble, each securing four fouls, one more, and they would be forced to the bench.

Halfway through the final quarter, Rebecca fouled out, with Saint Anthony delighting their home fans with their aggressive play and performance on the free throw line.

Center Kirsten Bell never fouled out choosing to allow Emma Sacatti to drive the lanes and feeding her center Cindy Marquez or laying it up herself. Saint Anthony ended the game five points ahead. Cindy total 16 points and 12 rebounds, and her partner Emma scored 19 with 15 assists and four steals.

"Look, Mama!" Dario pointed across the arena, Dorothy applauding her daughter's performance. "She sure looks happy."

"Who are you talking about, sweetheart?" replied Mrs. Sacatti.

"My friend Dorothy, she's standing right behind her husband."

"You can see her huh?" Palmira closed her eyes and through a huge telepathic thank you across the Sports Arena. Dorothy looked up and threw the Sacattis a kiss.

"She gave you a big kiss, Mama."

"God bless her, God bless you, Dorothy Marquez."

Eugenio, biting his nails throughout the game, waited outside the locker room to hug his daughter and ask if he could drive her home.

———————

Saturday morning, the girls were preparing breakfast for the convent nuns and the female residents when Betty's water broke. An ambulance was called, and Sister Barbara escorted the young woman to Cedars Sinai Hospital. Her mother was also called, and she joined the nun in the lobby. At approximately 1:15 p.m., it was announced Betty had delivered a 5lb. 2oz. healthy baby girl. Sister Barbara contacted the convent, knowing Mia must have sat on edge, wanting to know how Betty was doing. She was overjoyed to hear the news.

Mia knew Betty was close to receiving her G.E.D., only six weeks away from her first goal of completing her initial education. Her mother had placed her house for sale and selected a home down the road from the Sacatti's, only one mile from her place of work at Douglas. "I hope Sister Barbara lets Betty stay here until she completes her high school equivalent diploma," Mia expressed her thoughts to the young nun, Sister Kathy Webb, who had just completed her vows.

"I would suppose Sister Barbara would let Betty and her baby stay on. Her mother is in the middle of moving, and Sister would love to have her complete her G.E.D. I understand her new home is directly across the street from a college."

"Sounds like they moved on Harvey Way. Long Beach City is across the street.

"I can hardly wait to hold Betty's little girl. Did she name her yet?"

"She sure did, thank you for asking. She named the little girl after her mother, JULIA ANNA. I understand Betty wants to call her Anna to eliminate any confusion."

During the previous night, Friday night, under St. Anthony's safety rules, Mr. Sacatti was directed to the high school to pick up his daughter; once she exited the bus, she crawled into her parents' Plymouth and let her father know, 'Why the rule.' "Previously, girls told the coach their parents were there to pick them up, only to have a few jump in the car with their boyfriends.

"One of the basketball players, to the dismay of her family, hopped in a car with her boyfriend and didn't arrive home until 2:00 a.m. She told her parents another family would drop her off at home. She lied to them, and her parents called the police to search for their daughter. They faced false report charges and were lucky enough to have them dismissed."

Saturday, the Sacatti parents understood the safety rules and were geared up for the final match-up, a collision game ready for St. Pius X, poised to take back their only season loss. Eugenio dropped off his daughter, Emma, three hours before game time at 8:00 p.m.

He then headed toward the Sports Arena, hoping to secure better seats near the floor. Palmira, with Emma's help, packed three tuna fish sandwiches, a large bag of chips, and another three apples. Tucked into her heavy wool coat, Palmira passed security and settled her family into a cloak-and-dagger dinner on the floor of the arena unknown to floor security.

"Eugenio, I could feed our family for a week by what they charge for hot dogs and a drink."

"Mama, I'm thirsty now. Could we get a soda? Papa said he would bring three bottles." asked Dario.

"How about a refreshing drink of fountain water? It's free," replied Mrs. Sacatti.

When Dario and his mother returned, they found both St. Pius X and St. Anthony warming up on the court. "Hi, Emma! Mama just took me for a drink."

"Dario, you're not supposed to bother the girls. They have a big game and need to concentrate."

"You hear that little man St. Anthony needs to concentrate before Pius gives them a beating."

"Mommy, who's that woman? She thinks Emma's team is going to lose. Where did she go?"

All of the Sacattis, along with Emma and Cindy Marquez, stared with their mouths open. "She just walked through the arena wall," said Cindy, loud enough for the entire team to overhear her. Close enough, the Sacattis heard it, too, sitting only a few feet away from where the Saints warmed up.

"She does tricks just like Dorothy, huh Papa," said Dario, not entirely taken by the ominous entity.

Eugenio's head never moved from the wall. Emma saw her mother's handshaking and walked over to her. "We saw nothing. Mother, we're protected by our angels in heaven. Remember that and enjoy the night." She kissed her mother on the cheek and ran out to calm Cindy. "That woman, whoever or whatever she is, can't upset our play. We got your mother to protect us, Cindy. Don't forget that, and recall the nasty comments from a few Pius players in the newspaper. Their insecurity shows us who's the dominant team."

Dario looked across the basketball court and saw Dorothy sitting in the bleachers, staring at him. *"Can you hear me, little fellow?"* The boy nodded; he could.

"Good, I know who that woman is, dressed in a horrific outdated dress, how tacky. She doesn't represent good Dario. Her name is Helix, a twisted mess representing the other side. I aim to stop her if she interferes. You calm your mom and dad down. You hear me. I got you to get her to say her name out loud." Dario nodded again.

Dario tried to calm his mother. She shushed him. "It's tip-off time, honey. Let's concentrate on the play."

Chapter Thirteen
We never lose. We either win or learn.

Head C.I.F. referee Vincent Jordan tossed the ball up in the center circle. Cindy, standing on her toes, lifted her body only to slip and fall on a mysterious pool of water, landing hard on her rear end. After a back-breaking fall, she miraculously stood up as Jordan called an immediate time-out and asked to have the pocket of water cleaned up. Looking up at the ceiling, he and his crew tried to figure out the source of the wet drip.

Tip-off resumed this time. Cindy Marquez secured the tip to Emma Sacatti, who drove the court, leaping and sinking two points perfectly through the net.

Alice Payton of St. Pius, inbounding the ball, threw an erratic pass with forward Louise Auclair of Saint Anthony intercepting it, driving twelve feet toward the basket before flicking it to Emma Sacatti for the lay-up. With less than twenty seconds off the clock, the score stood at Emma Sacatti four and St. Pius X nothing.

Helix Crowfoot paused, *"She can't be that good; it's time I shut her down."* At that moment, Louise went flying, slipping on a suspicious puddle on the defensive side of Saint Anthony's court. She flew backward, slamming her back on the floor. Louise stayed down, unable to stand up. Tears rolled down her eyes as the arena doctor ran out to evaluate the extent of her injury. He called for a stretcher, and she was immediately carted off the floor.

It was Dorothy's turn. Ethical commands prevented her from injuring any of the opposing players, and creating a miraculous performance for the Saint Anthony team was also uncalled for at any time. Dorothy, however, knew this entity needed to stop her vicious tactics.

She entered Helix's mind, confusing the creature. *"Where are you from, and what's your name? I want you to know who you're dealing with in this arena. I'm Dorothy Marquez, a representative of God's kingdom. Now, I'm asking you again who are you!"*

Head referee Vince Jordan stopped the game after St. Pius immediately scored from the corner perimeter just as Louise flew backward through the air. "Where in the hell is that water coming from the ceiling?"

Maintenance director Albert Rodriquez knew of no leaks in the roof especially in two different spots. "We get the Lakers playing here when they're not on the road. All of our inspections are monthly during the season. If we lose Baylor or West on a fall like that, it could lead to a multi-million dollar lawsuit."

"How much do you think that girl is worth? Damn, one more mishap, and I'm calling the game," declared Jordan alarmed.

Vince Jordan continued the game continuously eye-balling the floor with his two other referees, at times missing crucial calls, especially those affecting the Saint's play. Helix laughed.

"One last time, who are you!" shouted Dorothy

"They call me 'Le Passe-muraille' pretty good at it, too."

"Not a name, so you pass through walls; you're an entity. I need a name!"

"My, the referees are missing the entire game. Oh dear, why is St. Pius ahead by five? What happened?" Helix let out a wicked laugh, not revealing her name even through her thoughts.

"You're forcing their heads down favoring St. Pius X. None of that is fair."

"You're right, Mrs. Dorothy. I need to put in their brain that 'they' could fall blistering and possibly receive a career-ending injury. Fear always works. Thanks for the tip."

With Vincent Jordan and his crew dropping their heads it further deteriorated any sense of control on the floor. By halftime, the score remained the same. Cindy Marquez wanted to fight back at the vicious fouls flung at her body anytime she was fed the ball in the base of the point. There she was, butchered, the Pius players taking advantage of the 'no-calls.'

Cindy stated her concern in the half-time locker room, "Coach, I got bruises. Even in the N.B.A., the officials would have called half of those fouls."

"We don't play dirty girls. I'm talking to the referees. They're either throwing the game or are afraid to fall themselves."

Dorothy stood unseen next to her daughter, her eyes glistening for Cindy and the team.

Tanya walked out to the referees, noticing they sat on the players' and coaches' benches, looking troubled and confused. "What in the hell are you doing? Two of my starting players are either not in the game or bruised beyond any minimal play."

Vince Jordan looked up, now defending his refs.

"We can't help it coach. Should I call the game? We can end it right now!"

"Couldn't you look up and follow the play? I'm sure with all of your experience you could help it. I can't risk any more of my girls getting hurt. Others are bruised, too. Given the opportunity, this team is brutal, not the same team we played before and not the same players we watched on film."

Back in the locker, a mere ten minutes before the girls were to take the floor, Emma brought up. "I don't think it's entirely the referees' fault, and I don't understand the play of the Pius girls. They're competitive but not outright cheaters. I don't think they might take advantage of the mysterious no-calls. Their minds and our referees are under some kind of control, right Cindy?

"Coach Errion, I told Cindy not to go out there for the second half. I think the St. Pius forwards broke her ribs; any more punishment, and God knows what will happen next. Cindy is beaten up, Coach, plain and simple."

"What happened? Did they break your ribs!"

"She cringed, coach, trying to swallow the pain. I told her she needed to tell you to leave the game, and she couldn't do it," said Emma.

True enough, Cindy refused to exit the finals, "I'm playing Coach Errion. Could I get a cushioned wrap protecting my ribs? Maybe the referee will extend the time."

Louise Auclair joined in, "I want in, too, Coach. I've stretched out my back for forty minutes. It's sore and probably will hurt even more tomorrow, but right now, I'm okay, and this is a historical night for all of us."

"Take a few warm-ups on the court, girls." She turned to their student trainer from Long Beach State and asked her to watch Louise. "Tell me if she cringes even in the slightest. You took a nasty fall. Goddamn, what's going on?"

"Cindy, let's get you wrapped. Emma run and see if you can get Dr. Clark in here. The rest of you girls hit the floor. Hurry, go now!"

Tanya Errion, who sent her assistant out to ask for an extension, was told, "Not a problem. I asked for the maintenance crew to check for any possible leak in the ceiling and they're checking it now. We told the crowd, so you got 45 minutes if we're able to proceed. At least we will see more concession dollars for the arena."

Dr. Clark, a loyal fan, having sent two of his girls through Coach Errion's basketball program, currently sent his youngest daughter to St. Matthews on 7th St. Reportedly, Dr. Elwin Clark felt his daughter, Rosa, a grade school phenomenon, could join Errion's varsity as early as next year. At 5'9", she towered over many of her opponents and still trained as a guard. She knew all of the ball handling tricks watching Emma play in her league in seventh grade.

Dr. Clark, a former N.B.A. player before washing out with an early knee injury, elected to finish medical school and start a family. And now, before he wrapped the girl, he felt Cindy's bruised ribs. "She's cracked three of them, coach."

"Can you wrap them with padding, and can she play?"

"I'll wrap it tight and place a triple layer where it hurts the most. Cindy can play, but I'll need to watch her. Let's get started, young lady."

Dorothy didn't need to guide the young man; he was trained well and brought up his three daughters just as well.

"You're going to feel a bit off balance, Cindy, but I'm sure you'll adjust. May I make a suggestion?"

"Sure, go ahead."

"Coach, this is going to take some time. You better get out there with your team. Emma, you can stay.

"I got a bit of advice for both of you," said Dr. Clark. "Use your elbow to your opponent's ribs. Hit them hard. You hear that HARD! They're playing N.B.A. defense; fight back discreetly. They cracked your ribs; pay them back without attracting any attention."

"But our coach told us not to play dirty, Dr. Clark," said Emma did not understand how the play of basketball could sometimes blend with the turbulent play of gridiron football.

Championship basketball always changed in the playoffs. "Watch the N.B.A. championships; those men step up their aggression. Until that time, *you need to* step it up."

"I don't have a problem not playing soft. I'm going to show those Pius forwards they need to knock it off. And I won't give those damn refs any obvious clue; I'm determined to elbow them goddamn hard," replied an angry Cindy.

"Atta girl. Remember you're fighting back, you're not initializing any bad play. Be careful, be discreet like I said.

"This should do it. How do you feel?"

"It feels tight!"

"Good! It'll loosen up when you play. Get out there, girls, and give them hell."

Can you take me to the toilet, Papa? Mama doesn't want to go."

"Yeah, I'll take you, Dario. Let's hurry up." Eugenio got up and reminded himself not to take his son's hand (Dario reached an age where only his mother could take hold of his small hand).

Both Eugenio and his son relieved themselves when Dorothy appeared to Dario. *"Just listen to me. I'll talk to you telepathically. I want you to help you help your sister's team, okay?"*

"Sure, okay!"

"Okay, what, Dario?" asked his father.

"You can't talk out loud, son. Just think it."

"Sorry, Papa. I changed my mind."

"You have to scream, GO AWAY HELIX, GO AWAY HELIX! You got that?" Dorothy instructed the young boy.

"GO AWAY what?"

"I'll spell it, then you say it. HELIX-H-E-L-I-X. GO AWAY HELIX. You got it now?"

"HELIX. I can say it now."

"But don't say it until I tell you. Shout, GO AWAY HELIX three times. 'I'll sit right near you."

"Whose HELIX anyway."

"She's that nasty woman you saw before the game."

"I don't like her, and she dressed funny, scaring my Mama and Papa."

"You'll set her straight, Dario; she won't listen to me." The boy smiled, claiming his newest apparitional power.

Emma and the rest of the Saints proffered their hands before the toss-up. Each of the St. Pius X Warriors ignored the gesture. *What's going on? They've never been like that,"* thought Coach Errion.

Two minutes later, Tanya witnessed a violent thrust to the lower back of Louise Auclair, sending her back to the floor of the court, sprawled in pain. To Coach Errion's surprise, head referee Vincent Jordan pointed to the offending player and called a technical.

Louise rolled on the floor in excruciating pain, then suddenly jumped up as if no vicious foul had ever occurred. "I'm fine, coach; let me stay in."

What in the hell is going on? Thought a befuddled Tanya Errion.

Louise sunk the penalty shot, lowering their point deficit to four. She then took the ball from Jordan and inbound it to Virginia Coughlin, who moved fluently as if unscathed. Virginia tossed a high lob into center, Cindy Marquez. A sharp pain hit the Saint's center in her padded side. "I see they bandaged you up, still feeling it, I take it," Warrior forward, Danielle Minsky whispered in Cindy's ear.

Instinctively set in her mind, Marquez balled her fist while sky-hooking the basketball with her left hand and banking it into the net. She came down, drumming her elbow into Minsky's sternum, throwing St. Pius X forward-backward and unable to breathe.

Chest pains were intense, eliminating any hint of basketball play. Danielle found she couldn't rotate her chest or even stand straight. A time-out was called by the coach of Pius and the girl was pulled from the game. Helped to her seat, Dr. Edwin Clark was called to administer aid. An ambulance was called, and she was taken to U.S.C.'s General Hospital.

Starting Warrior forward Regina Cawley shifted across to cover the Saints, Cindy Marquez. "No one ever saw it, Regina. You batter my rib cage, and suddenly, you're going to feel pain like you've never felt in your life."

Regina ignored the warning and smashed the back of her cupped hand into Cindy's head, causing the center to miss a rebound while triggering a swimming sensation in the skull. She fell to the floor, and St. Pius scored. Assistant referee Douglas Edwards waved off the basket, and Cawley was called for her 4th foul.

"What the hell are those girls doing out there? It's a war. My Cindy isn't out there to brawl. I never taught her to fight, yet those girls are hurting her," said Michael Marquez father of Cindy.

Connie Marquez replied, "I think my niece must have struck that girl they sent to the hospital. A reaction, I suppose, for those forwards pounding on her ribs. I hope Cindy survives this game in one piece."

"Fight back, girls, an eye for an eye and a tooth...no, that's wrong. You still are instilling hate out there, aren't you, Helix!"

"Are you talking to me?"

"You know damn well I'm talking to you! At least you laid off the officials. Our Saints may still win."

"I don't care who wins now. I'd rather watch a violent game, you know, like a blood bath. I need to step it up."

Injuring Cindy became too much for Emma Sacatti. Combining with her forward Louise, they penetrated the center circle, pumping in four consecutive shots. With a tie score, the Saints began to push the momentum.

Seconds later, Emma stole the ball from Warrior guard Lily Duran. She caught Louise from the corner of her eye, sprinting toward the basket fed the ball to her for an easy lay-up. St. Anthony went ahead by two. Lily, taking the ball inbounds, slipped violently on a puddle. Moments before, Louise flew across the same spot of the floor, safe and dry, even free of any sweat.

"I want you to know Dorothy, I can be fair. No interference hurting your team besides the smack to Cindy's head, and another starter for the Warriors' apparently kaput evened things up. Actually, that's two down for our Warriors. Shame on them for being so nasty in the first half.

"Whoo, I think she hit her head. There's a considerable amount of blood dripping from her hair."

"That's it, Helix. Are you ready, Dario? Start shouting HELIX, YOU MUST GO!"

Dario stood up, cupping his hands over his mouth, and shouted, "HELIX YOU MUST GO, HELIX YOU MUST GO, HELIX YOU MUST GO!"

"Why are you hollering, Dario?"

"It's that mean lady Mama. She's causing all the meanness and people getting hurt on the court. Dorothy wants us to send her back to H, E, double hockey sticks."

"HELIX, her name is Helix, Dario?"

"Yes, Mama."

"Then what are we waiting for? HELIX, YOU MUST GO, HELIX, YOU MUST GO, HELIX YOU MUST GO!"

Their voice doubled, attracting the boys, Ted Accenti and Ryan Finch sitting behind them. "Whose Helix?" asked Ryan.

"Who cares! HELIX, YOU MUST GO, HELIX YOU MUST GO." The blistering sound of HELIX YOU MUST GO swelled to the St. Pius X crowd.

Cindy's dad and auntie joined in, a deafening sound raising its pitch every second. Helix crushed her hands against her ears, appearing in full view on the court.

People who looked her way drew in their breaths as she dissolved directly into the puddle, disappearing below the floor. Any wet pool of water vanished, and the blood on the floor suddenly evaporated along with the blood on the back of the head of the guard, Lily Duran.

Louise picked the injured girl up. Lily thanked her, shook her head, and was ready to compete again. Head referee Vince Jordan waved his hands in the air and called his other officials into a huddle.

Next, he called together the coaches of St. Anthony and St. Pius X. Both Coach Errion and Trubisky of St. Pius nodded their heads in agreement. The game ended in an agreed draw. Too much of unexplained atrocities showered the entire two-and-one-half quarters.

Sunday papers across the region would announce the first called game ending in a draw in C.I.F. history. The mysterious events mentioned in the papers delaying the game multiple times could not be expressed as thoroughly as if all of the reporters were actually there. One of the local reporters, Bob Arthur of the Independent-Press Telegram, turned the bizarre game into a full tell-all non-fiction novel, CREATURE ON THE COURT achieving best-seller status in the N.Y. Times.

Mia received the news of last night's game ending in a draw. Excited, she dismissed the basketball game in favor of her newest update. "Mama, Betty delivered her baby yesterday, a baby girl. Both are fine and resting in the hospital."

"Did she give her daughter a name yet?" asked Palmira.

"I'm sorry, I didn't tell you, she did. 'Julia Anna' after her mother. They're going to call her Anna, so there's no confusion."

"Good idea. Betty's mother is a dear woman who went through too much grief and is happy again. She called me and told me she bought a house on Harvey Way, not to far from us.

"I understand she sold her old home in less than a week; now, her work is less than five minutes away off Carson Blvd. Did I tell you Mia, her work has a child care plan?"

"You did, Mama. And did I tell you the good sisters are going to let Betty stay here until she completes her G.E.D.? That's going to help me, too. My baby is due in eight to ten weeks."

"Mama, Mama, let me talk to Mia!"

"You'll have to hold on, Dario; we're in the middle of a conversation."

Her son backed away, leaving enough space for her mother to talk about what he thought were 'secret girl things.'

Finally, Mrs. Sacatti handed her son the phone. "Guess what, Mia, my friend said I was a hero last night. I helped get rid of the mean lady that bothered Mama and Papa and the whole basketball game..."

"Mia?" This is your mother. Dario is just speaking nonsense. "We are coming up today to visit you and Betty. I understand this is her last week before she takes her test for a G.E.D. You'll be all alone after this week. Did you make other friends? Okay...then we'll see you after 10:00 a.m. Mass. Yes, me too, goodbye."

Helix

Chapter Fourteen

The very first Easter taught us this:
That life never ends, and love never dies.

Dario did what he always did in the last few years: he woke up well before Mass, closed his eyes tight, and felt for the Easter basket sitting on the side of his bed.

On Saturday, just before the F.W. Woolworth closed, Emma and her mother dropped into the store to watch the manager drop the price of all the Easter candy as much as 80% off, especially the jelly beans, straw baskets, and paper 'Easter grass.'

Dario with his sisters, received a large chocolate Easter rabbit, chocolate marshmallow eggs, and jelly beans. The surprise of all Dario got five packs of the newest season, Topps baseball cards.

Unsuspecting his newest gift, he closed his eyes and fell asleep, only to wake to the sound of his mother wishing him a 'Happy Easter' and a blessed kiss on the cheek. "Time to get ready for church, sweetheart. Oh wait, what did the Easter bunny leave you!"

Dario smiled, picturing an oversized chocolate Easter rabbit and hopefully other good 'stuff,' some of it lasting more than a week, and placed inside his lunch pail.

Squirming, Dario survived the long Mass, reminded once again that this day was the most special religious event of the year, maybe even topping Christmas Day. Dario felt it was a tie, but now he found he leaned toward what Father De La Torre preached to the congregation (Father Gibson's rental priest). Five packs of baseball cards ranked that right up there with the best Easter ever, even when his mother let Dario eat all of his giant Easter rabbit in one day without yelling at him too much.

After walking home from Mass, the Sacattis sat down to breakfast and then waited for Julia Russo to walk to their house. Calling earlier Palmira shared she and Emma put together two Easter baskets for their girls at St. Agnes. Mrs. Russo thanked her for having forgotten about any treat for her daughter, Betty.

Eugenio drove to St. Agnes in the late Easter morning easy traffic in less than twenty-five minutes, Palmira allowing Dario to open one pack of his Topp baseball packs along the way. Emma protected the large basket for the nuns and other girls from the warm sun beating down on the '56 Plymouth.

"Everybody, I got Don Drysdale!" Dario shouted from the front seat.

That's wonderful, sweetheart. Now quiet down will be there in five minutes," his mother said, caressing his arm.

"Could I chew the gum, Mama? I won't spit it out."

"No, no, put it away and save it for later."

"Okay, I'll save it for later, Mama, when?"

"Never you mind, I'll tell you when."

Betty and Mia, holding baby Anna, met their folks at the door. Emma smiled, hugging Betty first and then kissing her sister on the cheek. Dario, not so much into mushy greetings, continued to stare at his Don Drysdale.

Mia handed the newborn to Julia and she kissed her grandchild as she held the baby girl tight. Mia's arms free embraced her mother and father. Looking down at her brother she asked him when was the last time he kissed a girl.

"Never!" said Dario, in contempt while caving into Mia's dozen kisses on his cheeks and forehead.

"Where's Sister Barbara?" asked Palmira.

Betty said, "She's eating lunch with the other sisters, girls, and a lady who said she knows your whole family."

Mia added, "She said she met all of you at the basketball game last night."

"She met us?" asked Eugenio.

"Yes, she said quite a few people met her," said Mia.

"We don't recall meeting anyone. What's her name?" wondered Palmira.

"Her name is Helen, a very pretty lady about your age, maybe even a little younger."

"Helen? I don't know if I know a Helen. Do you know of any Helen, Eugenio," said Palmira

"It's a common name, but I don't ever recall a Helen, especially last night. I could have been more focused on the game."

Palmera was now intrigued. "Mia and Betty, what does she look like?"

Mia spoke first, "For a woman so young, you'd think she knew how to dress."

"What do you mean, Mia?" asked her mother.

"Well it looks as though she still thinks it's the 1930's. An old cocktail dress."

Betty shared, "It's called a daizbella. And you're right; it was a cocktail dress, black, drab, and down below the ankles. We have a picture of my grandma dressed in something similar."

"What color is her hair?"

"That's easy black like her dress. She seemed nice, kind of sweet yet different," continued Betty.

"I'd say more like mysterious," said Mia, Betty agreeing with her.

Dario tugged on his mother's coat, "Mama, Mama, I know who it is!"

"SHUSH! You hear me, Dario you need to shush. Betty, do us all a favor asked Sister Barbara to come to the front room. Tell her there's a package waiting for her, and Betty, above all, look natural and don't look at that woman."

Betty left, and Sister Barbara returned to greet Mrs. Russo and the Sacatti family. "Sister, I need to talk to you outside." Emma looked anxious, her hands folding back and forth. Basketball games now held no immediate pleasant memories for her.

Sister Barbara followed Mrs. Sacatti out the front door. "Sister, the woman you're having lunch with may or may not be Helen. My family thinks she's a demon, possibly here to frighten Mia and Betty. She caused such concern at last night's basketball game the referee was forced to call the C.I.F. finals and decide on a draw. She affects trouble. Her real name is Helix. Say it and see what happens.

"Bring in this Easter basket for the nuns and girls. It's the package Betty said you'd received. Do you understand what I'm asking, Sister?"

"Helix, you say, and the Easter basket, thank you, that was thoughtful of you." Sister Barbara blessed herself and entered the convent, all smiles, holding the huge basket.

She returned to the luncheon with the nuns and expecting girls and presented the large Easter basket. There was a round of exuberant applause heard in the front room, followed immediately by a chorus of horrific screams.

Eugenio and Palmira rushed to the kitchen. Mia and Emma held Betty and Julia Russo back, as well as their little brother Dario. "Mama wouldn't let me tell you, Mia!"

"You need to listen to your mother, Dario, and shush!"

"It's okay, Emma. I think I know. That woman in there was Dorothy in disguise," said Mia.

"No, she's not! Dorothy is a nice lady, but that lady is mean. She ruined the basketball game last night," said Dario, offended by his sister's senseless accusation.

"Well then, whose she, Mr. Know it All!" Mia was frightened enough as is and didn't need her brother mocking the pregnant young girl due in a few weeks.

"Go ahead, Dario, you can tell these girls, but be nice. Both are very sensitive, not brave like you, little man," Emma said, counseling her brother.

"I'm sorry, Mia. Dorothy said I was brave last night. She called me a hero because she couldn't get that woman to say her name. If real people said her name, it would chase her away. So I shouted HELIX like I was told, then everyone started shouting it, and Helix appeared on the basketball court with her hands over her ears and disappeared in a puddle."

Emma continued her brother's eye-opener, "Betty and Mia, that's it in a nutshell. I can tell you more if you're ever up for it. In the meantime, that woman's horrible mission was to come here to trouble you girls and this entire convent. I'm sure she hates what these nuns do to serve expectant girls."

Betty, afraid, asked, "Will she come back."

"No, not if you know who she is and especially if you know her name, HELIX."

Screaming could be heard from the convent's dining room.

Betty and Mia joined hands and walked into the kitchen only to find pale-faced young girls and nuns shivering in their seats.

Sister Barbara, standing amongst the frightened crew of women, looked at Palmira and said, "Well, Palmira, you certainly were right; one mention of her name and POOF, she was gone almost as fast as Father Mc Kiernan's mass. Helix scared the daylights out of this group. Maybe one of you could explain who this woman was to the girls sitting here."

Eugenio and Palmira held back a smile at the McKiernan quip while the others, including Emma and Dario, weren't ready for any of Sister Barbara's wisecracks at this moment.

"Sister, if you have time, I think Dario and Emma could explain it best," said Betty, now holding her mother's hand."

"Well, girls, would you like to hear their explanation of this scurrilous demon?"

"YES!" Every one of them rang out.

For the next hour, with questions and answers mixed in, Dario (who still thought of himself as a hero) and Emma let the females of St. Agnes realize not to have any fear of this 'woman' ever returning.

A week later with Betty back home with her mother, Mia faced up to Sister Barbara O'Keefe. "Sister, I don't feel comfortable sleeping alone in my room."

"I'll move you in with Darlene Forrest; she's a year older than you and would probably feel better with a roommate. She's got an older sister, too, so she's used to rooming with someone at home. I'll get her to move in with you tonight; she's new to St. Agnes. I'm sure you'll enjoy her company. That will leave a room open. Space is getting tighter in the convent.

"Our insurance approved the reconstruction of the old facility. It's going to include an automatic fireproof ceiling sprinkler and a movement sensor installed in the front entrance and upper and lower windows to prevent breaking in."

Sister Barbara's update didn't seem to uplift Mia's spirit; she remained frightened.

She stood in her usual place directly behind third-grade teacher Mrs. Lilianna Holmes. *"Dario, I want you to do me a favor; you're a hero now. You know that, I'm sure."* Dario smiled, shooting through his teacher's head *This young boy appreciates my lesson on the planets.*

"I want you to talk with Emma; she's the only person I'm pretty sure Mia will listen to. Your sister Mia is frightened of that woman, Helix. Tell Emma I will always protect your sister. Nothing will ever terrify or harm her, including Helix. My guarantee.

"Do you understand me?"
"Yes."
"Yes, what?" asked Mrs. Holmes."
"Huh?"
"I said, yes what," reiterated his teacher.
"I was agreeing with you. I'm sorry, Mrs. Holmes."

She raised an eyebrow, not knowing whether to believe him or not.

"Dario THINK! Do not verbalize. What I don't understand is that every human being is blessed with a

guardian angel when they're born. Tell Emma your sister needs to pray to her guardian angel. Mia's angel will listen and is much more powerful than I could ever be. You still pray to your angel?"

"Yes. Dorothy, you're dead, so do you still got an angel?"

"I sure do! Once you enter heaven, you may or may not lose your angel. I still want to stick with Earth and do some good. Now remember what I said, talk to Emma and remember to say your prayer to your guardian angel."

"Okay! Angel of God, my guardian dear to whom God's love commits me here. Ever this day be at my side to enlighten me, to guard me, and to rule and guide me. Amen."

"I think you've been caught again, little man."

"Mr. Dario Sacatti, please stand up."

Dario stood and, aware now that he must have verbalized again, hearing the scattered chuckles in his classroom. "So your angel inspired you right now to say a nighttime prayer in the middle of the day?"

"I think I did because I wanted to better listen to you," said Dario, looking up at his teacher.

"Well, that's good to hear. Sit down and let your classmates see how well you listened. What is the third planet away from the sun?"

Dorothy reappeared and said, *"Tell her Earth."*

"Earth," said Dario, hoping Dorothy knew her science.

"Now, what planet is second away from the sun?"

"It's Venus, Dario. Tell her that."

"Venus is number two."

"What planet is closest to the sun?"

"That would be Mercury, little man," bailing out her little friend.

"That is the planet Mercury."

"Number four behind Earth?"

"We're looking at Mars, Dario."

"That planet is Mars." His classmates applauded his perfect score.

"One last question, Dario. What sits immediately behind Mars."

"You're about to sail out of this in one piece. Tell Mrs. Holmes, the HUGE ASTEROID BELT."

"The huge asteroid belt."

Scattered applause among the smartest third graders erupted into the entire class, applauding the student-guided by his almost guardian angel.

"You passed again, little fella. Let's keep your prayers inside your head and not out loud when I'm instructing the class. Now, everyone stand for the ANGELUS. The angel of God declared unto Mary..."

"And she conceived of the Holy Spirit."

On Sunday, Emma sat with her sister in the shade near the grotto at St. Agnes. "Mia, your brother talked to me and said you were scared."

"WHAT! How did he know that? Who told him?"

"He told me Dorothy would always protect you without frightening you. He said she's not like that rotten Helix. He also said, and I agree, that you need to keep your guardian angel in your nightly prayers. We were all born with our own angel, more powerful than a thousand Helixs."

"Are you sure, Emma? I'm afraid she'll come into my room and terrify me and my new roommate, Darlene."

"Believe me when I tell you, Mia, you're safe. I love you and wouldn't lead you in the wrong direction."

Emma and her sister left the grotto area and walked inside the convent to reconnect with their family and Sister Barbara.

Before retiring to bed, Mia first hugged her roommate, placed her head on her pillow, said a prayer to her angel, and fell asleep five minutes later. Completely exhausted, she hadn't slept in a week after Betty went home with her baby and the prized G.E.D.

Darlene Forrest was the present prize, offering the young girl companionship in the middle of the night.

Darlene smiled before she dozed off. The time arrived for her to set her deeds. She already affected the character of two of the pregnant girls residing in the convent. One of the youngest sisters also fell into Darlene's snare.

She smiled again, a crooked grin alluding to a devious covert plan to disrupt the entire convent and its spoiled pregnant residents.

Alarmed, Dorothy screamed into Mia's restless dream. *"SHOUT MIA! SHOUT OUT HER NAME! It's Helix, she's there! Scream her name now! HELIX! Helix, please shout, Helix, go away, go away forever!"*

"GET OUT HELIX!" Sweat dripped down to the angle of her lip. *"Get out forever, Helix, Helix, Helix."* She sat up in bed, almost frozen with fear and clearly not fully awake. "You need to get out now, Helix!"

The overhead light flew on, and girls from the adjoining room ran to Mia's bed. "Is she here, Mia!" Both girls shook with fright. "We gotta get out of here!" said Faith Buckley. Her roommate, afraid to lose contact with Faith, roared, WHERE'S DARLENE! HELIX TOOK HER!" Ellen Michaels dropped to her knees, hands over her face; she sobbed.

Alerted by the screams, Sister Barbara and Sisters Rosemary and Janet tore into the bedroom. A few of the girls down the hall slid under their bed, frightened by the sound of the name Helix.

"Where is Darlene? Where did she go? Faith, check the restroom down the hall."

Buckley ran, finding the communal restroom with its lights off. She turned back to Mia's room, her body juddering. "Was she in there?" asked Sister Barbara.

"Sister, the light was off. I didn't want to go inside!" Faith leaned into the arms of Sister Rosemary.

Ellen, on the verge of all-inclusive shock, screamed, "I want to go home! Sweat and tears engulfed her entire body. "My baby! I can't stay here!"

Sister Janet wrapped her arms around the miserable girl, whispering consoling words of hope into the teen. Mia fell back on her bed, thinking the same thing. What kind of protection was this, and where was Darlene, her roommate? Sister Barbara gathered up all the girls left in the convent and asked them to bring blankets and pillows down to the front living room. She slept on the couch while the teens, one by one, settled into an uninterrupted slumber.

She had suspected Darlene since last night. She spoke with her mother at home while Darlene napped, and Cecilia Forrest, a single mother, signed the release papers for the fifteen-year-old girl. Allegedly, she woke her daughter from her sleep and asked to get ready for her new temporary home at St. Agnes.

Mrs. Forrest excused herself for work and left Sister Bridget in the living room waiting for the young girl, Darlene. A few minutes later, Darlene made her presence with a large grin covering her face, and her belly showed as if she was supporting twins.

"Where's your sister?" asked the nun.

Darlene answered, "She's away at school."

That morning, Sister Barbara called the Ventura police department and talked to Detective Monty Philips, asking if he could check the property on 302 N. Billing. She stressed for him to call her back as soon as he was free. A fifteen-year-old girl was missing and purportedly lived at that address.

"I'll send out a patrol car that way right now and get back to you, Sister."

"Thank you, Detective Philips. Her disappearance has created a huge stir; we appreciate your help."

"Give me her name and a description of her in case she's there. Do you want us to hold her?"

"Yes, yes, detective, she's legally under our custody at St. Agnes. Her name is Darlene Forrest; she's about 5'3" and is very pregnant. Her hair is blond, quite long, 8-10 inches below her shoulders, and has piercing blue eyes."

"Fifteen and very pregnant. I'll let patrol know how serious this is. Will Darlene have a mother or father waiting for her?"

"As far as I know, she does, a single mother, Cecilia Forrest, who works in accounting at Perkins and Sullivan on the coast. Cecilia also mentioned an older daughter."

"I'll notify Darlene's mother, Cecilia Forrest, you say."

"Yes, Forrest with two 'r's. Have you heard of that company detective?"

"I sure have. Perkins and Sullivan is a big firm that's been around for quite some time. I'll get back to you, Sister, right away. What's your number?"

"Oh, of course. You can reach me at Hemlock 61367. Thank you, and God bless you, Detective Philips."

"You bet. I'll call you within the hour."

Chapter Fifteen
Nyctophobia

Sister Barbara's girls remained in fear of Helix, including the suspicious newest charge, Darlene Forrest. Where was she? Why would she disappear? Although not naïve, Sister Barbara sometimes set her heart in the wrong direction.

"Mia, may I talk to you?" asked Sister Barbara.

"Is it about Darlene, Sister?"

"Yes, it is. I'll be careful."

"Go ahead, for your sake. I haven't told anyone what I really feel about who or what Darlene is, but go ahead."

"What did she tell you last night?"

"Not a thing, just wished me goodnight and then smiled, not a real smile, I thought, more of a merciless grin not just in her mouth but her eyes too. They shined too much."

"How do you mean merciless?"

"I redefined it in my dreams. It turned into a malicious scowl. Darlene's incisors appeared to grow. That's when I heard someone shouting in my dream, 'Tell Helix she needs to go!' The teen girls next door told me I was screaming out loud. It was too real, Sister, and it all seemed to point at Darlene. I think she's Helix, only younger and different looking."

"Do you really believe that in your heart? Darlene is actually Helix."

"Sister, I'm positive she is. She worked her way back into St. Agnes, and if nothing is done, how will you ever again not suspect another girl at your door needing help? All of them could be potential demons."

Sister Rosemary entered the kitchen. "Sister Barbara, there's a phone call for you from Detective Philips."

"That house on Billing has been abandoned for eight years. Mr. and Mrs. Brad Forrest originally owned it. The home went down in a tragic fire, killing the couple. We never found a culprit, and the case is still on file.

"Cecilia Forrest was one of the victims still remembered fondly at Perkins and Sullivan. She had no daughters, only two twin boys fighting separately in Korea at the time, one in the Army and another, a Navy man on the ship, U.S.S. Missouri. Both are still alive."

"Detective Philips, I sat in that house and talked with Cecelia Forrest who at the time was late for work."

"You sure it was 302 N. Billing in Ventura?"

"I'm positive! The home was neat and clean, and she indicated she was single."

"I had one of the officers working in properties pull this file photo of her. We have a picture of Mrs. Forrest?"

"Could any of your officers send it to the convent? We don't have car transportation."

"I'll send someone now, Sister."

Thirty minutes later, Officer Glen Willis presented Sister Barbara with the photo. She looked at it and dialed the detective.

"That's exactly her. We sat down and talked, and she signed the appropriate papers, then got up and left for work. She told me she was late."

"Sister Barbara, this woman hasn't been around since '52, and our records show she never had a daughter."

"Detective Philips, the girls here are frightened. We all saw Darlene, and I maintain I saw Mrs. Forrest, the photo you have before me. Frankly, I'm perplexed, even afraid. I don't know what to think."

"I'll have my department double check on the address, and if a minor is using a false name, otherwise I'll call the L.A.P.D. and order a police vehicle to patrol your convent. They're going to need a photo of the girl. If she's still in the area, she won't be too hard to find. They'll be contacting your Hemlock number by tonight."

"Again, thank you, Detective Philips, and may God bless you and keep you safe. Goodbye."

"Goodbye, Sister Barbara."

Emma had just finished her fourth-period class and was ready to find lunch in the cafeteria. Now that basketball season was becoming more and more a thing of the immediate past, an occasional nod of appreciation didn't bother her except for the occasional hounding of Ricky Valenzuela, the Saints school newspaper sports editor.

"What was that thing in the corner of the court?" asked Ricky, who hadn't even bothered to attend the game.

"She doesn't know Valenzuela, so leave her alone," replied Ted, acting as a shield for Emma Sacatti.

Emma found it nice having a protective safeguard, wanting to stroll by her side. Ted, ever patient, waited for the day the Saints star freshman guard might change her stance on dating, especially now Mr. Accenti had obtained his driver's license. If she decided possibly her sophomore year would be more appropriate he knew he would wait. Ted could be persevering when necessary.

"Hello Emma, I'm so happy to see you!"

Emma looked up, surprised, as she sat down with Ted at one of the cafeteria tables. She briefly saw this pretty young woman once but never shared the same fear as her sister, Mia.

"Hello, Mrs. Marquez. Am I correct in recalling you?"

"Yes, very correct. Hello Ted, you played an expert season."

"Thank you, Mrs. Marquez," he replied, looking over at Emma, who seemed to stare right through the woman. Wanting to protect his hopefully future girlfriend, he asked, "And do you work here?"

"Oh no, I'm a medical doctor, and I am a good friend of the Sacatti family. I'm here to talk to Emma privately, if you don't mind. I hate to take away your lunch together."

"It's fine with me. Are you okay with that, Emma?"

"Dorothy, if you don't mind, I'd like Ted here by my side. I hope you understand. He can be trusted."

"Of course, I understand, young lady. I shouldn't be seeing you like this, but you weren't so adamant about not seeing me as Mia and your parents."

"Emma, would you care to do the introduction."

"Ted, this is Dorothy Marquez, Cindy's belated mother. Are you okay so far?"

"You, Cindy, Ryan's girlfriend!"

"One and the same. Cindy's mother never left this earth like most folks when they passed away. Mrs. Marquez..."

"Call me Dorothy."

"Dorothy stuck around to continue doing good for people on this earth."

"Thank you, dear. Go ahead."

"Remember the occurrence at the C.I.F. finals?"

"That flash! It appeared some lady...I won't go into it. It's what Ricky wants to report on, am I right?"

"Yes, you are. Dorothy prevented that inglorious entity from completely sabotaging the game. My brother, then you and Ryan began that chant. Only a human revealing her name can drive her away. Dorothy inspired my brother and told him what to do."

Ted stared at Dorothy before saying, "I never saw you at the game."

"No, you didn't, actually. Dario, for the most part, never did either. He was told only to listen until the time came."

"Can the the other students sitting in the cafeteria observe you sitting across from us," Ted continued.

"No, they can't. They can't hear me either; I'm talking to you telepathically."

"Are we making sounds they can hear?" asked an attentive Ted.

"You are the observant one, aren't you, young man? Yes, students can hear you, though, which is probably why they're wondering why you two don't always look at one another when you're chatting.

"Emma, despite your sincere effort your sister is panicked. Helix changed her form, something even somewhat ahead of my current capability. Helix now poises as a pregnant fifteen-year-old securing a place at St. Agnes and, God forbid, as of last night, rooming in the same room as your sister after Betty went back home.

"Mia was alerted in a dream by her angel, who alerted me. Every girl staying in the convent slept with blankets and pillows on the carpet in the front room with Sister Barbara sleeping on the couch. As of this moment, Helix disappeared after Mia screamed her name out loud."

"So this woman or thing is a demon?" wondered Ted.

Emma looked at the boy she was growing fond of and said, "Helix is a demon, a genuine menace causing destruction and panic wherever she is found. Please don't share this with Ryan or anyone, Ted. People might think you're crazy, and Dorothy, Helix has got me worried."

"Why just worried Emma, don't you feel fear?" wondered Mrs. Marquez.

"I don't know. Maybe I'm angered more so than being afraid."

Dorothy reached out and took hold of Emma's hand, "You, my child, are a living saint, someone Helix would staunchly fear."

"Mrs. Marquez, why would Helix fear Emma? I'm interested."

"Mr. Accenti there are few people not as subject to fear as others. Mia is very sensitive, Dario not so much. Mr. and Mrs. Sacatti are somewhere in between. Emma is an outlier set aside from the norm. It's not that you can't fear Emma; it's just that you'd probably be the last to do so, and that's what entities like Helix fear the most.

"Emma will always have something up her sleeve to diminish something as powerful as Helix."

"Aren't you that way, Mrs. Dorothy?" asked Emma.

"In a spiritual sense, yes, I am, as a human that I am no longer the answer is no. I can fight Helix, but I believe you could destroy her and even help her. I have misgivings about whether Helix is or isn't a demon.

"You, my dear transcend both spiritual and human qualities, a rare commodity.

"Emma, you have a God-given gift, and many people need your help."

Faith spoke first in the kitchen at lunch. "Sister Barbara, it's going to get dark, too dark tonight. Are we going to sleep in the living room again at bedtime?"

"Not unless all of you want to. I want to clear this up. Darlene is not coming back, so there's no sense in fearing the dark."

"I've feared the dark since I was four," said Ellen Michaels. I feared it in my own separate room in the resident house before it was set on fire, and I fear it now even with Faith in the same room with me."

"A few of you girls suffer an abnormal obsession, nyctophobia, extreme fear of the dark. It's time you got over it. Having a baby child is going to require rising endless nights, a few darker than others. Babies don't recognize darkness; they only recognize need.

"So what do you say, everyone, back to your rooms tonight? Your beds are more comfortable than the carpet."

"Maybe we could decide tomorrow; I don't mind the carpet," said Mia.

"Yes Sister, will decide tomorrow," the girls spoke as one.

"I'll take the couch tonight, Sister Barbara. You need to rest in your bed," offered Sister Rosemary, still groggy from last night's fiasco.

Sister Barbara nodded, thanking the older nun, then added, "Young ladies, I talked to the police, and they're sending out a patrol tonight to keep an eye on the convent. And I also talked to a veteran police officer, Detective Philips, and he reassured me Darlene Forrest, in all his years of experience, won't be returning to the convent. I also talked to Emma, Mia's sister, who reassured me people like Darlene or Helix, for what some of you called her will not return once she's identified."

Tina Welsh, a sixteen-year-old girl in her seventh month, spoke with fear, "But if Darlene was that woman who visited us who was Helix and then we find out Darlene is also Helix, what can we do if she changes shape? I'm frightened!"

"Let me first thank all of you for not alarming your parents. Helix is not coming back. All of you girls are protected by your angel blessed to you at birth. They will remain with you for your entire life. Make sure you talk to them before you go to sleep each night. They're there for every one of you more powerful than Darlene Forrest or the unexplained Helix. Don't forget that, ladies.

"Now let us say our after-meal prayer."

As darkness grew near, the girls carried their blankets and pillows into the front room. Sister Rosemary reassured the girls of the reason why she seldom felt fear. "Ladies, the

Lord is my shepherd, I shall not want. He leads me to green pastures. He leads me beside the still, still waters, and his goodness restores my soul. Psalm 23. It's far more effective than garlic or silver bullets. Shall I lead you threw it again, girls?"

All of them nodded, this time reciting it with her word for word.

———

After school, Emma finished her cleaning in the gymnasium by 4:00 p.m. Ted driving in his 1956 Ford coupe, parked his car outside the Lakewood library. Emma, a frequent visitor like her sister Mia and brother Dario, was lucky enough to secure a private conference room.

Dorothy, unseen by the library staff or public, thanked Emma and Ted for attending.

"Ted has a question for you, Dorothy," Emma said, sitting in the conference room.

"Yes, Dorothy, do you feel Helix is overhearing us at this meeting?"

"No, not at all. I'm focused on this place and the convent, as well as your home in Long Beach, Emma. I would know if she were around. You will see her soon enough at school. I placed that in her head. You are the one avenue for her entrance into Saint Anthony."

"She's coming to St. Anthony? I don't know if I would like that. How and when is she coming?"

"Let me clear something up first. I've done more than ordinary thinking. I've concluded I don't think Helix is a demon. What I found, I believe, is that she was a very troubled girl in her childhood, scourged throughout her life, turning her into what we think of as a beast.

"At your basketball game, she shared with me she didn't take sides; she just enjoyed creating trouble. I, however, got the feeling she wasn't enjoying it.

"Remember the puddle Lily Duran slipped on in the 3rd quarter, and when St. Pius X forward was later sent to the hospital. Both girls could have permanently hurt themselves, but both are fine today, including your forward, Louise Auclair. It was then I instructed your brother to start the chant to get rid of Helix. The sound of her name caused her to press her hands against her ears and disappear below the puddle, revealing herself to almost the entire crowd.

"At that point, in the 3rd quarter, your Saints team had the advantage. Even the officials appeared to neutralize in the 2nd half. Then suddenly, the head referee, Vincent Jordan, collaborated with the teams' coaches, and he suddenly ended the game in a historical tie, a wash where no one won and no one lost.

"What was her point? Helix lost on both ends."

"If she's not a demon, what is she?" asked Ted Accenti.

Emma interjected, "Hold that thought, Ted. I need to call my brother. He expects me home."

"It's been taken care of. I talked to Dario right before his lunch in the classroom. He knows you're busy and asked Roger if he could stick around until your mother and father arrive home around 5:30 p.m."

Emma smiled, saying, "You did that, Dorothy? You're like a regular telephone line."

"Ted, answering your question, Helix was once a lost human being who could never experience God's love the way most of us do. I need to find out who she was and where she lived. I suspect her name, Helix, was given to her by a confused mother and father. She apparently hates that name that followed her throughout her life. Emma, I think you're the girl who she'll convey this information."

"How will I even start, and when will I get time to talk with her?"

"I placed that in Helix's head. Like I said whether she knows this, and probably not, she needs you. Helix is going to accept a long-term substitute position at Saint Anthony, a 4th-period class where Ted can keep an eye on both of you. You will share a few lunch hours in her room since she won't be apt to attend the faculty room, preferring to lie low."

"What will I ask her, and won't she be suspicious?"

"Remember, Helix is not that astute. I believe she was a clever girl with above-average intelligence, but no more. You, on the other hand, are brilliant, Emma, clever and morally cunning. You have no desire to deceive her in the long run, only to assist her, a fervid human interested in assisting a defeated human being.

"To answer your question, Helix will arrive with your consent as soon as next week. Your fourth-period teacher, Monica McCarthy, put in for a transfer to the East Coast to settle down with her family. Helix will carry out her duties until the first week of June."

"What does Helix know about Biology?" wondered Ted.

"Enough to get by from day to day, but she will definitely need your help, Emma, ideas you can share with her during lunch. In the meantime, lightly probe her background. It shouldn't be too hard; your help will build trust."

"Will you be around in case I have a question?"

"Of course, but far enough away so she won't panic. I need to head to Mia and the convent. I see Sister Rosemary calmed the girls down and is prepared to replace Sister Barbara on the couch tonight."

Chapter Sixteen

Francine Crowfoot

Already a month into the season of spring, Emma and Ted were surprised to see a well-groomed young lady stroll into the fourth-period biology classroom, announcing she was taking the place of popular teacher Monica McCarthy. Although initially stunned, her class accepted the new long-term teacher.

Obviously nervous, she waded through the period, picking up where Monica left off last week. Francine reviewed what the students were taught as she did in the other periods of the day. She also introduced herself, revealing where she grew up and her mixed ethnicity of Irish and Kainai Blackfoot of Alberta. Her mother, an Irish immigrant, married her father, automatically granting her Canadian citizenship.

No other information was given, so Emma set out on

A series of carefully questioned insights into Francine's childhood to adulthood background. Emma thought bringing up her own grammar school background might help. Ted's first through eighth-grade experience at St. Barnabas in Long Beach might encourage Francine to reveal her elementary years.

Ted and Emma put their heads together, choosing to discuss their plan, interrogating the clever Francine Crowfoot. Ted commented first, "What a disguise this gal is much more than Dorothy's above-average status. I find her imaginative, crafty, and completely capable of handling sneaky high school students."

"We should be careful; Dorothy may have a habit of selling individuals a set of skills far much more than they're worth. When should we suggest eating lunch with her?"

"How many times did we stay in with McCarthy? Let Miss Crowfoot know that. We're popular basketball stars, she knows that. We can tell her we're tired of the phony hello's and how are you's. We needed a break, and Miss McCarthy gave us one. Besides, you got a million ideas about how she could enhance the biology curriculum."

Five pregnant teens huddled close in the living room of the St. Agnes convent. Three of the girls, including Mia, covered their heads with their blankets, acting as fallacious security, hiding from their fear of the ubiquitous Darlene Forrest.

On a starry night, the moon rose and set during the daylight hours, preventing any source of welcomed light from streaking through the living room. Shadows conquered the lack of light, crossing through the immense living room. Ellen saw them; Sister Rosemary, her eyes peering over her evening charges, caught it too. Light from the table lamp immediately flew on, capturing the suspicious shadow, a black feline rescued six years ago from the local pound. "Midnight, shoo, you can't be disturbing these girls. Now go!"

Mia smiled under her bogus shelter. *What they must have thought! And, look at me, hiding from what, fear? Fear manufactured in my weak brain.* She threw the blanket off. *It's hot under here. Damn it, I need to cool off. And that damn cat, scaring the girls. Wait, wait a goddamn minute, maybe Darlene possesses that black cat.* She tossed and turned until four in the morning.

When dawn arrived, emotions calmed the girls who decided to return to their beds with Sister Rosemary volunteering to bunk in the same room as Mia. The pregnant teens laughed at their fear, although harboring unspoken doubts.

Prayers became more heartfelt among all of the pregnant teens. *We can't be overly careful.* Each of the young girls laughed at breakfast with no topic, entering the conversation of retiring away from their bedrooms and sleeping for a third night in the living room. Sister Rosemary's suggested prayer to the girls' angels appeared to work. Dorothy, hovering near the young ladies, smiled.

Miss Crowfoot, may Ted and I ask you a small favor?"

"Of course, you're Emma, am I correct?"

"Yes. Ted and I were wondering if we could spend our lunches with you a few times every week. We both play basketball, and both of us did pretty well on the court..."

"And so each of you attained too much celebrity status like Bonnie and Clyde, you gotta lie low. I understand. I hear your teams went pretty far in the playoffs. I don't mind. I prefer eating away from the staff members. I got to figure out this curriculum before I lose control with the students."

"Organizing the curriculum in all my classes, it's my specialty. I find it similar to basketball, especially defense. When you can figure out a player's next move, you get them beat, picking up a steal, a charge, and so on.

"Biology is no different. One move through the curriculum at a time, find what interests the kids, involve them in the course, make all assignments clear, not too difficult, and move on."

"Have the students dissected an animal?"

"Like a frog or even a deceased baby pig. No, we haven't. We're now working toward that, you know, life science. I think Miss McCarthy felt uncomfortable cutting open a dead animal. I suggested grasshoppers just two weeks before she left. They're cheap and fit into the school budget."

"How do you know the budget?"

"I work here after school. My coach enlightened me on why we couldn't buy new uniforms, why our bus was thirty years old, and that we had to protect the basketballs as if they were gold, a few with little to no tread left on them."

"Sounds as if I should order the grasshoppers."

"I could do that, Miss Crowfoot. I act as a student liaison for my teachers, saving them time and trouble. I often did the paperwork for Miss McCarthy ordering supplies. Ordering grasshoppers should be a snap, so I'll just need your signature on the form."

"Wonderful, and Ted, what is your gift besides basketball?"

"At the moment, I'm hoping to attract Emma by helping her order the supplies. Other than that, I've maintained a 'B' average, unlike Emma one of the Saints straight A' freshmen."

"Almost boyfriend and girlfriend, I'm impressed you found each other."

"We became friends through basketball, and I was scheduled for this sophomore class as a freshman. Ted is in his second year and was assigned to fourth-period biology as I."

"Perhaps you should head to the office and begin the paperwork before your fifth period begins. You both don't share that class, do you?"

"No, Miss Crowfoot. Ted, you may stay. You're not allowed in the office at lunch."

"Thanks. Avoiding too many of our students would be nice. A few are wondering if I could autograph their notebooks."

With Mia down the stairs and into the office, Ted wired up his interrogation skills. "You're from out of the country, I take it. Up north in Canada?"

"No, actually from Oklahoma. My daddy migrated down when his people thought he needed to leave. Kind of a Popeye personality, always finding trouble, although I learned he fought only bullies beating up on Blackfoot nerds."

"So he settled in the great state of Oklahoma."

"Not at first. My father, Ben, wandered the East Coast and finally joined up with Teddy Roosevelt Rough Riders. He joined the Buffalo Soldier of the West in 1898 at the age of sixteen and stormed Kettle Hill with what a few historians refer to as San Juan Hill.

"Got my dad his citizenship and a bit of service money when he marshaled out of the corp in nineteen hundred. He met my mother, an Irish immigrant, a rough and tumble barmaid in Massachusetts who tried to kill him when he entered the women's restroom and tried to assault her sexually. He liked her sass and decided he'd marry her.

"My mother was attracted to my father's rough personality; he possessed the nerve of a riverboat gambler.

She married him in a matter of weeks. They moved to Oklahoma, where he found the farmland was cheap. A match formed in the depths of hell, don't you think."

"Wow, and then you came along."

"Yes, me and my brother Hyacinth."

The fifth period was announced through a loud, continuous bell. "Thanks for your father's interesting past, Miss Crowfoot," said Ted over the heavy racket.

Startled by the overwhelming loud alarm, Francine plugged her ears and asked Ted to shut the door when he exited, only to have her students stream through the threshold five minutes later.

Saturday arrived, and Emma found herself in the library with Ted. "This university contains the best references in America, from newspaper clippings to magazine articles. It's called microfiche a more accurate name for microfilm. We're going to find out how accurate our friend Francine was with you after I left."

Dressed in her typical yellow dress, Dorothy sauntered into the reference room. "How are two of my favorite students? Getting ready to study a bit of history."

"Are you familiar with this new concept?"

Emma replied," I was introduced to it in my honors history class. I was told U.C.L.A. is one of the first colleges to adapt it."

"I see you're perusing the Oklahoma City Times 1900. That's a little too far back, don't you think?"

"Mrs. Crowfoot slipped, forgetting what year we're in right now. She didn't realize there was no way she could have possibly grown up at the beginning of the century.

"So you think that 1900 may offer some clues?"

"Ted was told Ben, Helix's father, was eager to start farming coming from Alberta. We're looking to see any information that he lived in the area."

Ted and Emma poured through Oklahoma City Times newspapers from 1900-1912 when Ted hit on an article reading a Mrs. Riona Crowfoot had her husband, Ben Crowfoot, jailed for beating her. They mentioned her children's names as Francine and younger brother Hyacinth.

Ted looked over to Dorothy and said, "So Helix's mother was abused, and that year would put Francine at least fifty years old. She looks no more than thirty."

"Keep looking, Ted and Emma."

"Three weeks later, Ben was jailed again for abuse of his wife and sexual abuse of his daughter (this time they mentioned Helix). Which one was it?" wondered Ted.

"It appears the mother keeps running to the sheriff." Emma's curiosity matched Dorothy, a woman's intuition. "Why doesn't she leave the bum? The sheriff locks him up for a few days, and Ben gets out and abuses his wife and sexually assaults a very young Helix."

"Riona probably wasn't able to run a farm, and according to this article, Helix's age is around sixty or so," suggested Ted.

Two years passed before Ben Crowfoot made it back in the Oklahoma City Times. "Look at this: Ben was arrested for murder. No, I take that back; his twelve-year-old son was arrested for killing the sheriff, Ken Stauffer. According to the paper, Hyacinth caught the sheriff performing 'Amorous Congress' with Riona Crowfoot in his mother and father's bedroom while Ben was locked up. Sounds like they were having sex."

"Let me see that, Ted. 'Amorous Congress?' I've never heard of that. You Dorothy?"

"No! It appears to be a nineteenth-century polite wording for a forbidden act. What did they do with the sheriff?"

"Oh my gosh, it's more like what did they do with the boy! He was arrested and tried by a ten-man white jury. They describe the boy as 'colored' like his father. They found Hyacinth guilty and set up the gallows the following day."

"Did they hang him?" asked Emma.

"I don't know. Let's check the article for the following day. I can't believe how accurately this microfilm depicts the past.

"Nothing. What happened? Let me check the following day after this."

All three of the sleuths dropped their mouths when they read what happened. *"Deputy Gavin Roy saw Hyacinth Crowfoot walk out of the cell with his father, Ben. Deputy Roy shouted for them to halt when they began to run. Deputy Gavin Roy fired two shots, downing Hyacinth. According to reports, Ben then turned and aimed his pistol at the deputy, but not before Deputy Roy got off two more shots, wounding the armed husband of Riona Crowfoot.*

His boy was found dead in the street with his father disarmed and wrestled down by a half dozen law-abiding citizens. Mr. Crowfoot was hauled off to jail and is pending a trial for the attempted murder of the town's deputy, jailing another assistant deputy, and aiding and abetting a convicted murderer."

Confounded, Emma stated, "So the town is about to hang a boy for killing the adulterer Sheriff Stauffer, and they find out his father walked into the Sheriff's office with a gun and ordered the other deputy to free his son, shooting him, then locking up the assistant deputy."

"That pretty much sums it up. However, what happened to Ben? This so-called crime has got to have the town reeling and the Oklahoma City Times selling hundreds of newspapers."

Ted said, "Early twentieth-century justice in a racist town. It just hit me that if this happened in 1912, that puts our young substitute teacher around at least sixty-six years old. Can she jump in and out of different ages?"

Dorothy enlightened Ted and Emma, "Apparently so. I've seen her as a young lady, a pregnant teen, and now a young biology teacher with a slightly more mature face."

"If this newspaper is hot on the street of Oklahoma City, they're bound to report on the trial. Let's check."

Sure enough, the issue reported the following day that the city's judge ordered Mrs. Crowfoot to pick up her dead husband and pay two dollars for the coffin fee."

"WHAT!" Emma, astounded, couldn't understand the blind ignorance that appeared to run free and wild only fifty or so years ago.

"Read on, Ted. I'm shocked there's no justice!"

"According to what they wrote here is that since the 'law-abiding' citizens funded the gallows, the judge decided with the approval of the town council to utilize the scaffold and get rid of another n_ _ _ _ r."

"They actually said that, and the Times reported the word."

"Yes, the Times further stated they built the scaffold too high, and Mrs. Crowfoot and her daughter Helix witnessed a botched hanging."

"Oh my goodness! Did he live?" asked Emma.

"No, actually, the executioner and builders of the scaffold decapitated him. They placed his body and head into a cheap wooden casket and loaded it on the back of Riona's cart for burial on her property."

"Anything next? What about Helix? What happened to her?" wondered Emma.

"Should I keep looking?" asked Ted. "This might take some time."

Dorothy suggested, "Ted, let's go back to the reference librarian and find out the origin of the name Helix. I had never heard of that name and wondered what it meant. And why did her father and especially Helix's mother place it on her birth certificate if, in fact, they did?"

Helix never went to a typical home; she disappeared and wandered, finding a few places off-limits. *Did you have me banished from my favorite spots? What happened to freedom to roam on earth?* Helix brushed moisture mounting around her eyes.

"*Cheer up, Francine, feeling a bit down in the weather. Still upset over that goddamn name your daddy gave you. I'm here to help. I command twenty leagues of spirits. Join our team. I might be able to lift your banishments.*"

"Let me ask you, did my mother, father, and brother, Hyacinth, join your league?"

"Good question. The names in our league are non-gratis until you swear into the club."

"So they didn't join your stupid club. It's not like them, my brother, either."

"Oh, you need to start remembering HELIX, your brother killed, your mother was an adultress and your father raped you. All of that adds up to a gold star in our league."

"They never wanted any kind of star. They were victims their entire lives. They made mistakes and were blasphemed, treated as racist pigs, and killed for what reason?"

"YOU KILLED YOUR MOTHER, FRANCINE! You killed that man in that goddamn closet they called a room outside the bar where you worked. You killed the man your mother decided to live with, and to top off the end of your life, you swallowed a bullet!"

"Get out, Lilith, go away and leave me alone, leave me alone, damn it!"

Lilith left only to resume her devilish pitch at another time. Francine bent over and cried. Dorothy felt the girl's sorrow.

She never felt she prodded, interfering in the ghosted life of Helixa Francine Crowfoot, but this entity proved to skate the edge of misbehavior, erasing all dignity. A sixty-six-year-old delinquent serving a Class D devil. *What a sorry life*, thought Dorothy.

Chapter Seventeen

Young Helixa, Sixteen

Francine is troubled kids. I can feel her tears, and her heart is about to break. Let's find out why she hates the word Helix. And take it from there."

Emma put Ted in charge of the microfiche machine. "Here we go off to fish for the name Helix, AND HERE IT IS! Helix is a rare and real name. Its origin is unknown according to this info. Helix in Greek means 'twisted.' And look at it here: Helix is a boy's name.

"Do you think that's why she hates the name?"

"I don't think that a name no one has ever heard of would bother her unless it was solely used to ridicule her, which I expect. Look closer," said Dorothy.

"Emma, could you retrieve birth certificates from the reference librarian from 1898 to 1902? I think we will find Francine real quick."

Ted finally came across a pleasant description of the name Helix. "It says the name symbolizes creativity, intelligence, and a deep curiosity about the world. People named Helix are known for their innovative thinking, their problem-solving skills and their ability to adapt to new situations. It also says Helix values knowledge and unraveling the mysteries of life.

"Sounds pretty good to me."

Emma arrived back carrying four cubicles of film. Our librarian was very nice, saved me the trouble of going back and forth four times," commented Emma as she laid the enclosed film strips near the microfiche machine.

Ted rewound the film on the name 'Helix' and loaded it back into the tube. Taking the 1898 film of Oklahoma City birth certificates, Ted typed in Helix Francine Crowfoot and found nothing. Nineteen hundred and nineteen-one were similar. "Maybe we're wrong," said Ted. "She was probably born in the 30's." Ted threaded the last set of four films of nineteen-two and typed in Helix Francine Crowfoot. A similar name popped up. Helixa Francine Crowfoot. "It's her. Born to Riona and Benjamin Crowfoot."

Dorothy thought, "Helixa, a female version of Helix. A deep curiosity about the world? Riona traveled further than her husband to a new world where she was probably ridiculed on our own shore. His husband was too, once he left his Blackfoot family in Alberta, Canada."

"I think her father ribbed her when his wife, whom I'm sure she named her daughter Helixa, told him it was a female version of Helix. I think both mother and daughter suffered under his cruelty," said Emma.

Dorothy suggested, "Both of you, next week, make it a point to help Miss Crowfoot. Bits of kindness won't hurt her and also keep her from being suspicious.

"How are you going to spend the rest of your day?"

Emma, now sitting in one of the best reference rooms in America, told Dorothy, "I think we might want to learn how to dissect a grasshopper and, with my parent's permission, how to raise and feed a little pup."

Palmira was given positive notice that the sixty-five-year-old lead Medical secretary Wilma Burgess at the Dorothy Marquez Medical Center was about to retire in June. During the four weeks she worked with the mother of three, she admired the young mother's work ethic.

"Mrs. Sacatti takes the initiative and saves me quite a few headaches and worries. Besides, her shorthand is faster and more accurate than mine," she added, telling her boss, Dr. Vincent Miller, who oversaw the employment of personnel. "I thought with her on board, I could stick it out for a few more years, but I'm not getting any younger, and I want to find myself active with my grandkids for as long as possible. Doctor I'm going to recommend Palmira replace my position."

Vincent Miller noticed Wilma was correct; the medical center, although already running smoothly under a competent staff, had stepped up its efficiency since taking Palmira aboard. He decided once Mrs. Burgess's retirement was set in stone at the end of May. He'd relay the possibility of a promotion to Mrs. Sacatti.

"Your salary will be adjusted to help you tackle the added responsibility of your job. You, of course, may recommend to me a suitable replacement for your present position. Your new assignment, if you accept it will begin the first of June. Talk it over, Mrs. Sacatti, with your husband, and let me know by Friday if you'll accept Wilma Burgess's position."

Her eyes firmly on the road and her hands in a perfect ten/two position on the steering wheel, she pulled into her driveway at 5:30 p.m.

Palmira, shaking with excitement, met Emma first at the front door. "Hi, Momma, the roast is almost finished, and Dario and I set the table. Are you okay?"

"Honey, Wilma Burgess recommended her job for me to Dr. Miller. She's retiring in five weeks. She told me how much she makes, and then Dr. Miller asked me to take it!"

"That's wonderful, Mama!" Emma reached over and embraced her mother.

"Wilma takes in two dollars an hour more than I do. Even if I have to work up to that pay, I'll still bring home more than $160.00 a month. It looks as though my contribution at church is going to quadruple over our initial fifty cents in the envelope a few months ago. And never will I be forced to lose a payment in tuition costs.

"Are you still working that job at school?"

"I sure am. I enjoy it and Ted is taking me home now. He's got his license to drive a car."

"Sweetheart, you hang onto that money and chip in occasionally for his gasoline bill. God has blessed us, dear and someway we're going to thank Him."

A truck pulled in behind his wife's car, and Eugenio got out while at the same time catching Palmira in the air. "What's happened to you, dear? We inherit a million dollars?"

"Not far from the truth, my handsome man, I'm getting a big promotion at work. The pay's better; we got health, dental, and daycare insurance and well...well..." She shouted loud enough in glee as one of the neighbors opened her door to see if Palmira was okay. "I'm just fine, Mrs. Simmons! I got a promotion at my work."

Tina Simmons smiled, waved her hand, and wished Palmira a hearty "God bless you!" before closing her front door.

At dinner, Dario couldn't understand all of the excitement until his father announced, "Son, you've been a good boy getting your chores completed every Saturday and helping your sister around the kitchen. From now on, you're getting a twenty-five cent allowance every week, and when you turn ten, I'll increase it to fifty cents. You just remember not to forget your chores."

"Wow! Are we rich, Papa!"

"We're comfortable, Dario, not exactly rich," said his sister, Emma.

"Does that mean I can do whatever I want with my money?"

"What did you have in mind, Dario?" asked his mother, still thrilled about the promotion.

"I'm nine, and I still haven't got a Sandy Koufax card. I got a Don Drysdale and a team card of the Dodgers with a tiny picture of Sandy Koufax but no giant picture of him."

His father smiled over at his little athlete, a baseball fan of the Dodgers. Eugenio remembered how important card collecting was for him until, at the age of twenty-five, he found his mother, not a clutter bug, threw out his childhood soccer collection into the garbage.

"Sweetheart, I think your idea of an allowance for Dario is wonderful. I suggested to Emma that she hold onto her pay. Ted also drives her home now that he has a driver's license."

"Well, my, that's another good idea. Let me ask you, my intelligent young high schooler, what do you plan on doing with your extra funds?"

"With your permission, mother and father, Betty's neighbor's dog is going to have pups in a few weeks. She's a purebred, a Golden Retriever."

"My brother in Illinois owns three retrievers on his farm. It's all we ever owned. They're trained to round up his sheep and cattle."

"Papa, how long do they live? I read Golden Retrievers don't live long at all; 10-12 years is what I read," asked Emma.

"Not your Uncle Sal; his retrievers came from the same litter and are all seventeen years old as of a few months ago. He wrote they were as robust as when they were pups.

"Sal said they get the job done and love it. You need to find out if the mother and father are related. If so, I wouldn't want her pups. Also, find out if the grandparents are still healthy. You want what your uncle calls country dogs, no fancy pedigree and no championship lines. Champion dogs are too stuffy and often inbred. They got problems with the heart, hips, and eyes, thinking of only a few of their abnormalities."

"You sure know a lot about dogs, Papa," said Dario.

"I grew up on my parents' farm in Illinois after my father and grandfather escaped the brutal dictator Mussolini in 1932. A few years later, the war started. I volunteered and wound up here in California after fighting the Germans overseas.

I met your mother when our ship docked in New York and moved to the West Coast soon after. But yes, we had dogs trained and fed them well.

"You got to remember what I said. You do that and feed and exercise your dog daily he'll more than likely will live a long life."

"What does my Uncle Sal feed his retrievers?" wondered Emma.

"Never changed, the same thing I fed our dogs when we were young. Your grandfather insisted we never vary the recipe. I can write it down if you need it. I want you to know when I left to fight the war our retrievers were fifteen and sixteen years old. One of them lived to the ripe age of twenty-two."

"I'd love your recipe, Papa. My home economics class is expanding into dog recipes. The winning formula wins my teacher's own annual coveted Canine Ribbon. Mrs. Holden loves dogs."

"Get out a piece of paper and a writing pen, and I'll write it down."

Dario asked, "Papa, how about the dog food you make at work?"

"Well, son, it keeps a dog alive, and it's wet, goes down easier. At a nickel a can, it appeals to most families, including those ignorant adults who chain their dogs to a pole and leave them outside all year. If we owned a dog, I wouldn't recommend abusing an animal that way."

Looking up at Emma handing him a paper and pen, he said, "Okay, thank you, honey. Let me start."

Eugenio started writing: #1 meat- high-quality meat, not meat by-products. Meat like lamb (we raised them on the farm), real beef raised on a pasture, chicken, rabbit, eggs, and fish. A good mix will contain excellent fats, vitamin D, iron, and B vitamins. #2 Carbs and fiber- diced carrots, broccoli, blueberries, peas. All good, all raised on our farm. #3 fruits, vegetables, peanut butter, #4 herbs, and spices dogs love the taste- Rosemary, Parsley, Oregano, Basil. We bought Ginger and Cinnamon at the local market. Dogs need potassium, Copper, Zinc, and Anti-oxidants.

"Emma, check the ingredients on our dog food, and you won't find anything. People trust us, and as long as our nickel can keeps their dog alive, they'll buy it."

"Daddy, you could teach a life science class and your vocabulary; where did you..."

"My father, your grandfather was..."

This time, Palmira interjected, "Emma, I know you never had the chance to know your dad's father, but he was brilliant, an accomplished elder man. He succeeded during the depression when stubborn farmers failed. Those who listened to his theories succeeded. He was always a well-read man, a splendid human being. Your daddy and Uncle Sal learned those words from your grandfather; he was book-learned."

Sister Barbara waited at the front door of the convent, admiring the hard work laborers put in renovating the burned-out ruins of the old residents' house for pregnant teenage girls.

A grieving mother mounted the steps with her equally grieving petite daughter. "Her father forced my child to leave the house. Where could she go, Sister? My family lives three hundred to two thousand miles away. Thank you for helping her."

Tiny, yet obviously with child, the girl sobbed. "I don't want to stay here, Mommy. I want to go home. It's not my fault!"

"She won't tell us who the man was that impregnated her. My husband concluded our daughter is no more than a tramp." This triggered another stream of the girl's tears.

Mia, I accepted a new resident to St. Agnes. She's waiting with her mother in the living room. Could you show her around and, by all means, try and cheer her up, she's distraught. Her name is Catherine Siena, a twelve year old girl.

Comfort her? How could I do that? Sister, she needs Emma, not me; I'm a wreck. Mia uncomfortably stepped down the staircase, wondering what she would say. It hit her. *She's only twelve! She's younger than me.*

Sister Barbara introduced the mother and child, "This is Mrs. Siena and her daughter Catherine. Folks, this is Mia, one of our precious residents."

Mia politely proffered her hand to Catherine's mother forcing a welcoming smile to her face. Without giving it any thought, she found herself embracing the petite young girl. "Welcome to St. Agnes. I'll take care of you."

Sister Barbara not surprised by Mia's graciousness, smiled, proud to have chosen the then-youngest girl in the convent. "Catherine, Mia would be happy to show you around if you'd like."

Catherine looked up at her mother and hugged her. "Will you promise to visit Momma?"

"Yes, dear. Sister Barbara told me visiting is every Sunday, so I'll see you in a week, I promise."

"Will you tell Daddy I'm sorry?"

"I will, honey. I want you to know your father loves you. He'll get over all of this; I promise this, too."

She extended the embrace and let Mia take hold of Catherine leading her to another room. Catherine turned, her eyes still glistening, and blew a kiss to her mother. Mrs. Siena returned the kiss.

That evening, Sister Barbara sat with Mia alone in the girls' bedroom. "Mia, Sister Rosemary won't be staying with you tonight she deserves her own bed."

"That's okay, Sister Barbara. I'm going to miss her snoring; it relaxes me."

"You're kidding. I can hear Sister Rosemary through the walls."

"No, not at all. Why would I kid you?" Mia smiled, "It only annoys me when I'm trying to sleep."

Sister Barbara smiled and apologized, thanking the young girl for her patience.

"Sister, she was a Godsend to all of us. Don't tell her I mentioned she snores."

"Mia, I want to tell...no, ask you if you would allow Catherine in as a roommate."

"Catherine? Is she okay? What I mean by that you don't think she's..."

"ABSOLUTELY NOT! I completely checked out her family. A mother who dearly loves her and a father who momentarily accused her of being a tramp. She's eight and a half months pregnant, so her due date is about the same time as yours.

"Mia, she's scared. She won't divulge the father of her baby, which in itself could be a problem. She wears glasses because she's unceasingly near and farsighted and often crashes in the night because of her small bladder and the fact she forgets to put on her glasses. Did you notice she walked into the convent without them? I had to tell her to put them on and complimented her on them. I hope you do the same whether you like them or not."

Sister Rosemary entered the bedroom announcing to Mia her new roommate. "Sorry, you're going to miss me, sweetheart, but you are getting a delicate little treat. I know you two met, but Catherine is your new roomie."

"That's wonderful! I understand we share the same date with our babies."

Catherine didn't smile.

"Alright, I'll leave you too alone to get your rest," said Sister Barbara. Before she closed the door to the bedroom, she turned and indicated to Catherine that there wasn't any wake-up time. "Mia has kitchen duty, so she gets up early. Don't mind her unless you want to come down. Should I shut off the overhead light you both got bedside lamps."

Mia nodded, and the girls settled in under separate beds and covers.

"Catherine, I didn't see you in those glasses this morning. You look beautiful in them. I wish I needed glasses, especially like yours."

"Do you really think so? Sister Barbara said she liked them. When I first got them, the boys in seventh grade poked fun at me."

"Seventh-grade boys, what do they know? I'm a girl completely more sophisticated and a better judge of prettiness."

At 2:00 a.m., Catherine woke up delusional, shaking Mia awake. "Where am I? Where am I? Momma!"

"Catherine, I'm here. Don't be afraid, dear, you're at Saint Agnes Convent, and I'm here for you." She enfolded the thirteen-year-old girl in her arms. Catherine, somewhat lucid, calmed down.

"I need to pee, Mia. She scooted out on the other side of the bed, walking toward the closet door.

Catherine, you need your glasses." Mia took them off the side table while turning on the lamp. Handing her roommate the glasses, she said, "Let me lead you to the restroom; it's down the hallway."

Catherine entered the communal restroom and made her way into one of the stalls. After a reasonable amount of time, Mia asked if she was alright. There was no response. Refusing to leave the thirteen-year-old by herself, Mia peeked under the stall. Catherine looked down and smiled, and like a plastic doll, her eyes were distant, as if in a daze.

"Come outside, Catherine, if you're finished. We'll talk in our room. Remember, you don't have to worry about getting up tomorrow. The rules here can be slack."

"But what about you? You have kitchen duty."

"I'm a light sleeper. I survived a week with the loudest snorer in L.A. County. Let's talk."

Both lamps were on. Catherine sat still, wearing her 'exquisite' bifocals.

"Why did your father call you a tramp?"

"Because I couldn't tell him or my mother, I was raped."

"What! Rape is a crime, a serious one punishable in jail for years."

"He would have never believed me, and besides, it would have caused a huge fight with my parents."

"Could you tell me who the father is? I promise…"

"HE'S MY COUSIN!"

"Your cousin! Okay, I believe you. Is he close to your dad, his brother's son?"

"Kevin's the son my dad never had, a true saint, a high school football star and my rapist."

"Will you keep the baby?"

"No, no, my mother and I agreed to give it up for adoption to a good family where he or she will grow up happy. My child will never know his mother was a 'tramp.' She again smiled, her eyes empty."

Catherine Siena

Chapter Eighteen
Meat by-products, preservatives,
nitric oxides, and salt. Five cents.

Emma presented her worked-over recipe to first her father, Eugenio who approved of the contents. Next, she handed her

Home Economics teacher her recipe entitled "A Farmer's Dog," named after her father's childhood life on his grandfather's farm. She competed against twenty-five volunteer students out of one hundred and ten eligible sophomores and juniors. Dog food recipes, despite the well-thought-out lecture from Regina Holden, the majority of students didn't feel it was worth the effort for a single ten-inch silk ribbon.

A nickel for a can of dog food remained popular with the general public. There was no need to extend a dog's life; logistics weren't wrong; you just accepted dogs couldn't live forever, and you accepted it. Ditto went for cats, too.

Mrs. Holden reviewed the written recipes, many of them copied off existing cans and bags of dog and cat food. Only one of the recipes included a written explanation of why their food proved beneficial enough to help guarantee a healthy life combined with exercise and plenty of love. The name of Emma's food stirred up memories of Regina's own upbringing in the country.

It's complete! I don't know if Emma realizes her recipe could be a best seller, excellent for an advertisement campaign. By the end of the week, the animal lover and Home Economics teacher announced the winner and ran off over a hundred copies of the typed written exposé on caring for dogs (and cats).

Proud of the silk award she hoped would extend lives, Emma carried the ribbon home, protected in her notebook. Ted dropped her off at her house, but not before she gave him a peck on the cheek. "You're a swell guy, Mr. Accenti. Thank you again for the lift."

"She walked Roger home with Dario accompanying him pulling the award ribbon out of her notebook along the way. "Roger and Dario, this award I got at school hopefully represents a brighter future for cats and dogs."

"Not for Mr. Jenkins, puppy. He's got him tied up in the backyard and said he's going to use him as an attack dog for his business. He didn't even take him out of the rain and said he needed to toughen him up. My big sister built a shelter to protect him and told me she thought the rope was choking the poor pup. I know for one thing that little puppy has got sores around his neck."

"Did you call the animal shelter?"

"My sister, Sheryl, did and they told her Mr. Jenkins got a legitimate dog license and roping a dog and leaving him in the rain was not unusual. Sharon thinks all dog catchers hate animals and are cruel. We hear the puppy crying all night, and Mr. Jenkins won't feed him unless he stops."

"What's the dog's name?"

"You won't believe it, the German Shepherd's name is 'Lucky.'"

"Did you tell your parents?"

"Heck no! It wouldn't do any good; they play cards with them and our other neighbors every Friday night."

"Hmmm, what does your father think about dogs."

"He doesn't like them and won't let us have one. My momma is allergic to cats, so that's out, too."

When she arrived home, Emma prepared dinner, set the table with her brother, and waited for her mother and father. When Dad got home, Emma waited on the porch for him. She greeted him with a brief hug and asked, "Papa, do you know of a Mr. Jenkins? He lives on Clark."

"A Jenkins? No, I don't think I do. Wait a second, Bill Jensen, I know him."

"Randy might have mispronounced his name."

"Yeah, I know him. He goes through dogs faster than Mom uses up laundry detergent. Why?"

"Randy and his sister think he's abusing his puppy."

Eugenio said, "I don't know this as fact, but I think he's run all his dogs through some kind of illegal dog fights. Some of the boys at work probably know more."

"He told Randy he's training his dog to protect his business as a guard dog. What does he own, a junkyard?"

"He's a custodian. Works over at your mother's old job. You think he'd know better.

"What do you have in your hand?"

"I won the purple ribbon in Home Economics, the canine recipe award. Father, I typed up your ingredients and added what you said about why each food was important. That was a plus. My teacher ran off copies to hand -out to her students or the staff who wanted one.

"My question, Daddy, is, would you present this at work if they allow you to attend management meetings?"

"I could do that. I ought to give one of these papers to Bill Jenson; it'd do his pup a lot of good."

What Emma, her father, Randy, and his big sister didn't know was Long Beach Animal Control, with the support of the Long Beach Police Detectives, were investigating strong rumors concerning illegal dog fighting in their town. Following Bill Jenson in his car they found a suspicious broken down barn off the beaten path. Dog's yelping loudly, they suspected the source of Jenson's perverted hobby.

Arranging for a complete bust, they gathered enough police officers to surround the building the following week and close down the brutality inflicted on the poor canines.

A week passed, and Bill Jenson remained at home dining on two Swanson's chicken fried dinners. A week after that, police surrounded the barn, minus the abusive dog handler, only to find a chicken coop guarded by three nasty roosters. Someone filled in the police investigation with the devious lawbreakers, including Jenson, and most likely shifted the elusive dog-fighting arena to another county.

Three weeks later, the Los Angeles County Human Society took custody of Bill Jenson's German Shepherd while the police arrested him for animal abuse. Approximately two days after his arrest, the Sacatti family rescued a quiet and frightened puppy.

Eugenio announced to his family he was given the opportunity to present his idea at a management meeting, where still being the lowest on the leadership poll, management allowed him to speak.

"What did you say, Papa?" asked Emma, proud of her father.

"I handed them what you wrote and told them the ribbon you won for your project at school."

"Did you tell them about growing up on a farm and Grandpa's Golden Retrievers?"

"I wasn't comfortable talking too much; they're big shots. I just asked them if they had time to read your project and ask any questions that they might have."

This time, Palmira spoke, "Did they have any questions?"

"Only our president. He wants to talk to you on Saturday, Emma. I told him you could make it. If you're busy, I'll tell him you couldn't come that day."

"Papa, my paper was entirely based on what you did on the farm when you were a child. This paper is you, Daddy, not me. Most of the girls at school copied the ingredients from various packages and cans of dog food. I based my recipe on your experience and wisdom, Papa. You're the real person who should present what I typed."

Palmira voiced her husband's thoughts. "Emma you are your father's words. God gave you the gift of forming the right sentences at the right time. You speak what's in your daddy's heart."

Laughter came from the throat of little Dario. "HELP! He's licking me to death! Somebody's got to help me!"

Lucky the Sacatti's rescued pup was dancing around the mouth of Dario as he lay on the linoleum floor wrestling his new friend. Lucky splashed the boy with endearing wet kisses while the rest of his family laughed.

Mia's little child is going to worship that pup as they both grow up. Someday, Lucky, God willing, will still be around when her baby graduates from high school."

"You and I will shop for those ingredients tomorrow night and make a batch to take into my president, Harold Polk. Will wrap the dog food in cellophane and keep it cool in a cooler with ice on the way."

"I'll type up the ingredients on a label, and we can scotch tape it to the cellophane. Will call it A FARMERS DOG, *Specially made for* LUCKY. Does Mr. Polk have a dog?"

"He sure does, two of them, both Corgis. A smartbreed. I understand he loves them and exercises them twice a day. Which reminds me, you kids are going to need to exercise our little pup, Lucky."

"I already started this morning. I took Lucky with me and jogged a mile before any of you got up. He kept up and sure was tired when he got home. He instinctively ran to his water bowl. Afterward, I picked him up and placed him on Dario's bed, where he fell sound asleep."

"I hope he did his business on the run."

"Yes, mother, he sure did. I brought along a few paper towels and a small grocery bag and cleaned it up."

"I'm sorry I forgot; you fed him this morning before we all left?" asked Palmira, not trying to sound annoying.

"Yes, you remember I opened up a can of Skippy's and fed him what Papa told me to; one-quarter of the can, then I put him out back with his water."

Eugenio looked over at his son and said, "Dario, did you start teaching your dog new commands?"

"I did, Papa. May I get a treat?"

"Go right ahead, son."

"Come here, Lucky, TREAT! Lay-down." The pup hesitated, stared at the treat, then did what he was told. All of the Sacatti's applauded as Dario embraced the puppy.

Catherine Siena, a conscientious student, took well to the tiny three-to-one classroom environment. Her studies included General Mathematics, Earth Science, and English Grammar with an emphasis on presenting 'clean' papers in research. Catherine followed through on homework, as did the other girls. By 5:00 p.m., her studies and written work were complete. She chose to delve into the wealth of literature the sisters accumulated throughout the years. She preferred certain authors and found John Steinbeck one of her favorite writers. Mia introduced her to the famous California artist, and together, they would discuss the depressing final chapter of Of Mice and Men and the heart-rending journey of the Joad family in the Grapes of Wrath. His newest book, Travels with Charley, provided a comparative uplift.

Catherine wanted to know if Mia thought Steinbeck was a communist. "Our school would never allow that book not just because they thought John Steinbeck was a 'commie' but because of the 'cuss' words found in the story."

"John Steinbeck is a great American. Those who think he's communist are fools, and as far as the swear words, Sister Barbara has always told us it's not what you read that can hurt you; it's what you don't read. Besides, those swear words are written in the context of the story. We learned that in English.

"Someday Catherine, you and I are going to write like him. We're going to touch the hearts of America." Mia's prediction was not far off the mark because their English teacher noted how the two young girls could naturally put words together, creating magical sentences, paragraphs, and then short stories in teacher-given prompts.

Before settling into a good night's rest, Catherine asked Mia, "How could I keep my baby? I don't think I want to give my child up. I didn't do anything wrong, but I don't want my parents to know who's the daddy. I don't want my cousin anywhere near my boy or girl."

"Do you have any relative you can trust?"

"Yes, I do. She's my Auntie Grace. I think I could even live with her."

"Talk it over with Sister Barbara or Sister Rosemary. They'll help you. They've helped me all the time."

You two sure are persistent," said Miss Crowfoot as she looked up at the two talented basketball players.

"What do you mean?" asked Emma as she and Ted carried in the delivered grasshoppers for tomorrow's dissections.

"Come on, do you two feel I haven't caught on? You know well who I am. Who told you, Dorothy?"

"Miss Crowfoot, we have the grasshoppers. If it would make you feel more comfortable, we could show you how to dissect them for tomorrow's lesson."

"Yes, you could do that. I'd appreciate it, but let me ask you a question. Why are you so motivated to help me after what I did to your team?"

Ted looked over at Emma, taking her gently by the arm to help relieve the stress building inside her. "She knows Emma, she knows."

"Miss Crowfoot?" We weren't trying to..." said Emma before she was interrupted by the newest long-term instructor.

"Didn't your brother begin the chant? Aren't you more comfortable referring to me as...as Hel..."

Her eyes clouded. Miss Crowfoot, hurt by the digging memories of her father and the children she attended school with, stammered. Out of character, she placed her hands over her eyes. Hatred inside of Helixa Francine Crowfood subsided.

Emma offered the young woman a warm embrace. "Your name is Helixa, a beautiful name. We're told your name means you're intelligent, creative, and able to adapt. Your mother must have added the 'A.' Your father just bastardized it. He had no business doing that. Helixa is such a rare name even your students, as cocky as they were, wouldn't realize the beauty behind it."

Ted found a hopefully interesting historical fact.

"Oklahoma back in the day was filled with horrible bigots, most of them armed with weapons and ready to use them.

"You grew up in the middle of all this racist ignorance pushed heavily on you, your father, and your brother's dark complexion, too. Blacks in your neighborhood were treated with the same disdain. Many white children of that era were drummed into thinking they were 'better' and that there was no place for minorities such as yourself, your father, and brother to even reside in that town."

Helixa looked up and smiled at Ted. "He's a good boy, Emma. You did well for yourself.

"Let me ask you again: Did Dorothy tell you about my past?"

"Actually, I brought up to her the new microfiche research department in the U.C.L.A. library. She knew almost nothing, only that she surmised you weren't a demon. She read into your heart and mind, Miss Crowfoot you hinted at a trace of fairplay. Dorothy felt your horrendous treatment at our basketball game displayed in the end no favortism despite the fact you ruined the game. Not necessarily the act of a demon just the action of a confused girl."

"What did your research find?"

Ted spoke for him and Emma, "What we found first was through our discussions with you. You mentioned your last name, Crowfoot, an unusual name, and that you grew up in Oklahoma. That got us far into the Oklahoma Times back in the early 1900's."

"They kept vital statistics, births, deaths, and even important marriages," added Emma.

"And about my father, my brother, did you read what happened?"

"We did Helixa. Both were murdered."

"Did the paper tell you my mother sent me away from the house after they shot my brother and hung my father?"

"No, not a word," said Emma.

"I resembled my Irish mother. She told me to go to town, find a job and start over. I looked and found employment working the financial books in a saloon. Only fourteen, I knew my numbers. Olive Reynolds, the owner, was left in a pickle when her accountant, without notice, hopped on a train and headed back to Virginia, her hometown.

"It took me a week to figure out her mess and another week to straighten it out. I was always good with figures, but when I fixed Olive's books, she let me go. Olive said I was too young, and by then, she found out my father was Ben Crowfoot.

"I got the message my name was no good in Oklahoma City, so I went back home only to find my mother lying in bed with the deputy who killed my brother and was responsible for the lynching of my father.

"I headed straight to the kitchen where my father kept his pistol and walked into the room holding that shaking pistol and fired, killing my mother when she moved defensively over that damn deputy. I got off another shot as he flew from bed naked and shot him in the belly. He had enough strength to grab the pistol and shot me through the head."

"Oh, my dear God! You died a violent death!" Emma was stunned.

"Your entire family! All of you suffered!" Ted was equally startled.

"Both of you never read that, did you? I sat on my mother's bed and cried for three days, staring at the carnage. Finally, someone brilliant in the sheriff's office figured out 'what in the hell happened to Deputy Billy Carson' and found all three of us rotting and stinking up the place.

"After the deputy puked, he drove back to town and reported Deputy Billy Carson must have murdered us after I wrestled with him and shot him in the gut.

"That never made the news, I bet. Carson was a hero, as he snuffed out the entire troublemaking Crowfoot family."

Emma, dumbfounded, let Ted talk, but not before the fifth-period bell went off, sending Miss Crowfoot's ears mercilessly ringing.

Ted looked back and said, "Mrs. Crowfoot, we'll come after school and help you with the dissection of the grasshoppers."

Unlike what she had done since her mother taught her as a child, she thanked God for his blessings and welcomed her fifth-period students.

Chapter Nineteen

Lonnie Price

Dario, you need to remember to talk with me through your mind; otherwise, your teacher may get upset and wonder if you're off your rocker."

"Okay, that's fine!" said Dario, loud enough for students in the back of the classroom to hear.

"You agree to what I'm saying. That's fine, Dario, I'm glad to hear it. So what do we call the space rocks that periodically hit the earth."

"We call them meteors," replied Dario.

"I'm impressed, Dario. You didn't need any help on my part," said Dorothy while standing behind Mrs. Holmes.

Mrs. Holmes went on with her lesson while Dorothy spoke to the 3rd grader. *"Let your sister know that meeting too often at lunch in Mrs. Crowfoot's classroom doesn't give me a chance to talk with her. Can you do that, Dario?"*

"Yes, I'll do that," he replied, his voice much lower.

"Speak with your mind, Dario. Why do you keep forgetting."

"Dario, who are you talking to? You got me concerned now. I'm going to need to call your mother."

"Tell her you were answering her question if the children were listening and for everyone to sit up straight."

"Mrs. Holmes, I was..."

"No, no Dario out loud! My goodness."

"Sorry."

"Mrs. Holmes, you asked if the children were listening and I always listen and sit up straight."

"That's fine, Dario. I won't ask you if you were really listening as it's time for lunch. Everyone, please stand for the Angelus and the prayer before meals."

At lunch, Lonnie Price asked Dario if he was going to finish his peanut butter and jelly sandwich.

"I'll give you part of it if you give me part of your tuna fish sandwich."

"It's a deal! Here, take the whole thing. I'm getting tired of tuna fish."

Dario loved Lonnie's mother's concoction of extra mayonnaise with diced dill pickles and severed every bite. He, on the other hand, increased the torn part of his peanut butter and jelly sandwich and watched how Lonnie savored his partial peanut butter and jelly, too.

After lunch, the boys gathered on the various basketball courts in the asphalt schoolyard, with a few of them playing the forbidden game of 'slams' where they would throw the basketball at the backboard, sending opposing players a distance away to repeat the play. Some boys missed the backboard entirely which gave the game away to the other boy.

Father Gibson hated that game, which wasn't surprising. In the boys' view, it was harmless and didn't, as they saw it, cause any damage.

In Father Gibson's 'wise' point of view, it warranted a yank on the ear lobe, so when out of nowhere he appeared, Lonnie, whose ears stuck out the furthest, was surprised when Father pulled painfully on Lonnie's ears and told the rest of the boys to stand against the parish hall wall until the bell rang. Lonnie was sent to the principal's office.

"What did you do now, Lonnie?" asked Principal Killian.

"I got in trouble playing slams."

"Slams again. Say an Our Father and get back to class. Better yet, say an extra one for me." Lonnie left as Mother Killian shook her head and said to herself while returning to her classroom, *When in the hell is that priest going to transfer?*

When Dario arrived home, he and Roger took Lucky for a walk across the street on the rural community college 'new' sidewalk. "Lucky you sure are one 'lucky' dog to get saved like you did."

Lucky, doing his business hiking on the trunk of a large Fremont cottonwood, saluted Roger's statement in the best way he knew how. Completing two laps around the large community college school, Dario noticed his sister, Emma, hadn't arrived home yet. "She's usually home around four o'clock. I need to tell her something."

"What do you need to tell her?" asked Roger.

"That the lady in yellow needs to talk to her."

"Oh? I have a question for you. Does anyone ever ask you why you go to school a mile away when you got one right down the block?"

"Yeah, sometimes."

"Yeah, me, too."

Emma arrived home five minutes before her mother and father. "Roger, could you walk home by yourself today? I got to prepare dinner right away."

"Yeah, sure, not a problem. See you, Dario."

"I'll see you tomorrow, Roger.

"Emma, Roger, and I set the table for you."

"Thank you! You're both good boys."

"I talked to Dorothy today. She wanted you to use the cafeteria at school so she could talk to you. She has something to say."

"I wonder what she wants. Ted and I are spending too much time with our new science teacher."

Emma and Dario's parents arrived home a few minutes later. Emma reheated leftovers from two nights ago and soon served dinner to her family.

"You get up awful early to jog with Lucky. You okay with that?" asked Palmira.

"Not a problem, Mama. Lucky loves a little run in the morning. He's not only getting used to it he wants to pick up the pace."

"What happens when you stop getting up that early?" wondered Emma's father.

"It won't be for a while. I'm training for this upcoming season in volleyball and hope I'm in the best shape of my life for basketball. I understand we're getting a 6'4" transfer from San Luis Obispo. She'll be a junior and was All-League up north for Mission College Prep. We're gaining a top-notch center after losing Cindy Marquez to U.S.C."

"What's the girl's name," asked Mr. Sacatti.

"It slipped my mind, Papa. I'll ask Coach Errion tomorrow. I understand they already moved into a home near the beach. We're also getting a star guard. Her daddy played in the N.B.A. until he hurt his knee. Her name is Rosa Clark, and her father is Dr. Clark, our team doctor."

"Sure, Dr. Elwin Clark, we know him, Eugenio. He treated Louise and Cindy at the game."

Coached arranged for Rosa, Louise, and that new girl from S.L.O. to let us work out in the gym this summer. Ted's asking his coach if he and a few other players could join us. We got the gym until 10:00 a.m., and then I got to go to work helping to clean the school for September."

Friday, Emma enjoyed dissecting the grasshoppers in class, assisting anyone with Ted and Miss Crowfoot for a few of the students who cringed, even opening up a dead insect. "They're too large," commented one girl. "Do I have to do this?"

"Let me help you, Helen. Dissecting is mandatory, but I can understand why you're apprehensive."

Fifty minutes flew by, and Emma was eager to visit the lunchroom at noon. "Ted and I are going to the cafeteria today. Miss Crowfoot, wish us luck."

"Good luck, you two and say hello to Dorothy."

Emma froze. "You know she's coming to see us?"

"How can I not! That young lady carries a powerful aura. As I said, good luck and have fun."

"Would you like to come with us?"

"No, you two go ahead, I'll be fine."

Ted turned and said, "If you think so. We'll see you on Monday, Miss Crowfoot."

Dorothy was seated at one of the empty tables and welcomed the two young students. "She knows I'm here, doesn't she."

Ted smiled, saying, "She told us you have a strong aura."

"Hmmph! I was told that when I was alive. My husband, Michael, said I glowed."

"Oh look, here comes Miss Crowfoot," said Ted, a bit surprised.

One of the basketball players shouted, "HELIX! SHE'S HELIX THE DEVIL. EVERYONE RUN! HELIX MUST GO!" Lilith, disguised as the same girl who disrupted the C.I.F. finals, traipsed forward and ignored the panicked students.

Students started screaming. A cafeteria table lifted three feet off the floor, slamming down hard over five students hiding underneath.

Saint Anthony Vice Principal Judy Wilcox flew backward. "Where is that voice coming from? Where are you, my God, where are you!"

The true Helixa Crowfoot arrived in the cafeteria, was lifted off the floor, and flew five feet, slamming into a snack machine, surprising Ted Accenti.

"HOW DARE YOU TURN YOUR BACK ON ME YOU DIRTY TRAMP. NO ONE EVER LEAVES ME!"

Emma ran over to Miss Crowfoot lifting her off the floor. "Are you okay, Helixa!"

"I think so. Get out with Ted and save yourself. Lilith is a demon; she controls a league of over twenty of the cruelest people ever to walk the earth."

"What does she want with you?"

"She's getting closer, run!"

"I'm not going anywhere. You need to leave Lilith by the grace of God. I command his angels to take you away!"

"YOU! A mere child?"

Lilith grew closer as Emma raised her arms in the air, banishing the demon to the netherworld. Lilith was lifted and carried through the walls, heading south toward the ocean and flung in the water."

Ted now grew close to Emma, placing his arm around the distraught teen. "Did you see who it was, Miss Crowfoot?"

"Yes, Ted, I did. It was Lilith, a demon. She controls others and tries to continue to manipulate me."

"I saw her too, Ted. Hatred bled out of her face before she was swept away."

Helixa was astounded. "You saw her, Emma, you could see Lilith?"

Yes, I did see…"

"Miss Crowfoot, are you alright?"

"Yes, Mrs. Wilcox, I believe I am," answered Helixa.

"Students, please clear the cafeteria. Find a space outdoors; we just experienced an earthquake, and you're safe. Now go, GO, GO!

"You're bleeding on your arm, and it looks like your leg too. Could you two help Miss Crowfoot to the nurse's office and we'll get you fixed up.

"Do you have a fifth period?"

"Yes, I do; we're dissecting grasshoppers."

"Ted, once we get to the nurse, contact Miss Havelstine, our English teacher, and have her take the class. She's got a free period."

"I can help her pass out the grasshoppers and even assist any student who needs help. I've done it a few times."

"What about your class?" asked Mrs. Wilcox."

"I got my coach for physical education. I'll tell him what happened after school."

"You're referring to the earthquake, correct!"

"Of course, Mrs. Wilcox, the earthquake."

"And Emma, who do you have for the fifth period?"

"Home Economics with Mrs. Regina Holden. I can tell her in a few minutes. She'll understand the emergency."

"Good, now let's lift you, Miss Crowfoot. How's your back?"

"Just a little sore. I'll be okay."

Once inside, the school nurse took a look at Miss Crowfoot's injury as Ted darted over to Miss Havelstine's classroom and directed the first-year teacher to the biology room. Emma followed through with a phone call to her Home Economics teacher.

Finally, alone with the vice-principal in her office, Helixa and Emma sat down to answer a mountain of mysterious questions. Dorothy appeared to the two girls and helped guide them in their answers.

"Ladies, I asked the principal if she felt any rumbling, and she said no. That quake felt like a hard eight or nine. What frightened me the most was that strange voice. I looked behind me where it came from and didn't see a soul. Did you two see anyone."

"Tell her you saw no one."

Emma was impressed by how clear Dorothy's voice sounded. "No, no one. Did you see anyone, Miss Crowfoot?"

"I couldn't say. My head was in a fog after being thrown."

"Is your head alright, Miss Crowfoot? I could call an ambulance."

"No, I'm okay, just terrified by the impact."

"Did you hear a voice at all?"

"You need to answer an emphatic NO! I've cleared the heads of all of the students in the cafeteria. None of them will remember anything but a sudden jolt."

Helixa said, "A voice? I didn't hear any voice. I felt the jolt. Long Beach has always had pretty bad earthquakes, like the one my mother told me about in 1933. She said the whole town almost went down in it."

"I felt an earthquake also," said Emma, "We get periodic internal secluded jolts as if the inner earth beneath us was caving away. I experienced it when I was seven. It terrified my whole family, and our neighbors said they didn't feel a thing. None of it made the news either."

"Secluded jolts. Never heard of them. I spent a good portion of my life in Nebraska. I don't think I could get used to this. Please give me an old-fashioned tornado any day. At least you get a warning."

"Not bad, ladies. A secluded earthquake! That's one for the books."

"And both of you? You heard nothing?"

Emma looked at Miss Crowfoot. Both of them shook their heads no.

"Miss Crowfoot, all of us had quite a day. You have my permission to go home and rest. Will you be in on Monday? If not, I could arrange for a substitute."

"I think it best if I returned. I enjoy being around the students. May I ask if I could recline in the nurse's rest area until the end of the school day and then return to my classroom? I need to plan for next week."

"Sure, go right ahead. Our nurse won't be here; she leaves early on Friday."

"That's okay, Mrs. Wilcox. I should be fine."

Before Miss Crowfoot and Emma exited the vice-principal's office, Emma turned and said, "I'll sit with her until she's well enough to return to her classroom."

Judy Wilcox nodded her approval.

"Whose this, Lilith, Helixa?" asked Emma in the hallway.

Emma and Miss Crowfoot found Dorothy standing in the corner of the nurse's office, unable for anyone to see her if they walked in at any time.

Without hesitation, Helixa spoke first.

"She sided with me after I was shot, guaranteeing I would find justice for destroying the people who cursed me and my family in life. I took to her and found myself helping to create havoc in the lives of decent people in Tulsa, Oklahoma, the Greenwood District. Lilith was convinced whites needed to massacre hundreds of blacks while burning down their homes and businesses while I watched. She confused me, but the deep hatred for almost anyone overwhelmed me, and I went along with her evil acts, watching and even contributing when I thought it helped.

"I finally realized none of my perverse actions did me or anyone any good. When Lilith encouraged me to create a so-called blood bath during the basketball game, I caved in again.

"I'm sorry. I realize sorry isn't enough."

"Dorothy, to spare Helixa's employment here, how are we going to handle what the students heard, especially Mrs. Wilcox."

"Their memories of Lilith's haunting voice are erased, including Mrs. Wilcox, your vice-principal. They'll only remember the 'isolated jolt.' I still think your reasoning for the tremendous shake is classic. You have quite an imagination, Emma. You have my permission to call it the 'demon shake.' No one ever heard of it, and who knows, maybe we do have isolated jolts."

Lilith

Chapter Twenty
Skippy Processing Plant-North Long Beach

Crossing the small village road, she took Dario on her A.M. jog with Lucky, letting her little brother wake up early with her once again. *"The little guy sure is wide awake for such an early hour,"* she thought. Lucky remained patient, waiting silently for Emma to harness him across the street.

Stronger and faster, Dario challenged Emma every morning. She was surprised at how easily he paced Emma and their pup for a mile. "You sure have stamina, little man."

"Is that good?" asked Dario.

"It means your heart and lungs are very strong."

"It's because I run on the playground every day with my friends." Emma smiled and brushed back her little brother's hair.

By 9:00 a.m., her father pulled his truck up to the Skippy processing plant in North Long Beach. Emma hopped out of the truck carrying a styrofoam cooler containing the saran wrap custom fresh dog food toward President Harold Polk's office, trailing her father.

Harold greeted them from behind, just finishing his Corgis walk up and down the street. Emma bent down, ruffling the dogs' heads. "You look beautiful, little girl," she said, giving slightly more notice to the female pup, who seemed to enjoy Emma's attention.

"Mr. Eugenio Sacatti how are you. This must be your talented basketball-playing girl."

"Hello, Mr. Polk. I'm Emma, Eugenio's daughter."

"It's nice you both arrived on time. I hope my pups won't disturb us. I like to bring them to the plant after we take an early morning walk."

Eugenio remarked, "Mr. Polk, we brought a sample of the dog food inside this cooler."

Emma reached in and pulled out the saran-wrapped food with her homemade attached ingredients scotched tape to it.

"So this is the magic dog food that could give these pups a few extra years. That means a lot to me. I never heard anything about food increasing a dog's life.

"I did listen to your advice about picking out the right dog. I went to three breeders wanting documentation on the health of the parents and grandparents of the pups. Finally, one breeder gave me what I needed. These pups are gold. I walk 'em, and they got all their shots.

"My last two Corgis lived to eleven and twelve years old, what the actuality statistics agreed. I fed them Skippy's their entire life. I certainly do miss them."

"It appeared, Mr. Polk, you did all you could," said Emma.

"All except what I fed my Oliver and Ann. My dog food may fit the budget of hundreds of dog owners. It's not bad; then again, it's not the best. Who makes the best, you two?

"Let me ask you who has the time to make this day in and day out. Maybe a week's worth might do, but how long does your dog food last?"

"It can last a month on ice, Mr. Polk, and even longer if you freeze it. My papa never owned a freezer. I'd have to call my brother in Illinois."

Emma chimed in, "Mr. Polk, I understand you have refrigeration in your plant. You could make hundreds of pounds every day right here and have refrigerated trucks deliver it to the markets in wealthy areas. Your cost wouldn't hurt you if you charged less for a week's supply. People with money would be happy to purchase premium dog food."

"Do you think folks would buy it?"

"Only if you advertised. Rich folks probably own most of the color t.v.'s now. You'd let people know how this food will increase the lives of their beloved pets. And make sure you include in a pocket stand near the refrigerated food, a free brochure on how to extend a dog's life."

"This is all new Eugenio. Your daughter's quite the salesman. I should hire you, Emma, but then I'm lucky enough to have your dad on staff. Most ads on t.v. are for the same dog food; some of them are nothing more than empty calories.

"Well, Mr. Sacatti want to you say I put you in charge of production. I'm confident working with my processing engineer, and you'll lead my pups to a quality, long life besides putting more revenue into our company."

Mia accepted mentoring the young thirteen-year-old Catherine Siena. She found out Catherine was born on September 16th, and Mia's birthday was September 17th. "So we're the same age for one day," said Mia, adding, "I look forward to our big day coming soon."

"You're not afraid. I'm told the pain is unbearable," replied Catherine.

"If the pain is awful, the doctor gives you an epidural. It's, I understand, a piercing sting, but only for a few seconds."

"What's an epidural?"

"It's a shot in your lower back, an anesthetic to relieve your pain. I'm going to ask for one if I can't handle the throbbing ache."

"I don't know, Mia, I'm afraid of needles."

"Just think in seconds and count; it helps you forget about the needle. My mama taught me that when my school nurse lined up the students for their shots. I was always congratulated for being brave. You do the same, promise me?"

"I think so, I'll try and remember the numbers and count."

"That's it! Let's try it. Okay you're about to get your shot, ready? Now!"

Catherine counted slowly, "One, two, three, four, five. six…"

"Stop! Remember the numbers, not the needle."

Catherine, on her knees before expiring to bed was joined by Mia in bedtime prayer. "This isn't new for me, Cathy, but I confess I turned my back on prayer for too long.

Thank you for reminding me not to place God and my angel to the wayside."

Mia drifted into sleep within five minutes. Lately tiring, her pregnancy was a week or two away the baby's kicks reminding her that Mia's child longed for her mommy.

Dreaming through the comforting wave of Dorothy's unending love now usurped by an alarming vision of her little brother crying for his mother, Palmira.

"*Mama, please, Mama, I'm hot,*" he cried, still unconscious in deep slumber. In the room closest to her brother, his voice woke Emma first.

Pushing her blankets aside, Emma rushed to his room, careful not to startle her sleeping brother. Heat drifted off his body, alarmed she felt his forehead. Dario was burning up.

His sister rushed to the refrigerator freezer pulling out ice cubes and placing them into a dish towel. Emma rushed to her brother's bedside, placing the ice on his forehead.

Mia's eyes opened. Sister Rosemary stood over her, holding an ice pack to the young teen's forehead. Catherine stood nearby with Sister Barbara, "Catherine, grab a couple of shower towels and run to the ice bin in the kitchen and fill them with ice. Sister Rosemary, this girl is burning up.

Sister Barbara ran and grabbed the emergency kit in the hallway and returned moments later, securing a thermometer in her hands. Opening Mia's mouth, she secured the thermometer under the teen's tongue.

Both nuns watched as the ice pack appeared to thaw before her eyes. "Oh good God, Sister, is that steam!"

Sister Barbara pulled the thermometer out of Mia's mouth, and she gasped. "Sister Rosemary, her temperature reads…my God, it stopped at 107 degrees. Call an ambulance."

Catherine, with two other girls carrying bath towels filled with ice, ran into the room. Sister Barbara pulled the blankets back and asked the girls to dump the ice on Mia's body. They watched as the ice slowly melted away.

A siren sounded outside when an Emergency Medical Team rushed upstairs. "She's burning up, and nothing seems to lower her temperature," said Sister Barbara. All of the teens in the room cried, not understanding the emergency completely new to them.

Sister Rosemary cautioned the rescue team she was a week or two away from delivery. Mia was wrapped in cold, compressed wraps as the ambulance soared toward Cedars Sinai with Sister Barbara holding Mia's hand.

Emma tossed and turned, caught in a wicked dream. Mia was dying, burning up slowly before she expired.

"Mama, Papa! Mia is unconscious," Emma shouted in her sleep.

Dario heard his sister shouting and ran to her room. "Emma, Emma, wake up. You're having a nightmare." He shook his sister until she knew she was fully awake. "Emma, are you okay?"

She flew from under her blankets, holding onto her brother as she whisked both of them to their parents' room. "Mother, please wake up! You need to call Sister Barbara at the convent!"

"Why. What is it, sweetheart?" bellowed her mother, shocked an emergency suddenly awakened her.

"What's going on?" startled Eugenio, sat up rubbing his eyes. "Why are you two kids up? What happened?"

"Papa, please don't take this wrong, but I believe Mia may be in some sort of danger."

"How do you know this, Emma?" asked her father.

Dario said, frightened and perplexed, "Because she had a dream."

"What! A dream? What kind of dream, Emma?" wondered her father.

"Mia was burning up. It was as if I was there, Papa. It was as if I was standing there watching her burn up! Oh Momma, Papa, you need to call, call right now!" Emma fell across her mother's blanket, weeping.

Eugenio flew out of bed, raced to the kitchen phone, and asked the operator to dial St. Agnes Convent in Los Angeles. The phone rang three times before Sister Constance Maria picked up the phone.

Sister Constance let Eugenio know that Sister Rosemary was ready to call him after she calmed down the girls. "Your daughter was rushed to the hospital, Mr. Sacatti. She's burning with fever. Mia is at Cedars Sinai at this minute."

"Thank you, Sister, and tell Sister Rosemary I'm on my way to Cedars and not to call the house."

Palmira stood next to her husband. "Shouldn't you call Cedar's first? Find out what happened."

He called and was told his daughter was there in the emergency. Palmira told Emma to watch her brother as the couple rushed to the hospital, Palmira praying along the way.

Emma lay down with her brother, in and out of sleep, when she heard the phone ring. She ran from bed to the kitchen phone, "Hello Emma, it's me, Lilith. Don't ever tangle with me again!"

Emma heard her father's truck pull in behind the Plymouth, arriving back home on Sunday morning at 5:00 a.m. She met her parents at the door. "Mia's fine, Emma," said her mother, Palmira. "You were right she did have a monstrous fever. According to Sister Barbara, Mia's temperature rose to at least 107 degrees. Cedars personnel recommended she purchase a new thermometer. According to the Emergency Medical team report, Mia was bound in cold wraps on the way to the hospital. The heat from her body steamed up the encased wrappers.

"Once she was moved to the emergency ward, your sister shook with the chills although her fever, now 101 degrees, persisted. Mia was now wrapped in blankets to keep her warm."

"How's Mia's baby?" worried Emma.

"They found her child safe," said Eugenio. "Testing suspected your sister may have suffered from food poisoning; the nuns and boarded girls who ate at the community convent seemed fine. "As of now, no other person at St. Agnes experienced any discomfort."

Palmira spoke before the exhausted parents climbed back into bed. After a few more tests, a couple of possible infections were negative. "Cedars confirmed your sister must have experienced what your father told you: food poisoning. It had to be something Mia ate without the knowledge of the convent or any of the teens."

Eugenio calmed Emma before they all headed back to bed. "The teens and sisters didn't experience stomach disorders, so that part is good. If Cedars can't find anything with testing, your sister will head back to the convent tomorrow. Now get back to sleep, Emma."

Lilith's phone call raced through Emma's mind. *"You can't win. My angels are far more powerful than you. Stay away from my family and all my friends. Keep away Lilith in God's name."*

Lilith cringed down in the depths of the Pacific Ocean.

Emma walked her brother almost a mile to attend the 9:00 a.m. Mass. Father Gibson's homily centered around thanking parishioners for considering Richard Nixon during the last November election. "He's a good Californian and loyal to his wife. Think about him in the future."

Word was already out; Kennedy's relationship with 'Jackie' was less than honorable.

What's that got to do with Christ's words, especially at a children's Mass? Probably a few of his top financial supporters wanted to hear his diehard bluster.

She walked her brother to Ralph and Virginia's mom-and-pop market located inside the village after Mass. Dario's allowance burning in his pocket. "My friend Lonnie told me Mr. Ralph sold the best baseball cards and that I shouldn't be shopping outside of the village. I told him we didn't have a pharmacy, so we had to go there sometimes. I'm going back to Dr. Sloane; even Mr. Ralph has good cards. Dr. Sloane will have the last packs of the year."

"Are you talking about the end of the baseball year high-end cards?"

"Yep, and she said she'd save me some."

"She did, I remember. So you got yourself a whole quarter. How many packs are you going to buy?"

"Can I spend it all?"

"It's your money, Dario. Spend it all if you wish."

He laid down his quarter, bought five packs, and said a silent prayer. Dario waited until he left the market to open his pack, watching another boy flicking 'commons' into a trash barrel.

"Those are great cards for lagging; the more you have , the more you can save your Willie Mays, Mickey Mantle, and Don Drysdale's. I'm going to get them when he leaves."

He waited and lunged into the trash barrel, pulling out a dozen or so cards before nervously opening his packs. "Out of 25 cards, I got a Brooks Robinson, an Al Kaline, and Eddie

Mathews. Still no Koufax. I did get a metal baseball coin of Whitey Ford, but he's not that great anymore."

"Koufax may be in the high series packs of September, Dario. Maybe you should buy only two to three packs and save your money until then and buy the entire box from Dr. Sloane."

"I'd be in fourth grade by then. Do you think it will work?"

"It might Dario. Buying two to three packs every week should help you find out. Maybe you'll win one when you're lagging your commons against a wall."

"Naw, my friends would quit before taking a chance on a Koufax, even a Drysdale."

Arriving home after Mass, Emma and Dario found their parents getting ready for the 11:15 a.m. Mass. "Did you kids say a prayer for your sister?"

"I did, mother. I think she'll be alright," said Emma.

Dario didn't say a word he had forgotten. He'd wait and say one after his parents left for church. *I just thought about praying for a Koufax card. God probably will punish me.*

Ralph and Virginia's Lakewood Village

Chapter Twenty-One
Donovan Fisk-Goodbye and Hello

Control your meager dominions, Lilith. They're waiting for your commands, and why did you let a mere woman control your presence? Goddamn you, now go!"

Lilith ventured from the depths of the ocean, sticking her head out of the waves and breathing in the fresh air a mile out from the shore. She attempted to board the surface of the land but was thrown back.

"Damn it! I'm coming for you, Helix. How dare you defy me." Lilith felt ill; her stomach curdled, and she began to vomit. I can't be sick. What in the hell is going on?"

Lilith called upon her so-called single 'region' of a malicious and vile 'entity.' "Find Helix and destroy her. Send her away to oblivion. Deliver her to the depths of distress and sorrow.

A well-behaved but seemingly not the sharpest tool in the shed, Donovan Fisk controlled the imaginary thoughts of other members of Lilith's league. "I don't think they hear me."

"Just keep an ear out for all of them, Donovan. I already am having difficulty with damn Helix Crowfoot. Why did she turn on me? Find out Donovan, and also look for that bitch, Emma Sacatti. She attends high school on the surface, and Helix is a goddamn teacher. Go, go and find them both! Get the others to assist you if you need help."

He flew fast as if beaming across the universe. He sprawled across Long Beach, his sense flashing on the suspected high school in question. He walked into the biology room, invisible to the students. Helixa looked up to the corner of the room, her mouth dropped. *"Donovan, what are you doing here? Please leave."*

"PLEASE? What's got into you? You sure changed Helix. And what in the hell is wrong with you? Lilith is waiting for you over the ocean. Let's go now."

Donovan, a bumbling robber of two stagecoaches, shot and killed one and wounded two Wells Fargo drivers before he was beaten after wrestling a purse from a rather large female occupant of the stagecoach. She stabbed him multiple times after knocking him out. Two weeks later, after recovering from his injuries, the town of Westmont, Texas, hung him.

"Who the hell are you? Get out right at this minute!" alarmed Emma screamed telepathically; however, the position of her face told the students around her that she was panicked. Her desk moved backward, toppling the desk behind her. She rose from her seat and was flung backward, her head hitting the wall beneath the windows on the west side of the room. Students screamed as Ted lifted from his desk in the back of the room and ran to the aid of Emma.

Dorothy set foot in the room and, combined with Helixa, cast the appalling and foul Donovan from the high school and far out into the ocean.

Wiping out the biology students' memories, Dorothy and Helixa hovered over Ted, assisting an unconscious Emma Sacatti. "Someone run to the office and have them call an ambulance." Three students darted from the room as the other freshmen and sophomores nervously talked about the earthquake they just felt.

"I hear this is the 2nd one this week. I wasn't in the cafeteria, but I was told a secluded tremor shook the entire lunch room," said Melanie Baines, a freshman honor student.

Her friend Angie Franke declared, "I was there! It scared the heck out of me, and now this! I'm frightened."

Ten minutes later, ambulance personnel knelt next to Emma, now revived. "How are you feeling?" said a young attendant. A few of the girls cooed over the handsome ambulance driver.

"I think I'm okay; I hit my head," replied Emma, still a bit muddled.

"Can you stand up? Let's check."

Emma stood, wobbled, and fell in the arms of Ted Accenti. "We need to take her to St. Mary's Hospital for observation." Vice-Principal Judy Wilcox held the student's hand as the ambulance worker loaded Emma on a stretcher.

After contacting the school office, Wilcox rode in the emergency vehicle with Emma, reassuring the girl everything would be alright. "It's been a terrible last few days. I was told your class felt an earthquake."

"Yes, Mrs. Wilcox, a powerful one."

"I can't understand it. We have to have a sinking hole underneath this school. Two in four days, and yet this one mysteriously on the second floor. I understand no one below you felt a thing. My goodness, it's beginning to send chills up my spine.

"Ted is following us and will drive me back to school once you're settled. It appears they're going to keep you overnight, so I need to contact your parents when we arrive at St. Mary's."

―――――――

Where in the hell is Helix?" wondered a perturbed Lilith.

"She teamed up with Dorothy and drove me back here."

"WHAT! What is wrong with you? You're a coward, Donovan, a goddamn chickenshit. I thought you were tough, and two girls forced you back to the ocean."

"I injured Emma. She's got to go to the hospital, I'm sure of it."

"Emma, the girl who plays with the angels. A mysterious girl. You were once more than a pathetic human being, Donovan. Her angels can't work against you now."

"I don't know she shouted at me, and not a student heard her. Where does she get that kind of power? I can't figure it out. I think I caught her off guard."

"Perhaps I should utilize Lamia. She's killed dozens of female patients as a nurse, young, old, weak, and strong, and you're worried about a teenager. You're pathetic, Donovan. Why do I get all the losers!"

"That girl's got some kind of power, Lilith."

"Oh, go to hell, and I mean literally, go to hell, you wimp."

"But you promised you'd never send me to hell. I like roaming the earth, Lilith. I'll do what you say. She's gotta be in the hospital, not far from the school."

"Then do what you got to do, Donovan. Do you want me to send Lamia to hold your hand?"

"Well, actually, it's not a bad idea. It might bring back a few good memories."

"Yeah, you're right. Not bad thinking for an idiot. I'll send her, too."

Donovan waited until he was out of contact and hit the shoreline. "Why did I get stuck with her? No wonder Helix dropped out."

Wandering into St. Mary's, he immediately bumped into Dorothy Marquez. "I thought we sent you out to the ocean. What are you doing here?"

"It took two of you to do it, Dorothy," replied a cutting Donovan while not too sure of himself.

"Donovan, I believe the young girl sitting in the second row could have done the same.

"SO! Did Lilith send you here to trouble Emma?"

"She's a pain in the ass. She threatened to send me to hell if I didn't come here."

Helixa appeared in the lobby. "She can't do that, Donovan. She's a Class D demon and on probation with all the Class A types. Her time on earth is numbered. It would be best if you dropped her like I did. You spent all those years with her and should know better by now."

"I can't; she's sending Lamia that stupid killing nurse. Lamia will go back and tell Lilith I crossed her, then it's HELL for me!"

"Have you ever seen Lamia, Donovan?" asked Helixa.

"Well? No, I haven't, but I hear about her all the time."

"She doesn't exist, and Lilith doesn't run a league. She couldn't even handle a two-bit rodeo. She fooled you, Donovan, and she can't send you to hell," replied Helix.

"How do I know that you're the one trying to fool me Helix."

Irritated, Dorothy said, "Her name is Helixa, Donovan. Say it, or we'll send you back to sea."

"Okay, fine! Helixa. You wouldn't lie to me, would you?" Tears fell from the entity's eyes.

"I don't lie anymore, Donovan, I can't. Instead of bothering Emma, you could learn from her like I did, and Dorothy next to me would help you, too."

Entering Emma's room, she relaxed in bed, waiting for testing. Ted returned after dropping off Mrs. Wilcox at the school and guessed why Emma was suddenly staring ahead at what most people thought was empty space.

She greeted Dorothy, Helixa, and the so-called 'villain,' Donovan Fisk. *"You wouldn't be here, Donovan, unless something came up."*

"Go ahead, Donovan, what do you say?" pressed Dorothy.

"They hung me for killing a Wells Fargo stagecoach driver and wounding the guy sitting next to him. He shot at

me FIRST, and then I got beat up and stabbed. Not a fair deal back then."

Dorothy and Helixa stood there with their mouths open before the former Oklahoma teen said, "Emma, Donovan was always ten cents short of a dime. Right, Donovan!"

"Huh? I never had a dime in my pocket for more than a day. Stealing anything was the only thing I managed to do."

Emma held back a good laugh and let Ted know who was there and asked the three if they might reveal themselves to her friend.

Ted let out a sigh of relief and worried Emma's staring forward had nothing connected to her head injury. "Hello, Dorothy and Helixa. It's nice to see you here."

"You're that kid! I've seen you before at your school," said Donovan.

"And you must be the jerk who hurt Emma and threw the entire classroom into a frenzy. What are you doing here!"

"I'm getting protection. I don't like Lilith she bothers me."

"I don't know who in the hell is Lilith, but you owe Emma an apology!"

"SORRY!"

One word and it appeared his head went blank. Notably, with a mentally deficient I.Q., Donovan would have been provided a bit of solace even in a 1961 atmosphere. Instead, in 1877, Texas placed a rope around his neck and hung him until he choked to death.

Soon after, Eugenio, his wife, and his son walked into the room. Only Ted remained and greeted the Sacatti's. With Emma, he completed his assignments due the following day and spent the rest of his evening waiting for the testing on Emma's head.

A physician, Dr. Eugene Yap, arrived in the room with good news. Mr. and Mrs. Sacatti, your daughter only experienced a minor concussion; she'll be fine and ready to leave the hospital with you tonight."

Dear Lord, first your sister Emma and now you. What's going on, honey? And be honest with your father and me."

"Not now, Mother, let's wait until we get home.

Things were looking up with both Eugenio and Palmira's current employment. Her husband met with Harold Polks food engineer, who controlled the safety of Skippy dog food every week. Now, Johnathan Grouse felt his healthy 'real food' dog meal for dogs could work not placing any financial damper on his boss's company. Harold was excited, wanting to place the healthy food on his Corgis' everyday diet.

Dr. Miller over at the Dorothy Marquez medical clinic praised Mrs. Sacatti daily and then...

Dario brushed his teeth and was sent to bed. Emma sat down in the living room with her parents. "St. Anthony never experienced a secluded cafeteria earthquake. As far as I know, one most likely doesn't exist. Momma and Papa, for some reason, we've been attacked by what Dorothy calls a Class D demon who was permanently exiled deep into the ocean."

"My God, Palmira, this sounds like one of those 'B movies showing at a Drive-In. I would have never believed Dorothy existed if I hadn't seen what I saw and then the confusion at the basketball game. We go to church every Sunday and every day during Lent. What could a demon want with us?"

"It started as an innocent prank to get back at Dorothy and her insisting on remaining on earth performing good deeds like for both of you Momma and Papa.

"She's also connected to our basketball team with Cindy playing center during the school year. So this so-called demon sent one of her dominions to trash our year. That dominion was a troubled girl who passed away fifty years ago. She was the entity we saw at the C.I.F. game.

"She's now my biology teacher."

"WHAT! We have to pull you out now!" shouted Palmira, waking her son, Dario.

"It's complicated, Mom and Dad, something that I feel can lead to a happy ending, a sort of mystical relief."

Dario, now awake, appeared in the hallway, "Momma, I just spoke to Dorothy she told me everything is going to be alright. She told me she and Emma will keep anything scary away from our family and friends too."

"Good Lord, did you see her!"

"Naw, I just heard her in my dreams. I'm not allowing myself to see her except in my classroom."

"What in the hell!" said Eugenio.

"Now, Honey, watch your language," said his wife.

Calm, Eugenio asked, "What do you mean? Does she appear to you in the classroom?"

Dario looked over at his sister, silently asking for permission to speak. Emma nodded her approval. "Only I can see her in my classroom, and I don't talk to her with my voice. I just have to 'think' talk. She's always nice and tells me what I need to tell Emma. She also helps me when I need help that's why my teacher thinks I'm really smart."

"Yes, Mrs. Holmes does think you're bright. Son, Dorothy doesn't frighten you, does she?" wondered Palmira worried for her boy.

"No, I like it when she visits, not like Father Gibson. He scares me when he walks into the classroom. He's always mean to Mrs. Holmes."

Donovan joined Helixa inside the Catholic church in Long Beach. *"I find peace here, and I'm not frightened when I wait in the morning inside your classroom.*

"Let me ask you this: do you ever think about falling asleep? I used to like that. I used to like that a lot, Helixa."

"Fall asleep in here, Donovan. You're safe, and don't worry, I'll protect you."

"Thank you, Helixa, you're a real friend."

"You are too, Donovan. Go ahead and stretch out on the pew, you got long legs."

Donovan Fisk

Chapter Twenty-Two

Catherine Siena

Early Monday morning, Emma, after taking Lucky for a 5:30 a.m. jog, picked up the phone, grabbing it in time, giving up one half of a ring, and increasing his parents' much needed sleep.

"Hello, may I help you?"

"Is this Mrs. Sacatti?"

"No, this is her daughter. She is asleep right now. I can take the message."

"My name is Mrs. Cathhart. I'm a registered nurse at Cedars Sinai, and we're releasing your sister Mia today. We completed all the necessary testing, and she and her unborn baby appear fine. I'll follow up with a call to Sister Barbara at St. Agnes to have someone pick up your sister."

An hour later, Emma shared the news with her parents. Overjoyed, Eugenio went to work whistling in his truck along the way. Palmira wrestled her son awake, fed him breakfast, and dropped him off at school. Not able to whistle, she hummed her favorite Doris Day tune, "Sentimental Journey."

Sister Barbara, up much of the night praying in the

chapel for the recovery of Mia Sacatti and the girl's baby was relieved when meeting the young teen with a close embrace at the hospital.

"I only remember my brother burning up, Sister. I must have panicked, dreaming of him melting in front of me."

"You're fine, Mia, but we have to figure out why your dreams are so strange. We'll pray on it. Now, let's head to the convent in Father Kessler's car. He's new to the parish. Catherine was worried about you. She joined me a few times in the chapel."

Back in her new home, she greeted the nuns and girls. She moved forward and hugged Catherine. "Maybe this week for both of us, Mia. My baby's kicks are getting stronger. He or she sure wants out, but you know I'm still scared. Petrified might better describe how I feel."

By Friday, Catherine's worries culminated. After lunch, yellow fluid gushed down the pre-teen's leg. Embarrassed, she noticed the smiles on the nuns' faces. Her teen friends, not too familiar with the sensation, viewed breaking her water with a grimace.

Father Kessler was on call and pulled his Plymouth Fury near the front door of the convent. Sister Barbara, Catherine's steadfast strength, accompanied her to the hospital in the spacious backseat.

Catherine's cervix thinned, and she began to open; contractions were not noticeable. Five hours later, with Sister Barbara holding her hand, the twelve-year-old began to push, breathing and relaxing to ease the pain. Her cervix widened to seven centimeters. She immaculately practiced what Sister Rosemary taught her in childbirth class.

At 7:00 p.m., her mother choked up and walked into the birthing room, infolding the girl she gave birth to in her heart not too long ago. "Your daddy is waiting in the lobby. He recognizes his behavior was wrong. I hope you will forgive him."

"Momma, Momma!" Catherine screamed, her heart leaping with garbled joy and second-stage agony. Sister Barbara placed Mrs. Siena's hand into the delicate palm of Catherine.

Catherine screamed again. "Breathe hard, Cathy, breathe hard, in and out. I love you, my baby child."

"She's not wide enough. You're going to need to stretch at least two centimeters."

Catherine's eyes soaked, screamed a third time, her voice carrying down the hallway.

"I'm going to give you an epidural, sweetheart. Do you mind?"

"No, no, I can take it. I don't care if the pain is unbearable."

The needle entered her lower back, "One, two, three, four."

"You took that well, Catherine. Where did you learn that?" said her doctor, Richard Le Gaspi.

She gasped; a sudden stream of relief filled her body, her screams turning to grunts. Dialating one more centimeter, she continued to push while both her mother and Sister Barbara continued to coach her major contractions.

"Would you consider a Cesarian doctor?"

We try to avoid it. Catherine's cervix should handle the birth if the child is smaller than normal.

Catherine pushed again this time a tiny head appearing. "Three more times, Catherine, you're good with numbers."

"ONE!" she pushed, showing those around her bravado. "TWO! Only one more doctor, right?"

"One more, dear, just one more!" Doctor Legaspi said, now part of the cheer squad.

"THREE!!!" her voice was heard down the hall and around the corner. The baby's head clearing the cervix continued to break through. "She's a beautiful girl, Catherine!" said Dr. Le Gaspi. "I can tell she wants her mommy."

Renado, Catherine's mother, cut the cord as Doctor Le Gaspi gave the baby a whack on the butt, startling the tiny four pounds three-ounce girl into her first earthly breath. A curdling sound, one that would notify the mother, baby Cielo (her given name) would long for her mother's arms for weeks to come.

Emma and Ted attended the stirring graduation of Cindy Marquez, her brother Carl, Cindy's boyfriend and captain of the boy's basketball team Ryan Finch. Emma greeted all of the seniors who had spent mostly four dedicated years at the school.

"It's off to U.S.C. for you and your brother Carl. I understand the school also wants to see Ryan go there."

"I'm trying to talk him into it. His father would rather see him at U.C.L.A. under John Wooden."

Ted offered a more realistic plan. "An offer from a national champion coach you might want to rethink about him transferring away from a top contender?"

Back to school for the freshmen through junior students, Emma found herself attending classes from 8:20 a.m. until 2:30 p.m. and continuing to end the school year in biology with her now self-admitted boyfriend, basketball star sophomore Ted Accenti.

In their biology class, while mentored by the freshmen girl, Emma was tired of staring at Donovan Fisk, who was told to sit in the corner and not move until Helixa's day was finished. He didn't mind. First, he knew he was protected from the hands of the devil, Lilith, and second, he enjoyed picking up tidbits of information into his frail mind. "Do you think Lilith is an Algee?"

"The word is algae. A-L-G-A-E. Spell that, Donovan."

"I can't."

"That's alright, it's not important, and to answer your question, she's more of a fungus, a kind of mold that attaches to the body and can lead to death, possibly even death through cancer."

"I don't think I want to talk about that anymore. I do like birds and other animals. Could we look at pictures of different birds?"

"We could do that. It's the last week, Donovan. I'll show what we call a movie to the children in class. You could watch birds all day moving around as if they were alive."

Dorothy, are you okay with this Donovan fellow? I can't seem to read him like I do Helixa. Is he hiding his feebleness, and will he hurt my family or my friends?"

His mind is thin as well as his thoughts. He's a good man, a human being who never found justice as a youngster or as a man. Although not entirely innocent, he chose to survive in Texas the best way he knew how until a Texan town took his life.

"He can't be mentored and morally coached as you did Helixa, but he does have a basic set of principles, Emma. He's capable of grasping goodness. He wants it, and you, myself and Helixa can provide him with decency, a real feel for life as he was never given while on earth."

Emma looked at Dorothy and said, "That sounds like

Helixa without the capacity to establish a decent life without the stealing and robbing?"

"The only thing he ever taught himself to do. Remember, his capability to think carefully was robbed from him at birth. And then, he lost his mother as a small child. There's so much injustice in this world. Someone needs to help turn it around."

On Tuesday morning, Emma helped set up the projector. Miss Crowfoot had secured a copy of North American Birds on her own at the public library. Although not seen by the general public Donovan tagged along secure by Helixa side.

Sitting in his usual spot in the classroom, he enjoyed the film immensely. In no time, students heard the songs of the Hermit Thrush, the American Robin, the Texas Song Sparrow, the Baltimore Oriole, and the Rose-Breasted Grosbeak, all in unison with the greatest bird whistler of all time, Donovan Fisk.

Students looked to see where the beautiful sounds were mimicked, certainly not the cheap ten-volt speaker students strained to hear its narration. But Emma witnessed the genius who pursed his lips and whistled the sounds of God's birds. Birds he talked to as a child and as a grown man surviving the late eighteen hundred western state of Texas.

"Mr. Fisk you do have a wonderful talent, a gift." He looked up and smiled. The students, with the exception of Ted, wondered who the girl in the front-row corner seat was talking to. Helixa knew, too, and winked at Emma.

Hours later, far after dusk fell on the city of Long Beach, Donovan Fisk leaned on a pew with Helixa Crowfoot inside the dark church next to Saint Anthony High School. "I like this church, Helixa. It relaxes me like the hills in Texas."

"What were you doing in the hills?" wondered Crowfoot.

"Listening to nothing at night."

"You like the quiet, I take it."

"Like the inside of this church. It's where I used to sleep when the noise outside the barn I slept at got too noisy."

"At night, Donovan. What kind of noise went on in your town."

"Bandits and cowboys would ride into town and fire their guns. They scared me, Helixa. Those mean boys would have shot me if I let them see me standing by the haystack. Drunk, all of them liquored up. I couldn't sleep, and I never learned my lesson."

"Never learned your lesson? What happened?"

"I became pals with the robbers. They gave me my first gun and told me to rob a stagecoach if I wanted to get into their gang. So I tried, but the stagecoach got away.

"I thought 'Texas Jack' would kill me, but he didn't. He gave me another chance because he was nice. So, the second time, I really messed up, and I never saw Texas Jack again."

"You were stabbed and arrested, right?"

"Right. I got put in jail."

"Donovan, you can relax here. You know what this soft thing is called?"

"Yes, I do. A nice man they called 'the jailer' gave me one so I could sleep. Usually I put my head on my hands and went to sleep. It sure was soft, and I fell right asleep."

"They're called pillows and are filled with soft feathers. You can lay your head on this tonight."

"Are we going to see that magic movie on animals tomorrow Helixa?"

"We sure are it fits in with my unit on mammals and birds. You did a terrific job today whistling those bird songs. Did you like the library where I took back the film on birds?"

"I sure did. It's big and has got all the books ever made."

"Just about. Now, if you like, close your eyes, and I'll wake you up when the sun comes up."

"And you're going to protect me, huh Helixa."

"I'm going to protect you, Donovan."

"I like it in here; it's dark, and it's like I can see the stars with the candles in the front, except I can't see them when I'm lying down."

"No, you can't, but they're peaceful."

"They're peaceful, Helixa."

———

Mr. Siena, finally, after an hour or two following the birth of his granddaughter, visited his sleeping daughter in the birthing room adjacent to the hallway on the second floor.

"She's asleep. Do you think we can still take her home?"

"Not now, Mr. Siena. She's going to need a couple of days to recover."

"So you'll let me pick her up then?"

"It depends on you, Renzo," said Renata, Renzo's wife and grandmother of baby Cielo.

"What do you mean it depends on me!"

"I was forced to look for St. Agnes. Remember, you wanted to throw her out. You called her a tramp, and now you want to take her home," Catherine's mother said, raising her voice.

Sister Barbara intervened. "Your daughter is a saint, everything good but promiscuous. What happened to her was vile. Whether you believe it or not, your daughter was raped. A vile act she never extended upon the child. She could have cried for an abortion; however, she extended at the innocent age of twelve motherly love to her unborn baby, something a few women twice her age couldn't do.

"Your daughter was never a tramp; I'll repeat, she's a living saint."

"Well, who in the hell raped her!"

"We can't tell you. Catherine will not let that man ever enter her life and even consider taking custody of that child."

"Why can't she tell me? Damn it, I'm her father? I find out who did this, and I'll beat the hell out of him."

"That's why you can't know Mr. Siena. Your anger appears to have mastered your fist. Have you ever struck anyone, including your wife and daughter," said Sister Barbara, now concerned about Catherine and the baby.

"That in the hell is none of your business."

"Renzo, when we signed Catherine over to St. Agnes, we awarded them custody of our daughter until they deemed it was safe enough to bring her back."

"WHAT! That's tantamount to kidnapping. You can't do that. I'll get the police to bring her back. You'll see! Let's get out here, Renata, before I lose my goddamn temper," he reached out and grabbed her arm.

Three days later, Catherine returned to the safety of St. Agnes. "Sister Barbara told me I could stay here until they clear the paperwork with my mother's sister in Cambria. Now I understand she's afraid to take me in. She thinks my father will drive up and grab me, and with his temper, God knows what he'd do to my aunt." She turned and checked on her baby sound asleep in the crib next to Catherine's bed.

"And Mia, I don't know how long I can stay here. I don't want a foster home. I hear a few of them are abusive and are only doing it for the money. Mia, I don't want to be adopted. What if the father is just as bad as the one I got."

On their knees before bed, both girls prayed for some relief, some hope that satisfied Catherine and offered her infant child happiness. "I was thinking my friend Betty Russo, who delivered her baby just before you arrived, might be a good family to move in with, especially now with what faces you."

"What's she like? Does she live near here?"

"She lives about a block from my house. Her mother is single and very sweet, like Betty. If, for some reason, that doesn't work out for you, there's my house. Both Betty's mother and my mom have childcare coverage so that you could go back to school."

"Would I ever see my mom?" Tears started to form in the twelve-year-old's eyes.

"You know something, Catherine, this could work! Betty's mother, Julia, is single and works all day in Long Beach. Your mother, who is a stay-at-home mom, could move in to keep Betty and Mrs. Russo company and spend the day keeping the house nice."

"You really think that would work. My mother keeps a spotless house and is a terrific cook. Betty and her mother would come home to a clean house with dinner ready on the table. She's also good with babies if they ever need her."

"I think it could work in either of our houses. Catherine?

" How long have we been on our knees?"

"Long enough for me to know you're the smartest girl I ever met."

"Do you think so? Well, you and I have something to share with Sister Barbara tomorrow. Let's get to bed we got a lot to dream about."

Dorothy smiled down at the girls. *That girl always was as brilliant as her sister.*

A week later, after tossing their idea around to Sister Barbara and letting Emma know about their plan when she visited the following day, Mia's water broke in the lunch room. Sister Rosemary said, "It must be something about our lunch that stimulates initial labor. I'll get Father Kessler's car keys; he's busy in the church and won't miss his Plymouth."

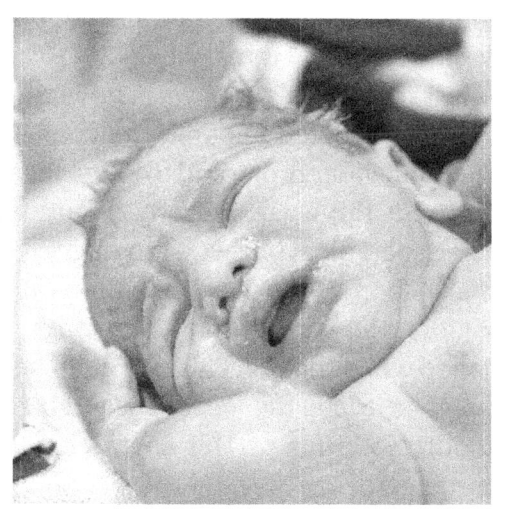

Chapter Twenty-Three
Little Barbara Rosemary Sacatti

Three of the now 'experienced' girls cleaned up the mess on the linoleum floor on Saturday at 1:00 a.m. while the nun went to retrieve the Plymouth Fury.

Not wanting to miss the birth of Mia's baby, Sister Rosemary drove steady, gripping the stirring wheel in the proper 10/2 position. Again, Sister Barbara sat with the serene thirteen-year-old in the back seat. "You look calm, Mia. Catherine was a bit nervous."

"I figure Betty and Catherine are fine and happy and that I won't wind up the same. I might have the doctor give me an epidural; Catherine said it really helped."

Because Sister Barbara's girls were generally in their early teens, she was instructed to admit the young girls into the hospital once their water broke and they reached the first stage of labor. For Mia, this was a welcomed caution.

Arriving at Cedars Sinai Mia was immediately assigned a room on the third floor. Within an hour, she went into her second stage of labor. Her contractions were longer and strong. Mia groaned while she bravely positioned herself into learned relaxation tips, trying the most comfortable position. "Breathe in and out, sweetheart." This time, Sister Rosemary coached the young teen.

Her baby moved down the pelvis as her cervix effaced and dilated. In an early second stage of labor, Mia began to push. After twenty minutes, her baby crowned, and Dr. La Gaspi encouraged Mia to push hard.

"ONE!"

"Another counter!" said Dr. Le Gaspi. "Keep it up, young lady, two to go."

"TWO!"

"Your baby's almost here, one more girl. I understand you taught..."

"THREE!"

"Just one more time, little lady, one more time!"

She pushed while gripping Sister Rosemary's hand, she shouted, "FOUR!" Her baby slid out.

"You have yourself a baby girl, my dear."

"A baby girl, Mia. Curls, dresses, dances, and beautiful long hair like yours. Only a few years away, sweetheart."

"I'm so happy, so happy. Dario wanted a baby girl; he said he already had too many friends and didn't want a brother touching his baseball cards. A GIRL! Wait until my family finds out!"

"They're on their way, the entire family, including Dario," said Sister Barbara. "Your labor was quick, and no epidural."

Emma finished her summer workout with Louisa Auclair, the incoming freshman phenom Rosa Clark, and the transfer from up north 6'4" Tanya Bailey. Ted joined the group with two of his varsity class stars competing with the girls.

Mia was sent to the convent the following day and found Catherine's mother waiting with Betty and her mother Julia. "Sister Barbara telephoned us, and we were more than happy to help," said Mrs. Russo as they helped pack Catherine's personal belongings. Holding her newborn Mia was unable to hug the trio of women and offered a peck on each of their cheeks.

It became apparent Mr. Renzo Siena wasn't willing to give up his lifetime misfortune of carrying an appalling temper. According to him he was fine and told his wife, "Good riddance. I'll see you in hell."

Mrs. Siena failed to tell her daughter how her father reacted, only the news that Julia Russo was more than happy to have her daughter and granddaughter move in with them. Catherine suspected the heat pouring off her father's head.

"We'll be down the block from each other. All three of us will be able to walk our babies up and down Harvey Way," said Mia, her eyes wide open.

A tissue to her eyes, Sister Rosemary's heart ached, saying a final farewell to the last and longest resident of St. Agnes. "Come and visit when you can, Mia. Could you help her with that, Mr. and Mrs. Sacatti? And, of course, you two,

Betty and Catherine. Your girls are going to grow up together and make fine citizens. I hope I'm around to see them graduate from high school. I know Catherine and Mia I won't miss your graduation. And Betty, I pray you graduate from college in a few years."

Mia handed her baby to her mother and hugged the older nun, both of them soaking each other's shoulders. "You sisters and all the girls here will remain in my heart forever. You truly, Sister Rosemary and Barbara, are God's angels here on earth."

Mia's lovely words brought another episode of tears to many of the people in attendance, including the dear entity Dorothy Marquez. Sister Barbara drew her emotions deep inside.

―――――――――

Early morning jogs started again at 5:30 a.m. with the growing and rambunctious pup, Lucky. Emma picked up her pace as Lucky easily equaled her stride.

After a quick breakfast, she hitched a ride with Ted Accenti and headed toward St. Anthony. With the renovation of the forty-year-old basketball gymnasium, the group of seven future boy and girl varsity stars was limited to half-court play.

Ted found Rosa Clark, a freshman out of Saint Matthias Elementary School off of 7th Street in Long Beach, displaying one of the most prolific ball-handling skills he ever witnessed. His morning workout partners agreed with him.

David Sparks, a 6'3" returning senior starter, agreed, stating, "My family visited my grandmother just after Christmas in Pennsylvania, and Pop took me to a high school basketball game in town. We saw a young kid play, and he put on a show like Rosa here. His name is Pete Maravich. I didn't think I would ever see anything like the way he moved the ball, but Rosa, I think you top him."

She dribbled as well as Bob Cousy of the Boston Celtic and could move the ball instantly without looking at her teammate. Dr. Clark warned the kids if she's on your team always expect the ball before it dings you in the mouth or nose.

She never faded her shooting. Rosa's hand-eye coordination found the rim from 12 to 18 feet away over 45% of the time. She at no time seemed to miss at the free throw line, completing 95% of her shots.

Dr. Clark shared with the summer basketball players while his daughter retreated to the ladies' room, "I've seen her make fifty in a row time and time again. She looks at a rim fifteen feet away, and her eyes tell her it's less than a yard. She's phenomenal, but you'll never hear it from her; Rosa is modest like her mother."

Playing four on three, the girls versus the varsity boys, 5'9", Rosa put up twenty points, recorded over eighteen assists, and hit the basket, recovering nine rebounds. The St. Anthony girls team, with the addition of Rosa Clark and 6'4" transfer Tanya Bailey was destined to hold onto their shared C.I.F. title (outright tying it this year) and perhaps attend the nationally top 8 tournament in Kansas at the end of the Southern California season.

All seven students agreed on running their practice routine through exhibiting skill sets in dribbling exercises, passing and moving, and retrieving a pass while following with a distant shot or lay-up. Players were leery of Rosa Clark's 'sneaky' bullet passing one of them, crazing Louise Auclair's nose and causing blood to trickle. "We need to follow your father's advice, Miss Clark," said Ted, impressed by the fourteen-year-old protégé demonstrating her advanced play in front of the other players.

She demonstrated extraordinary dexterity by driving forward, stopping on a dime, and moving up with her arms extended 90 degrees for a picture-perfect jump shot.

"My God, fellas, Rosa's got Jerry West's move." Rosa used to the positive comments smiled while continuing to pass off to Emma Sacatti, who easily laid up another basket.

Somewhat overheated in the warm gymnasium, they broke practice and geared up for a four-on-three scrimmage. Dr. Elwin Clark applauded the play of all seven players, looking forward to another promising year for the boys and girls teams. Sitting behind him, without his knowledge, sat Helixa Crowfoot and Donovan Fisk.

"I never saw people playing with a ball like that, Helixa. They put it under their legs while running. How do they do that."

"It's what they all practice, Donovan. Practice, practice, practice."

"Do you think I could do that?"

"Maybe, maybe not. You might get bored and quit. Most people do. Those kids are pretty special, and they seemed to stick with it."

"I think I could give it a try."

"Let me ask you this, Donovan. When you were a kid, how much did you practice those bird calls."

"I don't think I had to practice. I just puckered up my lips, put my tongue under my mouth, and whistled. I did have to listen to the birds if I wanted to sound like them. Maybe I practiced a little."

"I bet you a dollar to a donut none of those kids could whistle like you, sing like a bird. Would you like to trade?"

"No, I would like to share. Those kids could teach me, and I could teach them. Do you think they'd help me?"

"You're almost there. Right now, those young kids can't see you."

"It's because I'm a ghost, huh?"

"Yes, Donovan, people would consider us ghosts."

"I was always scared of ghosts, Helixa."

"Don't be; not all ghosts are bad like Lilith. Some are good and help folks like Dorothy. Anyway, my friend, you're beginning to change. Remember those students in my biology class? They could hear you sing like a beautiful bird."

"They heard me, huh, Helixa."

"They sure did, and you wanna know why because what you did was a good thing. The more good you do the more people will begin to see you like a person and not a ghost. Can you be good and not think of doing terrible things like robbing and shooting people?"

"I sure can, and I'm going to try. Where did the kids go?"

"We were talking so long we must have forgotten about them. Dorothy told me they all got jobs cleaning up the school this summer."

"I can do that. I used to help sweep Mr. Morgan's store in Texas."

"That's not a bad idea. Let's talk to Dorothy first, and maybe she could talk to Emma. The school could always use an extra hand, a by-gone entity or not."

A bright late spring morning, and Mia, tired from little rest the night before, still crawled out of bed at 8:00 a.m. on Monday after hearing her sister rise at 5:30 a.m. for an early jog with Lucky. "How about another walk, little fellow," she said, brushing the dog's forehead while fixing oatmeal for her and Dario.

Dario now slept in Emma's room to give his sister more space with her new baby. The boy was up and awake again. "Could I go with you, Mia I won't talk with your girlfriends."

"Sure, you can lead Lucky on his leash and harness while I push the stroller to Betty's house."

After fixing her infant a warm bottle of milk, she followed through burping her baby, Rosie named after the saintly nun at St. Agnes. Forty minutes later, she set the baby in the stroller, fluffed the blankets, and pulled the carriage sun visor, shading the tiny newborn.

Mia and Dario met up with the other young mothers pushing their carriages. By the way, Catherine's eyes were lit up. The thirteen-year-old could tell her friend welcomed her new home, one hopefully filled with peace.

"Good morning, Mia. Your baby isn't keeping you up, is she?" asked Betty, more accustomed to sleepless nights with her newest adopted sister, Catherine Siena.

Mia batted her eyes, "Wait 'til school starts in September. Do you think they'll learn to sleep through the night?"

"All I know is Catherine and I share a room, and our babies work off each other. One wakes the other, and they begin to cry together. One, two, and three in the morning, it doesn't matter."

"Do what Emma did for me: get a transistor radio and ear plugs, tune into K.R.L.A., close your eyes, and burp them. It drives out the constant crying and settles their colicky stomachs. My mother tells me babies always get gassy, so get used to it."

"Catherine has a mini tape recorder. You could tape your favorite songs. I'm going to run out and buy two earphones at the student union across the street.

"Did I tell you, Mia, I registered at Long Beach City College? I'm taking a political science course. It counts as one of the classes I need for an Associate of Arts degree. I understand that an A.A. degree is worth no more than a box of Cracker Jacks. After two years, I'm going to transfer to a university and get my bachelor's."

"That's wonderful, Betty. By the time you graduate from college, Catherine and I would have worked our way through high school. Let me ask you two something: how do your mothers get along?"

"My mother, Julia, adores Renata. Your mother Catherine is a natural housekeeper and a workaholic. She doesn't leave a thing uncleaned. Bedsheets, wash, and now dirty diapers. And can she cook? My mother comes home to the best-cooked meal she's had since she grew up and left my grandma's house. Catherine, your mother spoils us; she's too good to be true."

"I'm happy to hear that. My father rarely gave her a good word like he always reminded her, 'I expect you to do your job, just like I do mine.' Not the best of praise for a mother who spent her life trying to please my dad.

"And Betty, you and your mother are dear lifesavers. I found my mother crying because she was so grateful for her current blessings. Thank you."

The three moved along the sidewalk, talking endlessly about their babies when a truck pulled alongside the heavily shaded curb with a diaper service advertisement on the side. Dorothy, overseeing the girls at the time, knew the man driving the truck was a scammer, a stocker preying upon young girls. "What's he doing in the village? He's not welcome here."

Dorothy rounded up Helixa and asked her if Donovan was ready for his first good deed. Surprised at his response, Donovan welcomed the challenge.

Getting out of the truck, Jeffrey August tripped over the branches of a Laurel Sumac bush growing parallel to the ground. Falling on his face, he broke his nose. Betty rushed up to him and noticed a pistol that fell from his side lying on the dirt road. She picked it up, wondering what to do with it, when Mia shouted, "Hold him at bay!"

Betty quickly picked up on Mia's queue and threatened to shoot the man if he moved. He dropped to the side of the sumac bushes while holding his nose. "Who is he?" cried Catherine.

"I don't know, but any man carrying a gun can't be good," said Mia loud enough to pull a few neighbors from their home.

That's when the diaper service driver decided to lift from the bushes and attempt to take off, only to have Betty pull the trigger back and fire a round in the air. "The next round goes through your skull. I told you DOWN!"

A vigilant neighbor contacted the police, and within a few short minutes, Long Beach Police arrested the man striking a blow against one of the Southland's most criminal pedophiles. A tow truck took the stolen vehicle to the yard until the Tidee Didee service picked it up.

By the time the police interviewed the girls at Betty's home, all three of them laughed off the ordeal. "Where did you learn to fire a gun," asked Mia still overcome with emotion.

"I never held a gun in my life. I thought when it shot, we were all dead."

Catherine added, "Then you shouted you were going to put a bullet through his head. No, instead, you said skull. That sounded like one of those westerns on the television."

"What made you think he was a criminal, Mia?" asked

Betty.

"I don't know. What again did I say?"
Baby Rosie

Chapter Twenty-Three
Donovan Fisk

Your first genuine good deed, Mr. Fisk. You handled it without any incident, revealing your presence. Donovan, you're on

your way to sainthood."

"Those girls used some fancy words, too. I handled how they would have captured an outlaw, though, didn't I?"

Helixa said, "My goodness, you had me scared the way those girls were talking, and you probably realize Donovan, you're responsible for locking up a truly bad man, worse than the man who tricked you into robbing a stagecoach."

He smiled, proud of his achievement. Dorothy and Helixa smiled along with him.

"Are you ready for your custodial duties at the school in Long Beach," asked Miss Crowfoot."

"I can do that. You just tell me what to do."

"Tonight, when it's dark, lay out all the equipment for the boys and girls to polish the floors. After you watch them, you can wax a floor or two and save the school the trouble of not finishing. How does that sound, Mr. Fisk."

"No one ever called me Mr. Fisk."

"Just Donovan, huh," wondered Helixa.

"Sometimes stupid or retard, and if they were nice, they called me Donovan, like that nice jailer man. He held my hand just before they hung me. I remember telling him about my momma and my dog, Dewey. Momma used to tell me that one day, we'd have a dozen chickens in a barn and a cow to milk every day. I sure miss those two."

That evening, Donovan pulled out the heavy buffer, extension court and wax and bucket. He then stacked the chairs and desks in the hallway. After clearing seven classrooms, Donovan Fisk retreated to the empty church with Miss Crowfoot, who offered him a pillow. He watched for a minute or two the reflection of the offered church candles reflecting off the ceiling, then fell asleep dreaming of his mother, who kissed his cheek and sang to him a lullaby.

All seven of the hired summer student employees found out that not only did the night custodian pull out the necessary cleaning equipment but also pulled out all the desks and chairs on the upper left side of the third floor.

Ted was the first to marvel, "They sure got a hard-working janitor here at night. We'll clear out the right side why you girls wax and buff the floor."

By the completion of the day, Emma and her friends completed the first floor.

After practice on Wednesday, again they found all equipment pulled and ready to use. Chairs and desks were arranged in the hallway again on the left side of the second floor. The boys spent the day emptying the student's desks and chairs on the right side of the school's middle story.

"Whoever this man is, we need to give him our thanks or some kind of gift if we don't see him," said Louise Auclair.

Tanya Bailey snapped her fingers and declared, "I'll bake an apple pie. I'll bet he'll like that."

"I'll make him some of my famous Rice Krispy treats," said Rosa Clark.

On the 3rd evening, Donovan found he broke out in a sweat, clearing the left side of the first floor. "Helixa, I don't remember when I got all wet working so hard."

"It's a sweaty sign from heaven. You're turning more and more into a human being, Mr. Fisk, one of God's finest."

"Do you really think so, Miss Crowfoot?"

"Yes, I do, Donovan; I believe in miracles."

Pepped up, he worked harder, emptying the student chairs and desk on both sides. In the early hours of the morning, he lay his head on Helixa's soft pillow and fell asleep close to the only woman he ever loved, his mother, Hannah Fisk, *"Goodnight, my precious child; God loves you."*

Early morning gymnasium routines jumped each day to an uncanny level. Tanya Baker leaped and dunked the basketball, imitating the move of 6'3" Ted Accenti.

"I've never seen a girl dunk a basketball, not even a small beach ball. Wait until the coach sees what you can do," said Emma.

"I'd appreciate it if you kept it to yourselves. I don't think I could duplicate it in a game."

"Sure you could; you just need to work on your breakaway ball-handling skills. We'll keep at it until you're confident. Think of yourself as a guard, and your confidence and poise will build."

Emma added, "Ted's got a point. You're 6'4" tall and a truly great center. Turn yourself into a ball handler and amaze the crowds even further. We got eight weeks and we'll help you. Rosa's now on our team, the best ballhandler in the history of C.I.F. We'll watch what she does and imitate her. What do we say, guys and gals."

They all nodded, joined hands, and hollered SAINTS!

When practice ended, Tanya Baker revealed her baked apple pie. "I baked two. I didn't want to torture you people. I also wrote the janitor a note, although I don't know his name."

The other basketball players also didn't have a clue.

Rosa Clark pulled the Rice Krispy treats from her backpack. "My mother felt the same as Tanya. We made a few extras for all of us."

"Would you look at this? He cleared both sides, and there it is, all of the cleaning tools pulled down to the first floor," said Ted's teammate, 6'4", Alex Bradley.

All three boys moved to next week's building number two, completing the moving of desks and chairs on the right side of the first floor. All three of the girls completed the left side of the classroom floors before breaking for lunch. "Where should we put the pie and Krispy treats," wondered Rosa.

"Well, we're almost completed with building one why don't we place it in building two with a note next to the desserts," said Emma.

Dorothy stood near Emma and informed the up coming sophomore the custodian was none other than Donovan Fisk. "Sweetheart, he's trying to win the heart of his Maker. Helixa tells me he's gone full bore ahead, practicing good deeds, a sort of Penance. You should mention his name he'd be delighted.

"Also, I want to remind you Donovan was responsible for helping your sister and her young friends in capturing that brutal pedophile. Don't tell her though Mr. Fisk helped them."

At lunch, Tanya Errion dropped by to check on the working athletes. "You're finishing building number one!"

"Yes, coach, we pulled through with the help of the night custodian," said Rosa Clark unaware of the mystical man working toward pleasing his belief in a virtuous God, but also pleasing himself.

"Rosa, Saint Anthony High School doesn't employ a night janitor, we can't afford one."

"But every day when we get to work..."

Mrs. Errion intervened, "Stop right there. Your father told me how humble you are. You're going to fit perfectly with our team, and I want to say you are working as quite a team moving through your morning and afternoon work. I'm proud of all of you. Allow yourself credit for working so hard."

Emma stopped Rosa and the other girls and boys and thanked the coach for complimenting them.

"I gotta go. I'll leave you seven on your own. I'm going to let the principal know what a fine job you're doing."

She left, and Emma told the basketball players, "I believe Coach Errion is misinformed. The janitor's name is Mr.

Donovan Fisk, and he'll be pleased with the thank you note and treats."

Two hours after dusk fell over the school, Helixa pointed out the note to Donovan. "Could you read it to me?" he asked.

"Of course, my good man, it says,

"Dear Mr. Donovan Fisk,

Thank you for your tireless help in relieving us of all the work ahead of us, cleaning, waxing, and buffing our two buildings. We are now ahead of our work and will be able to work on extra chores at Saint Anthony, like painting a few of the outer walls. Painting the walls was work set for the December vacation season. You are responsible for students seeing a clean and possibly newer painted campus.

We left you a few treats. We hope you enjoy them.

Sincerely yours,

Tanya, Rosa, Louise, Emma, Ted, Alex and Tim.

"That's for me! A whole pie! Those kids are nice, Miss Crowfoot. And what's that next to it?"

"I don't think either one of you is familiar with that dessert. They're called Rice Krispy treats. It's made from a twentieth-century cereal with something called store-bought marshmallows. Try one," said Dorothy.

"Can I eat one? I can't touch human food, can I?"

"Sure you can, Mr. Fisk. You're one step closer to humanity. Take a bite!" said Dorothy.

Donovan bit into the treat, and his eyes lit up. "This tastes good, Helixa. I've never put anything in my mouth like this. You should eat one, Miss Crowfoot."

She took a small bite, and her face imitated her new friend, Donovan. "This is tasty!" What do you call these, Dorothy?"

"Again, we call them Rice Krispy marshmallow treats. Check your box address at the post office first, and then ask the Home Economics teacher at Saint Anthony to make you some. She'll most likely be happy to help you."

After finishing buildings one and two, the summertime working students received permission to paint the outer first-floor utilizing eight-foot ladders to reach the initial upper part of the building.

Finishing the first floor, the look of the building, although only one-third finished, looked pleasing until showing up one morning to complete their work; they found the 2nd floor completed on both buildings.

Confused, the students shook their heads. Again, Emma cited Donovan Fisk as the hero behind the paint job. "I heard he paints at night with appropriate lighting."

"Hell, that's dangerous. Up that high at night!" said Alex, astounded by the quality work.

"And quicker than what we did for the first floor," added Rosa.

Emma said, "We need to bake him another pie and those Rice Krispy treats. It's my turn I'll prepare both."

Ted, who understood who Donovan Fisk really was offered to help. "We'll prepare it at my house said Emma and present it on top of the equipment tomorrow night."

Alex said, "What I can't understand is we never see the guy, and why doesn't the girls' coach know about him working here?"

"Not hard to figure out here Alex. Teachers and coaches are usually the last ones told what's going on with personnel. I bet she still doesn't know."

Emma glanced over at her friend Ted and threw him a surreptitious nod.

At dusk the following day, Helixa found lying on top of the painting equipment another delicious apple pie sitting next to a dozen or so Rice Krispy treats.

265

"You're gaining more favor with the kids, Donovan. How is it you paint so well? Were you a professional painter in your time?"

"Nope! I only whitewashed the side of the jail because I had to before they hung me. After I worked for a half hour the sheriff grabbed the brush from me and said I did an awful job. I never painted before."

"Well, you certainly seem to know what you're doing. One of the kids thinks you did a better job and faster, too."

"I watched them for a long time. I can't read or write, but I know how to watch. I'm good at that."

"I noticed that Mr. Fisk. You appear to observe and then perform. You're a very smart man, Donovan."

"No one ever said I was smart. People like to call me names."

"Your performance on this building proves they were wrong.

"I need to ask you a question. Would you mind looking like you did when you were twenty?"

"I don't know. I never got a good look at myself. I saw a little bit, though. First, I tried looking in the water, but it was too brown. Once, I started to see myself in a big glass window, and I was told to keep walking before I could see anything. I know I wasn't twenty years old I was a lot older then."

"Donovan, I checked my mailbox at the post office while you were painting. The school wants to hire me as a biology teacher this September. Could you help me? Would you like to do that?"

"I can't read anything, and I can't write either. Those important people find out, and I'd get in trouble."

"Donovan, I want you to know this is not what I looked like before I lost my life. I looked different, but I feel comfortable in my present body. You could change too when the time comes. Could Dorothy talk to you?"

"Okay, Dorothy, I'll listen."

Dorothy Marquez just finished influencing her daughter's thoughts. She thought if Cindy transferred to U.C.L.A. it would be a bad move. Her daughter needed to stay close to her twin brother. Besides, U.S.C. women's basketball had a better coach.

Dorothy felt Cindy would soon move away from her infatuation with Ryan Finch and find new friends at the University of Southern California university.

"Donovan, you're going to be able to appear and disappear at will. If you assist Miss Crowfoot, you're going to need to appear as a well-dressed graduate student studying to obtain a high school teaching credential. Spending time in the classroom is mandatory, and I could arrange to make that happen."

"You want me to be a teacher?"

"A teacher's helper. You'll assist Miss Crowfoot in the classroom. Just watch her, then respond."

August found the seven varsity players laying off their team practice and pulling back to individual drills at home. Emma increased her morning run to two miles, preparing for the game of volleyball in September.

Lucky was growing more every day and keeping up with Emma on the run. Dario, ready for fourth grade, decided to join his sister when he could get up. Mia, one of the lucky mothers, found little Barbara generally slept through the night making sweet gurgling sounds well into the morning hours.

Although Catherine and Betty's babies were still learning how to adjust throughout the night, Catherine's mother helped take over the task of baby care during the day.

Her natural maternal instincts appeared to creep back with the addition of the two infants. She still, despite the extra responsibility, maintained a spotless home.

Renata felt the girls could use some extra rest as school started in four weeks. Betty's once a week three hour class ended a week ago. "One down, Mom, and nineteen to go before I transfer to a four-year college."

Donovan, now posing as a twenty-two-year-old college graduate, was sent to SHERRY'S for MEN and fitted into a new suit. Dorothy acted as his older sister and paid for the completely new look, from shirt to tie to socks and shoes and, of course, the wool suit. They then shopped at Sears for more informal dress shirts and pants, giving him a new everyday look.

"You saw yourself in a mirror today, Donovan. What did you think?"

"No whiskers on my chin. I look like a kid."

"What you look like, Mr. Fisk (and remember, that's what the students will call you), you're a handsome modern young man."

"You're going to have to sit down with Helixa, and she'll review with you the curriculum week to week."

"Curriculum, you call it, huh? I'll do my best."

"And Donovan, you did a terrific job painting the 2nd and 3rd floor. I believe the principal believes the pastor in the rectory financed it. Will leave it at that."

Donovan asked permission to walk around town so people could see him. He felt good in the open air near the beach and dug his toes in the sand for the first time in his life. When he settled down at night in the church, Helixa fitted him with new pajamas. Folks don't sleep in their clothes, although for you, it wouldn't matter. I got you a blanket, too. Sleeping like a human is a good way to pretend you really are one. It'll get you used to thinking like a person."

"I like being a person again, Helixa. I went to the ocean today and sunk my toes in the sand, but something really bothered me. I hope God's not mad at me."

Helixa, worried for the transformed young man asked, "What happened?"

"All the people at that place were practically naked. I tried not to look, but there were so many of them."

Helixa Crowfoot smiled and said, "I thought the same thing when I first saw how people failed to dress at the beach, especially the females fully."

Donovan, weary, changed the subject, "I'm tired, Miss Crowfoot, and I really like these bedtime clothes; they're soft. I sure hope I can visit my mother tonight in my dreams. It's as if she's here in church with me."

She is, my good man. Your mother is getting closer and closer.

.

Chapter Twenty-Four
Donovan Fisk

Let your mother know Emma, my successor, Dr. Miller, is planning on handing out big bonuses just before Christmas. Palmira will be looking at more than enough to purchase gifts for her husband and the kids. I'm going to place in his head giving your mother a reasonable raise. Your family, with the added addition, could use the money."

"Thank you, Dorothy. Your kindness is always appreciated."

"Dr. Miller loves Palmira's shorthand skills, fast and accurate."

"She tells me Dr. Miller's patience has grown my mother's understanding of medical terminology. I'll make sure my family hears of the promising news."

"It appears your sister is moving along well at St. Anthony. I see she joined the volleyball team."

"She did. However, only nine girls in the entire school wanted to play, which I can't understand. Mrs. Holden, my Home Economics teacher, coaches the team. She's dedicated and sold on the sport and, above all, happy to coach us. I don't know why additional girls don't want to try out."

"So, how is your sister doing as a player?"

"Terrific, she can dig. Another team sends a girl to slam down a volleyball; Mia is capable of digging it out. She played a half a season at St. Cyprian's before quitting. My sister did practice digging against the wall at school at recess and, at times at lunch. She's now part of the team, and I'm proud of her.

"I talked Louise Auclair to join the team, and most likely, our most talented players, Rosa Clark and our spike sensation 6'4" Tanya Baker, were eager to start the season."

"I heard Mia placed her baby with infant care."

"That's right. Momma takes the baby inside the daycare center on her way to work."

"Your father is creating more interest at his employment site. He mentioned to the board that they should print coupons to encourage the public to create a habit of purchasing that promising dog food."

"I know I recommended it. The newspaper got coupons for all kinds of food and products. Coupons will pick up interest."

"He also suggested to the board to create a small store outside the plant. 'Factory fresh, Factory direct, Factory price.' Hundreds of cars pass that plant every day. Drawing in the public to purchase the higher-cost food without the need of a coupon would stimulate interest with people normally not able to afford full price.

"Purchases would explain why that food is important and why exercising your dog is just as vital to the longer life of their pet."

"Makes sense. We don't make it at home anymore. Papa buys it before leaving work at a discount and takes it home to Lucky. They should continue to open it up to the public; they'd sell more of it."

"Does your father sample the dog food?"

"He sure does, only A Farmer's Dog food, not the can of Skippy. It's got essential and quality human food. None of it is processed, so it's fit for human consumption. Of course, the mix appeals more to the dogs, but the president of the company wanted continuous quality control, so my father volunteered to test it every week. Not a whole lot, just a half of a teaspoon full. He constantly emphasizes this diet will keep dogs active, healthy and feeling good."

"Your father's enthusiasm sure has gotten him ahead. Thank goodness you saved Lucky and brought him home. Your pup stirred up a whole new diet for our canine angels."

"You know you're right. Our little Lucky jogs with me every morning. He loves the run, and after the police arrested that pedophile, Lucky will soon protect me when I run before the sun comes up."

Adjacent to the biology classroom, Donovan was asked to clean the science laboratory before the students got busy inside it performing various experiments.

Mr. Fisk learned by watching, and the handsome new teacher's aide assisted the week-to-week research the students performed.

"Miss Crowfoot, a few of the girls are asking me questions I don't feel good about answering," said the younger-looking Donovan.

"Questions? What in the world is on their mind."

"They want to know if I'm married."

Helixa laughed while asking, "So what do you tell them."

"I don't tell them nothing."

"Anything, Donovan, the word is anything. When you say the word don't you don't say the word 'nothing.' Don't and nothing are both negatives. Double negatives are wrong. 'Instead, you say, 'I don't tell them anything.' Do you understand what I'm saying?"

"I only understand the less I say, the better off I'll be."

"Don't worry about those girls; it's just an innocent infatuation. Those girls will have a crush on a half dozen boys in a few weeks."

"I heard that word from Dorothy some time ago."

"Are you referring to infatuation?"

"Yep, that's the word."

"Well, if you have to say anything, tell those girls you're happily married, and you love your wife with everything that you can possibly find in your heart."

"But didn't you know I never married a girl?"

"That's okay. It's alright to play let's pretend. It'll keep the girls off your back."

"So pretend? I can do that!"

Donovan carried on as if he found a girl, fell in love and got married. In the fewest words you could manage, he let those teen coeds know he was forever happy. What pleased him most of the girls felt happy for him and wanted to meet the fictitious girl, Ida, *Ida as in 'Ida' believe you, Mr. Fisk, but who names their daughter Ida in 1961?*

Honor Gibson, a proficient and curious fifteen-year-old student, asked Donovan, "How come you rarely talk, Mr. Fisk? I can tell from the way you speak you're from Texas. Am I right? My cousin Tommy is from there and stayed at our house one whole summer and you sound like him."

Donovan chose to nod while handing out papers to the students.

By the end of September, students accepted Mr. Fisk and certainly appreciated his help. However, one student seemed to suspect the teacher's aide couldn't read. Not wanting to prod him, he couldn't help but think why, when Donovan faced a question in a book, he would back off and throw the responsibility to Helixa.

Frank Banning, however, wanted the aide's opinion. "Mr. Fisk, I can't agree with what this textbook is trying to say. I can't entirely approve of it, and it appears Miss Crowfoot doesn't have a problem with it. What's your opinion?"

Dorothy appeared to Donovan, calming his fears. *"Donovan, the boy wants to know if a cell is arrested during mitosis. At this stage, distinct chromatids are visible at opposite poles of the cell. The book tells us which stage of mitosis does this describe. The book tells us it's Metaphase. The answer is ..."*

"The book is wrong, Frank; the answer is Anaphase."

"That's what I thought, Mr. Fisk."

"I'll let Miss Crowfoot know, she probably misunderstood."

Donovan walked over to Helixa and whispered in her ear when Dorothy joined the two, stating, *"Helixa, young Mr. Fisk knows his stuff on Cell Division. I'm proud of you."*

"I almost got caught. Thanks for giving me your help, Dorothy."

"Why don't you return to the laboratory? Donovan students may need your assistance. Anyone asking your assistance with the textbook and Dorothy will be there to assist you."

Donovan moved to the lab adjacent to the biology classroom. *"Dorothy, I don't think our friend will be around for the full semester his mother seems to get closer almost every night. I've seen her praying at the altar rail."*

"Has Donovan seen her?"

"No, he would have told me. His mother only seems to appear to him in his dreams. Donovan talks about that quite a bit. He attributes his wonderful dreams to the feather pillow I gave him to rest his head."

"How long do you think it will take for his mother to cross Donovan."

"A week, a month, a year. I hope it's after January when his assignment is up."

Dorothy, noticing a student who handed Mr. Fisk a textbook, flew across the room to the former Texan's aid. *"Read to her so she can carry on with her experiment."* Donovan picked up the book and feigned. *"It says: Stem cells are basic cells that can change to any other kind of cell that our body needs. Most cells in the body begin as stem cells. Then they grow into the tissue of other body parts."* Donovan finished reading and continued on his own, "Kathleen, tell me what you are observing under the microscope."

As he rested his head on his soft pillow, Donovan contemplated the course of the day while reflecting on the intermittent lights reflecting off the ceiling of the church. "*I was asked why I didn't talk much and she knows I'm from Texas. What kind of teacher doesn't talk much?*"

"*That's not hard to understand, Donovan. You're new to the job and nervous. Besides there are a lot of people who aren't much at talking.*"

"*That makes me feel better. You know, Dorothy came through for me twice today, Helixa. What would we do without her?*

"*Do you think she could find a way toward my mother?*"

"*Do you mean to heaven?*"

"*I guess I'm asking too much.*"

"*No, not at all, Donovan. You're a good man. God would be happy to have you standing next to your mother, Hannah.*"

He smiled, set to tune into another dream, a small boy in the arms of his precious mother once again.

Sometimes, my good man, I feel the same way. Helixa sighed and fell into a deep sleep.

Why don't I take you both? Your mother, Riona, is waiting for you on the other side. Until then, sleep well, my dear, and think about it.

Into its third week of league play, St. Anthony already beat the so-called 'powerhouse' St. Pius X. Involved on the deeply talented team included a transfer from Louisville, Kentucky, six foot two inches Sally Ann Wade, a powerful striker with five years of volleyball experience. The Saints tainted the Pius X team with two 15-7 and 15-6 defeats. Mia scored two aces with her sinking curved set. Emma, proud of her team and especially her little sister, looked forward to an undefeated league season.

Ted, whose basketball coach was out on jury duty, pulled Emma aside after the volleyball competition and asked his friend when he'd be allowed to take the pretty girl to dinner.

"Mr. Accenti, when I turn sixteen in April. My parents are strict, especially my mother. You don't want to disappoint them, do you?"

"No, of course not, so I got six and one-half months until I can ask again. I'll wait."

"Like my mother told me, 'Be patient, my little girl, that Ted is a keeper.'"

"She said that! Well, if you think it's true I'm happy to wait.

"I noticed your sister is as cute as you. The guys are talking about her."

"Well, you tell them she's hands off. She turned fourteen last week. Two more years at least."

"Well, I think I should be pleased dropping you two off at home, are you ready?"

xxxxxxxxx

Emma rose from bed, her forehead dripping sweat. Pressing her hands on the sides of her head, drifting past her sister sound asleep, and into her brother Dario's bedroom.

Standing over his bed, she declared, "I love you, Dario. I love you, Dario! Oh, please watch out; the ceilings coming down!" The third time she shouted, loud enough to wake her brother.

"It's okay, Emma, you're having another fever dream."

It's what his mother explained to him, yet still not taking the terror out of him. *Maybe a devil has taken over your body.* He closed his eyes and drew his blanket over his head, waiting in dread for his sister to leave the room.

SILENCE!

Dario flew out of bed, praying he wouldn't collide with Emma in the long hallway. Dashing down the hallway, he curved right, eventually reaching his parent's bedroom. "Momma! Momma! Emma's having a fever dream! She was in my room talking crazy."

Awoken and startled from her sleep, Palmira moved out of bed, rushing to Dario's bedroom while Eugenio placed his massive hand over the small boy. *Papa will protect me.* The 3rd grader instantly dove into a deep sleep known only in early childhood and innocence.

Palmira turned from Dario's bedroom after checking the floor and closet and headed toward Mia's and Emma's room. Checking under the bed and again in the girl's closet. Quieting Mia back to sleep, she flew across the hallway, beginning to panic. *She didn't fall downstairs, did she? Oh dear God, what if she's outside!* Temperature's outside hovered in the low 40s, with a wind chill, lowering the cold weather to thirty-two degrees.

Skirting left, Palmira checked an empty restroom. *Dear God, don't let my daughter have left the house. Protect Emma, Lord!*

Overwhelmed, she tore toward the kitchen, tripping on Emma crawling on the tile floor and flying head first into the kitchen cupboards. Blood dripped freely from her brow. Palmira grabbed a kitchen towel and pressed it firmly to her forehead while crawling back to her daughter, Emma.

"Momma! The ceilings coming down." She cried, holding her mother tight while biting down on her lip.

"Don't worry, precious, I'll stop it. Shh."

"Momma, I have to go to the bathroom."

"Let's go to the restroom, honey. First, let me get an ice pack for you out of the refrigerator. Stay seated and rest your head against the wall."

Palmira got up and opened the refrigerator freezer, pulling out a frozen homemade ice wrap made of cotton tape. She semi-thawed it under lukewarm water and placed it securely around Emma's head.

Gently lifting her daughter, Emma stumbled, pressing her hands against her ears. "Momma, they're coming, billions. It's the end of the world, Mommy." Tears flowed from the thirteen-year-old eyes, stinging the wound on her split lip.

Finally arriving, the young teen sat on the toilet, relieving the urine pressed up in her bladder. Palmira prayed the cold press would lower the fever with her delirious daughter. "Momma, they're almost here, trillions, trillions!" Emma let out a loud moan.

Palmira placed her left hand over the compress as she placed her right hand over Emma's arm. "We're okay, honey, we're safe."

"We're safe, huh, Mommy." Palmira's daughter appeared to calm down. "I have a fever, and they can't get us."

"No, dear, they never will get us. Are you finished? Let me help you up, and we'll lie down together in bed."

Palmira gently guided her daughter back to the girls' room, continuing to press the compress against Emma's brow.

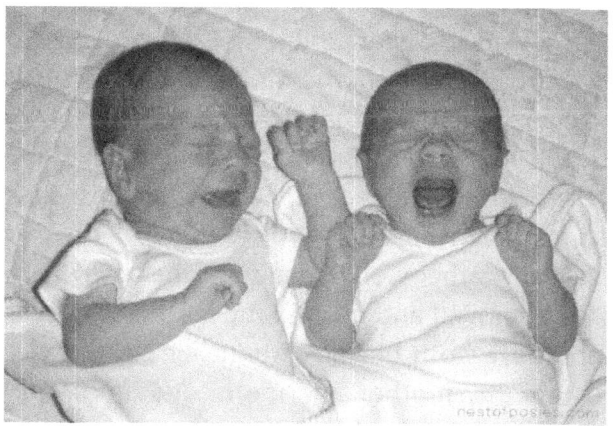

Climbing in bed together, Palmira eased Emma into a quiet sleep, her daughter's fever easing down then back up during the dreadful night. Palmira promised to take Emma to her work, visiting Dr. Bishop first thing in the morning after dropping off Mia and Dario at St. Cyprian's.

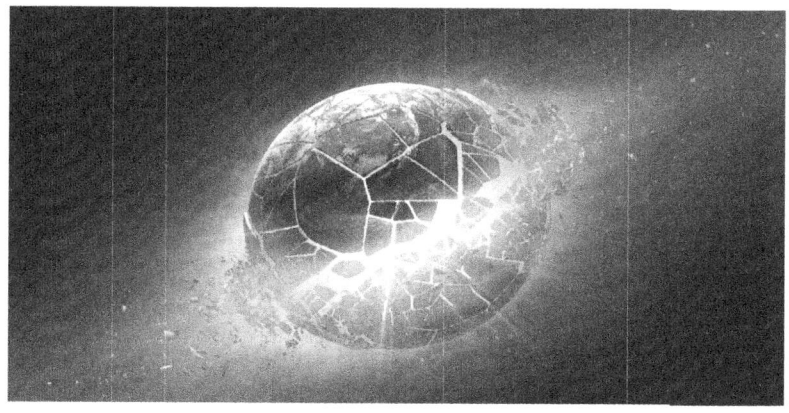

xxxxxxxxxx

Chapter Twenty-Five

Precious sleepless memories.

Catherine struggled in Sister Bridget's 8th-grade classroom. Sister knew of the baby at home and felt the pressure of a small thirteen-year-old girl may have mounted too much pressure on the young child. Bridget also knew of the rape; a boy four years her senior and nephew to her unsuspecting father was the unknowing culprit.

"Sister, my father would tear apart the boy if he found out, just like he shoved and pushed my mother on occasion. My mom and I are both better without him in the picture. Mrs. Russo took my mother and me in. It's an act of God protecting us, Sister Bridget."

"It sounds like you two found happiness, sweetheart. Why are you struggling in class?"

"I can't concentrate well enough to complete my assignments, and the baby keeps me up half the night. Betty, the other girl I live with, you know of her; she's not sleeping much either but does well taking college classes. "What's wrong with me, Sister?"

"Not a thing is wrong with you, sweetheart. Life has not treated you fairly yet you still carried on. Could I keep you after school? I have a girl who will tutor you and get you back on your feet. You know her, she's Evelyn Marquez, a very humble and polite girl. She has a cousin attending U.S.C., a basketball player. I think Evelyn may follow in her footsteps."

"Won't she miss practice if she helps me?"

"Her coach won't meet with the players until December, and the volleyball coach can't be here until 4:00 p.m. That will give you plenty of time to finish your work. Also, I'd like to suggest you join the volleyball team after your homework is finished."

Catherine smiled. A new day dawned for the young girl troubled with doubts who felt so alone in a new environment. Her near future seemed bright.

Receiving help from the niece of Dorothy Marquez brought more confidence to Catherine than actual academic awareness. She couldn't focus on completing assignments, and now, with Evelyn by her side she began to move ahead in Sister Bridget's eighth grade.

Although not completely athletic, she found a spot on a team with players more than proficient in the game of volleyball. Many of the girls on her team showed patience, assisting Catherine while gradually honing her potential.

Nighttime cries from little Cielo no longer troubled her. At such a tender age of thirteen, Catherine's maternal instinct grew with her friends Betty and Mia.

Not terribly inclined to visit Derek's family, Evelyn did, however, enjoy the occasional Sunday get-togethers at Grandma Marquez's home off of Vermont, on New Hampshire in Los Angeles. "Sister Bridget at my school in Lakewood assigned me to help one of my classmates."

"That's nice, sweetheart. What's her name?" responded Vivian Marquez, mother of Evelyn.

"Catherine Siena. She's new to the school and was kind of down not knowing anyone. Sister thought if I helped her after school, she'd cheer up. Do you know something, though? She didn't need much help; she just needed a friend.

"Sister Bridget talked her into joining volleyball, something Catherine has never played, but she's coming along fine."

Catherine! Oh dear, I didn't know she might feel depressed. Thank you, my dear niece, for being her friend. I'll have to check on her and Betty, as well as Mia.

"I see you have decided Helixa. I'll be happy to escort both of you through the light. Your mother will be happy to see you again. She often talks about you. She tells me you are the love of her life and beyond."

"Hannah, I only ask that you wait for Donovan and me until the end of the semester; that's when your son's supposed assignment is up, and I can put in for a permanent leave to see my mother."

"Of course, time is of no essence, Miss Crowfoot; a month is like a day. However, I will inform your mother you are on your way she'll be delighted."

"Is that you, Momma?" cried Donovan, his head resting on the soft pillow.

"Your mother, Hannah, is very close; she will be taking both of us to heaven, my dear Donovan, very soon. Until then, picture her in your dreams, and she will talk to you."

"Okay, I can do that. Good night, Miss Crowfoot."

"Goodnight, Donovan."

Chapter Twenty-Five
Bernadette Fisher

He was surprised to hear the voice across from the short hallway leading into the classroom. Who was she, and what did she want? Lamia's voice echoed in the ears of Donovan Fisk. Not a typical sound, she exuded a form of hatred, a revulsion, and it frightened him as he buried his youthful face.

"Where is Mr. Fisk? I'm here to take him to hell."
"And you, my young lady, are whom?"
"Lamia, and don't question me, Dorothy."
"Ahh, so you do exist."

Hearing her name, Donovan dashed into a crowded closet and prayed to his mother. A science lab empty of students found them sitting politely, taking notes, and viewing a planned film. Dorothy discussed telepathically with the obvious entity. *"One of Lilth's charges, I take it. We thought she only made you up."*

"Never mind about her, where's Mr. Fisk?"
"I'm afraid you missed him. He left this earth to be with his mother in heaven.

"I'm more concerned about you, Lamia. Having Lilith as a pal can't ever be a lasting friendship. How did she rope you into her schemes? I could probably stir you away from her."

"Don't try and butter me up. I'll be back!"
"Miss Crowfoot, Lamia is no good. You should find yourself treading carefully with the likes of that woman."
"Bernadette Fisher, you could hear us!"
"Loud and clear, Miss Crowfoot!"
"So you're clairvoyant, I can tell."
"Very much so; I've been this way my entire life."
"Did she frighten you?"
"No, not at all. I've grown accustomed to wandering spirits. However, as I mentioned earlier, Lamia is a handful. Miss Crowfoot, she's a demon."

"What! A demon. My dear God, will she find Donovan?"

"I blocked Mr. Fisk from her mind. She can't bother him as long as I'm around."

"You can stave off Lamia's aggressiveness?"

"No, not me, my angels. They're far more powerful than Lamia."

"You remind me of a girl named Emma. She's a grade ahead of you."

"I know her well. She's the basketball star. I also know she is clairvoyant.

"Emma walks with the angels, and neither of us can stop Lamia from finding Donovan and finding you, too."

"We talked so long you missed the film, Bernadette."

"I can focus on two things at once. I heard the film enough to get by with what was said."

"Could you arrive early before school, around 8:00 a.m.? I'll arrange for you to meet Emma."

"That would be fine. I look forward to meeting her."

"Bernadette, could you retrieve Mr. Fisk from the biology laboratory? He often hides in the closet when he's afraid."

Bernadette, a former eighth-grader at an unknown school on a shadowy street, was happy to rescue the handsome young man strolling into the lab. Opening the cupboard and letting Donovan know all was safe.

Summoning Emma to her classroom, she found Dorothy tagged along understanding Lamia did exist and turned out as a demon. "My goodness, Helixa, she'll be impossible for us to thwart her aggression."

"That's why I wanted to talk to Emma. Dorothy and Emma, I want to introduce Bernadette Fisher, a freshman

Honor student and a clairvoyant. She walks with the angels, Emma."

"That's good to hear. Nice to meet you, Bernadette," said Emma. Dorothy nodded, showing her approval of the remarkable girl while shaking the student's hand.

"I understand you have your own set of angels, Emma. We should make good friends. I want both of you to know a deadly demon entered this room yesterday, most likely deadlier than what I hear was your previous demon, a Class D presence by the name of Lilith.

"Lamia ranks ahead of her and is powerful. She wants to destroy Mr. Fisk and probably Miss Crowfoot, too. Alone, my angels will defeat her. With your help, Emma, we could send her back to hell for good."

"What would you like me to do, Bernadette? I'm rather new at this, although I was able to send Lilith permanently back to the ocean and away from the school."

"I snuck into Lamia's thoughts; she's planning a huge earthquake if she doesn't find Mr. Fisk. If we send her to the ocean, she'll trigger a tsunami that will swallow half of Long Beach. She needs to be sent to hell.

"Miss Crowfoot told Lamia that Mr. Fisk now resided in heaven with his mother. She didn't buy it. I asked my angels to block her thoughts so she couldn't find him.

"We need to contact her now. My thoughts will attract her here before school begins." Bernadette concentrated on luring the demon with the thought of sitting near Donavan.

Lamia appeared, a lubricious smile stretching across her face. "I see you delivered Mr. Fisk. Not enough. I need to take you all, and aren't you a young, handsome fellow, Donovan! I'm happy to meet you."

Bernadette and Emma sat quietly while Dorothy and Helixa stared at the entity, their mouths gaping. Donovan shook, tears flowing from his eyes. "Not hell, Helixa! I've seen it when Lilith wanted her way. It's hideous, it's horrific, all of you, ungodly." He placed his hands over his face, trying to hide, hoping Lamia would go away.

"Now's the time, Emma." Each of the girls called upon the help of their angels.

"What's wrong, young ladies something blocking your mind?"

Despite what the demon said, she fought while falling back and struggling to stand erect. "I'm not leaving without that bastard." Donovan couldn't look up.

Their heads felt as if on fire. Emma and Bernadette wondered how long Lamia could resist. "Leave this earth back to hell with you forever," shouted Emma.

Lamia fell, writhing yet maintaining that unearthly grin. "Where are your angels, girls?" she said, slowly losing strength.

Bernadette strained, "Both of us, Emma!"

"Stay with your thoughts, Bernadette. Lamia is fading. You have no right to torture anyone or anything. Back to hell with you, Lamia, back to hell forever."

Groaning, she reached out and touched Donovan. He screamed in agony, calling for his mother. Her hand left his wrist as Lamia looked up, pain circulating throughout her body. She pointed to the exit doorway, shouting, "It's you! Damn, it's you!"

Everyone turned around, surprised to see the young freshman standing beneath the threshold. "Off to hell with you, Lamia. God's angels do not need for you here!"

Lamia flew in the air, her body slamming against the divider separating the windows. Hovering back a few inches toward Donovan, she slammed again against the barrier, her back seriously failing before she flew out the window and down below.

A quiet peace beset the biology room. Donovan stared her way. *Who is this girl*, he thought.

Mia? Emma's sister turned pale and forced herself to sit at a desk.

Emma ran to her younger sister and held her. "She's terrified Dorothy, you must know that."

Dorothy completely erased from Mia's mind the previous ten minutes and flew toward Helixa.

"Why am I crying, Emma? I just wanted to bring your lunch to you you must have grabbed mine instead."

"It's gotta be your sinuses, Mia. It's that time of the year. Miss Crowfoot, do you have a tissue?"

"She appeared petrified, Helixa, the poor girl's so afraid of me," said Dorothy who herself felt chills up and down her spine.

"It's important Donovan and I leave. Look at him shaking like a leaf. Erasing his memory doesn't work like it does with Mia."

Mr. Fisk, filled with trepidation, said, *"I don't want to stay Dorothy. Lamia is the devil, and she'll take me to hell as soon as she can. My mother will get me. She told me she would when I fell asleep in the church."*

"Mr. Fisk, please don't leave the kids. We love having you around. You're smart and never hesitate to help any student who needs your help," remarked Bernadette, encouraging her surreptitious ruse.

Clearing her eyes with a tissue, Mia said, "I can hear all of you. Dorothy, I can't see you, but I know you're here."

Emma moved to comfort her sister. "They mean well, Mia. Dorothy, Helixa, and Donovan won't harm you or anyone; they're here to offer their help. Find it in your heart to believe me."

Candles flickering under the statue of Mary, Queen of Peace, drew Donovan's thoughts forward. "Who's this lady Helixa?"

"I don't rightly know, but what I do know she's most likely what people say is Jesus mother."

"I must know her my mom mentioned Jesus all the time and his mother and daddy. Mary was his mother."

"What drew you to the front of the church? You always stayed near me, hugging the pew."

"I was afraid. At first, I thought that statue was a real woman. I wasn't afraid of the cross with Jesus hanging on it. I remember we had a smaller one when I was growing up.

"Miss Crowfoot, my momma, Hannah, stood in front of this statue in my dreams at night. This is where she is going to take me to heaven. You too, she told me. You're going to see your momma. Her name is Riona. That's what my mother told me.

"Do you think we could sleep up here in the front of the church? I'm not afraid anymore because you take good care of me like today."

"I'll be right up there, Donovan. Let me bring your pillow and blanket."

Gathering in nighttime sleep both Helixa and Donovan heard the slamming of a door on the upper south side of the church. "An old man entered the church clothed in beat-up rags. His face covered with a grey beard he limped toward the altar rail and knelt.

Bowing his head he blessed himself as his lips moved in quiet prayer. *"He doesn't seem to have a place to stay, Donovan."* She looked up at the stained glass window and could see a heavy fog settled over the entire church as well as circling the Long Beach shoreline.

"Miss Crowfoot, he should sleep here. It's cold outside. Can I give the man my pillow?"

"Let him discover it, Donovan, or else you'll frighten him." A quick brush of her hand and the pillow appeared on the pew closest to him. The soft, iridescent candlelight moved the senior through the reddish glow as he spied the pillow and decided to stretch out on the church pew, thanking God for seeing after him.

"He's holding on to himself with his arms. I think the church might be too cold. He can have my blanket. Should I cover him up?"

"Drape the blanket quietly over the pew; he'll find it."

Dorothy appeared to Donovan and Helixa, "Get ready, she's coming," she said just as Hannah stood under the station on Mary waiting for her son and Helixa.

Thunder roared inside the church as lightning crackled around Lamia now hovering in the back of the building.

"Do you feel you always have to make a loud entrance, Lamia? This church is actually sanctified," said Dorothy.

"I see you drew in someone else. I'll take that woman and the rest of you to hell."

"We have a fifth. Are you interested?"

Donovan, now a seven-year-old child, cried on the side aisle of the church just as his mother walked up and surprised him. "Momma, momma!" He grabbed her and held on.

Lamia roared with sickly laughter. "Hold on! Who in the hell is that old man? I imagine he can stay. I don't need any worthless bum."

Standing and walking to the middle aisle, the 'old

man.' spoke to Lamia. "You don't recognize me, do you? I could have easily chased you away in the morning and wouldn't have needed any help; however, a church always grants permanence toward getting rid of major ulcers such as you, Lamia."

"You must have remembered Bernadette Fisher, that cute young freshman girl. She's changed Lamia and called you forth once and for all. Goodbye to you," Dorothy said as the 'old man' Bernadette Fisher flew in the air, took hold of the beast, and disappeared from St. Anthony church, never to walk the earth again. Once again, although now limited, they deceived Dorothy and her friends.

"Is she gone, Mama?"

"Gone for good sweetheart." Hannah took her son's hand and nodded toward Helixa, "You come along too, sweetheart; Dorothy has taken care of everything."

Helixa turned and blew a kiss to Dorothy, who flew one right back.

"Are we going to heaven, Momma?"

"We sure are! There's a dozen chickens and a milk cow in the barn."

"And it's our big barn, isn't it, Momma."

"Our very own son."

Up the highway, Donovan could hear the faint sound of a dog barking. "It's Mr. Dewey, our dog!"

"Yep, none other than Mr. Dewey, and we got him on a strict, eternal diet. It's so tasty I think you might like it too!"

On Friday morning, October 1st, 1961, Dorothy Marquez, now Miss Dorothy Mullenger walked into her biology class as the students and staff supposed she had done since the beginning of the school year. All memories, with the exception of Emma Sacatti, were erased. Mia, the lone suspect, felt comfortable under Miss Mullenger's instruction.

Typically, Ted and Emma walked into the biology classroom at lunchtime. "Quite a show and touching performance you missed last night, Emma. Helixa and Donovan went to the beyond with Mrs. Fisk, and our friend Bernadette Fisher, disguised as a broken-down senior citizen, drove Lamia directly to hell."

Confused, Ted scratched his hair, wondering out loud, "Can someone tell me who is Helixa, Donovan, Lamia and this woman or girl Bernadette Fisher."

"I'll fill you in later, Ted. What you are presently experiencing has only happened here for a few hours. I have a question for you, Miss Mullenger. How'd you come up with such an interesting name?"

"Not hard at all; I'm Donna Reed's first cousin!"

"Donna Reed, the actress?"

"Absolutely, yeah, sure, why not, the one and only."

Ted's eyes lit up. "She was wonderful in 'It's A Wonderful Life' and now the 'Donna Reed Show' on television."

"Well, Mr. Accenti, if I see her, I'll tell her what you said."

"If you ever see her! You must share dinner with her every Sunday. Do you think you might get an autographed picture?"

"I'll see what I can do only if you keep my relation to Donna an absolute buttoned-up secret."

Ted feigned, zipping up his lips. *What a day! Miss Mullenger's first cousin is Donna Reed!*

Dorothy missed the camaraderie of the Oklahoma girl, Helixa, and the innocent young man, Donovan, from Texas. She wondered how they accepted life in heaven. *I can't picture Mr. Fisk sitting around and listening to an angel's harp. He'd prefer the innocent, quiet life sitting there chewing on a piece of straw and admiring the abundance of chickens and maybe even a cow or two in his barn.*

I'd bet he'd like a good ice-cold root beer, too. What did they call that drink back when...sarsaparilla? That's it! And now I suspect Helixa Francine probably would like the same thing. She's an Oklahoma girl!

Chapter Twenty-Six

Dorothy Mullenger

I realize Miss Mullenger is actually Mrs. Marquez; it's no secret to me, Emma. I also know she's only taken over the classroom for a week now. I do miss Mr. Fisk; however, I never could grow close to Helixa after what she did at the convent.

"I couldn't grow confident that Dorothy completely brought her around. I know it sounds wrong, but she terrified me."

"How are your other classes, Mia?"

"I enjoy coming here; most of the students are more mature and behave themselves in the classroom. What I really enjoy, thanks to you, is joining a team sport. Each girl plays with spirit and shares it with all of us, including the team we are competing against. Baked cookies after every game with our opponent. Who's idea was that?"

"That's Rosa Clark's idea. She said they practiced it at St. Matthew's. It reduced the tension, sometimes swelling up in competition."

"Well, anyway, volleyball, more than my academic classes, has helped me with my confidence, especially after leaving the protection of the nuns at the convent."

Emma reached over and hugged her before leaving Mia's bedroom for a good night's sleep. "Don't forget to say your prayers, Mia; your daughter is a sleepy angel. Tomorrow, I'll walk with you with little Rosie."

That morning at 5:30 a.m. Lucky scratched at the side of the bed, waking Emma. "Hmmm, Mr. Clockmaster, you're going to have to distinguish between Monday through Friday and Saturday morning. On Saturday, we go for our run at 6:00 a.m. Let your brother sleep for another half hour."

Dario, now up, asked her sister, "Is it time to jog Emma?"

She reluctantly nodded.

"Hey Lucky you know how to tell time?" Dario climbed out of bed, looking at the clock on the side of Emma's bedroom table and not completely understanding Emma's Saturday morning routine.

Emma, seeing her brother already up, rose and slipped on her sweatpants and top. Dario did the same as Lucky became frisky, wagging his tail east and west in rapid succession. He knew not to bark; that was a learned and forbidden reaction early in the morning.

Crossing the street, the trio took off on the smooth sidewalk circling the community college. Lucky, taught to run by Emma's side, lapped at the cool air as the wind passed his alert nose.

Dario, stronger as he participated more and more with his sister, started to build a runner's physique, his arms moving effortlessly by his side and his heel-to-toe action routinely planted on the smooth cement sidewalk.

"Dario, all of us are going to start sprinting the easier sides of the school. It will help you move faster on your fourth-grade football team. Are you ready? Go!"

Eighty yards later, they let up on their stride. "How's your team doing at St. Cyprian's?"

"We won two and tied one. Our coach, Mr. Roman, says we're the best team he's seen in a long time."

"Who's the team you tied?" she asked.

"St. Cornelius, they never lose, but they didn't beat us either like everyone else. I caught a football spinning in the air and ran it back a long way before they pulled my flag. My coach told me that was a hard catch to make, then rubbed my hair.

"Our team is going to play them again, probably for the championship. If we win the next three games, we're all going to get a trophy. That's why I want to get better."

"What position do you play?"

"I run a lot on offense, Greg Schneweis and me, we do almost all of the running. My friend Mick, who's bigger than most older sixth graders, is our best blocker."

"That sounds fine, Dario. Now, are you ready to sprint again? Let's go!"

After four laps around the circular nine-hundred-yard college, sister, brother, and Lucky tiptoed back into the house, took separate showers, and slid back into bed for another rest with a tired Lucky, fresh with water and a constitutional lap around the backyard, slept with his best buddy, Dario.

Up again at 8:00 a.m. Emma secured the baby carriage from the garage and joined Mia, walking baby Rosie down the street toward Betty and Catherine's home. The three mothers, along with Mia's sister, greeted each other before wheeling their buggies across the street, repeating the nine-hundred-yard circular track Emma covered that morning with Dario and Lucky.

Shade covered most of the route since the community college planted Pepper trees near the edge of the sidewalk. The babies, Rosie, Cielo, and Anna, appeared to enjoy the cool, fresh air of the morning, all cooing in unison.

"Do you think the babies recognize they're lying in separate carriages," wondered Catherine, the youngest of the three.

"What do you think, Mia?" asked Emma.

Mia leaned in and whispered, "My baby sometimes talks to me at night."

"How so? And do you know it's her?"

"Telepathically. Words are never shared. If I found any maternal instincts at my age, they're speaking to me at night."

"What is she trying to tell you, Mia?"

"More like what she's trying to warn us."

"Warn us! How does an infant warn her mother?"

"It troubles me, Emma. Dario sees Dorothy routinely and talks to her. You are far and away, steps ahead of him and me. Where does this come from? Is my daughter psychic? When does it start."

"I can't say, listen, Catherine and Betty have fallen far behind. They appear engrossed in their own conversations. So tell me, what's Rosie warning?"

"We're under thick, dark clouds. They swoop down on us and bury our thoughts. It's a deadly wall of what appears as poisonous fumes ."

"Catherine and Betty are catching up. Would you like me to move into your bedroom tonight?"

"Would you! Better like I'll give Dario's room back and move into our old room together. You might be able to hear her. She never wakes up; however, I feel her mind is humming messages and warnings. As I said, they're coming around too soon, Emma."

"You two girls set a hot pace. Two high school athletes, what could we expect," said Betty, staring at her adoptive sister. "You're not crying, are you Mia."

"I've got allergies, and I think these Pepper Trees are taxing my sinuses."

Their carriage walk ended with another hug while wishing each other good luck in school on Monday.

Saturday night, Dario moved back to his old room, falling asleep like most little football players. Within two minutes, a soft purr exited his lips and nose, dreaming of another miraculous catch, this time running the distance for a game-winning touchdown.

Asleep, the sisters talked softly so as not to wake the baby. "What may I expect, Mia?"

"Soft pictures erupting into a cataclysmic eruption of earth. I read St. John's Revelation at the convent Emma, and it feels somethings on the way."

"I never like that passage. It goes against Christ's final words of peace and hope. Revelation is a favorite of doom and destruction preachers. It scares the heck out of most folks buying it. I really never liked it! Your dream may be no more than what you read, and now it's troubling you.

"Why do you think this dream stems from your baby?"

"I see other forecasts crawling back and forth, brimming with hate. It's not an infant's vision; Rosie's being fed by another being, but still a warning, not a threat."

"I will open my mind to Rosie's thoughts. Please rest tonight, Mia, I'm listening."

A sigh of relief left Mia's lips as she closed her eyes and drifted into innocent dreams, one serving an 'ace' in volleyball.

One a.m. in the morning, a voice permeated the girl's room. *"My auntie! How are you, Emma?"*

Birds chirped as a mother bear fished out a brook trout from a lazy river, food for her cubs.

Tips of pines swayed in the morning breeze, gently caressing the forest. An eagle floating on a jet stream eyed Yellowstone Falls, spilling its waters into Yellowstone River. There, the massive female grizzly stood watching the waters , waiting to strike again, then again as her small cubs stayed safely behind, observing their mother's play.

"Caldera!"

Emma woke, her eyes wide with her heart racing at 120 beats per minute. She stared at the crib. Her niece was sound asleep, purring like a kitten. *My niece! No, this isn't coming from you, Rosie. You sleep tight. Something or someone is talking to Mia and me, and I'll find out.*

A caldera, she read a few existed in America, one being the giant caldera at Yellowstone, the potential of a supervolcano that would affect the entire world. Lives in the United States, especially Montana, Wyoming, Idaho, and much of Colorado, would be wiped out.

Yellowstone's supervolcano is dormant, not ready to stir for a dozen millennia. So what's the warning? Is Mia familiar with a caldera? Probably not. Does she realize the drastic potential of Yellowstone National Park changing the entire earth's climate? I hope not. It's time I found out who invades our dreams, especially through an infant child. Are you back, Lamia, or something stronger, evil, and calculating? I need to talk with Dorothy, no, I mean Miss Mullenger.

Monday at lunch, Mia and Emma walked into Miss Dorothy Mullenger's biology room. She was busy finishing a liverwurst sandwich, a delicacy that seldom crossed her taste buds for over twenty years.

"I'm fully alive working this classroom and enjoying my students but nothing can beat an Oscar Meyer liverwurst sandwich on Wonder Bread. Heaven has no equal," Dorothy said, smacking her lips.

Emma bit into an apple while her sister declined to eat lunch. "Miss Mullenger, Mia, and I heard what appeared as a voice and explicit pictures coming through her infant daughter Rosie."

"What! Rosie, your little girl?"

"Miss Mullenger, she's warning me of something. It comes in pictures of impending doom, dark clouds pressing down on me, followed by a tumultuous erosion of our earth."

"And you say your baby speaks to you in your dreams."

"Very few words, mostly devastating scenes, as I said, nothing evil, only a cautionary warning. Why am I seeing this?"

"Dorothy I saw it too, maybe more explicit. Rosie started talking to me, one sentence, 'My auntie! How are you, Emma?' And then a forest scene with a waterfall and wildlife. Then Yellowstone was mentioned, and a caldera. Are you familiar with a caldera?"

"Yes, generally mentioned when associated with a supervolcano. Yellowstone has long been said to contain a caldera. If it ever blew, God help us, especially those folks living within five hundred miles of it. There would be a violent earthquake. Clouds would rise and block out the sun."

"Does it sound like a warning? Through an infant? Something is out there using that baby too, to…"

Dorothy interjected the perplexed Mia, "A diversion. Whatever is haunting your sleep is trying to reroute your mind and send you and Emma on a detour. It recognizes your ability to thwart even the devil. A demon doesn't want you to prevent what it has in mind.

"Yellowstone isn't going to blow; it's dormant."

"You think Lamia is back?" asked Emma.

"No, she couldn't be our Bernadette Fisher was an angel sent by God to protect us. Our entity may not be up to any good. I don't know. Continue to listen, girls, and get back to me."

After school, volleyball went without the usual spirited RAH, RAH! Mia went through the motions, as did her sister Emma. "You two girls look lifeless," said their coach, "This Friday might place us in second if we lose. I need both of you up with spirit the rest of this week."

"You okay, Mia?" asked Rosa. You appear down. Is something bothering you and your sister? She's usually the fireball on this team."

Emma intervened, "Mia's been sick and is trying to hold her stomach. I'm worried about her. She may have the flu."

"Mia, you should see a doctor, maybe even stay in bed. We got a big match this Friday, and besides, the flu could be contagious. We should wear masks and prevent breathing in germs."

Mia, caught up in her sister's fib, found herself telling one of the volleyball player's best athletes, "It's not the flu, Rosa. I have a severe case of sinus congestion that happens every fall. I'll be fine. I need to clear out my nose."

Ted dropped the sisters off at home, and Mia went directly to bed not from any physical ailment but more of an emotional impediment. Emma prepared dinner, and Dario set the table for the family after returning with Lucky for the dog's late afternoon walk.

Forty-five minutes later, Mrs. Sacatti returned from work after picking up baby Rosie. Eugenio rolled in ten minutes later. "Where's your sister, Emma?"

"Her sinuses are acting up. She's resting in bed."

"Warm the bottle. I'm going to check on Mia," said Palmira.

Palmira walked toward the girls' room with the baby when she found Mia talking to someone off her bed. "Mia, could you introduce me to your friend? Hi, I'm Mrs. Sacatti."

"Nice to meet you, Mrs. Sacatti. My name is Tien Anh I'm a friend of Mia."

"A friend, how nice. Where did you two meet?" said Palmira as she handed the baby to her daughter.

"I met her when she delivered little Rosie, and there she is, a beautiful big girl."

Emma walked into the room, stepped back, and ambled forward a few steps, handing the baby bottle with a diaper to her sister.

Tien winked, telepathically introducing herself to Emma, *"I'm Tien Anh, an old friend of Mia."*

"I see you met Tien. She's a dear friend and dropped by to visit."

"Well, we need to set two more plates on the table, Emma. Tien, you're welcome to sit down to dinner with us. My husband and I are honored to have another friend for dinner."

"Whose the other friend, Mama," asked Mia as she fed Rosie.

"Ted, I saw him driving his Ford on the way home from child care and waved him over. That young man has done so much for you girls I thought it would be nice to invite him over. It'll give your mom and dad a chance to get to know him better."

Mia stared over at Emma as Emma stepped her mother into the hallway. "Mother, Ted doesn't know about Mia's baby, and I think it would be best to keep it that way."

"Oh dear! You better tell Tien not to mention she was at the hospital when your sister delivered the baby."

"I'll do that, Mother."

Mrs. Sacatti stepped back into the room and let Tien know she looked forward to her husband meeting the new friend.

Three bells signaled the front door engaged a visitor.

"Should I get it, Mom?" said Dario, peering through his bedroom window. "It's Ted!"

"Go ahead and welcome him to the front room. Make sure you tell Emma first."

Dario stuck his head into the girls' room, announced their visitor, and then stared at Tien before running to the door.

"Come on in, Ted. Emma will be right here. Are you her boyfriend?"

Ted smiled, not too sure what to say when Emma walked into the front room, saving him an explanation.

"It's so nice you're here, Mr. Accenti. I should have invited you a long time ago. I'm sorry I didn't think of that."

"I thought his name was Ted?" said Dario.

"It's his last name a lovely Italian name like us."

"Are you going to be a Mrs. Accenti someday, like Mama is a Mrs. Sacatti?"

"You ask too many questions, Dario. Why don't you see if your mother needs help."

"Okay, but who's that girl in your room? I've seen her somewhere."

"Again, with the questions. Hurry up to the kitchen."

Ted, let me escort you to the dining room to meet my father sitting at the dinner table. Mom is busy in the kitchen and will meet you shortly.

Eugenio stood up, proffering his hand. "So this is the talented Ted. I've heard a lot about you. Here, have a seat."

"It's nice to make your acquaintance, Mr. Sacatti. Emma told me you helped your company secure a patent for your childhood dog food recipe."

"It was Emma's idea. I owe my promotion at work to her enthusiasm and brains. She actually talked our president into making what's become a pretty popular dog food."

Mia accompanied Tien out the front door. "Let your parents know I appreciate the invitation but 'mother' expects me at home. And have no fear, my dear Mia. I'll take care of everything."

Mia offered Tien a hug before she watched her head out to the Cadillac convertible, sitting in front of Ted's car.

She waved to Miss Mullenger, sitting behind the wheel as she headed into the mist before disappearing.

Chapter Twenty-Seven
She hummed the melody of guidance.

Mia walked into the dining room carrying her daughter while toting a milk bottle. "Hello Ted so nice you could make it for dinner. This is our baby Rosie, our newest addition to the family. Ted stood up until Mia made herself and the infant comfortable.

"Where's Tien, sweetheart?" said Palmira, wondering where Mia's friend went.

"I'm sorry, Mother her mom expected her at home for dinner. I walked her to the door with Rosie."

"She sure has a nice car, a big one. I think it might be a brand-new Cadillac. I saw it when I looked out of my bedroom room at Ted on the porch and then over to the big car parked in front of Ted's old Ford. Her car is what they call a convertible.

"And you know what, Ted, Rosie is Mia's baby. She's just four months old."

A quiet interlude swept the table until Ted said, breaking the ice, "And a very beautiful baby like all the girls in this family."

"Well, thank you, Ted, that's awfully kind of you," said Mrs. Sacatti.

"So, Mr. Basketball, how is your team looking this year? I might be able to attend a game or two."

"Promising, we have the potential of winning the league championship. I should add not as promising as your daughter's basketball team. Women's Sports Magazine has them ranked #3 in the entire country."

Dinner progressed well, mostly centering on basketball and volleyball dominating the topic. Dario finally squeezed in an "appropriate" tidbit, letting Ted and his family know his fourth-grade team remained in first place."We only got crummy Our Lady of Refuge and Fatima left since we tied Cornelius, and they lost to St. Joseph. We win both of these games, and everyone on our team gets a trophy."

"How about your baseball cards? Got a Koufax yet."

"No, I don't. Are we going to Doctor what's her name at the pharmacy? She told me she'd save a whole box. I saved up with my allowance."

"How many in a box," wondered Mr. Sacatti."

"Twenty packs, and I saved a whole $1.00."

Emma corrected her brother, "If I go with you, Dario, you're going to have to remember her name. It's Doctor Harriet Sloane, a pharmacist who's been more than good to our family."

"Okay," he said, not wanting to miss what he thought of as once in a lifetime experience trying to secure the coveted Sandy Koufax card. "I said enough Hail Mary's trying to get one. Mrs. Holmes said it would help me a whole year ago."

"Anyone ever get one, Dario?" asked Mia as she helped feed her child.

"Yeah, David Edwards. He got two of them. He's the luckiest kid in the whole school. Lonnie has a zillion baseball cards but no Koufax."

Well, after finishing dinner, Emma finally rose from the dinner table, asking permission to escort Ted to the door. "We both got quite a bit of homework tonight so he and I are going to need to get started."

Mr.Sacatti stood, "Well, nice meeting you, Ted. We want you to know you're welcome anytime."

"My sentiments too, Mr. Sacatti. Hope to see you soon," added Palmira.

Ted politely shared his sincere thanks and left the kitchen before exiting the front door with Emma.

"Ted, could you not repeat what Dario…"

"Say no more, Emma; my lips are sealed. Please let your mother know how nice it was of her to invite…"

Emma quickly planted a kiss on Ted's cheek. "You're a wonderful friend, Ted."

"Thank you! First a delicious dinner and then an even more delicious kiss. I will savor both, my sweet Emma. Oh, and tell Dario it was a Cadillac. That girl Mia was talking about must have a set of wealthy parents."

Ted turned and floated toward his coupe. A significant day for one of the Junior stars of the St. Anthony basketball team.

So it was Donovan who sent you down here?" asked Dorothy as she spirited the '60 Cadillac convertible De Ville up Arbor Road toward Lakewood Blvd.

"He's quite the young character were happy to have him. Wants nothing more than his modest farm and a long hay straw to gnaw on day and night. Spends part of his day feeding his chickens and milking his cow. She's named Josephine."

"Whatever happened to Helixa?" asked Dorothy.'

Lives in the same house with Donovan, her mother, and Donovan's mother, Hannah. All sleeping in a two-room, one bath farmhouse. Simple folks. They spend the day cleaning the house and mosying around their garden outside. I have to say, so far, they're pretty successful and content, too. At night, they watch the stars and talk about nothing in particular."

"Old Donovan's taken an interest in the Sacatti family."

"That and some, especially the baby, Rosie. According to him he didn't take 'fancy' to Lamia entering that baby's dreams and bothering Mia. Ask me to see you and put a stop to that wicked woman."

"I think he knows I don't hold any real power staving off the devil," said Dorothy.

"Oh, I'm sure he does, probably thought it would be real nice for you and me to get together, maybe talking to you about joining us upstairs.

"Where are we going, by the way."

"I'm sleeping inside the old St. Anthony Church. Helixa gave me the idea. It's peaceful and absolutely quiet. Who knows, it might motivate me to give up my stay here on earth."

"We can go up right now, Dorothy."

"No, I still oversee my clinic and I heard Dario praying the Hail Mary. He's hoping to latch on to a Sandy Koufax baseball card. He's been wanting one for a long time."

"Did anyone ever tell the boy Sandy Koufax is a devout Jew?"

Dorothy replied, "Dario would recite the SHEMA daily if it meant opening a nickel pack and finding Sandy staring at him. Besides Tien, I have a daughter and son playing basketball and football at U.S.C. I do love watching them and would miss seeing them at the games. And Emma, her basketball team is one of the best in the country."

"You might convince me to settle down here, Dorothy."

They often talked while kneeling in the darkened bedroom before they crawled into bed. "So, when did you first see Tien?"

"Right when Ted dropped us off from practice. Found her in our room," said Mia.

"Did she frighten you?"

"No, not at all. She must have some calming effect on people. Tien was here to tell me not to worry, that Donovan requested for her to help me."

"Donovan, huh? Did you ask her how he's doing?"

"Tien was a little vague but happy to have him up there."

"Well, no more our homework. I'm ready to gonk out vague 'is it good or is it a bad' type dream. I'm glad and tired of it all until tomorrow morning. I think I'll forgo my early morning run. Do you think Lucky will mind?"

"I think he'll want to remind you. He doesn't get homework."

Not actually knowing how to tell time, Lucky still woke at exactly the 5:30 a.m. hour and brushed up to Emma's side, letting out a soft sigh. "Kicking in your instincts, huh, fella? Okay, I'm up; let's go."

Emma sensed the morning air, a heavy ozone. Lucky, do you think we got some kind of storm pouring in?" She looked down at her German Shepherd pup and noticed his nose sticking in the air. "Let's make it quick. I'm not about to run in the rain." Emma noted the stars still dominated the early morning sky, not a cloud anywhere, not even brushing the far horizon."

After school, the smell of a storm in the air picked up. "I hope it pours," said Tanya Bailey, "We need the rain after this dry summer."

Expecting to hear the patter of rain on top of the gymnasium roof, the girls felt a sudden jolt followed by a roll. "Take cover in the hallway, girls," shouted their coach. Dropping to the ground, the team crawled. Ted, alone in the stands beginning his homework, trailed the girls.

As fast as the volleyball team made it to the hallway, the quake seemed to have had enough power to wake up the community. Waiting for an after-shock that never arrived, the principal entered the boys and girls gym and announced practice was over. "Girls' for your safety, head on home."

The volleyball coach, Mrs. Holden, tried to appeal the principal's call. "Mrs. Verdugo, this isn't 1933; we'll be alright."

"I can't take a chance. Did you smell the air and still no rain. Something's up, and we're not taking chances. Girls, you're going to have to shower at home."

———

"Ted, we still have time," said Emma. "One of Dario's two big games is today. If we leave now, we should catch the second half."

After a brief drive, Ted approached Pan American Park in his 1956 Ford Coupe. A few seconds ticked off the start of the second half with Our Lady of Refuge leading 6-0.

Sailing high into the cloudless sky, the football spun, twirling end over end. A dizzying spec in the air waiting for Dario Sacatti to retrieve it; he paused, focused, ready to sprint forward.

Brushing his hands across his school pants, he eliminated the sweat on his palms. He flicked his fingers, relaxing his anticipated grip. Fielding the difficult catch, he dashed forward following a clean block by huge guard 4th grader Mickey McCorkle.

Dario spun eliminating the defense from pulling his flag lying flat on the boy's side. Down the sideline, he ran darting past two of Refuge's fastest runners, only to have his flag pulled with less than ten yards from St. Cyprian Falcon's goal line.

Two plays later, quarterback David Edwards ran it into the end zone, tying the score 6-6. Following the Falcon touchdown, an equally high-spinning kick-off soared into the darkening azure sky off the powerful toe of Lonnie Price.

Waiting, the Our Lady of Refuge's fastest sprinter, Carson Fullmer, looked nervous, unsure of the gridiron ball's rotation. Dropping at an uncomfortable angle, Carson lost his grasp, fumbling the ball on Refuge's seventeen-yard line.

Dario dove for the loose football, recovering it after two opposing players pounced on his back late, wrestling the ball away from him.

Referee Jack Gunningham awarded the ball to the Falcons, enforcing his call by shouting, "The ball was dead. Cyprian recovers on the seventeen-yard line."

Dave Edward's stepped back on offense lofting the ball toward the corner end zone. Dario, racing past Fullmer, leaped into the air, snatching the ball, falling passed the goal line, and digging up the grass with his knees.

"No detergent on the market will take out those grass stains," said Mia later that evening. She was more concerned about Dario ruining his salt-and-pepper uniform pants than him catching a game-leading pass.

Twenty minutes later, the game ended with St. Cyprian's winning the game by a touchdown. "We should have killed them," said Dario. "Cornelius beat them by twenty, and we beat Cornelius the 2nd time."

Emma said, "Be happy you won, young man. You played a great game."

"How come you made it? Didn't you have practice?"

"They called off the girl's practice because of the earthquake," said Ted, rubbing Dario's hair. "Didn't you feel it?"

"It was a tiny one. We hardly felt a thing."

Mia then shared, "Ted's radio news station said it was a 4.9. That's pretty powerful."

"In any case, Dario, I'm going to reward you by loaning you a dollar. We're headed to Dr. Sloane and her pharmacy. I don't think she could hold onto your baseball cards any longer."

Dario took to the announcement as if he had just woken up to Christmas morning. "I'll pay you back as soon as I get home."

I haven't seen any of you in quite some time. And who is this handsome young man?" asked Dr. Sloane.

"Dr. Sloane, this is our good friend Ted Accenti. He plays basketball like me over at St. Anthony."

"Well, it's good to meet you, young man. You certainly look like a basketball player. How tall are you?"

"I'm six foot three inches and still growing. My father is six foot five inches."

"Well, I hope you play well; I've always liked the sport. And you, my little man, I bet I know what you're here for a few packs of baseball cards."

"Dr. Sloane, if you have a whole box, I saved up a dollar from my allowance."

I do have a whole box. How many packs do you think are in a box?"

"There are twenty packs; that's why I have a dollar."

"Actually, Dario, there are 24 packs in a whole box. I know you're looking for a Sandy Koufax, and these are late series cards, series #6, to be exact. I had one boy find one when I first opened the case in September. Buying an entire box might increase your chances; you never know."

Emma answered for her brother, "I'll be happy to help you, Dario. You can pay me back when you get your next allowance."

"There you go, young fella, your good sister increasing your chances. You'll have to let me know if you find one, a Don Drysdale, too. I understand he's a tough card."

"I got a Drysdale last year, but none so far this year," answered the fourth grader.

Dr. Sloane reached low behind the counter and pulled out a complete box of 1961 Topps baseball cards. Never purchasing more than five packs, Dario's eyes sparkled. Christmas in late October and the last series which most boys ignored because of football.

Dario pulled out the wadded dollar bill his sister gave him when given to him on the football field. Dr. Sloane noticed the deep grass stains on the boy's knees. "Playing a little too hard, Dario."

"I played in a football game, and we won. We're going to get a trophy because we're champs."

Mia corrected her little brother."You still have one more game against Fatima."

"Maybe, but they're so bad they had to forfeit a game because they didn't have enough players. I'll show you my trophy when I get it, Dr. Sloane."

"And your Sandy Koufax, too. Have you said your prayers?"

"That's what my teacher last year asked me. I say a Hail Mary before I open every pack."

"Keep up the prayers. Koufax could use a few. And Mia! My sweetheart, how have you been?"

"Fine, thanks to you and all your help. St. Agnes welcomed me and helped me bring about a healthy girl. I named her after two of the sisters."

"Wonderful to hear. I understand an angel paid a visit to your home. She's not what I expected, though; Tien, however, did help me not to panic during that quake."

Mia and Emma looked at each other, surprised and confused. They offered Dr.Sloane a dear hug before exiting the pharmacy. Two giant question marks hovered over the sister's heads.

Dario, unaware of Dr. Sloane's statement, asked Ted if he could open up two packs of the 1961 cards in the junior's Ford coupe. Accenti led in the two Hail Mary's.
Dr. Virginia Sloane

Chapter Twenty-Eight

We learn geology, the
day after an earthquake.

Why would Dr. Sloane mention Tien? What good would it do," asked Mia, kneeling before saying her evening prayers.

"I don't know; it appeared off the cuff. Maybe Dr. Sloane wanted to reassure you to have some confidence. She did say Tien helped her, too. I wouldn't worry about it, like your angel told you not to fear. What could happen."

At 2:00 a.m., an aftershock occurred that same night, waking the baby and the Sacatti household, as well as the rest of the community. An unusual 5.2, most post-earthquakes, although troublesome, seldom shook harder than the first. This quake, however, felt different, as though pushing vertically from beneath. A few people reported feeling as if their home jumped a foot or two into the air.

Scientists at the Cal Tech seismic laboratory in Pasadena were baffled, completely thrown off by the nature of the quake. Initially, yesterday's afternoon quake held a typically horizontal thrust with a typical push slightly upward as it struck buildings sitting on top of the earth's surface.

This quake, rare if mostly unknown, pushed entirely upward as if two massive hands beneath the earth pressed against the surface of the Long Beach/Lakewood community. Interestingly enough the earthquake registered only a minor insignificant blimp outside the area and felt more like a rolling tremor for less than a few seconds.

Eugenia, out of bed after the first thrust, rushed his family and dog into the downstairs hallway before checking for damage. Finding no obvious loss, he turned on the television. He received immediate information as well as learning folks were clogging the emergency switchboards, as reported on the local newstations operating again after shutting down at midnight.

Cal Tech could not explain the mysterious circumstances behind this event. Sources of how deep the tremblor originated from eluded the scientists.

"I thought their new seismic system could track the whereabouts of an earthquake. They seemed not too convincing where it began, except underneath Long Beach. I wonder if it will make the morning newspaper."

"I doubt it, sweetheart. They print that and deliver it out well before dawn," said Palmira, curled up on the couch next to her husband.

"Mama, Rosie is fussy. Can I heat her up a bottle?" asked Mia.

"Stay in the hallway, kids, I'll get it," replied Mrs. Sacatti.

Returning the bottle to her grandchild, Palmira fell to the floor before slamming up against the wall of the hallway, hitting her head. Emma reached out and caught her mother, saving her from further injury. Another aftershock hit the city, the most severe of the three.

His house still thumping up and down, Eugenia crawled toward the hallway as a large picture with an antique frame fell on his back. "Are you alright, Papa!" screamed Dario. The baby started crying as the house bounced for nearly a minute.

This time, the Sacattis could hear windows shattering in the front parlor, the light stand fell, and their beloved curio crashed to the floor. Dario sobbed, joining his baby niece while grabbing onto his sister Mia. Lucky, coiled in Emma's arms, shook in silence.

Schools were postponed the following day the majority of campuses inspecting any damage. Mia called the Russo household and got Mrs. Siena on the phone. "Sure, they're both up and a little shaken up from last night's quake. How is your family doing, Mia, any damage."

"My father told us we lucked out. The bay window pane in our living room shattered, along with a few other items. How did you fare?"

"Besides a figurine shifting two inches we haven't found any damage as of yet. That motivated Mrs. Russo to head to work. Did your mother and father do the same?"

"As you know, my mother's a receptionist and figured quite a few patients might show up today at the medical clinic. My dad hesitated at first, then left for work. He's a plant supervisor and figured he needed to be there."

Betty came to the phone, relieved her friend was okay. "You're not going to believe this, Mia, but our babies slept through both quakes. Of all nights, and they never woke up. How did your baby do?"

"Cried and wailed. Just the opposite, Rosie's sound asleep now. Betty, would you and Catherine care to take our little ones out for a carriage walk?"

"We loved too, considering we were allowed to get some sleep after the major rattling of the house. What about you? Aren't you exhausted?"

"I think the walk might do me some good, and Ted's coming over to assist Emma in replacing the front window. Papa left her some money. It's going to cost $65.00 to replace that huge pane of glass plus two other small windows. Thank goodness Ted's handy around the house. My father will be happy when he gets home.

"I have a question. Did you say your house 'rattled.'"

"Yeah, why."

"Our's acted as if it jumped!"

"Jumped! That's weird. Well, maybe our's did too."

All three girls, with Dario leading Lucky, secured on a leash, met with their carriages at the crosswalk on Harvey Way.

Crossing the street to the shaded community college, Catherine commented, "Still hot, and it's already late October. These trees are a Godsend. I haven't seen Lucky in a while," she said while kneeling to hug the affectionate pup. And how are you, Dario?"

"I'm fine. Usually, I run before the sun comes up with Emma and Lucky. Our dog is really fast, like me. Did you know I won my football game yesterday, and I'm going to get a trophy."

"No!" said Catherine and Betty.

"Actually, he's got one more game before his team is declared champs," replied Mia.

"Yeah, but they're crummy, so we're going to slaughter them.

"Betty, I got a box of Topps baseball cards at my house and my mom said I can open them when I get home. Ted's going to help me try and get a Sandy Koufax."

"Well, good luck to you. I hear Koufax did well this year."

"He broke the major league record with the most strikeouts in a year. He got 382 plus 26 wins and a 2.04 earned run average."

"Wow, you sure know your stats, young fellow," said Catherine, fascinated by the boy's knowledge of mathematics.

"That's why I have to say a Hail Mary for every pack I open. Ted said he would help. I opened two of them yesterday in Ted's car. I have twenty-two more packs to go!"

Catherine turned to Dario's sister, "How's Ted doing, Mia? He's so cute and tall. Is Emma dating him? She's a sophomore now."

"She's a sophomore, alright, but told him she couldn't date until she turned sixteen. I don't know why Emma's holding out. When she turns sixteen and still doesn't want to date him, I might work my way personally into his life. He's too attractive to pass up, and Dario, you better keep quiet."

"Why? Ted is going to marry her someday."

Mia pushed her baby carriage in silence as Catherine and Betty noted a possible secret crush on the 6'3" basketball player.

Once home, Mia retreated to her bedroom, not wanting to come in contact with Emma's 'boyfriend.' "Rosie, you realize how much I love you, but as of now, I don't think any boy would want to take us on, and me still only fourteen years old. I'll grow up an old maid."

After taking careful measurements, Ted picked up Emma and took her to his father's referred steady glass factory. "My father comes here when it comes time to install windows. Their quality and prices beat most of the competition."

"Your father's a local contractor?"

"Mostly a carpenter. He feeds out work to local electricians when he requires three or more bids. I'm proud to say my father can pretty much build and service any house on the block. I'm not proud to say this, but earthquakes have always been good for my dad's business."

After picking up the acquired glass, he prepped the broken windows, showing Emma how to assist him. After Emma pressed the glass into the standard grooves, Ted applied the putty leaving the large pane of glass for his final installation.

Dario sat on the porch reciting Hail Mary's faster than a Koufax fastball. "You need to slow down, little guy. Those prayers might fly passed Jesus's mother. She won't get what you're trying to do! Breaking it up into two parts and concentrate on the words, that way, it will assist Koufax in his next rotation next season."

"HAIILL MMAARRYY..."

"Not that slow. How about opening the cards and promising a decade of the rosary afterward? I'll help you after

Emma and I finish placing this large window pane and puttying it secure."

"Hey, Ted, I got a secret Mia told me on the walk. It's about you and..."

Ted intervened, "Dario's secrets are not supposed to be for anyone to share. You keep it to your..."

"Hey! I got another Don Drysdale! Koufax has gotta be next," shouted Dario as he held up the Topps card.

Emma smiled while she backed up her friend, "Dario, did you hear Ted? You tell a secret someone confided in you, and you'll never get a Koufax."

"All right, I'm sorry. I won't ever tell."

After an hour of puttying the bay window, Ted suggested he check the foundation of the house. "Your house lifted up and down, right?"

"Yes, up and down over and over," replied Emma.

"I checked your foundation, and the foundation on the southeast part of the house slipped. Your house in that corner is sitting on half the block."

"What can we do?" asked Emma.

"We'll get your friend Dorothy and she can lift the house and place the southeast section where it belongs."

Ted cupped his hands and started calling for Dorothy. After not receiving a response, he said, "You don't think they made her go to work today, do you?"

"Ted, I don't think Dorothy is capable of lifting a ..."

He smiled, and then he bent over laughing. After gathering himself and withstanding a gentle sock to his shoulder, he said, "How about I build a frame and set it under the foundation and pour some quick set cement inside it? That'll secure the foundation. Will make a quick trip to your hardware store."

His Ford coupe slowed down, coming to a stop. When Emma turned to her left to see the expression on Ted's face, she sat there frozen. "Ted, Ted, are you okay?" Panicked, she realized he didn't move. A residual smile crossed his face. "Ted!" She grabbed his arm.

Icy to the touch, she screamed for help while opening the car door. She looked up and down the block and found two neighbors who looked as if they were breezing away the day in some form of talk. "Please help me!" she shouted, only to find they stood as statues, unmoving and still no more than human images.

She ran up a porch and pounded on the door. A young child answered, looked up at Emma, and halted. His mother, coming from the kitchen saw her son stiffened at the front door. She clutched his shoulders, looked up at Emma, and ceased to move; the housewife's eyes gazed in astonishment.

"Ma'am, ma'am! Oh dear God, help me!"

She ran next door. There was no answer at the door. Hearing the sound of water running in the backyard, she opened the fence gate and dashed toward the rushing water , finding an older man holding a hose, flooding the area of his lawn. Emma shut off the water while discovering the neighbor didn't move.

She ran back to the '56 Ford Coupe, finding Ted, his hands still glued to the steering wheel in a ten/two position. Placing her hands on his face, she found he couldn't respond; however, his chest moved out and in as if his breathing continued. "Oh, Ted, what have I done!"

She searched the houses on her neighborhood block until she found one with a screen door and the front door wide open. Emma tested the screen and found it was unlocked. She crept in, hoping someone unfamiliar with what was occurring outside might in some way help her.

She looked from room to room until she found an elderly woman napping in bed. "Ma'am, ma'am." She gently touched the lady's shoulder until the woman awoke.

"Is that you precious?"

Emma noticed the woman was blind and decided to calm her with a gentle fib. "No, ma'am, I'm from the police department sent here to check on you. Are you all right?"

"Yes, I'm fine. Is my Carol okay?"

"She's doing just fine. We just experienced another earthquake, and Carol wanted me to check on you." It suddenly occurred to Emma that if this woman couldn't see, would she be okay to step outside?

Noticing the land phone on the side of her bed, she phoned the police. A desk sergeant answered. "Officer, I'm inside a house with an elderly woman…"

"Don't go outside or stare out through your window!" he shouted into the phone.

"I now realize this, sir. However, whatever this thing is, it hasn't affected me. I do have a question: the woman I am with is blind. Could I take her outside to a safer place?"

"Are you blind, too? We've gotten calls for some reason; blind people are not disturbed by this menace."

"No, officer, I can see," replied Emma.

"Can you get to the police department? We're on Clark Ave. We have a doctor who slipped in from Lakewood General blindfolded I'd like him to check you. Only God knows what's causing this."

"I'll do my best. I'm only…," Emma looked over at the blind woman. I have never driven a car, but I think I could manage one. It will take some time."

"All right then, and be careful. Whatever's out there is sinister enough not to respect life."

"Ma'am, I'm going to help you outside, and we'll head to another home first and then to the police department, where you'll be safe."

"That's fine. My daughter works next door at the hospital. She's a registered nurse, and with all this shaking, she must be really tied up. Oh, and I didn't get your name. My name is Mary, Mary Walsh."

"I'm so happy to make your acquaintance, Mrs. Walsh. My name is Emma Sacatti."

"Happy to know you, Officer Sacatti. Did I tell you my husband was a police officer, worked out of Southgate, and was injured in a shootout and forced to retire? He died five years ago, and I still miss him. And his rugged face, the most handsome man I ever touched with my hands. He knew I was blind when we married and still took care of me."

"What was his name? He sounds like one of God's greatest saints."

"James Walsh, my Jimmy; I truly loved him. I still do. Are you married, Emma?"

"No, I've never married. Mrs. Walsh, I'll guide you toward the door and place you in my vehicle. You'll be safe at the police station."

"You won't need to assist me, darling; I've memorized every nook and cranny of this house. Let me get myself ready, and I'll go with you."

"That's perfect. I'll get you ready to hop in the car. I'll be right back."

Emma ran out the front door to Ted's Ford coupe. She reached in, trying to pull the heavy boy from the vehicle and place him in the back seat when a patrol car alongside. Two officers with dark sunglasses climbed out offering to add assistance to the young teen.

xxxxxxxxxx

Her fever rose, yet she still slept, her mother's arm placed tenderly on Emma's shoulder, comforting and unconsciously reassuring her daughter in her sleep.

Fear not, Emma, Mama, and I will protect you, soothed the eighth grader's blessed guardian angel.

Emma blinked twice, restless yet not disturbed.

xxxxxxxxxx

"Ma'am, let us take him out and place him in our car. He appears one of the victims."

"Oh dear God, I can't thank you enough. Officers, a blind lady is waiting for me in that house. Could you help her, too?"

"Of course. I see you're not wearing dark glasses. Are you okay?" asked Officer Bill Rollins. "And also your name, ma'am?"

"My name is Emma Sacatti, and I don't know why, but this nightmare hasn't affected me. I need to go home first. My brother, sister, and her baby are stranded inside. I hope they're okay."

We'll take you there after we help the woman out of the house."

Officer Cyrus Bellanger walked toward Mrs. Walsh's home, introduced himself, and escorted her off the porch while Rollins placed Ted's unconscious body in the back seat of the police car. "Cyrus, why don't you take Mrs. Walsh to the hospital first with this young man? I'll take Emma home and check on her family."

Lakewood's police car disappeared out of the village and down Arbor Road and headed towards Clark Ave, northeast of their present location. Officer Rollins started up the 1956 Ford coupe and proceeded toward Harvey Way, less than a half-mile away.

Dario, tired of not finding a Koufax, took his remaining packs of baseball cards into the house, carrying his other cards in the Topps carton.

"Any luck, Dario?" asked his sister Mia as she warmed a milk bottle in a pan filled with water on the stove.

"Not one! I knew Mrs. Holmes was right. I should pray first, then open the pack."

"Maybe you're right. We don't have school today, so why don't you relax and turn on the television."

"Good idea! I never get to watch the regular cartoons or cowboy shows because I have school." He turned on the black and white set and immediately started changing the five available channels. "News, news, news. Not even channel 13 has anything good," Dario shouted from the living room.

All news from every channel! Tien understated herself. What's going on? She told me not to let Dario leave the house and then disappeared. "Dario, turn the knob to Channel 2, 4 or 7. I'll be right in."

Feeding Rosie, she walked into the front room and observed her brother's eyes glued to the set. "Are you okay, Dario?"

"Something's happened right here where we live. Something happened to almost everyone!"

It's what Tien tried to tell me before she said my family was safe and to keep an eye on Dario. What's going to happen to us? Oh my God, what about Catherine and Betty and their babies?

A car drove into the Sacatti driveway. Mia flew to the door and looked through the screen, noticing it was Ted's car. She saw her sister jump out and head to the porch, but who was that police officer getting out on the other side?

"Thank God you're okay Mia," she kissed her sister's

hair as the baby became uneasy. "Where's Dari...There you are, little fellow." Emma knelt and hugged her brother.

Officer Rollins noted that this mysterious revulsion escaped the Sacatti children. *What was it they possessed that practically affected the entire town?*

"Mia, this is Officer Rollins. He wants us all down at the police station and maybe even the hospital to check why this horrible plague never included us."

"Dario, why don't you get your book? We may be awhile," said Mia.

"Could I bring my packs of baseball cards I didn't open up?" He looked up at his sister with tears beginning to crowd his eyes.

"Of course, you bring your open Topps cards, too. Maybe you'll find your reward, Dario."

Mia turned away, the baby crying as she placed three bottles in an ice chest. Emma retrieved three clean diapers. "Mia, did Mom or Dad call?"

"Yes, thank you for reminding me. Papa just called me before the officer drove up in Ted's car. Daddy said he would tell Mama we were alright. He said he'd be home after his boss ordered the closure of the plant at noon. His men were ordered to wear the dark sunglasses brought in by the company, whatever that meant. Papa, though, should be home soon. Can we wait until he gets here?" Each sister looked over at Officer Rollins for permission. He told the girls to relax with Dario and the baby as he made a call to the police station.

Their attention turned toward the news update every few minutes. News reports appeared to grow bleak as the Sacatti girls prayed for their dad to return home. Five minutes later, Eugenia's old truck pulled up out front. He exited his vehicle with dark sunglasses covering his eyes.

Hustling to his front porch, he panicked as his son opened the door and met his father outside. Emma explained for some reason, his children and perhaps Mom and Dad were immuned. "I can't quite explain Papa. You may want to check with Mia. She might know. First, please meet Officer Rollins. He's taken good care of us."

"Mr. Sacatti, it's good to meet you. Your children demonstrate an interesting phenomenon that Lakewood General Hospital and the Lakewood Police would like to examine and question. Your daughters wanted to wait for you to arrive home before we set off to the Clark Ave. station. I encourage you to come along. I understand they packed items for the baby."

"Yes, let's head on out, but first, let me call my wife and let her know we're alright and where we went."

Eugenia followed the police officer to the hospital while Dario said a quick Hail Mary and opened another pack of baseball cards.

Chapter Twenty-Nine

Self-confidence and more so a blessing.

Tien brushed by a thought with Dorothy, devoid of real answers. "You spent over eighteen years looking over this town as an entity. What are your thoughts on the present malady?"

"I feel somehow Lamia is behind this, operating in her cozy corner of hell. You protected the Sacatti family, so she's finding retribution through earthquakes and now this trouble."

"What's interesting, Dorothy, no one has lost their life, although, through natural attrition, 2.6 people pass away every day. It's almost a divine presence that has shadowed this town in the last two days."

"Divine!" That's your territory, Tien."

"Miracles do happen, however, but not like this. Generally, we leave acts of nature or human interference to those who walk this earth. Cures for disease and legislation that protect individual rights are purely through the goodness of people.

"On the other hand, wars and evil dictatorships are the result of mankind gone leery of human decency. Curing a war creates as much destruction as natural earthquakes.

We're waiting for people to find ways around war and more methods to warn ahead when a natural disaster is about to strike.

"War and suffering might end when destructive people reject evil, ease their egos, and head toward what we see as goodness. Whether that includes sincere prayer or not depends on what's hidden in the heart of the individual."

"I take it you don't think Lamia is involved in this. You feel it's entirely manmade," wondered Dorothy.

"In the past, severe problems that affect large groups of people blame God's retribution or the active vengeance of the devil. Look at the headlines of today's Independent, GOD'S WILL? Evangelists are spouting the end of times, claiming people have sinned and God is striking back. All of this is false, Dorothy. However, this is different something not known to human history, and why only in the Lakewood, Long Beach area.

"Scientists will study it and try to find a logical reason for this chaos. Yet, I know there is no logical reason why this occurred. It came and went in less than a day. People found frozen in place are now going about their business at this moment. Individuals are packing churches, offering thanks, and praying for guidance in the future."

"It appears Lamia is laughing in hell, a unique ploy to cause suffering and doubt without taking a life. She's at it again."

"You answered my question, Dorothy. Lamia was given free rein to abuse the people here in town. Her interference anywhere needs to stop now."

———

Sitting quietly at the Sacatti dinner table, baby Rosie lightened the despondent family by raising her hands and shouting what she heard time and time again, a word that sounded like Koufax,

"What did she just say?" asked Mia.

"It sounded like...like Koufax?" replied Mrs. Sacatti.

"Yeah! Sandy Koufax. I'm going to find one. Rosie knows, doesn't she, Papa?"

Everyone looked over at the baby girl and laughed.

"Say it again, Rosie, maybe I'll get two. Can you say Koufax? Say, Koufax," pleaded Dario.

"KO, ko az," Rosie responded as she grinned, watching her family applauding one of her first words.

Each member of the Sacatti family clapped as baby Rosie joined together her hands with the rest of her family.

Emma decided it was wise to start up some sort of conversation. "Mama, the last two days at the clinic must have taken a lot out of you."

"It was actually quiet. We were surprised until we learned that going outdoors caused that sleeping sickness. The doctors were stilled unable to come up with any diagnosis. We were ordered to sit tight and not leave the building. I was relieved to hear your father's voice and what some people were doing to thwart the problem. And God found favor with all you children when I found out this plague or whatever it was didn't affect you.

"By the way, I understand Ted's doing fine."

"Back to normal, Mama," and Emma continued, "Since school is out until next Monday, he's set to correct the slippage in our foundation tomorrow morning," said Emma. "We're headed to the hardware store tomorrow to pick up some cement. Ted told me he already took measurements and built a frame to fit underneath the house."

Eugenia spoke, "Let me give you some money and a little extra. I was hoping you could take him to a nice place for lunch. He's a good young man. Try not to forget Emma."

"Oh, and invite him to dinner too," Palmira added. "Ask him early so it doesn't upset his mother's plans."

"WHEWWW! Here comes the bride, all dressed in..."

"That's enough, Dario, eat your dinner," scolded his mother.

Tien visited Mia and Emma, announcing herself with a friendly hello on the recommendation of Dorothy. "Good evening, girls. I hope you found some calm after Lamia's wickedness."

"That was quite a scare, and we were spared the physical cataleptic lapse," said Emma. "I've wondered if those who were affected are struggling with this."

"I compare it to waking up from a sound sleep, nothing more. Your friend Ted's memory of driving and next blacking out is unfeasibly vague. He and thousands of others are recovering. I'm happy to see you seem pretty good. What are your plans for tomorrow?"

Emma started first, "Ted and I will finish upgrading any damage to the house. I'll help him secure the corner foundation of our home. He sure is quite the handyman."

"Don't forget lunch and dinner," replied Mia, hoping to sit across from him at the dinner table.

"Who are you guys talking to," asked Dario, wandering into their bedroom.

"Hello, how are you, Dario?" asked Tien, greeting the young boy.

"I'm fine. You're Tien, aren't you the angel who beat up the devil."

"More like setting the devil in its place."

"Can you stop earthquakes? They scared us and wrecked our house."

"I don't have that kind of ability at this time."

"Can you make magic? I like magic."

"I might, but not too hard, mind you. What do you have in mind?"

"Well, I was wondering if you could..."

"Don't say it, Dario. It wouldn't be fair to the other boys," warned Mia.

"It was fair to David Edwards. He's got two and won't even trade for his extra, except for a Mantle and Mays."

"I take it he collects baseball cards. Typical boy. Go ahead and ask me, Dario."

He looked over at his sister before thinking, *Maybe Mia's right it wouldn't be fair. I wonder, though, if she can read my mind. KOUFAX!* "Never mind, Tien, my sisters are usually right it wouldn't be fair." *KOUFAX!* He repeated in his head.

Emma said, "You heard your sister, little fella; now go to your room, say your prayers, and climb into bed."

"Mother nature never caused our crust to slip or, in this case, bounce up and down; Lamia was responsible for our two earthquakes. Even worse, scientists probably won't make any gains studying this newest phenomenon.

"That woman's hand created this disaster from the corner of hell. Lamia cost you and your boyfriend time and money not including the fact she cost your cities millions.

"Lamia has violated God's laws on earth, laws curtailing the good nature of typical folks. She comes across as a violent dictator, fortunately not tolerated by our Maker or his strongest angels above. Humans can take out a tyrant, and we all look forward when none of those vicious despots exit.

"We do listen to prayer, and in the end, good will always prevail. Lamia is now 100% shut down. Not one person or thing on earth will suffer from her vicious hands.

"Girls, be careful though evil men and women still walk this earth. Good night now, say your prayers and give my regards to your parents. And, before I forget, let Dario know he needs to persevere."

Tien left, and the girls dropped to their knees as they did every night before starting their prayers of thanks, but not before one or the other shared her thoughts.

"Emma, do you trust everything Tien says? I mean, she's made promises before and look what happened."

"I understand what you're thinking. Trust is a pretty heavy thing to hold onto when you really are not fully acquainted with someone. Let me ask you this: do you fully trust me?"

"I trust what you tell me is from your heart. You mean well, Emma, so when it comes right down to it, yeah, I can say you earned my trust."

"Mia, do you think I can fully trust you?"

"My actions have not been honorable. I disappointed you, Dario, and Mama and Papa. No, how can you trust me?"

"But I do. You've made mistakes, some more egregious than others. I've made mistakes, too; however, neither of us is perfect.

"Yes, I trust you, Mia, and more importantly, I love you because I know you. You're a good mother, and you love your daughter. That counts sister. I think love is bigger than trust. Look at Peter in the bible. He denied Christ three times and yet Jesus turned over his whole church to him. We can do the same, forgive, and show compassion.

"Maybe the question is, do we love Tien? Maybe not as much as if both of us knew her.

"Let's say our prayers. I'm getting up at six since we don't have to get up early for school. I'll harness up Lucky and maybe wake Dario. He wants to pick up his speed for that trophy he's aiming to get.

"Good night, Mia."

"Good night, Emma."

———

Wednesday evening flew by quickly, and by the time Emma rolled out of bed, her parents were up preparing for work at 6:30. Lucky had waited the extra time not to disturb the girl he dearly loved.

"I'm headed out, Mom and Dad. I'll see you tonight."

Palmira rushed to the front door to remind Emma to invite Ted over for dinner.

"I won't forget Mom. He'll appreciate the invite." Emma started on her three-mile run, not waking her little brother probably caught up in his dream of coming across a Topps, Koufax. Lucky the Sacattis German Shepherd, growing bigger every day, kept pace as his ears and nose caught the refreshing morning breeze.

"We're coming up on our sprint, Lucky. You ready! ONE, TWO, THREE GO! They flew down the short end of the community college, Lucky's tongue saluting the air.

Off on the long straightaway on the other side of the college, they settled unto what Emma thought might be too brisk of a pace. "You okay, little fella?" As typical, the bugger pup kept his stride heeling alongside his master. She slowed down anyway. Within less than a minute, Lucky and Emma would be flying down the opposite short stretch on the north side of the campus.

Before completing a thousand yards on their first lap, she noticed Dario waiting with his mother on the college sidewalk. "You didn't wait for me, Emma; I wanted to run."

"Hop aboard, little guy will be sprinting in thirty seconds."

Dario geared up for the all-out run, his arms moving in perfect sync on each side of his body. He ran like a boy four years older than him with shoulders square, head level, and knees lifting above his torso. *If he's not a halfback, he'll make a great sprinter,* Emma thought consciously while widening her pace, trying to stay by her brother's side.

Emma brushed her brother's hair with her hand after the run.

"Our game is not for another week because of the earthquake and stuff. We're going to beat Fatima's pants off, and I'm going to score more than one touchdown. My coach, Mr Roman, thinks I'm getting faster. You do, too, huh."

"I'll be the first in our family to recognize your speed, Dario. Staying with you on those sprints set my legs moving faster than I normally do. Over the weeks, you have developed a new set of wheels. I might have Ted join us to test you. But, Dario, confidence is good for all of us; however, you need to keep your progress to yourself. Remain humble, and God will triple your blessings."

They headed into the house, finding out that Mia had started up a warm breakfast. "Ted called and knew you were probably out running. I told him to head on over, and we'd have breakfast waiting for him."

"Thank you, Mia. I should head to the shower," said Emma.

Dario looked at his sister and replied, "Why, you don't smell Emma. You still smell good."

"Now, how would you know how I smell?"

"I could smell you when you when we ran. You smelled like flowers."

"Thank you, my good young man. I like to stay that way for our guests. You don't need help, do you, Mia."

"No, you go ahead, Emma, I'll be okay. Rosie is still sound asleep in her crib."

Emma walked upstairs to the Sacattis' only bathroom to take a quick shower.

"Dario, that flower you smelled on your sister is called Yardley rose powder. I fall asleep to that lovely fragrance every night. It's Emma's favorite, actually. Papa buys it for her every Christmas and on her birthday in April."

"She sure puts on a lot lately because I don't know if I ever smelled it when we ran. Maybe she wants to smell good for Ted."

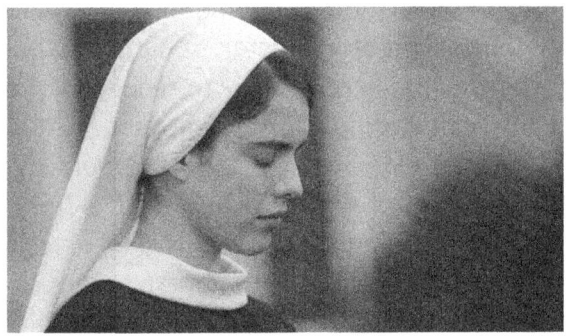

Mia, although not disagreeing with Dario, thought, *Whatever happened to her desire to become a nun.*

Dario moved to the refrigerator with Lucky in tow. The boy pulled out a package of A Farmer's Dog, cut out an appropriate slice, and set it in Lucky's food dish. After his pup wolfed down the food, Dario let the dog outside in the backyard.

Chapter Thirty
Laughter left his wrinkles
in the right place.

At 6:45 a.m., the front doorbell sent its message throughout the Sacatti household. Lucky scampered to the door, barking wildly. His nose detected a special guest, one the dog loved immensely. Lucky then started to squeal loud enough for Mia to tell the dog to stop. "Why are you so annoying, Lucky?"

She opened the door to her new candidate for 'striking boy of the year.' Ted crossed the threshold, again to the aggravating high-pitched squeak of the Sacatti dog. Ted bent down and took Lucky into his embrace. "How are you, little fella? Do you smell my cats?"

Mia guided Ted to the dining room behind the kitchen. "Breakfast sure smells good," he said while finding a seat at the table.

"I sure hope you like it," said Mia. "Emma just finished up in the shower she'll be right in. She thought she caught Ted staring at her when she found out Dario stood directly at her side. "Dario, why don't you take a seat? Emma told me you ran hard today, so you have got to have your hunger up."

"I do. I'm hungrier than the people in China."

"Dario, I don't think we've ever been that hungry," replied Ted.

"Lonnie Price said that at school and all our teacher said was stand for the Angelus. My fourth-grade teacher doesn't really like boys, so she must have been hungry."

Ted shared tongue in cheek, "Well, in that case, little partner, 'I'm so hungry I could eat the back end of a skunk.'"

"Ted, what are you trying to teach that boy? Your little joke will be all over the school." Ted looked up and saw Emma.

Dario laughed and bent over while wiping the snot from his nose with his hand. Mia threw him a napkin to clean up. "I'm tellin' that one as soon as school starts again…the back end of a skunk. All the boys will love that one. I think I'll tell it before lunch. If Mrs. Hamilton didn't get mad at Lonnie, she wouldn't get mad at me."

"I wouldn't be too sure of that, Dario," said Mia, throwing her brother another napkin while asking, "Dario, did you wash up?"

"Mama made me take a bath last night."

"Now, young man! Wash your hands thoroughly and your face, too; you still have snot on it."

Dario got up without a word until he remarked, "You sure smell pretty, Emma," as she entered the dining room.

Again, he stresses how beautiful she smells. What's wrong with him? Mia now sat at the table a troubled smile crossed her face.

Finished supporting the foundation of the Sacatti home, Ted looked happy to accept the luncheon invitation yet turned down the invitation to dinner.

A clear voice circled his brain, indicating to him that Emma never could make any commitment to the 6'3" young man. According to Mia's dubious suggestion, Emma's committed to God, a devout nun waiting in the near future, married not in the upcoming years to Ted but to Christ Himself.

No, no, not true. Who are you? Who in the hell are you placing these thoughts in my head?

Yet, the thoughts persisted, immersing his brain like wildfire until he could no longer take the heat, gripping the sides of his head and trying to prevent an internal explosion.

Never fear, young man; her sister longs for you. Look at the way she stares, makes you breakfast, and hangs her head when her stupid brother interferes with his God-awful empty comments. She's the one for you, committed and ready to say YES!

Look Mia's way and drop your obsession with this stubborn Emma Sacatti. A kiss on the cheek, come on, you want more than that.

Dinner would be too much. He needed to think, to rearrange his thoughts. Did Mia really have a crush on him? She was just as beautiful as her sister! She needed a man. Mia wasn't the type to raise that kid for the rest of her life. She would never hang her single status on a permanent shelf, not with a sole child in the picture.

Yet, she was fourteen, Mia wouldn't be sixteen until September of her junior year. Would Ted have to wait that long?

Of course not, Ted. You'll be a healthy senior just a corner around adulthood, and keep in mind Mia doesn't hold the same values as Emma. She's different, morally open to new adventures, and experienced, ripe for a curious boy like you.

Ted, I need to talk privately to Miss Mullenger. I hope you don't mind."

"No, not at all." *I'll look for Mia in the cafeteria she'll enjoy my company.*

"Dorothy, I needed to talk to you today about something that is bothering my sister and, frankly, me too."

"You're always welcome in here, Emma. What's on your mind?"

"Mia and I want to know how well you know Tien Anh."

"Our angel? She called for me to the church at night. I found her disguised as a homeless older man. Donovan and Helixa were there, it's where they normally retired at night. Next, to my surprise Lamia appeared hovering over the back of the church.

"According to Tien, it was a trap to lure Lamia into a church and dispose of those evil wretches permanently into hell.

"She shows up as a friend on occasion. That's, however, all I know of her. She's not here, is she?"

"No, I would feel her. She's not around," responded Emma. "Mia told me Tien visits her, letting my sister not to worry that everything is going to be alright. Then what happens? Two odd earthquakes lift the entire community, creating what we thought was hundreds of thousands of dollars in damage. We later found out the quakes only caused minor damage.

"Next, a mysterious plague overtakes only the Long Beach and Lakewood communities. And we found out who is totally immune to its devastation: our entire family.

"Not to worry? Everything is going to be alright? What kind of angel would tell my sister and even me that kind of thing?"

"That sounds like a legitimate concern. Have you talked to Tien as of late?"

"I needed to bounce this off you, Dorothy. We're not sure we trust her. Not to worry? What's next?"

"You're one of the few people I've ever met who can call forth angels to assist you. However, you never contacted Tien; she just showed up at the church.

"Do you think Donovan contacted her?"

"Thinking of it, why would he? He couldn't have had any knowledge of what we were experiencing. I don't think Helixa knew either.

"Tien told us Donovan was busy collecting eggs, milking his cow twice a day, chewing on a straw, and watching the sunset and stars at night, that I believe.

"What I couldn't understand was how Helixa would be content sharing a house with Donovan and his mother. Helixa was back with her mother, but a two-bedroom, one-bath house? Helixa was much too active to accept a leisurely day on a farm. She enjoyed teaching biology to the kids and so did Donovan."

"Don't forget Donovan missed his mother," said Dorothy. "I believe Helixa, too, was eager to reconcile with her mother. Now, they're in heaven where their legitimate desires are satisfied."

Emma wondered, "Could you call them back, Dorothy? I think both of them miss teaching."

"I honestly think Donovan and probably Helixa couldn't leave their mothers once again."

"How about bringing them along?"

"What good would that do, Emma?"

"We could set them up in a beautiful four-bedroom home in Long Beach right near the ocean. I know Donovan loves the water; he's told me so. And you wouldn't have to teach anymore and concentrate more on your family and the medical clinic. We could also solve for once and all if Donovan actually contacted Tien Anh."

"I could contact the once living. What would you want me to say?"

"Tell them to come back and try living in Long Beach again, to bring their mothers. They could live near the ocean in a larger home, and make sure you reassure them they could work together again here at school."

"All that, and do you think they'll bite? Do you realize Donovan is living comfortably as a seven-year-old?"

"Convince Hannah he needs to come back as a young man. She can do that, and maybe you could hint Mia and Emma are in trouble."

Volleyball and elementary school football teams were rescheduled. Emma and Mia faced the newly opened St. Joseph's all-girls high school in Lakewood. Closer to dozens of competitive Catholic elementary schools within a couple of miles of St. Joseph, the school found applications in access.

Built on a former five acres of dairyland, St. Joseph started with a freshmen class and worked up to a complete high school three years later.

St. Anthony was leery of the strength of this new Parochial School. They knew the combination of freshmen and 'all-girls' did not attract a wealth of distractions. Boys on campus did not shake up the complete focus these girls dedicated to the sport, at least in the first year.

St. Anthony's bus rolled onto the St. Joseph campus, ready to compete outdoors against mostly fourteen-year-old girls still dressed in their school uniforms. Mia found three of her old friends from St. Cyprian's all of them demonstrating wicked serves since they first discovered volleyball in fifth grade.

"Emma, these girls are fully experienced going back four years, you should know that. I was a cog in their well-oiled machine, never possessing a definite interest in the Cyprian squad. I eventually got bored and quit the team. Emma, these girls are good!"

Junior year, Tanya Bailey circled her team around her, repeating what Mia shared with her sister. "Rosa Clark let me know she faced St. Cyprian's twice. Those girls we're facing today have strong serves, one of them Eileen Cruz, who has developed an overwhelming curve. When have we not crushed teams with consistent serves? We are a highly competitive high school that has been around for over forty years. An opponent can rarely serve up an ace. Today, these girls are going to find that out. Get ready to dig and put these youngsters away."

A wicked serve fell toward Emma Sacatti, who dug it out, setting up an even more malicious spike from team captain Tanya Bailey. Terrified, the young freshmen team from St. Joseph never recovered.

Substituted into the match, Mia impressed her former teammates, serving up an ace, something the young team had not yet measured up to in their freshmen year.

With permission from Vice-Principal Judy Wilcox, Ted was permitted to drive the Sacatti sisters to their brother's football game at Pan-American Park.

Three-quarters passed, and Ted, Mia, and Emma found their brother standing on the sidelines with a smile on his face. "We're beating them 36-0. I scored two of our touchdowns like I said I would."

Scoring a lone touchdown Fatima celebrated as if they won the game. Within five minutes, the game ended, with both teams lining up and congratulating each other.

Dario hopped into Ted's Ford coupe, comfortably reclining in the back seat. Mia pushed herself to the middle of the front bench seat as Emma sat shotgun, wondering what was going on with her younger sister, even Ted didn't seem to mind Mia brushing up against him.

Dario pointed out, "Hey Mia, you're sitting in the wrong seat."

Even Dario picked up on the seating arrangements. What's going on? Thought Emma.

"Dario, you still have your quarter from Saturday," asked Mia.

"Are we going to Dr. Sloane's at the pharmacy!" Mia's brother sat up in the back seat. "Do you think she still has baseball cards? Football already started, and the World Series is over."

"It won't hurt to check. Let's find out." Mia appeared to savor sitting next to her newest crush.

"Why don't you three drop me off at home, and I'll get dinner started." Emma, eager to leave the car, came up with an inverse plan for Mia and Ted to remain together, alone, while Dario entered the pharmacy to purchase his baseball cards.

Not too subtle about it, are you, Mia. Just don't get yourself pregnant again. What a horrible thought. How could she think such a thing of her sister?

Dropped off at her parents' house on Harvey Way, Emma exited the vehicle. Mia turned and suggested Dario climb up front. "Not over the seat, Dario. Get out of the car and climb in where your sister sat."

Within ten minutes, the trio reached Dr. Sloane's pharmacy. "You go in by yourself, Dario. You're a big boy now."

He hopped out of the car, fidgeting around in his pocket for his quarter. *Five packs! My last chance. Dave said he'd trade his extra Koufax for a mint Mickey Mantle. Please, please, guardian angel help me at least get one.*

As the automatic door of the pharmacy opened Mia's lips pressed against the wet mouth of Ted Accenti. "I've always loved you, Ted." She couldn't stop. Kiss after kiss, the couple melted into each other's arms.

"Mr. Dario Sacatti! How are you, my friend? I might know what you are here for. Topps cards and not the football kind, I take it."

"Do you have any packs of baseball cards left, Dr. Sloane?"

"I believe I do. I saved a few for you, my friend, not as many as before mind you. What do you have to spend?"

"I got a quarter from my allowance."

"My good friend, then I think we're in business. I'll pull the packs up, and you can select the ones you want. Let me ask you, though; you didn't find one Sandy Koufax in that whole carton?"

"No, I didn't, and my sister's friend told me I shouldn't say any Hail Mary's until AFTER I found the Koufax. It didn't work. I didn't even get a Mantle or even a Willie Mays like I did before. I got a Mays when I only bought two packs."

"I can't say I agree with that fellow. Is that him in the car," she said, standing firmly on her toes and looking over the counter.

"Probably, he drives a Ford."

"Oh my!" she said, watching Dario's sister, Mia, zealously kissing the boy embraced in her arms.

"Dario, you take your time; you've bought too many packs not to get the card you want. I'll be right back."

Dr. Sloane walked briskly out of the store and placed her hands on the hood of Ted's car, pushing her palms down and distracting the couple. "You two stop. Mia, your brother's in there, and you! Aren't you Emma's boyfriend?"

She turned around and walked back into the store, shaking her head. Dr. Sloane found the 4th-grade boy had decided on four of the five packs.

"Dr. Sloane, could you pick out the fifth one for me? You got lucky hands."

"Dario, I'm going to pick out two more packs and give you one free." She feigned as if she had given it some thought and slid into the boy's original stack of Topps two more packs."

"Wow! Thank you, Dr. Sloane. I'll pay you back when I get a nickel."

"No need for that, son, just tell me how you did."

"Dario thanked her again and left the store."

"Hop in, Dario, and sit next to Ted," said Mia, standing outside the Ford and opening the door for her brother.

His face lit up, "You'll never guess what happened! Dr. Sloane gave me a free pack and told me all I had to do was tell her what I got. Boy, what a great day this has been. I scored two touchdowns and got a free pack of cards. And my coach, Mister Roman, said we're all going to get our trophy at the Sports Banquet in three weeks."

"That sounds like a good day to me," said Mia, scooting more toward the car door than her brother sitting in the middle.

"Ted, I decided to say a Hail Mary before I open a pack. That's how I got my Willie Mays. And do you think if I get a

Koufax, I could call Dr. Sloane? It would be easier." Dario thought it over and answered for himself. "I think I should call her even if I don't get one."

Quiet on the ride home, Dario finally said, "I'm going to open them before I go to sleep; that way, I can concentrate on my prayers."

Eugenio and Palmira returned home; the dinner table was already set, and a roast was finishing in the oven. Mr. Sacatti showered first before reminding his son he should take a quick shower next.

"You must have rolled around in the grass, son. Now, put on a new set of clothes and underwear."

Dario, to the interest of his parents, controlled the tableside jabber. "I scored two touchdowns in the first half. We were ahead 36-0, and Coach Roman pulled out us starters. He said he doesn't believe in slaughters, but if Fatima got close, he'd send us back in, and you know what? He never did. They were so crummy."

"We don't tolerate that kind of talk," said Palmira.

"Sorry. Our Lady of Fatima scored a touchdown at the end of the game, and they were happy but not as happy as us.

"Papa, I think I could be a player on the Rams because I know how to catch, and Emma says I'm fast."

"Girls, you've been so quiet, not a word out of you. Didn't you play that new school in Lakewood?"

"Yes, mother, we did. A number of their players attended St. Cyprian's," replied Mia.

"Mia, your father, and I thought about sending you there. An all-girls high school might have suited you well. However, we felt separating you from Emma wasn't such a good idea."

Emma noticed her sister's face turned a shade of red. *Why not send me to St. Joseph? You could have Ted all to yourself without me getting in the way.* Mia thought.

Finishing their homework without sharing a word, the girls showered ten minutes apart finally settling down for bed. Kneeling, they whispered their prayers while Dario, in his bedroom, recited his first Hail Mary, popping a stick of the pink Topps gum in his mouth.

Common, common, a common Milt Pappas. Big deal. Dario recited his prayer slower with fervor, more than the prayer before his game with Fatima. Heaven hung its grace within his room, a blessing ready to sprout its angelic wings inside the pack of baseball cards. Boom! Another stick of gum was pushed into his mouth. He tasted a miracle, one comparable to Lourdes, maybe even to the three children at Fatima.

Common, wait! A Willie McCovey! Common, common, now Eddie Mathews, oh my God, Mickey Mantle! Oh, thank you, God, thank you. Two packs and three great cards. He could almost feel the same glow the three children felt in Portugal.

Should he go on? He wondered. *No, I'll open them in Church. I'll look at the statue of Mary and then open one pack. And if I don't find a Koufax, I'll trade my Mantle and Eddie Mathews for his extra Koufax. He likes Mathews and loves Mantle even more. He'll do it.*

He fell asleep, a smile crossing his face. "*What a day, what a lucky day.*"

"I'm sorry, Emma. I really am sorry," said Mia, unable to fall asleep.

"What are you sorry for, Mia? I want to know."

"I convinced Ted you weren't interested in a long-term relationship, that you...well...that you are committed to your promise to join the novitiate and become a Sister of Mercy. Wasn't that what you told me?"

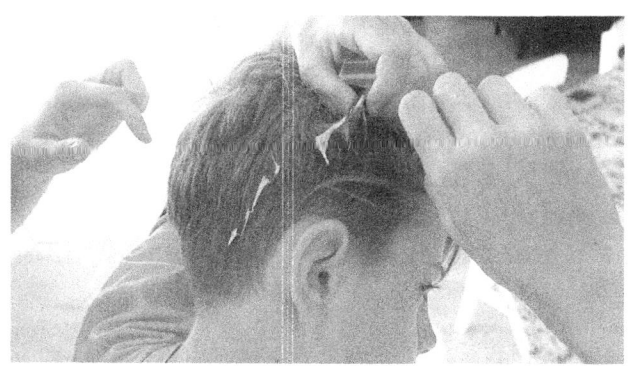

"I was a seventh grader. Don't kids change their minds? You hurt me, Mia, you really hurt me! Did you kiss him?"

"Yes, I did, and he told me he liked it. It's more than you ever did, even telling him you wouldn't date him until you turned sixteen!"

"That's mother's rule, not mine."

"Mother's rule! That's your rule, Emma. Mama wouldn't care if you dated Ted."

"I gotta get up to run, and Dario wants to join Lucky and me. GOOD NIGHT!"

"I'm sorry, Emma. I want you to know Ted still likes you."

Chapter Thirty-One
Olive oil did the trick.

Oh dear God, Dario. You wrapped two sticks of gum across your pillow and, oh no, through your hair. How am I going to get this out? Doggone it! You stay right here." Emma arrived back from the kitchen and bathroom carrying a small glass of olive oil and her old toothbrush.

Dipping the toothbrush in the olive oil, she scrubbed his hair. Lucky sat nearby, unmoving. Dario's hair was soaked with the precious oil the family normally used to cook. "Now we wait and hope for the best. No running for us today. Sorry, Lucky, your brother doesn't listen to his mother and sisters. "What were you thinking, Dario? Shame on you."

He felt bad. First he receives three of Topps finest cards, and what does he do? Dario disobeys three of the people he loves dearly. *That's a sin, Dario, a grievous sin. Maybe you should give the cards to Norman Saudee. He's poor, and his family won't let him collect cards because they cost too much.*

Emma waited five minutes and tried the side of his head with the most gum. She found the gum easily sliding off. Within two minutes, she removed the offending Topps by-product from his head. "Now, my good man, you're going to wash your hair with shampoo and get rid of that smell, then you're going to 100% remove that gum from your pillow. I'm going to take Lucky on his run.

"You better do a good job, Dario, because I'm going to check."

"I'm sorry I disobeyed you, Emma. I'll never do it again."

Emma entered the bathroom with her brother, scrubbing her hands with soap before heading out front to the outside securing Lucky in a harness.

I said I was sorry, and if I never chew gum in bed again, I guess I can keep my cards. I'll give Norman a bunch of my commons. He'll like that.

———

He brought his cards to school, placing them safely in the pocket of his binder, preventing any chance of them creasing. He decided not to let on to any of his friends, his Mantle, McCovey, or Mathews. Looking at them alone in the church was enough.

Dario finished his lunch quickly, choosing to carry his binder for a "religious" visit to the iconic large statue of Mary located on the front left of the church facing the altar. He fingered the packs and drew them out of his binder. "Hail Mary, full of grace..." He closed his eyes, envisioning the Jewish leader of the Los Angeles Dodgers. "...us sinners, now and at the hour of our death. Amen."

Slowly, he unwrapped one of the four packs left from last night. He looked up at the statue when Tien appeared before him. "You remember me, don't you, Dario."

"You were at my house visiting my sisters."

"Wow, what a great memory. I see you're beginning to open your packs of baseball cards."

"I got one opened already."

"Now, don't let me hold you back; go ahead and sift through it."

Ready to delve into the cards, a voice was heard from behind. "Who are you talking to, Dario? You know we got a basketball game against Room 9. Come on before we run out of lunchtime recess."

Lonnie Price, his Room 10 pal, walked up and glanced down. "Shit! You got a Koufax! You got a Koufax, Dario!"

Dario broke out with a huge grin. "It's a miracle, Lonnie, an honest-to-gosh miracle."

"Look through the rest of the pack!" Sure enough, a Willie Mays popped up. "Shitcahoona! Dario, what a pack! You said a prayer like Mrs. Holmes told you last year, didn't you?"

"Yeah, I did; I said a prayer, Lonnie!"

"Well, let's get out and tell the boys. You're one lucky kid."

Dario placed his cards and remaining packs back in his binder and left the church with his old friend, asking Lonnie not to tell anyone until after school.

"I liked that, Dario, not so much your foolish baseball cards but your friend's obscenities, although I couldn't quite make out 'shitcahoona." Tien laughed anyway.

———————

Tien moved quickly to the lunchroom of St. Anthony High School, where she found Mia and Ted sitting, once again, in the cafeteria. "Hello, Miss Sacatti. I'm so pleased to see you again. Who's your friend?"

Mia, not extensively happy to see her suspicious angel, half-smiled and said, "This is Ted Accenti, one of the school's top basketball players."

"Top player, oh my. My name is Tien Anh a close friend of Mia. I'm glad to meet you. How's your sister, Mia?"

"She's fine, Miss Anh."

"Oh, call me Tien and you too, Ted. I hope Emma's spiritual calling to the noviciate is still in place. As you know, not too many girls are choosing a religious life nowadays. What a blessing that girl demonstrates day to day. And you two! What a delightful couple, like two peas in a pod meant for each other. Well, I have to go. I'm so happy I met you, Ted, and I'll see you soon, Mia." Tien winked as she exited the cafeteria.

In an instant, unprovoked, Mia grabbed Ted by the side of the head and delivered a deep kiss, one most likely not accepted by the school's administration.

Eewws and ahhs immediately surfaced, especially when Ted returned the kiss. "I love you too, Mia!" he said loud enough for students to hear them throughout the entire lunch area.

"Alright, you two lovebirds to my office now!" shouted Vice Principal Judy Wilcox.

Inside her office, Mrs. Wilcox asked the two to sit down. "I don't have to tell you that public displays of affection are forbidden, at least when you carry it to that extent. Both of you need to control yourself. Mia and Ted, I'm surprised you went too far. What's got into you!"

Tears poured from Mia's eyes. "I don't know. I wish I knew," she said as she dabbed her eyes.

Ted, more composed, told the V.P., "We were working on an apology for...well, we wanted to apologize to Emma when this woman walked up to us..."

"What woman?" asked Vice Principal Judy Wilcox.

"Her name is Tien Anh," said Mia. "She's nothing but trouble. She shows up, and a few minutes later, after she leaves, we're in trouble."

"What are you trying to tell me? She made you do it!"

"Yes!" Mia blurted out what looked to both of the two as the truth so fast it appeared to floor Mrs. Wilcox.

"You're saying...what was her name?"

"Tien, Tien Anh. She comes out of nowhere and makes positive promises. She's a liar, Mrs. Wilcox, a terrible liar."

"So she lied to you, and you two decide to embrace and kiss foolishly."

"That was never my intention, ma'am. That woman possesses some kind of control over people," said Ted.

"You saw her, didn't you, Mrs. Wilcox?" added Mia.

"Honestly, I didn't see any adult inside that cafeteria. And Ted, you should be doubly ashamed of yourself. I thought you and Emma were boyfriend and girlfriend. Now this!"

"I was told she found a calling to the religious life. That's why she kept putting off dating me."

"What! You give Emma and Mia a ride home every day. You're telling me she won't date you?"

Mia said, "She won't date him. She made up a rule saying she wasn't allowed to date until she turned sixteen. My mother and father idolize Ted and they wouldn't find any problem with my sister going to dinner or even an occasional movie or canteen dance with him.

"Emma told me three years ago she had a calling to the convent. As you know, she's very devout. But Mrs. Wilcox, what she told me last night, seemed to change all that. It's why we were set to apologize."

"Apologize for what? For what you did? I don't understand. Listen, both of you are good students and involved in activities. You go about your apologizing and stay away from each other in the cafeteria. Now go!"

Placing his binder on a stairway away from basketball play Lonnie swore to his friend not to give away the miracle occurring inside the church. Koufax and Mays summed up the answer to Dario's heartfelt prayer. *And to think I got three more packs!*

Room nine played a hard three-on-three game. Two of their players starred on the football team. Sweat poured from the boys' faces, their shirts beginning to soak through their armpits. The score tied at 8-8, each basket counting as one point, Dario made the winning shot as the bell rang.

Dario picked up his loose-leaf folder, walked into his classroom, placed his binder on his desk, and was immediately told by Mrs. Hamilton to head to the boys' restroom to wash up. Lonnie Price and David Edwards, equally dripping with sweat, were ignored.

After taking off his shirt and wiping down, he returned to Room 10, sitting and fidgeting with his binder before opening it up. He noticed only his pencil holder and binder paper. Dario flipped the loose leaf folder around, then around again before shouting, "GODDAMN IT!"

His entire class turned around to face him. Mrs. Hamilton stood rigid, her hands on her hips, her lips pressed straight. A moment later, she said, "Mary Ellen, will you march this young man to the principal's office? Shouting God's name in vain, Dario is one of Our Lord's most grievous sins. Now get up and go!"

The boy picked up his binder and headed to the door, Mary Ellen leading the way. Reaching the office, he was told to sit until Mother Killian was available after school. An eighth-grade teacher, as well as the school's principal Dario's wait surpassed two hours.

Sitting uncomfortably in the wooden chair he moped, next planning murderous activities against the thief. He concluded it couldn't have been Lonnie, his friend was playing the basketball game with Dario the entire time.

But what if Lonnie mentioned the cards to another student, promising to split them up after school? But he knew he kept a constant eye on the binder. No one came near it, not during his entire game. The thief would have to possess lightning speed. Impossible, he thought. He looked again through his binder, practically tearing it apart.

"What are you doing, Dario?" asked the assistant secretary, Mrs. Lois McGuire. "Are you so upset you're willing to destroy a perfectly good binder? Now stop it, or I'll call your mother."

Did the cards and packs fall out? His mind raced. How? *I wouldn't put those packs and cards in my binder if I knew they would fall out. They were zippered in and attached to my three rings. Whoever stole my Topps would have to click open the binder and then pull out the pouch. And that pouch was hidden in the middle between all the binder paper.* Frustrated tears formed in Dario's eyes, finally dripping down his cheeks. His hands began to tremble, and he turned pale.

Lois looked up and rushed to the boy's side. "Are you okay, Dario? What happened to you?"

At the same time, Sister Bridget walked into the office after school to check the mail. "Why are you crying, Dario?"

"He was sent here for saying the GD word in class. Mrs. Hamilton wanted him to wait for the principal."

"Mother Killian is busy today. Father Gibson wanted to talk to her in the rectory after school. Dario, walk into the principal's office; I'll be right with you."

"No mail today, Lois?"

"He hasn't arrived yet. He must be a substitute today."

Sister Bridget turned and walked into the office. "What's troubling you Dario, and your hands are shaking."

"I'm crying because I'm mad."

"That's why you said Goddamn in class?"

"Yes, but I wasn't thinking when I said it because I know saying God's name wrong is bad. I did everything Mrs. Holmes taught me, and then some rotten kid stole my cards."

"I don't quite understand you, Dario. Calm down, then start over."

"Last night, I said a real good Hail Mary and got a McCovey, Eddie Mathews, and most of all a Mickey Mantle. So, I decided not to open my other packs and open them in church. I figured saying a Hail Mary in front of the statue of Mary would work, and it did.

I got a Sandy Koufax, and my friend Lonnie Price saw it. Now, someone stole my cards and my three unopened packs. Those cards are really hard to get."

"Do you have any idea who might have taken them?"

"At first, I thought it was Lonnie because he was the only one who knew I had them. But it couldn't have been him; he was with me the whole time playing basketball."

"Did you leave your cards lying around on the playground? That's one way a thief could take them."

"I put them in a zipper folder in my binder and kept my eye on it the whole time I was playing."

"Well, I'll talk to Miss Hamilton and let her know you were upset. Dario, say a prayer to St. Anthony; he's the patron saint of lost things. A prayer to him might ease your mind. I'll see your teacher right after school."

She dismissed the boy, sending him home with the primary-level students whose mothers lined up their cars to take them home. Dario walked with his head down, not so much thinking of how he might pray to the man who found things but more to the boy he'd sock in the nose when he found who stole his cards.

Tien Anh smiled, reading his thoughts.

Cindy Marquez's twin brother Carlos claimed he slipped on soap in the shower room, hitting his head on the tile floor. Evidence of any soap could not be located. What faced the U.S.C. team was losing a starting freshman offensive guard on a winning John McKay team, ready to face the powerful Notre Dame Fighting Irish.

Dorothy Marquez hovered over her son in the hospital, watching her husband and daughter Cindy help care for the boy diagnosed with a severe concussion. Out for the season and losing a year of eligibility, Carlos wasn't released from the hospital until three hours after he watched Notre

Dame's defense crush S.C.'s offensive line beating them in Indiana 28-7.

Five years of tackle football and never a major injury. What happened, a fall in the shower? Slipping on mysterious soap that no one could find. What was going on? Dorothy thought about Emma's and Mia's suspicions. It was time for the spiritual entity, Dorothy Marquez, to seek help.

"I'm happy to see you three together; thank you for relaying the message, Mia. Helixa is back with Donovan they'll be taking my place on Monday. I purchased a large two-story house near Ocean Ave. with four bedrooms and two baths. Riona and Hannah, Helixa and Donovan's mothers came with them. A fourth important divine being tagged along. He goes by the name Ben and was Donovan's angel up until Texas hung Fisk.

Ben is an angel and may have some important information. I want you three to visit the house on Saturday, and he'll fill you in. Ben is a good man, and Donovan and Helixa will tell you he resided with them in their humble home in heaven."

"Is he a true angel, Dorothy?"

"In fact, he is. Ben is Donovan Fisk's former guardian angel and still seeing after Mr. Fisk whether the former Texan resides in heaven or on earth."

"That's good to know your power on earth only extends to humans, not to....well, you know what I mean."

"I do, and that's one reason why you two sisters should meet him and the other four."

"Okay, we'll do that," said Emma. "What time?"

"Before 9:00 a.m. Donovan wants to go to the beach with Ben. Mia, your baby Rosie, if you want to bring her along."

"Mrs. Marquez, I'm sorry to hear about Carlos." Mia walked over and embraced her biology teacher.

"Thank you, sweetheart. Giving up this job will help me focus more on my own children. I could have caught my son before he fell."

———————

Ted pulled his Ford up to the given address at 8:30 a.m. Dorothy waited out front in one of five rockers, moving back and forth on her exquisite wrap-a-round porch.

At a cost of $45,000.00, Dorothy held the mortgage, easily dropping fifty percent of the down payment on the exclusive house in an A+ neighborhood. Controlling equally A+ stocks, Dorothy stayed financially in the black and ahead in predicting what companies excelled forward and what companies she knew to avoid.

Emma's eyes went wide when she noticed two middle-aged men lounging in identical rockers wearing nothing more than what most 'hip' Californians referred to as tourist tidies. "Donovan? Is that you!"

"Yes, it is Miss Emma, and this is my friend Ben."

Ben stood shuffling over to Emma, Mia, and Ted, his hand graciously extended. The three of them noticed his belly covered half of his skimpy cotton yet publicly legal underwear. "You two plan on crossing the street dressed, or should I correct myself and say 'undressed?'"

Dorothy stood and let her friends know you could take Donovan out of Texas, but he would always remain an unsophisticated hick. Donovan saw those embarrassing bathing suits in a fashion magazine and swore he wanted the same. Ben, always on Donovan's side, agreed. Now they risk being arrested for indecent exposure."

"I don't think they're illegal, Dorothy, and why isn't he the handsome, debonair young man the students adored in the classroom."

"Oh, he knows he'll have to change before walking into school, maybe one of you could get him to change right now, him and Ben."

Mia spoke up, "Donovan, you look like a fool. Don't be stupid; people will laugh at you, and you'll never gain any respect. Put on surfer shorts; there acceptable."

"What are surfer shorts?"

"They're longer and hip and go back to what you looked like when you taught. A few girls might notice you on the beach and introduce you to their older sisters."

Donovan, for earlier explanations, wasn't swayed by catching the eye of a few young girls. He did, however, seem to find a bit of interest in 'surfer' wear. Donovan asked, however, what did 'surfer ' mean.

"It's a boy or a girl who balances themselves on the top of a wooden or foam board and rides the waves," explained Ted.

"Could you show Ben and I," asked Donovan.

"Sure, how about after school next week? Seal Beach has better waves especially inside the wedge. I'll show you."

"Could you take us today? I can't drive your cars, and I don't think Helixa will let me go when I'm working."

"Sure, no problem. Emma and Mia, however, wanted to ask you and Ben a few questions."

"Then come inside and meet my mother, Hannah, and

Helixa's mother, Riona. I don't think you've seen Helixa in a while. She's busy in the kitchen with our mothers."

He and Ben led the three young students inside the 3200 square foot home, massively larger than what a simple man such as Donovan thought of as an adequate resident.

Coffee on the morning stove permeated the nose of the young trio. A hint of apple fritters from the oven also greeted Mia, Ted, and Emma.

Helixa walked out of the kitchen and threw her arms around her former students. "I missed you so much! Please sit down. You sit too, Donovan and Ben. You thee youngsters, I want to introduce you to Riona and Hannah, two of God's most beautiful ladies."

She called out, and two middle-aged women dressed in full linen ankle-length skirts exited the kitchen with Hannah carrying a tray of coffee cups and Riona handling a kitchen towel wrapped around the handle of a large pot of coffee. Hannah, relatively shy, and Riona, full of spirit, were both happy to serve the young visitors.

"Our daughter and son, now two teachers! What a blessing," said Riona, pouring three cups of coffee while Helixa entered the parlor with a tray of warm fritters.

"Now relax, and I want you to enjoy what people ate for dessert in the nineteenth century. The coffees from a can bought at your grocery store," said Helixa.

Ted took a deep bite, hungry after missing breakfast. Donovan spoke up, "Let them talk now, Helixa; Ted's taking Ben and me to a beach with big waves."

Emma spoke up, looking over at Helixa, Donovan, and Ben. "Have any of you ever heard of Tien Anh? She tells us she's an angel."

Not one of the three ever heard of Tien. "We're sorry, Emma, we couldn't help you three."

"Can an angel shape change from an angel to another angel."

"Sure!" answered Donovan, "I'll be doing that when I walk into the classroom, and I'm not even an angel."

"Have you ever heard of Lilith?" asked Mia.

"Lilith! Yes, sure, she's what we refer to as a demon," said Ben. "A weaker demon easily handled by me or any angel."

"Should I ask Tien if she's Lilith?" Emma, now intrigued by the suspicious nature of Tien Anh, wanted to know more.

"You won't have to," said Ben, "I'll know her. Does she visit often?"

"At ill opportune periods. Tien promises us our lives will experience pleasant times, then we run into calamities. Odd earthquakes, an unknown plague..."

"And my son slipping on nothing in the shower hitting his head on the tile. Carlos suffered a severe concussion and was hospitalized. Whomever Tien is, she's toying with us."

Ben suggested, "Send her to your classroom and let her know you're upset with Carlos's injury. I'll be there as a student in your room."

"But remember, Helixa is taking my position on Monday. Ben, if this is Lilith or God forbid Lamia, both of them despise Helixa and would be glad to see her in hell."

"Good, I'll be waiting for Lilith," said Ben.

"What if it's Lamia?" asked Dorothy.

"Never heard of her. However she may be stronger than Lilith but still not a problem for me. Neither one of them has any business disturbing you folks."

Chapter Thirty-Two

Mr. Ben Fisk

Good morning, Dario. Why the sad face?" asked Tien, a sardonic sneer streaking across her face. *"No luck praying to your lost and found friend."*

"No luck, Miss Tien. I can't understand. I was told if I asked St. Anthony, he'd find my cards. I don't even care about the packs; I just want my Koufax and Willie Mays back. Even my Eddie Mathews were all stolen from my binder."

Tien stood in the back of the classroom, standing near the window next to Lonnie Price. *"Let me stand in front of you; your teacher is ogling you."*

"Mr. Sacatti, what do you find so interesting staring out that window? Tell me what I was presently talking about."

Dario looked up at Tien, hoping for an answer found she did nothing but grin. *"No answer, huh? I think you might be in trouble."*

"Good morning, Tien; it's so nice to see you here. Here to calm down, Dario? Someone stole his baseball cards yesterday."

"Hello Dorothy, I'm pleased to see you too. The poor boy is in a jam. He wasn't listening to his teacher."

He was listening to you. "Dario, tell Mrs. Hamilton that in order to add unlike fractions, you have to find a common denominator."

Dario repeated the advice. Mrs. Hamilton found that Dario was nothing more than lucky and chose to ignore it until she was ordered to bring up to the class minutes before lunch the baseball theft of Friday.

"I'm impressed, Dorothy, you are perceptive."

"I'm so glad you're here. I removed myself from my job because of my son. Helixa took over and is back. She told me she's afraid and wanted your help...remember Lilith or Lamia and her run-on with them."

"I'll move over to the high school when I'm finished with Dario's teacher. She's an old grump. Why don't you let her know I'll be there in ten minutes? I'll see you there."

"Thank you, Tien. I'll let Helixa know you're on your way. Donovan will be there too; he's assisting her again."

"Donovan, too, huh?"

Dorothy said goodbye to Dario as he stood with the class and said his prayers before meals. Afterward the students were told to sit again while she went over what Sister Bridget asked Mrs. Hamilton to do.

"Friday, someone stole Dario's baseball cards. He was so upset he took God's name in vain. Dario, tonight you will write 100 times, I WILL NOT TAKE GOD'S NAME IN VAIN. It's the least you could do.

"Now, if anyone stole those cards, I'm going to let you return them to my desk today or tomorrow, and I won't say a word. Stealing is against God's seventh commandment, although I'm relatively positive baseball cards don't count as stealing, so..."

Lonnie Price shouted out, "And there were three full packs of cards too."

"Lonnie, if I wanted to hear from you, I would have asked you to speak, so shut up." A few of the students froze.

"Get ready to line up for lunch. Girls will go first. You boys stay seated until the last girl leaves the room."

A few seconds later, the boys stood and rushed to the door, the larger students winning the sprint.

Tired of their nonsense, she shooed them down the hall as Hamilton closed the door and joined the lay teachers in the lunchroom.

Alone in Room 10, Tien flashed her magic, and lying on the teacher's desk was the zippered pouch containing Koufax, Mantle, Mathews, and Willie McCovey, plus three unopened packs of 1963 Topps baseball cards.

Twenty minutes later, Mrs. Hamilton walked the corridor back to her classroom accompanied by Sister Bridget. "Dario appeared stressed, Abigail. I hope he gets over the loss."

Hamilton said, "He'll forget about it and hopefully focus more on his studies."

"Isn't he doing well?" asked Sister Bridget.

"He could do better, as well as his friends."

Unlocking the door to her classroom, she sauntered over to her desk, her eyes bulging at what she found sitting in the center of her teacher's table top. Hamilton turned and ran to her open door, "Sister Bridget, please come back!" hollered Abigail.

Bridget turned, alarmed why Mrs. Hamilton would be so excited.

"The cards, the cards are here lying on my desk!"

"Well, isn't that good news? Why are you so upset."

"I locked my door; how did they get in here so fast? Only Mr. Roman, our custodian, has a key to every classroom. Do you think he stole those cards!"

"Shh, soothe yourself, Abigail. How would Frank know you wanted them back on your desk? And I know he comes to the convent and eats lunch with us every day. He's there now."

"Do you think someone hid in the closet?"

"I doubt it, but let me check."

Sister Bridget walked back to the closet and opened every door. No one appeared in the classroom.

"Sister Bridget, maybe he left. I'm scared."

"Don't be frightened, Mrs. Hamilton. Are you going to give the cards back to Dario?"

"Back to Dario? Well, yes, after he turns in his assignment tomorrow, one hundred standards on, I WILL NOT TAKE GOD'S NAME IN VAIN."

"Good idea. Dario will learn a lesson from that. What are you going to do with the cards?"

"I'll place it in my attache case and lock it. Tomorrow after school he'll walk home a happy boy, although I want him to sweat it throughout the day."

"Good thinking. Well, you have a good rest of the day, Abigail." Sister Bridget left the room and headed toward her eighth-grade classroom.

You're frightened, ABIGAIL! Tien threw her head back and laughed. *It looks like there's more in store for you and that little shit Dario Sacatti.*

"Hello, Miss Crowfoot, and I see Mr. Fisk. How are you, sir?"

"We're both fine, Tien."

"Did Mrs. Marquez tell you about her son Carlos? That's why Donovan and I are here."

"Where is Dorothy? We were supposed to meet here."

"Her son had a seizure and is back in the hospital. Dorothy is devastated."

Carlos, a seizure? This is better than I expected.

"My heart goes out to her. My goodness, back in the hospital. Which one? I'll need to visit the poor boy and offer condolences to Dorothy."

"Dorothy didn't say. It's why Donovan and I are afraid. We were happy to come back and assist her, but what happened to Carlos? We feel Lilith is still active, and only you could stop her."

"Why aren't you helping Tien? You're getting lazy!" shouted Donovan, disturbing the lone student sitting in the front row.

366

"Mr. Fisk, accidents happen, and since you want to include this kid, you can't blame me for any unfortunate disturbance with the Marquez boy or the Sacattis'.

"And who is this kid anyway? Did he miss a homework assignment?" pointing to the lone student in the room.

Ben, disguised as a fifteen-year-old kid, stood up and turned to the veiled Tien Anh, walking toward and creating apprehension in the surprised pseudo-angel.

"I've heard enough even with my back to you, young lady. I know who you are. Helixa, this is Lilith, a weak demon."

"I am no such thing as what you call a demon. My name is Tien Anh, an angel…"

"Enough! Lilith, you don't know what you're talking about.? Who's your friend using you to create havoc in this city and against the Marquez and Sacatti families."

Tien smiled, "Why? What are you going to do with me? Are you a friend of these two losers?"

"I'm sending you to hell for good. You don't tell me who you're working with, and I'll find her anyway."

"Who are you?" Tien said, backing away from 'the kid.'

She disappeared from the room Ben never moving from where he stood. "I summoned two angels to carry her to hell forever. She'll no longer trouble you two or anyone else. What I'm concerned with is what entity also exists. Lilith is too weak to carry out her evil conduct. She'll let her know I'm looking for her. She won't know who to look for, however, Helixa and Donovan, I never revealed myself."

"Ben, Donovan, and I are back with our mothers. Perhaps we need to go back and take Dorothy with us. I'm afraid of this demon, Lamia. She's too powerful, and I can't think of anyone who could defeat her but you," said Helixa.

Emma walked into the room, overhearing Crowfoot.

"Ben, Lamia never exited. Tien invented her.

Donovan spoke up, "Wasn't it you, Emma, who sent Lamia away from the school into the ocean."

"No, that was Lilith," replied Emma.

"Emma, you did that! A human sent Lilith flying into the ocean. You must have a rare influence over other angels." Ben looked impressed.

Dorothy now appeared after talking with Emma, Ted, and Mia in the cafeteria."She mentioned that to me. Emma never took any credit for what she did. She said it was her angels that interceded for her. And come to think of it, Mia, her sister, seemed to find she possessed the same gift."

"Both of them with a set of angels guiding them; I rarely come across two individuals much less sisters with such powerful gifts. If Lilith was sent to the ocean by angels, that's where she resided. May I ask what ocean?"

"Right outside our window, although Donovan and I did see Lamia in church one night hovering in the back. That's when Tien (Lilith) drove her out of the church."

"A ruse! Lamia was never there. Tien put on a show fooling both of you."

"Donovan, you and I will keep our eyes out for any repercussions. None of you should worry. I don't think anything will happen, and I'll protect you all."

"I don't know Ben. You didn't do me much good in Texas. I choked for five minutes until I was gone."

"Justice was served Donovan. You listen to those stagecoach robbers. You were foolish enough to carry out their dirty deeds and never listen to me. Look where it got you."

Emma brought up an idea, "Mr. Ben, have you ever given thought to teaching high school? Our administration has tried to hire a fully qualified chemistry teacher since

September, and all they found were multiple substitutes, all still attending school."

"Hmm? A chemistry teacher. I could more than handle that. My education far surpasses what you people refer to as an advanced education. What university do you think I attended?"

Helixa said, "How about Harvard? It's back East where I told my principal I wanted to move to until I decided to come back."

"Harvard? Nah, that's too stuffy. How about Yale in Connecticut."

"Yale's not stuffy?" said Dorothy. "You could always attend Princeton."

"Princeton, that's too prissy!" responded Ben. "Besides, I like Connecticut. It's a peaceful state. I'm not particularly fond of Massachusett and, even more so, New Jersey."

Emma, pleased to welcome Ben aboard on the teaching staff, wondered, "How long will it take you to produce a diploma? And in California, you'll need a high school teaching credential with Chemistry as your specialty."

"No wonder your school couldn't find anyone. To answer your question, Miss Sacatti, I have all the documents in my possession right now. I'll be happy to instruct students on the same campus as 'my brother' Donovan Fisk."

"So now you're brothers? Congratulations, Donovan," said Helixa.

"CONGRATULATIONS! He's the so-called brother who watched that Texas sheriff put a rope around my neck."

"It wasn't the sheriff Donovan; it was Paul Atmyer, the executioner."

"You hear him! Why can't Helixa be your sister and leave me alone." Donovan appeared livid.

"Because we've always been brothers. I cried when they hung you and stuck by your side afterward. You finally listened to Miss Crowfoot and, in effect, listened to me.

"By the way, where's the chemistry classroom? I want to check it out before your principal hires me."

"What makes you think she'll hire you," asked Donovan, still a little peeved."

"She'll hire me, little brother, because I attended YALE!"

"Your classroom butts up with this one, and your laboratory is behind your classroom," replied Miss Crowfoot. "Let me escort you to the principal's office after school. And Ben, I think it might be a good idea if you were my uncle. Schools would have a difficult time handling me living with you boys?"

In the days ahead, the school was delighted to hire such an excellent teacher. The students prized Mr. Ben Fisk, almost as handsome as his brother Donovan.

Instead of residing in the church, all three of the newly hired science teachers resided comfortably in their 3,200-square-foot home just off Ocean Avenue in Long Beach.

Emma and her family slept comfortably at home, with no unforeseen wickedness crossing their lives. And, according to reports from Harvey Way, Ted picked up Emma Sacatti on a Saturday evening and took her to see one of Long Beach's most talked about movies, THE SOUND OF MUSIC. He was wise enough to have her home 15 minutes after the film finished and long enough for Emma to plant a kiss on Accenti's lips.

xxxxxxxxxx

Emma's temperature dropped to 103 degrees, although her brain continued to sprint through her splintered skull. A touch streaming into Emma's head told her nothing would harm her.

"Sleep tight, my dear. Emma felt the comforting, reassuring hand of her mother on her shoulder, placing the eighth-grade student into a deeper REM sleep

xxxxxxxxxx

Good morning, Mrs. Hamilton. I finished my standards last night." Dario handed the teacher his I WON'T TAKE THE LORD'S NAME IN VAIN neatly printed as told.

"And did you complete your other homework?"

"Yes, ma'am."

"Good. You're going to have to wait until after school to see if anyone turned in your baseball cards."

"Yes, ma'am."

"Go outside now. I have work to do, and class doesn't start for another twenty minutes."

Dario walked outside, his shoulders sagging. *"Place the cards on my desk at lunch or after school, and I won't say a word."*

She never had any intention of getting those cards back. She locks the door at lunch and then locks it after school. How's anyone supposed to get in?

The poor boy felt like screaming out a few choice swear words, but he held back. Dario took Sister Bridget's idea and offered up a prayer to St. Anthony.

Hours dragged throughout the day when, at last, Dario faced his teacher again. "Listen, young man, when I give these cards back to you, you're going to promise never to bring them to school again. Do you completely understand me!"

"Yes, Mrs.Hamilton, I promise." His stomach did flips.

No trading was necessary with a Koufax and a Mantle; he was, to his knowledge, king of the collectors.

She opened her attache case and panicked. The cards were missing. *What! Where in the hell could they have gone?* "They're not here, Dario; I must have left them at home. I'll bring them here tomorrow. You go home now."

Sweat beaded down her forehead. *"I never took those damn cards out, and how did I ever get them anyway?"*

That evening, Mrs. Abigail Hamilton tore apart her apartment across the street from St. Cyprian's on Clark Avenue. Only a four-room home, she started in the bedroom, even lifting the mattress, and proceeded to the closet. Abigail realized none of it made sense but shifted to the small living room, looking over, under, and behind her couch before removing the cushions. The bathroom and kitchen weren't spared, and before she dozed off to bed, she realized the school had taken on a haunting, a mysterious ghost occupying room 10 and bent on driving the sixty-five-year-old widow insane.

I can't stay there! God forbid, whatever it is, it might follow me. What if it's here in my apartment? She bit her nails while kneeling to pray. "Angel of God, my..."

The following morning, in Abigail's room 10 classroom, after notifying the principal she needed to leave her school position next month for employment in another state, she stated, "My sister isn't doing well, and she wants me to move in with her." The excuse had some merit as Abbey, her sister, lived alone in Colorado and would welcome Abigail.

Mrs. Hamilton, in the meantime also came up with the idea of the children writing a scary Halloween story. *"That should appease whatever is spooking this room."*

"Children, tonight you will think of a Halloween story.

It is allowed to be scary, but don't overdo it, and absolutely no blood and guts. At least 100 words and no more than 200. Your paper is due Thursday morning."

Again, Dario braved another long day finally standing before his teacher. If he was going to take on declaring himself one of the King of Baseball Cards, he needed to practice a little humility first.

"Mrs. Hamilton?"

"What! What do you want, Dario?"

"You told me you'd bring my baseball cards today."

"Well, mister, I couldn't find your miserable cards. Now get out and leave me alone."

Dario left the classroom, tears crushing his eyes. Lonnie waited for him outside. "First, she tells me she left them at home, and then Mrs. Hamilton says she couldn't find them. I prayed so hard for those cards, and now they're gone. She's a witch, Lonnie, a damn witch."

"Are you swearing again?" asked Sister Bridget walking nearby.

He held his head down, expecting the nun would be compelled to punish him. "Lonnie, you head on home I need to talk with your friend.

"Tell me what happened, Dario, I'm listening."

"My teacher stole my cards. She said she had them, and so I waited for two days, then Mrs. Hamilton told me she couldn't find them and told me to leave her classroom."

"Dario, let me talk to Mrs. Hamilton. If I don't get anywhere, I'll talk to Emma, your sister."

Sister Bridget walked into Room 10 and listened to the whole story of Abigail Hamilton. "On my honor, I have no idea where those cards disappeared that's why I'm leaving. Confidentially, Sister, between you and I, this classroom is haunted."

"Let me go over this. You're not holding those cards to punish the boy?"

"How dare you! Of course not. I still have three days, so leave me alone."

Sister Bridget apologized and walked out of room 10, confident the veteran teacher told the truth.

Mrs. Abigail Hamilton, now alone, sat at her desk and sobbed, her hand covering her chin and mouth.

Chapter Thirty-Three

Ben Fisk, Seal Beach Wedge

Emma, Mia, and Ted found the new debonair Benjamin Fisk sitting in the biology room at lunchtime.

"Hello, Mr. Ben," said Emma.

" Well, hello back to you three. How are you doing?"

"Mr. Ben, I have a question for you, but first, I want you to know my brother Dario has been depressed for the last few days. Someone stole his prized baseball cards last week. Sister Bridget called my house and told me the whole story."

"What happened?" asked Ben.

Emma now had the attention of the three entities. "What Sister told me was unusual enough to get Dario's teacher to resign at the end of this week. She feels her classroom is haunted.

"Dario's baseball cards suddenly disappeared right under his nose. He carefully protected coveting them like they were gold, and then next, poof they were gone. By the end of the day, the baseball cards were lying on the teacher's desk, neatly arranged by Dario in a plastic zipped-up pouch.

"That in itself spooked the teacher. She always kept her door locked when she left her classroom. Then suddenly, out of nowhere she sees them placed on her desk. Without hesitating, Dario's teacher placed them safely in her attache case, which also contained a combination lock. At the end of the school day, she promised my brother the cards AFTER he wrote standards for taking the Lord's name in vain."

Emma went on to finish the story that spooked Dario's teacher, Abigail Hamilton, far enough to get her to quit at the end of the week and far enough for Dario to relapse into even more misery.

"That's quite a lengthy story, Emma. What's your question?" wondered Ben.

"I think Lilith haunted Mrs.Hamilton's classroom. Do you think she had anything to do with stealing those baseball cards?"

"It's possible. Sounds like another of Lilith's stupid tricks."

"Could you get them back?"

"Lilith should be in hell. I don't think it might be wise calling her back up."

"Poor Dario, Emma, and I have never seen him this way. Mr. Ben. He loved those baseball cards and even told us he said a prayer before opening a pack. Now he's offering up prayers to St. Anthony."

"Hmm, maybe Anthony is asking for my assistance. Who were on those cards?"

Emma perked up! "A '64 Koufax, Mantle, Mathews, McCovey and..."

Mia cried out, "And I think a Willie Mays!"

"What do they look like? Wait a minute, bring your brother here, and I'll read what's cooking upstairs."

"Could you come to our house? We don't think Dario could make it here during the week."

"Maybe not. Come to my house instead, near Ocean Avenue, tonight. I'll begin teaching on Monday and need to focus on the curriculum."

Both girls looked at Ted and he nodded approval. "What time, Mr. Ben?" asked Emma.

"Well, before it gets dark. I don't want any student living in the neighborhood misinterpreting why I would invite you two into my home. Bring Dario, and we'll meet on the porch."

Ted drove over to St. Cyprian's after school and asked to relieve the boy from basketball practice. Emma's boyfriend let her brother know there was a man, a sort of detective, who could help locate Dario's baseball cards. "He needs you to answer a few questions describing the cards stolen, including the three packs, zip holder, etc. Can you do that, buddy?"

"Yes, I'll do my best. Ted, do you like my sister?"

"I sure do. Emma's a swell girl, why?"

"Because I saw you two kiss on the front porch before she unlocked the front door."

"You peaked, huh? Well, let me tell you something, Sport, in a few years, you'll be doing the same thing."

"I don't think so; the girls in my class aren't as pretty as my sisters."

Ted pulled in front of the gymnasium and picked up the girls waiting in the front. A quick drive to Cerritos Ave. near Ocean found Ben and Donovan lounging on the front porch, this time dressed appropriately and looking much younger and refined.

"You must be Dario Sacatti," said Ben Fisk. "A bit down, I take it because of your lost baseball cards. I think I could be of service if you concentrate on me. Can you do that?"

"Yes, sir, I can do that."

"Okay, now tell me, what's the first card you'd like to

think of?"

"My Sandy Koufax, he plays for the Dodgers."

"Koufax, huh?" Alrighty, think of that card until you see him in your head."

"What's next?"

"Three more. Mickey Mantle of the Yankees, Eddie Mathews of the Braves, and Willie McCovey of the Giants."

Mia intervened, "How about Willie Mays?"

"I still have my Mays. I never took him to school."

"Alright, Dario. Let me go over this. Mantle, Mathews, and McCovey, am I correct?"

"Yes, Mr. Fisk, those are the players."

"Anything else?"

Emma joined in, "Ben, three packs of Topps cards were also stolen. Ted bought a pack on his way over here."

"That certainly helps," Ben said, eyeballing the pack of cards. "Okay, my young man, I found your missing cards."

A chorus of "SO FAST!" went out at the same time.

"There lying safe inside a briefcase, all four cards and your three packs. A pouch of some kind is holding it."

"It's got to be in my teacher's OUT OF SHAPE case," said Dario.

"OUT OF SHAPE case. I don't understand," responded Ben.

"He's referring to her attache case," said Emma.

"Attache case. Oh! I get it. Yes, attache case is another word for briefcase. You bet, young man, those cards are in her OUT OF SHAPE case."

"But she said they weren't there!" said Dario, worried her teacher was keeping them hidden.

"Not anymore, Dario. A woman by the name of Lilith kept them hidden from your teacher. They're back now; you need to know no more.

"What's Lilith doing here?"

"Now, Ted, are we headed to the Seal Beach wedge on Saturday? I'm ready."

"You're going to need a surfboard first. You can use mine until the stores open the shops at 9:00 a.m.," replied Ted.

"So I take it you're picking me up at 6:00 a.m.."

"Yep, at the crack of dawn."

"Oh my goodness, that early!" exclaimed Emma. "I'm barely even up that early on Saturday. Why at the crack of dawn?"

"It's when the surf is at its best, and besides, there are no crowds, just surfers."

"Why do they call it a wedge," asked Dario.

"It's called that because the wave hits a jetty or a breakwater, and the wave doubles in size."

Mia asked, "Won't the water be freezing?"

"I'll let Ben wear my wetsuit," said Ted.

"I won't need it. Give it to Donovan."

"Ted, I didn't know you surfed," wondered Emma.

"I did every summer until I worked with you last June."

Mia continued, "I've seen that wedge, Ben; it might be too dangerous for you."

"No, not for me; remember, my skills are angelic. It's Donovan I'll have to protect. He's an amateur."

Ted said, "Speaking of that, Ben, we could always surf the soup at Bolsa Chica."

"Where's Bolsa Chica, and what is 'the soup.'"

"Bolsa Chica people usually call tin can beach because of the litter, and the soup are small waves no more than two to three feet high."

"Not for me. I want the biggest and most dangerous waves, and besides, I'll protect Donovan."

"Yeah, like you did in Texas!" clamored his friend.

"So Saturday! We'll be up and waiting on the porch," said Ben.

"Let me join you; I'll run along the shore," Emma said.

On Thursday morning, a nerve-racked teacher called in Dario Sacatti before school started. "Listen, young man, your baseball cards were found in my attache case. I'm going to give them to you with the promise you won't take that binder of yours out of your hands for the entire day. And you won't be allowed to show them to your friends, and you won't play basketball today; you'll hold that binder with your life. Do you understand!"

"Yes, Mrs. Hamilton, I understand, and I promise."

Mrs. Abigail Hamilton handed him the pouch, the cards and packs resting in perfect shape. His hand shook as he placed the cards in his binder. Dario's heart palpitated. If not so young and in perfect condition, he may have flopped over unconscious.

Thank you, St. Anthony, thank you! You're the best! One more gift of thanks flooded his mind. "Thank you, Mrs. Hamilton, you're a real nice teacher."

"Okay, fine, just keep your collection to yourself until after school. Now, line up with the rest of your class outside."

Dario kept the recovery of his baseball cards to himself, not drawing any unwanted attention as he held his binder tight against his chest. By afterschool, he revealed to his friend Lonnie what his binder actually contained. "I knew it!" said Lonnie Price. "You got them all, what we saw in church?"

"All of them. Let's head to Sister Bridget's room; she wants to know." Off to the upper-grade classrooms located on the north side of the school, the 4th-grade students ran to room 14.

Dario stood outside Sister Bridget's classroom until she was finished reviewing any problems with tonight's homework with a handful of her students. Finished, she looked to her left, "Dario, I see you're waiting. Come on in. What do you have in your binder pressed up against your chest."

He smiled, his grin lighting up the classroom. "Don't tell me. Did Mrs. Hamilton locate your Koufax and friends?"

Choked up, he only nodded a 'YES!'

"Well, that's wonderful, my young man. And Lonnie, what do you think of that?"

"I'm glad, but I don't think any person stole them. I think something strange happened; it's Halloween time."

"We won't spread that kind of news, Lonnie. I'm sure there's a more sensible explanation."

"Not with our teacher she's looked different. She won't stay very long in her classroom unless kids are there."

Dario found his voice, "We were asked to write a Halloween story but not too scary. I'm going to write one tonight and make you and my teacher stars in the story."

"Oh my, me a star! Well, like your sisters, I take it you possess a terrific imagination. Keep it mild, my good student."

"I will. There will be no blood and guts because Mrs. Hamilton won't allow that, and she's a good teacher."

"That's good to hear. Would you care to show me the cards you prayerfully earned?"

Dario did so as Lonnie looked on, still astounded by the incredible find.

"I have to call Dr.Sloane now I found my Koufax."

That night, Dario broadly changed his opinion of Abigail Hamilton. "She never tried to trick me; she only hoped I would learn a lesson, and I did."

Mia, Emma, and Palmira smiled while Eugenio was more interested in a second helping of his wife's rigatoni with Italian sausage.

"I'm going to write a Halloween story and make my teacher and Sister Bridget famous. I already wrote it in my head."

"Get started early, Dario; what's in your head may not translate on paper," suggested Emma.

The story in his head was translated word for word on paper. Dario decided to spend the rest of the evening placing his most valuable cards into heavy plastic shields. "Not one bent and almost perfect centering."

Before he knelt for nighttime prayers, his sister, Emma, suggested he reread his story and erase any grammatical or spelling errors. He lay down and began reading:

A True Story
By Dario Sacatti

Every year, the whole school at St. Cyprian's School on Arbor Rd. was asked to go to church and pray for the repost of souls of people who died. It was Halloween time, and this wasn't just a time for trick or treating. Some of the kids only cared about candy, so the teachers made us pray, especially for our relatives and important people like President Kennedy. So we bowed our heads and let the eighth-grade girl lead us in prayers that most of us already knew. Without a warning, the statues began to float in the church. Before we knew it, my teacher, Mrs. Jones, floated to the ceiling and couldn't get down. The girls screamed, but not the boys, who looked around proplexed. Before there was a riot Sister Mary raised her hands and said, "Statues back to where you were and be still." She looked up and said, "Mrs. Jones, come down!" and my teacher fell on the floor with a plop. But she wasn't hurt. That night, the girls were too scared to go trick or treating at night, but not the boys; they went trick or treating and got a lot of candy.

THE END

Following early morning on Thursday, Dario handed in what he thought of as a literary gem. "She's going to love this, but I hope she's not too scared because I put A TRUE STORY."

He waited to share the story with his friend Lonnie Price and equal baseball card legend David Edwards.

"What's it about?" asked Lonnie.

"I'm not going to say until Miss Hamilton lets the top boy and girl read them out loud to the class. She's gotta pick me, and no one helped. I wouldn't even let my sisters see it."

———————

He sat in the high school cafeteria at lunchtime, wondering if she would accept his invitation to see THE SOUND OF MUSIC on Saturday evening. A musical leaning toward the feminine gender, she was sure to want to see it.

It didn't seem fair that after almost a full year, he'd be filled with apprehension, wondering if she would turn him down. If Emma had never existed and only Mia represented the young female side of the Sacatti family, she would gladly tell him she'd go, only knowing the junior teen for two months.

But she presently noticed Mia sitting off to Ted's far left, engrossed in conversation with new Loyola basketball transfer Scott Baio.

"Why are you so quiet, Ted? Did the cat catch your tongue?" asked Emma, inexplicably reaching out and taking his hand.

She's touching me all on her own. Has she changed? "I was wondering if you might want to see that new Julie

Andrews movie Saturday night. I know we just went last Satur..."

"I loved to Mr. Accenti, and let me get the tickets."

"You really will go? That's terrific. I couldn't let you pay for the tickets; it's not how I was brought up."

"Okay, then I'll buy a popcorn and a drink, and we'll share it!" Emma poked a glance over at her sister.

Ted felt relieved he might have been off kilter. She was changing. First, a dinner, a movie, and now another film at the Crest Theater.

"Ted, do you know who my sister is talking to? I've never seen him on campus."

"He just arrived and is already getting comfy, I see. That's Scott Baio, our newest 6'3" basketball player. A transfer from Loyola of Los Angeles. His family just moved into Long Beach, so he's basketball-eligible.

"Scott's got a huge set of hands and can grip a basketball. He dunked on us last year, fast-breaking down an open court. He, to put it plainly, can leap.

"I understand his father is a radiologist and took a job over at Long Beach Memorial. Scott lives off 1st Street in Belmont Shores. His father probably makes good money."

"He's looking over at us and waving. Should we get up?" wondered Emma.

"Yeah, why not practice starts on Monday so I might as well get to know him better."

"Hello, Scott and Mia. Scott, this is Mia's sister, Emma, and an equally terrific basketball player."

"So I heard. Two beautiful sisters. I certainly wound up at the right school."

"We're lucky to land you here at St. Anthony. All first team conference as a sophomore guard, I had a heck of a time trying to guard you."

"How about you, Ted? First-team sophomore guard you played like a pro. Your jump shot duplicated Jerry West of the Lakers. I hope we can team up on the floor. I understand your partner guard is still here."

"Alex Bradley, he was picked as an honorable mention and showed up this summer to enhance his skills. We teamed up with our center and three of the girls, including Emma, here. Coach stayed away as C.I.F. rules forbid official summer practice."

"So he's even better. Is there room for a forward?"

"The way you leap! We're going to go far, Scott."

Scott Baio

Chapter Thirty-Four
Mary Ellen Schivonie-4th Grade

Fame would have to wait as Dario settled into a long, dragged-out Friday only rescued before lunch with the announcement from Abigail Hamilton that today would be her last day. A few of the girls moaned while the rest of the female students kept their calm. The boys imploded mucus creeping down their noses as they furtively applauded their teacher's revealing message.

Dario picked at his lunch, waiting for his afternoon class. Finally, the bell sounded and the students in orderly boy/girl lines walked into Mrs. Hamilton's final afternoon in the 'haunted' room 10 classroom.

"Students, your Halloween stories were imaginative, and I'm pleased more than a few A+ papers were earned. I, however would like to call up Dario Sacatti first."

He stood up proud. *An A+ waits until I show it to my family. Maybe our school newspaper might like it.*

Abigail Hamilton picked up Dario's paper from the pile neatly stacked on her desk, wadded it up and threw it to the floor. "SACRILEGE! Now pick it up and take it to the office. Mary Ellen, follow him. I don't want to see him in my room ever again!"

Dario and his classmate walked down the hallway while Mary Ellen shared her feelings. "Dario, I wasn't one of the girls who moaned. I don't think she ever treated most of the boys with respect. Do you think I could read your story before we reach the office?"

Dario stopped and handed the wadded-up paper to the girl he suddenly found attractive. Perusing the neatly written Halloween story, she looked up and said, "You sure do have an imagination, and I want you to know I like it." She finished with a kiss on his cheek.

He floated the short distance to the principal's office.

"Mr. Sacatti, you're back," said Lois McGuire, St. Cyprian's assistant secretary. "I just received a call from Mrs. Hamilton. What did you do this time?"

"He wrote a sacrilege," said Mary Ellen Schivonie.

"Do either of you even know what a sacrilege is?"

Both 4th graders nodded no they had no idea what blaspheming the Lord might be.

"Is that the paper in your hand, Dario? Let me take a look at it. You say here the word repost, the real word in context is repose, the repose of souls with an 'e' at the end instead of a 't.'"

McGuire read on, holding back a snicker as she moved down the story. "You have another error, Mr. Sacatti. You wrote 'proplexed' you meant perplexed, 'the boys were perplexed.'" Again, she read to the end, no longer to hold in her smile. Hand over her mouth, she finally let out a roaring snort while covering the mucus released from her nose.

Startled, the head secretary looked up from her ledger. "Mrs. McGuire!"

"I'm sorry! Dario, this is for an adult hilarious. So the boys weren't afraid, yet the girls were frightened."

"And they didn't get any candy."

"What an imagination!" said McGuire, placing a handkerchief over her nose.

"That's what I said. I think it's a good story, and I don't think there's anything wrong with it," remarked Mary Ellen, trying to defend Dario.

"Well, my Mr. Dario Sacatti, you can't stay here; our principal was called out today. You need to head to Vice Principal Sister Bridget's classroom. She's no longer teaching eighth grade. She moved to the sixth grade next to the library. I'll call her; she'll be expecting you."

Dario knew the sixth grade, like the eighth grade, was clear across campus down long corridors. Mary Ellen would walk next to him, and he more than valued her company.

"I think Sister Bridget might like your story. She's not grumpy like our teacher."

"Before we get there I want you to know I always liked you. Some of the other girls think you're swell, too."

What a great day for me to get in trouble, and I still don't know what I did wrong or what a sacredige is.

Dario and Mary Ellen stood before Room fourteen's open door. When students' heads turned toward the fourth graders, Sister Bridget's attention turned to Mr. Sacatti. "Mary Ellen, thank you. Please return to your classroom."

"Yes, Sister Bridget. And good luck, Dario," she whispered before turning back to room 10.

"Let me see that paper in your hands." Sister Bridget stood in front of her classroom and silently read Dario's Halloween story. A smile crossed her face before asking Roger to escort the fourth grader to the library. "Find Dario a book he'll read while waiting for the end of the day."

Sister Bridget loved to read, and she loved every student in the school to do the same. When she was reassigned to the sixth grade, she was also given the responsibility of ordering new library books for the school while helping her students keep the library in an orderly state.

She loved the job, and her student, Roger, one of the most prolific readers in the school, often recommended current novels that children would take too. The boy responded with a one hundred percent terrific track record so far early in the school year.

"I'm going to recommend S.E. Hinton's THE OUTSIDERS. She's a woman teacher, and her students asked her to write a book since she felt there wasn't enough current children's literature out on the market, so she wrote that book. You'll like it," said Roger.

He handed the almost two-hundred-page book to Dario, who would start on it in Room 14 and finish by Monday.

When Dario looked up from the book he had started, only to finish by next Monday, he noticed only five minutes were left before the bell rang.

Walking home with Roger, Dario said, "I'm almost halfway through the book. You sure know how to pick them, Roger."

"When you're finished, I've already picked out what you should read next. It's titled, Where the Red Fern Grows."

"What's it about?" asked Dario.

"Two dogs named Ann and Dan and a boy named Billy. Wilson Rawls wrote it. He's kinda new and knows how to put together a good story. Most of the older kids read it, but I know how smart you are. You're going to like it a lot.

"How was your story? I told you the more you read, the better you'll write."

"I think my story is…well, at least pretty good. My teacher thinks it's a sacrament."

"I think she meant a sacrilege. Sister Bridget told me what it's about."

"It's about our whole school going to church at Halloween and statues start to float in the air."

"That's no sacrilege. I had your teacher two years ago. She's a gripe. She never liked boys. I used to read every day, and she never acknowledged my effort, so I quit until I got to 5th grade, and everything changed. You're going to like Miss Davis.

"Anyway, how come you don't have football practice today?"

"What? Practice? I forgot! We gotta a game today, and I walked halfway home. I gotta get back now."

"Let me hold your book, Dario; I'll put it in your mailbox."

Dario ran toward Pan Am Park, cutting across Pierce Avenue, his lungs on fire. He arrived just as the first quarter ended.

"Why are you late, Dario?" asked Coach Frank Roman, his 4th grade coach.

"I…I" Dario couldn't lie, at least not to coach, besides Heaven's saints rallied around Dario, blessing him with a Koufax and Mantle card. "I guess I forgot, coach."

"Well, get in there! Call 2-4-16 in the huddle."

St. Cyprian's quarterback faked a handoff to their halfback, handing off the football to Dario Sacatti. Darting toward the sideline, he waited until his blocking halfback broke midfield. Dario heaved the football toward Greg Schneeweis, who retrieved the ball high in the air, scurrying across the field for the team's first touchdown, tying the flag football game 6-6.

Dario noticed two of his classmates cheering on the sideline. One of them was Mary Ellen with her friend Mary Payne from Room 11. Both girls found him staring their way. The former Mary blew him a kiss, not too common for a 4th grader.

Their final game ended St. Cyprian's 24 and Beatitudes 6. Dario knew his team already captured a league championship. However, nothing would satisfy his youthful memory other than an undefeated season. Mary Ellen stayed near the team after Dario's opponents climbed into their cars and left the park.

Mary Payne was the first to congratulate Greg Schneeweis for his three touchdown catches. Nudging up to the young boy, she caught his attention, hoping he might return his interest. Greg, however, told her thank you, turned, and ran toward his house nearby.

Dario offered to walk the girls home, both living a block away on Fidler Avenue. Mary Ellen and her friend Mary were delighted.

Not knowing what to say, he let Mary Ellen, Room 10's jabberjaw, take over the conversation, exaggerating to her neighbor the 'sacrilege' paper turned in earlier. "He's better than Nancy Drew, and someday he'll write books for other kids. I hope I will be around to congratulate you, Mr. Sacatti."

"How about our football game?" he wondered. "That was no sacrilege."

Mary Payne, one of Room 11's brightest students, snickered. "Dario, do you know what a sacrilege is?"

"Something bad?" he responded.

"Well...yes. It can be not nice. A sacrilege means when you say something bad about God or the church. What Mary Ellen told me is that you didn't do that. So your story or your football game wasn't a sacrilege."

"I don't like doing bad stuff that's how come I got my Sandy Koufax."

Puzzled, both of the girls wished Dario a good weekend, both of them retreating, while giggling, into Mary Ellen's house.

Lucky the Sacatti dog never fully understood time, especially when alone in the house. Whether by himself for an hour or even six hours, he longed for companionship, promising one hundred percent canine love. When Dario arrived home first, Lucky squealed, dancing around the backyard with fervor.

"Come inside, Lucky, and I'll put on your harness. We're going for a walk."

"WALK!" Lucky's limited vocabulary understood that magical word. Love combined with nature's plentiful odors on the campus trail, and Heaven just opened its gates to one of its favorite four-legged saints.

By late afternoon, Emma and Mia arrived home, followed by Palmira and Eugenio.

"Dario, I found a book in the mailbox. Is it yours?" asked the boy's mother.

"A book? Oh yeah! Roger left it for me."

Lucky, excited to see the rest of his family continued to twirl around the house more hyper than usual. He appeared to recognize tomorrow was Saturday, and his family, or at least some of them, would remain near him all day whether washing clothes or weeding in Lucky's favorite dirt out in the yards.

Saturday, though, found Emma crawling out of bed earlier than usual, preparing to accompany Ted to the beach with Ben and Donovan. "No run today, little guy. Dario will take you on a walk with Mia and the baby. You go back to sleep with Dario and don't wake him."

Lucky appeared to understand obedience and retreated to Dario's room, lying on the carpet next to the boy's bed.

———————

Six in the morning on a Saturday that's even a bit early for me," said Emma as Ted drove away from the Harvey Way house in his Ford coupe.

There are a few surfers already in the water at the crack of dawn, even a few die-hards before the sun comes up."

"How can they see? It's got to be pitched dark out there in the water," responded Emma."

"I wouldn't know. Surfers probably wear flashlights on their heads. The earliest I ventured out was 7:00 a.m., and even with my wetsuit, I froze.

"You heard Ben; he doesn't get cold, and evidently, men upstairs who weren't ever human learn fast."

Ted arrived fifteen minutes late and found Ben and Donovan on the front porch rockers, drinking hot coffee and watching the sunrise lift above the horizon.

"Hi, fellas. You gonna put on a shirt, Ben," said Ted.

"Why, I'm going into the water."

"I couldn't talk him into it," replied Donovan. "I'm wearing a jacket and sweatpants, and if it weren't for this hot coffee, I'd be freezing."

Twenty minutes from Long Beach along Pacific Coast Highway, Ben asked permission to roll down the coupe's back seat window. "It's a bit stuffy in here," he said.

"Good thing you were one of God's good angels; heaven's got better weather conditions. Sure, roll it down. You want Ted's jacket, Donovan. I'm turning the car's heat on upfront."

Gladly accepting the jacket, Donovan wrapped it around his chest.

"There she is, Ben, the Seal Beach wedge off to the right," said Ted.

After crashing into the breaker, ten-foot waves appeared doubled in size. Surfers sitting on their boards in the right spot rode the wave and, in seconds, spun out before it crashed into the jetty.

"If you don't spin out, you and my board will smash into those rocks. Should I tell you, Ben, you gotta be careful?"

"I'll watch first and show you how fast I can pick up."

Donovan took off his jacket and covered his swimsuit with Ted's rubber wet suit. "You sure this will keep me warm?"

"Compared to not wearing one? Yes, it will considerably, Donovan. If you still feel cold, get out of the water and join Emma and me for some hot coffee she made this morning."

Ben jogged toward the water carrying a ten-foot Gordie board over his head. Laying the board on top of the surf he paddled out far to his right toward the jetty. "He blends in well, Emma, with the veteran surfers. You goin' out, Donovan?"

"I'm going to need that hot cup of coffee."

Nine o'clock rolled around, tripling the amount of surfers sitting on their boards waiting for the next wave. "It looks crowded out there. I hope no one crashes into another surfer," said Emma, worried about Ben.

Donovan, gathering up his nerves, now enjoyed body surfing the smaller waves gliding them toward the shore every few minutes. "Ben's been out there for two hours he's taken to the sport. I wonder if he wants to purchase his own board?" said Ted as he took a bite out of Emma's peanut butter and jelly sandwiches. "These sure are good. It's funny how sitting on a beach can make food taste so much better."

"How about a banana when you're finished."

"Yeah, sure. Nothing like a banana to go with this sandwich. You know, I read where Elvis loves a sliced banana on top of his peanut butter sandwich."

Emma looked up and saw Ben and Donovan walking toward the couple. "I want a board just like this one, Ted, new or used. I take it the stores are open."

"Let's head over. Emma and Donovan, we'll be back in 20-30 minutes."

Rows and rows of surfboards lined the walls and racks of Harbour Surfboards on Main Street. Gordie, Bing, Carbonell, Dewey Weber, Chuck Noll, Harbour, and Jacobs were the names of just a few of the many famous brands in 1962.

Ted pointed to the Gordie "Gordie the Only Way to Travel," a take on the 60's Western Airlines commercial that seemed appealing to Ben. "This is what you rode today, Ben."

"Well, then let's get it." He pulled out his wallet, froze, and then turned around, facing Ted. "Ted, you and your family are safe. Let Emma know she and her family will also be okay." Ben turned around again, this time vanishing. His sudden disappearance didn't affect anyone near Ben except for the now startled Ted Accenti.

"Ben! Ben, where are you?" Ted stuck his arms out as it feeling for air.

"You okay, buddy?" asked a concerned customer.

"No! No, I'm not. Oh, good Lord!"

Chapter Thirty-Five
Tsunami hits Seal Beach, California

Ted dashed out of the surf shop, heading toward Emma. Alarm overwhelmed the young man. Shouting for his girlfriend, he found a stricken teenager frozen to her beach blanket, staring at an empty wetsuit.

"Donovan, where did you go? Where did you go, Donovan!" Ted knelt next to her, throwing his arms around Emma. She moved her head; her empty eyes now beaded on a panicked Ted.

"Donovan was just here, Ted, peeling a banana, and next he disappeared into thin air. Where's Ben? Ted, all at once, this is too much."

"Ben vanished in front of me before though he told me our families are safe."

"SAFE! What does that mean? Is Lilith back!"

"I don't know. What's going on, Emma?"

A mass of beachgoers screamed as a heavy wave crashed to shore, throwing water far up the shoreline, coming within a few yards of Emma and Ted's spot. Others closer to the shore were swamped, their blankets and towels dripping wet.

Another large wave fell, wiping out former places of beachgoers sunning and relaxing.

"High tide at ten in the morning! Something's wrong, Emma. Quick were heading toward my car." He swooped up Emma's thermos and picnic basket. Emma scooped up her blanket and Ted's wetsuit as they proceeded to dash to safety.

A twenty-foot wave hit near the shoreline, tumbling people who previously wanted no more than to dip their toes in the wake of a gentle wave. This time salt water licked up to Ted's coupe as well as other vehicles.

A small child thrashed in the deeper water, ready for

the receding wave to pull her out to sea. Ted dashed toward the girl, diving into four-foot violent surf, yanking, pulling, and creating nightmarish chaos.

Ted reached forward, grabbing her by the hair and pulling the terrified four-year-old to his chest, holding her head above water. Pulled toward the open waters, he caught into another larger wave, riding it to shore while covering the girl's mouth. He lurched forward, struggling to gain footing, when Emma grabbed his free hand pulling him to the parking lot now under a foot of water.

The mother of the girl struggling in the water reached up, screaming for her daughter. Ted ran and jumped back in, this time successfully clutching the woman's arm and escaping the deadly pull of the rogue wave. Panting, she boosted her body, reached out, and held onto Ted Accenti as the young man swept her off her feet and carried her to safety.

"Mama! Mama!" the young child cried through a flood of tears. Mother and daughter connected as Emma handed the child to her 'Mama.'

"You saved her life, mister. God bless you." Sinking to her knees, she cried as salt water ran up to her and her daughter's knees.

"Get in the car! Everyone!" Emma opened the door and pushed the girl and her mother in the back seat. Ted peeled out, driving parallel to the ocean until he was able to make a quick right north on Seal Beach Blvd. A rumbling sound shook the car, bouncing the occupants up on their seats. "Step on it, Ted!" shouted Emma as she looked in the rearview mirror, witnessing a huge one-hundred-foot tsunami approaching the coast and Ted's Ford coupe.

He pressed down on the accelerator as the car leaped. Saltwater crashed four hundred yards behind the vehicle.

Both the mother and daughter cried as they held each other in the back seat. Water swept forward, crushing all living and non-living things in its path. Traveling faster than the coupe, the water finally slowed its deadly advance as Ted made a quick left turn on reaching a calm North Sunset Beach. Traveling further north, he reached Long Beach, cutting south toward Ocean Blvd. and the house on Cerritos Ave., mortgaged by Dorothy Marquez.

"Helixa and her and Donovan's mothers may be in danger," said Emma as she turned to calm the mother and daughter.

Ted hopped out of his car, noticing an 'Open House' sign secured firmly in the front yard. Emma turned in the front seat of the Ford coupe and introduced herself adding, "And your names?"

"I'm Ruth Gomez, and this is my daughter, Aaron. Please to know you and your friend."

Emma, noticing Ruth's daughter was still upset, asked the mother where they lived, hoping to offset the tragic circumstances.

"We're from Norwalk further in. This outing was our first visit
to the beach. We hopped on a bus early this morning."

Aaron, calmer, asked, "Is the beach always this scary?"

"No, not at all sweetheart. Usually, it's quiet and peaceful. What you experienced today will probably never happen again."

Ted walked through a wide open door, running into a female realtor walking from the kitchen with a cup of hot coffee. Her face looked frazzled.

"Oh, hello, how are you? I didn't think anyone would come by today and was thinking about locking the front door and going home to my family."

"So you heard. Catastrophic!" said Ted.

"I watched bits and pieces after listening to a newsbreak on the radio. A horrible tsunami, drownings, and thousands gone. That wave seemed to wipe out that little city. I don't think I can even talk about it." She courageously stuck out her hand and introduced herself. "My name is Rebecca Clauson, and you."

"I'm Ted Accenti, a friend of the people who owned this house. Miss Clausen, why don't you sit and relax? Your hand is clammy, and you don't look too good."

"Oh, thank you, Ted. Could you sit too? I sure would welcome some company at this time."

"Let me run out to my vehicle my girlfriend and a mother and daughter are waiting for me. I'll bring them in."

Ted returned seconds later with Emma and Mrs. Gomez standing behind the teen, still bewildered. Miss Clauson, this is Emma, my friend from high school."

Emma spoke up, "And this is Mrs. Gomez and her daughter Aaron."

"Come in, come in! You'll have to excuse me. I just heard of the devastation at Seal Beach."

Aaron broke out in tears, holding on to her mother's side.

"We were there, Miss Clausen. Ted rescued both of us."

"Oh, dear God! Please sit, Mrs. Gomez, and relax here on the sofa. I'll get some coffee. What would Aaron like."

"We're fine; we just need time. It was my daughter's first visit to the beach, and then this."

Ted asked permission to turn on the radio thinking the women and girl couldn't handle the visuals. He turned the sound low while Emma started up a conversation with Mrs. Gomez and Miss. Clausen, who preferred everyone address her as Rebecca.

"Call me Ruth. I own a home in Norwalk northeast of here."

"Norwalk?" asked Emma, half listening.

"Norwalk, yes, a newer community similar to Lakewood, not too far from you."

Rebecca intervened, "So Ted, you're a high schooler may I ask what high school and also who were your friends that lived here?"

"Yes, Emma and I attend St. Anthony down the road, and we must have just missed our friends, the Fisk," he said lifting his head away from the radio.

"The Fisk? My records indicated an elderly couple owned this home for over forty years. They raised their five children here; however, this place has been vacant for over two years."

Ted looked over at Emma, who shrugged, although not entirely taken aback. "We shouldn't be too surprised who are science teachers will be on Monday."

"We're going to move along, Rebecca would you like for us to wait while you lock up?"

"Yes, thank you. I won't be long."

Five minutes later, Ted was back on the road, heading toward Norwalk to drop off Ruth Gomez and her daughter Aaron.

Pulling up on Stearn Ave, Ruth Gomez's husband was waiting on the front porch holding an infant with a police officer calming the father of two down. Looking up, an expression of joy crossed his face. "RUTH! And my baby girl Aaron. Thank God!"

The couple embraced, tears spilling on each of their shoulders.

"Daddy! Daddy!" Aaron sobbed as she grasped her father's leg. Mr. Gomez handed the baby to his wife as he lifted his little miracle, muffling her to his chest.

Relieved, the Norwalk police officer left in his car as Ruth introduced the teenage couple. "Would you and Emma please come in?"

"I'm sorry, we need to rush home and check on our families," Emma said, anxious and hoping to find her family safe, as well as Ted's parents.

Pulling up on Harvey Way, Emma rushed into her house. Mother was busy cleaning out the stove, and Mia was feeding her newborn a bottle. Outside, Eugenio and Dario were busy weeding the flower bed. Ted walked in a minute later equally amazed at the calm in the Sacatti household. "It's as if nothing ever happened today, Emma."

"Ted, turn on the television," asked Emma.

Channels 2, 4, 5, 7, 11, and 13 all tuned into normal programming. "What's going on, Ted!" Emma shouted.

Palmira walked into the front room. "Honey, are you alright? You didn't even say hello. Hello Ted, how are you."

"Mother, did you hear anything on the radio or watch on TV?"

"No, I've been busy all day in the kitchen and with the laundry. How was your day at the beach?"

"Mother, could you call everyone in? We have to talk."

Palmira, worried, rounded up the family, all of them seated in the front room, mesmerized by the look on their sister and daughter.

"Dario, get up and get your sister a glass of water. Ted, do you know what's troubling my daughter?" asked Palmira, placing her arm around Emma's shoulders.

"Mr. and Mrs. Sacatti, Emma, and I experienced a huge tragedy at Seal Beach."

"Dear God!" Palmira gasped as she covered her mouth."

Ted looked over at Emma, and she spoke, "Mother, everyone, we witnessed a huge tsunami as Ted drove hard out of town. The wave engulfed the entire city. Hundreds lost in the rogue wave."

Eugenio latched on to his wife, Palmira, who trembled with fear. "Turn on that channel, Ted; we need some news."

Channel after channel, not a shred of evidence popped up. News or no news as typical of an average Saturday afternoon.

"Try the radio, Mr. Sacatti. They reported the devastation in detail."

Eugenio turned to the all-news station. A weather forecast, report on traffic and college football scores, nothing more."

"I don't find any of this amusing, you two. We feel frightened, and we're not crazy, you know, so stop it!" Mia rose on the couch, baby in hand, and left the room.

"Mother, Dad, Ted, and I aren't imagining this were stunned, and I don't think I can get over this. I need to talk to Mia in our room. Ted, could you fill my parents in on what we experienced."

Eugenio looked over at his son, "Dario, go outside and finish the weeding."

She walked up into the bedroom just as her sister put little Barbara down for a nap. "Mia, Donovan vanished right before my eyes. Ted said the same thing about Ben when they were in the surf shop. But there's something even more important: Ben's final words to Ted were that our family and Ted's family are safe."

Emma explained the wave, the rescue, and visiting Dorothy's home near Ocean. "All of this is a nightmare, and somehow nothing happens to us. Nothing happened to anyone, it appears."

"We'll find out on Monday, won't we? So let's not talk about it anymore, okay." Mia sat livid on the edge of her bed arms folded across her chest.

Monday morning surprised Mia, Emma, and Ted. Although flummoxed, they accepted the end result. Mia lost her science teacher to someone who had allegedly been on the staff since the beginning of school in September. Mrs. Florence Barkley, a former science teacher at Woodland High School in Iowa, welcomed Long Beach's weather and the well-behaved students.

Ted and Emma found their science teacher also no longer addressed their former chemistry class. Jordan Matthews, a popular new recruit from Banning, California, again signed on before school began in September.

"We'll meet at lunch outside under the eaves in the senior yard. Hardly anyone will be there, and we need the quiet.

At lunch, the three students skirted into the empty schoolyard, sitting comfortably in the shade of the eves. "They're gone, Emma, they're really gone. Why would they leave?"

"Let me answer that for you, Emma." Ben Fisk strolled into the courtyard, standing in front of his friends. "I pulled all your friends, including Dorothy, into heaven to protect them. Lilith is up to no good. She's orchestrating help from below. I've requested an angel to protect you and members of your families."

"What about Dorothy's family, especially Carlos and Cindy?"

"All of them are protected. Mia, one of your angels, is Anathiel, one of God's proudest, most loyal angels. Talk to her often; she'll listen. Ted, I selected Angelo. He's a messenger of God and will also protect you."

"Whose Emma's angel," worried Mia.

"Like you, her angels are abundant, including me. We will all protect you, sweetheart. Before I fade, be kind to your teachers; they're dedicated, and your grades are the same. And taking the doubt out of your head, Mia, Ted and Emma experienced everything they said, but I need to add Lilith's orchestrated help is fully capable of illusions. Emma, you and Ted suffered from hallucinations. Seal Beach is safe. There was a real estate woman in Dorothy's home, yet Ruth and her daughter Aaron didn't exist. Enough said. Beware all of you."

Ben vanished.

Chapter Thirty-Six

Emergency Test Siren-1962

Monday turned out as one of the best days for Dario, and for the majority of boys in Room 10. Mrs. Abigail Hamilton had now moved and was not a grumpy member of the St. Cyprian's Elementary school staff. What a pleasant day.

And his teacher, Miss Carol Rose, a flower, a fragrant blossom unfurling her love of children with a smile and gracious personality. "Dario, Sister Bridget turned over this crumbled paper to me and wanted my opinion. God gave you a brilliant imagination, son. I realize All Souls Day and All Saints Day have passed, but you deserve recognition. Would you care to read it to your classmates?"

A hand shot up. "I'd love to read it for Dario, Miss Rose. I'm the only one in this class who ever heard it, and I loved it!" Mary Ellen Schivonie, one of Room 10's most prolific readers felt helping Dario might draw more attention to her.

Finishing his essay with perfect cadence and distinctive passion, the students applauded Dario, a few patting his back.

"Could you rewrite it, Dario, so that I can display it on the bulletin board," asked his teacher.

On that Monday at 9:00 a.m. Long Beach's alert siren sounded. Miss Rose, confused, was told her students needed to duck beneath their desks with their hands over their heads. "You're supposed to hide under your teacher's desk, Miss Rose," shouted three of the girls used to the loud wail of the siren.

For those in the know, especially the adults and older upper-grade students, the siren routinely sounded on the first Friday of every month at 10:00 a.m. Many in the school panicked. At the height of the Cold War and a mere year following Kennedy's election, the Cuban Missile Crisis found its way to the front page and now unnerved the veteran teachers and their older students. "Turn on the radio, Sister Bridget," pleaded one of the sixth-grade pupils. Her class listened to typical everyday news, including updates on what was going on in Cuba.

"Randy, jog to the school office and tell the secretary to announce the siren is off-kilter and all is well." Her students were relieved an atomic threat wasn't real in their young pre-teen and early teen minds.

When the siren stopped, the boys in room 10 thought it was 'really neat,' while the eighth graders referred to the office announcement as 'cool.' Peace in Long Beach, in any case, was secure, so why the siren mishap?

Because the air raid siren was so loud, Sister Bridget decided to call the local police station, who certainly heard it a half mile away on North Clark Ave. "Ma'am, we don't know what you're talking about; there was no siren. We would have been alerted if it went off."

She hung up the phone, confused, looking over at the school secretaries. "Both of you heard it, am I right?"

"Of course we did. Why don't you call the fire

department? They're next door to us," suggested the head secretary.

"That makes sense, thank you, Rita." Sister Bridget dialed the fire department located within fifty yards of the school.

"Emergency siren. I'm sorry, Sister Bridget we never heard a thing. Have you called the police? If the siren is down, it needs fixing."

"It's not down; we heard it at school loud and clear. Now we're confused."

"I'll call the county and have them check it thoroughly. Is there anything I could do?"

"I suppose calling to have it checked would help. Thank you, Captain Hanks."

That evening news would carry the exciting announcement to his family and the entire community. Not since 1960 did the siren 'misfire' and create a schoolwide stir and overwhelming proof at the elementary school that everyone heard it, not including the police and fire departments nearby. The siren, recently renovated, sounded off schedule. Its routine emergency practice warning an hour early on the same day the entire school was herded to 10:00 a.m. First Friday Mass.

Emma looked over at her sister who in turn was already staring Emma's way. *Expect illusions and hallucinations.* They both wondered did this count as a demonic, impish encounter.

Prayers that evening included Anatheil, Ben, and other heavenly entities, and the very next morning, the girls walked through what they thought was a typical day at school until...

"Someone chase it out the window!" shouted freshman Rosa Clark. A large, though harmless bat flew unmolested throughout the St. Anthony gymnasium. Players, including the coach, ran in circles, teasing the Hoary bat toward an open window.

Emma and Mia stood miffed in position on the volleyball court. Players screamed at Ted, sitting in the stands near the open window to help. "Help with what?" he shrieked. "What are you girls talking about?"

Moments later, the volleyball team stood still. "My goodness, that thing was huge," said 6'4" Tanya Bailey. "Ted, could you stand on your toes and close that window."

Mia and Emma knew enough not to comment. Both signaled their secret to Ted, who motioned his covert understanding with his hand.

Coach Regina Holden continued to drive the practice forward, standing on a platform and hurling volleyballs down at her players. "DIG, DIG, DIG," she continually echoed in the gymnasium. "Mt. Carmel girls are tall and can spike. Expect the volleyball to come your way at bullet speed. Dig girls! Dig! Atta girl Mia good hustle.'"

She broke up the typical routines with a close of, "One hundred in a row girls." This time, the St. Anthony varsity team served one hundred serves without missing over the net as Coach Holden counted down to zero. "This Friday, we beat the girls at Mt. Carmel and we start playoffs in our own gymnasium; keep that in mind. It's at night, which means moms, dads, and boyfriends will be packing these stands." She looked at the only boy in the stands. "Am I right, Ted!"

"Right as that bat that flew through the window!"

Every girl chuckled as Tanya sparked the team with "BEAT MT. CARMEL!" With the girls and coach joining her for the second and third time.

After a quick shower, Emma and Mia joined Ted in his Ford coupe. "This time, a bat flies in the gymnasium. None of us saw it, am I right," said Emma, wanting to settle the obvious illusion. "What's next?"

"Lilith's deceptive tricks aren't funny. Her demonic antics need to stop. What if Coach Holden complains and asks the school to hire an exterminator?" said Mia.

"Bats can also carry rabies, and who knows, your coach may wonder if that bat was pregnant. Lilith could hurt our school. We're a restrictive budget."

"That's an excellent point, Ted. I'll discourage any idea she might come up with that ghost of a bat."

Ted commented, "Who knows, the school may take it out on her penny budget.

"By the way, Mia, Scott brought your name up during basketball practice. Are you still interested in him?"

"It appears he's interested in quite a few girls. I saw him talking to Kathy Haynes, one of our junior homecoming princesses. Isn't she dating Mark Musser?"

"I guess so. I don't keep tabs on things like that."

"Well, tell him I'm not interested. There are plenty of girls who could fall in love with his face."

Ted dropped off the girls and headed home. Emma immediately started up dinner while Mia and Dario took Lucky for his second walk of the day. She met her two friends pushing their carriages.

Betty was the first to hug her friend, "Mia, it's good to see you. How's your freshmen year coming along?"

"I've adjusted well and joined the volleyball team. How are you two girls doing?" said Mia as she joined Catherine in an embrace."Your babies have grown!"

"And I bet yours has too," said Betty.

"She's 16lbs. and is a little over two feet."

Catherine started screaming enough to alarm Dario and the girls. Lucky barked defensively. "My little Cielo stopped breathing; she's turning blue!"

Betty and Mia looked down. Betty's eyes went wide while Mia saw only a content baby sound asleep. Dario's sister calmly picked up the baby while handing Lucky's leash to her brother. She gently patted the baby on the back, offering an earnest prayer to her angel, Anathiel. *If I ever needed you, Anathiel I need you now. Please intercede.*

"Whoops! Cielo just spit up. She's fine, Catherine, don't get so upset."

"Oh, thank you, Mia, I thought..."

"Well, now you thought wrong. Cielo's fine, maybe a bit colicky. I felt gassy movement in her diaper."

"She turned blue, didn't you see her lips, Mia?" asked Betty astounded at the sudden change.

Please help me out, Anathiel, and thank you for your aid. "Her lips looked fine to me, no worries, except for the mess on my shoulder."

"Oh goodness, Mia, come to my house. We're the same size, and I'll get you a fresh blouse."

Now, never mind. Give me one of Cielo's fresh diapers, and I'll wipe it off. We're all mommies and the first to understand a simple spit-up."

Dario, now mastering the leather leash of his dog Lucky, moved forward in the opposite direction of Betty, Catherine, their two carriages, and the babies. Lucky's nose, signaling a wealth of former canine pals, led the way, stopping now and then to salute a tree or post.

Mia, still ill at ease over her frightened friends' illusive encounter, asked her brother, "Dario, I need you to tell me, did you hear that siren at school?"

"Sure, it was loud, and it scared the girls. All the boys were laughing at them under their desks."

"You sure you heard it. Your friends didn't persuade you?"

"What does 'persuade' mean?"

"Encourage you to hear something you never actually heard."

"Oh no, I heard that siren alright. We thought the Russians were going to bomb us, but the siren was only fake."

She never doubted what Dario told the family earlier, but why did he hear it. Wasn't he protected from hallucinations or misguided deceptions creeping into the air? But he said he liked it; he laughed with his friends. Could that be the difference?

Mia walked another half block with her brother before turning and heading home.

―――――――

That night, Mia dreamt of a rope dangling from a cross beam installed in her bedroom. *"I'm going to do it first and then you, Emma. When Mom and Dad wake up, they'll be happy."*

She placed the rope tight over her neck and signaled for her sister to kick the chair out from underneath her. Falling, her legs swung as she choked. So this how it feels, she thought.

The rope grew tighter, and Mia panicked as her sister laughed. Dario walked into his sister's bedroom with Lucky, next pointing and laughing with his sister Emma. Lucky let out a playful bark while merrily wagging his tail.

Mia's tongue hung out while her eyes bulged from their sockets. "That's even funnier, isn't it, Dario," said Emma, slapping her brother's back.

Mia woke from the nightmare, sitting up in bed and breathing hard while grasping her neck. She stared into the darkness when Emma's face appeared before her. *"You had a dream, Mia, a nightmare. It's okay. I'm with you."*

Dario handed his sister the rope. "Do it again; that was a crack-up." This time, Emma forced the rope around Mia's neck while she and her brother forced Mia on the stool. "Go ahead, Dario, kick it out!" *Mia swung again, this time her eyes finally popping out of her sockets.*

"Yeah, we did it, Emma. Mom and Dad will be so happy getting rid of that nasty bitch."

Emma shook her sister's shoulders, trying to wake her without startling her. "Come on, wake up, Mia, you're dreaming."

Mia's eyes twitched before opening them. Tears formed in her eyes as she reached out and held her sister. "It's you, Emma. I thought I was dying then...then."

"Only a dream, little sister. I'm with you."

"That's what you said!" and Mia began to shake.

Emma slipped into the bed with her sister, holding her tight for the rest of the night. At 5:30 a.m., she slipped out of Mia's bed, woke her brother, and started on their morning run with Lucky.

Sitting in the back of the bus on Wednesday morning, Mia went over her dream with Emma. "That's an awful nightmare, and it included Dario and you laughing at my terrifying battle with a rope.

"And you and Dario helped," Mia said, wringing her hands together.

"From what Ben told us, this is out of character. Can Lilith affect our dreams?

"First, you make me aware of Dario and the siren and how he laughed with his friends in the face of potential danger, then Lilith or whatever piggybacks on that, and you find your brother laughing as you battled through your nightmare."

Arriving at school they found Ted was absent that day. "Ted, not here! He's never gone from school. Why didn't he tell us," said Emma, worried about her boyfriend.

By the fourth period, they received their answer. Vice-principal Judy Wilcox called the sisters into her office to report the tragic news.

"Girls, I realize how close you were to Ted Accenti. I need to share this with you." Emma's face paled as she held her sister upright, trying to prevent her from fainting."

Vice-principal Wilcox stood up and returned with two cups of water from the cooler. "Go on, Mrs. Wilcox, tell us."

"Ted's father took the boy and his mother to school and work that morning. Ted's car was stuck with a mechanic while being fixed. His father missed a turn on Seventh Avenue, swung back into traffic, and a station wagon destroyed his car. All three members of his family were killed. I'm so sorry. I've called a doctor to give each of you a sedative to relax you. Both of you are in my prayers and may God rest their souls."

"DEAD! No, that can't be true. Emma, this is another illusion like last night."

St. Anthony's school nurse walked in and offered to take the girls to her office to lie down and wait for the doctor. "I've laid out blankets for you two. Come with me, please."

With the help of the nurse and vice-principal, Mia and Emma sleepwalked into the nurse's large office.

Fifteen minutes later, the sisters asked if they could move to the cafeteria to sit next to their friends. Instead, they slipped into the near-empty senior courtyard, hoping to see a sign from their friend Ben Fisk. He was waiting for them under the eaves. Relaxing, his arms stretched out on the bench. Embracing both, he comforted them both and then announced, "Houston, we have a problem."

"Houston! What are you talking about, Ben?"

"Oh, never mind, that won't be quoted until April of 1970. A mistimed, senseless metaphor. What I'm trying to say is I tried to slip it into your vice-principal's talk, which, by the way, never occurred. Didn't you hear her tell you Ted's car was being serviced at a mechanic?"

"Yes, she said that!" stated Emma, gripping her sister's hand.

"I thought you both knew Ted. Again, my mistake. When would Ted and his father ever take their cars to a mechanic? Get it, they wouldn't. Ted and his parents are fine. He just had a bad toothache and is checking into the school office right now."

Both girls got up to rush to the office. "HOLD ON! Both of you. I'm not finished; stay seated."

Ben explained the glitch. "Lilith sent an operative to create havoc, bleeding illusions into the very people we're trying to protect."

"Why do we see everything odd, including today," asked Emma.

"As I said, you have a multitude of angels watching over you. I'll admit I never had the strength to stop Donovan's hanging, and now Lilith sent a demonic messenger tricking all of us. By the way, here comes your boyfriend."

Talking out of the side of his novocaine-filled mouth, Ted gave a cheery hello to his old friend while the girls rushed up, planting kisses on his cheeks. Emma stared at him and blurted out, "I love you, Ted!"

"Wow, what did you tell them, Ben? I love you too, Emma!"

"Ted, I told these girls to watch out for any mysterious misconceptions. They were both victims of one this morning."

"Me too; I swore I forgot my wallet at home, and here it is sitting in my back pocket. Let me buy all of you lunch in the cafeteria I owe you one. Join us, Ben."

"I'm working on this mishap, but we're all going to get it done." He disappeared, at least to the three of them.

"What does he mean by 'we' and 'mishap' what happened?" Ted said, escorting the girls across the yard.

Eugenio watched as one of his workers slipped and fell, flying backward over a four-foot barrier built to prevent any mishaps inside the Skippy plant. Rueben Flores hit his head on the cement floor below. The other workers went about their business as if nothing happened.

Eugenio, unaware of any so-called figments of his imagination, rushed down the stairs screaming someone call an ambulance. A worker took the emergency phone and dialed zero. Within minutes, an ambulance arrived, placing Eugenio on a stretcher.

"What happened?"

"You passed out boss. We gotta a lot of heat up there, and I guess it got to you."

"How's Rueben?"

"Boss, I'm Rueben. I'm fine, Mr. Sacatti; we're just a little worried about you."

"Get me down from this stretcher and get me a glass of cool water, and I'll be fine."

Rueben looked up at the emergency team and nodded to unstrap him as he assisted his boss, Eugenio, to his small office. "It's hot in here too, boss. Could I suggest you get yourself an air conditioner?" Rueben flew open the second-floor window and it seemed to let in more heat.

"If you boys can't get air, neither will I. I promise you I'll ask the boss again for air conditioning."

Eugenio's fainting spell was reported to the C.E.O. of Skippy's and now A Farmer's Dog manufacturing plant. "He fainted! My God, it was ninety degrees today. How hot is it in that plant, Carlson?"

"Over a hundred and five. Men have carried on with their work in that kind of heat in the past, sir."

"You think so. I heard one of our workers quit his job and went back to Mexico and died. He was only forty-two. I always wondered why he passed away. Did we give him heat stroke?

"And another thing, Carlson, we have a refrigerated section of our plant for A Farmer's Dog. We can't have part of our force suffering in the heat while others can work comfortably in a refrigerated unit. We need to cool down this entire plant and keep the unrefrigerated section at 74 degrees. Get on it now, Carlson. I want it finished before Christmas.

"And another thing, install fresh water coolers now."

Within the week, word got out what the president's plan was, and the staff gave credit to their new floor boss, who in turn credited the C.E.O. of Skippy's dog food.

Table talk swirled around the Sacattis dinner table that week. First, Eugenio telling of his hallucination and recovery at the store plant, and then Emma quieting down the family, warning them of future, even dramatic deceptions that might hamper their family. Mia nodded in agreement as Dario tilted his head, not quite understanding the so-called threat.

"Emma, what you heard about Ted is terrible; I can't think of anything worse, but it was 105 degrees at your dad's work. Any man employed under those conditions may have collapsed. And getting air conditioning installed! That seems, for those men, a blessing."

Friday morning a first arriving employee unlocked the doors to the Dr. Dorothy Marquez Medical Clinic. Palmira set up at her desk ready to close the week and mentally prepare for the weekend.

A Long Beach Police vehicle pulled their car in front of the clinic. Two officers exited and entered the building. Alone at her desk, Palmira welcomed the officers despite the gloomy expressions on their faces.

"Good morning, officers. How may I help you?"

"Are you Palmira Sacatti?" asked Officer Winslow, his eyes fixed on the mother of three.

"Yes, I am. Is everything okay?" Palmira halfway stood now, concerned about a police presence in the early hours of the clinic.

"Please sit down, ma'am. We need to tell you Dr. Miller suffered a fatal heart attack today. His wife found him passed away in bed. We need to talk to you, so you're going to have to close the clinic."

"Dear God, Dr. Miller was a saint. What about his wife and his son."

Winslow looked over at his partner, "Officer Penn?"

"Mrs. Sacatti, they're, as you might expect, upset, and Rachel Miller is currently being calmed by her sister. Dr. Miller's son took it hardest and is currently under sedation at Lakewood General Hospital on Clark Avenue."

"Please excuse me, officers. I'm going to need to visit the restroom I think I'm sick." She left the office area, her face turning pale as her eyelids drooped.

"Did you see how those sweet, rosy red cheeks turned white? And her eyes sank like she believed us. You ready to leave this place?"

Dr. Miller swung through the door, calling for his secretary.

"I'm here early, Palmira. Are you in?"

A moment later, she appeared with water dripping from her pale face; she swooned, losing her footing. Dr. Miller ran up to her, folding his arms around her and leading the young grandmother to her desk chair. He walked over to the water cooler and offered her a cold drink.

"Dr. Miller, I was told you were...where are the police? They're gone! Their car must have driven off."

"Mrs. Sacatti, let me give you a mild sedative; you're beginning to go into shock."

Their bus left the school grounds by 2:30 p.m. St. Anthony girls' volleyball had no intent of losing to the Mt. Carmel Conquisidors of Los Angeles.

Tall, lanky, and athletic, the Mt. Carmel team was ready to take down the undefeated Saints. "Let them dig out our spikes; we welcome the challenge."

Coached to return vicious spikes those at 'bullet-streaked speed,' the Saint Anthony felt they were ready to pull out anything fired down at them. Their bus pulled to the curb on Hoover Street near Florence Avenue. Exiting the bus, one of the girls ducked as shots were fired. The entire St. Anthony team rushed into the Conquistadors gymnasium shouting "bullets fired."

Police were called and sectioned off the area with yellow tape. A liquor store robbery down the road left the owner severely injured, who, in relentless response, fired his own weapon at the escaping thief.

Fears tempered down, especially when police apprehended the criminal. St. Anthony's final volleyball game proceeded forward.

With a few successful spikes, Mt. Carmel quickly succumbed to defeat 15-3 and 15-5. A non-competitive third game was played, giving the Conquistadors a moral victory 15-12.

Climbing inside the bus afterward, Mia questioned whether there was a robbery and if shots were clearly sent in the air. Coach Regina Holden stated, "Mia, I talked to the police personally. This neighborhood is subject to crime. I feel bad for the Mount Carmel girls."

Mia persisted, "Who did the cops look like?"

"Who do they look like? Well, let me think...one of them was young; peach fuzz covered his chin, and his hair was slicked back almost a very light brown. I noticed his ears; they were tiny without lobes.

Thinking of the other officer, he must be looking at retirement, his face drawn and bored; it was as if he went through this nonsense too often."

"Thank you, coach. I hope you don't mind my curiosity."

"It's okay, Mia; we experienced too much today."

Mia looked over at her sister, Emma, and whispered, "No earlobes, Emma. What do you think?"

"Tiny ears without earlobes. She wanted us to know. It's Lilith, what's she doing back?"

"Oh, Emma, if she's out, our protection must have broken down."

"I'll talk to Ted when we get back to school; he said he'd wait."

Ted appeared in a good mood; his coach was back from Jury Duty and his team was able to practice back in the gymnasium. "As far as anything unusual, we were fine, and I was okay, nothing out of wack.

"You don't believe your police officer's set of small ears and no earlobes constitutes a semi-disguised Lilith, do you? How many people are born with big and small ears and no earlobes? Come on, you girls are getting a little paranoid."

Paranoia went out the window when they arrived home. Palmira partially recovered from her early morning scare about why two Long Beach police officers would report a false fatality scared the wits out of her.

"I was told Dr. Miller suffered a fatal heart attack; his wife discovered him dead when she woke up. My God, what a nightmare! And their son was allegedly in shock recovering at Lakewood General Hospital.

"I was forced to excuse myself and retreat to the restroom. I vomited, spitting up my breakfast. When I returned, the officers disappeared and their car was gone, and there my boss stood, Dr. Miller, alive and well, his entire family just as safe."

Again, Mia looked her sister's way. Emma spoke first, "Mom, could you describe the officer?"

Palmira gave her daughters the same description as their coach.

"Mom, we need to discuss this as a family. We're headed toward some calamity."

"Damn it, what are you talking about, Emma!" demanded Eugenio. "If these table time discussions aren't true, then what happened? Now, you want us to have another family discussion. Let me know what's on your mind now."

Excusing Dario from the dinner table, Palmira walked her son to his room to peruse his baseball card collection, now protected in plastic sleeves.

Emma started with Dorothy an entity not afraid to appear in public from time to time. Her parents nodded, accepting the phenomenal experience. Next came the frightening experience at the basketball game and Dario's chant that "Helix must go."

Earthquakes, a deadly plague that spared and avoided the Sacatti family. Mia, as she fed her baby, reminded her parents of the terrifying fire consuming the building next to the convent where the mysterious girl was rooming with her. And how Helix turned against the influence of the devil and eventually settled in as both Emma's and Mia's biology teacher.

"Stop right now, both of you. God would not approve of all of this nonsense. Our country is already experiencing enough trouble with the communists, Khrushchev, and Castro and you're worried about the devil.

"A DEVIL! What is this filth? We pray nightly; we just prayed before we ate, and we attend church every week. Where in the world do we invite the devil into our lives? You girls forget this drivel and go about your business with school, and Mia continues caring for her child.

"Kennedy is speaking tonight on television. Why don't we see what he has to say."

Earlier, a U2 Spy plane detected newly built installations in the countryside of Cuba. Spot launchers, missiles, and transport trucks indicated that the Soviets were building sites to launch nuclear missiles capable of striking targets across the United States.

In a dramatic 18-minute speech, Kennedy shocked millions of Americans, including the Sacatti family, revealing 'unmistakable evidence' of the Cuban missile threat. Kennedy announced the U.S. would prevent Soviet ships from entering U.S. waters and demand Russia remove the nuclear missiles.

Dario, only a 4th grader, couldn't completely understand why his mother was crying. "Is that why our siren went off at school? Are the Russians going to bomb us, Daddy?"

His father replied, "Our devil comes in the form of two evil men, Nikita Khrushchev, and that weakling Fidel Castro."

"Momma, don't cry," Dario said, holding his head on his mother's lap as he felt his tears running down his cheeks.

Emma, embracing Palmira, asked her sister, "Mia, could you get the rosary beads hanging off the handle of the curio cabinet?"

"Today is Friday, everyone, so we will concentrate on the sorrowful mysteries, asking God to deliver us from the evil of the Soviet and Cuban leaders and bring about world peace."

Emma calmed down her family and led in prayer; her parents, brother, and sister never were so devoted to every Our Father, Hail Mary, and Glory Be. Even baby Rosie appeared to sense the emergency and remained silent in the arms of her mother.

Mia and Emma pressed to their knees before bed and prayed that Kennedy might inspire the world and talk Khrushchev from a worldwide nuclear holocaust.

When they woke, it appeared Kennedy's hope to solve the crisis was set in motion.

Saturday, Emma met with Ted after she finished her morning chores. They walked for an hour around the community college. Emma did not want to remove herself far from home. She asked her mother if her family could attend Mass with the Accenti family and invite them over for breakfast afterward.

"I think during these tumultuous times, that may be a good idea. Did you ask Ted what he thought of that?"

"He agreed and thanked you in advance in case you thought it was okay."

On Sunday, a majority of the 9:00 a.m. congregation remained after to recite the rosary. Father Gibson recited the Glorious Mysteries. Almost every parishioner held rosary beads as they delivered each prayer with sincere devotion and piety.

After breakfast, the Sacatti and Accenti family sat in front of the television, watching every word shared by the nation's favorite newscaster, "Uncle" Walter Cronkite.

"He's like a member of America's family," stated Eugenio.

Despite his accurate and unbiased information, the two families went to bed that night again on their knees, asking God for some form of hope.

―――――――

Monday morning, Ted picked up Mia and Emma in his 1956 Ford Coupe. Arriving at school fifteen minutes before the bell sounded, the trio noted no hallucinations or typical visual illusions.

By 4th period, Mia walked into her Biology class while Emma and Ted walked together into their chemistry classroom. T.V.'s set in almost every classroom appeared to calm the ever-increasing tension. All went well when teachers and a few students froze, staring out the 1st, 2nd, and 3rd floor windows.

A huge mushroom cloud lifted into the Los Angeles sky, followed by a rush of crushing concussive air. Los Angeles and surrounding cities, including Long Beach and Lakewood, no longer existed. Dario never experienced folding his hands over his head and hiding under his desk. His classroom, as well as the entire school, disappeared within the nuclear wind.

Eugenio and Palmira, who lived their lives as a prayer, found themselves standing together on a modest farm with a dozen or so chickens and now two Holstein cows in need of milking. "I won't ever forget my childhood on father's small farm. It was my responsibility to care for the chickens, feeding and gathering their eggs every morning. Such a wonderful farmyard duty. It was as if, as I am now, in heaven."

"Ever milk a cow before Mr. and Mrs. Sacatti? I'll show you how." Donovan was so kind and helpful.

Ted sat on the small porch, scanning Dario's terrific collection. "I have never seen such a perfectly centered Koufax, Dario. Ever think of trading him?"

Emma, Mia, and her baby, Rosie, watched as Ben's dog rounded up the chickens, marching them to their pen. A nearby rooster stood nearby as if to say, "They never listen to me." Little Rosie couldn't hold back her laugh.

Mrs. Accenti helped Riona and Hannah with the dishes as her husband relaxed with Ben chewing on some perfectly blended tobacco and spitting it into separate spittoons. "It's like they did back when. It's good, isn't it?" asked Ben.

"The best, my good man, the very best," responded Mr. Accenti.

———

Within the middle of the country, silos opened up, releasing thousands of nuclear weapons headed toward Moscow and major Russian cities. Cuba was now flattened and never again a threat to the United States; however, two hundred to three hundred foot waves engulfed the missile shredded east coast, collapsing its tallest buildings.

Millions upon millions suffered the holocaust while a threatening radioactive cloud rested over the rest of the United States, including major parts of Canada and Mexico.

America's strongest economy in the world would now fail under the nuclear disaster, and Russia's stolen empire would now split up into individual countries, many under a new democratic rule. Neither country could possibly lead other countries. Their leaders, now defunct or killed, proved their inept power decisions, willing to sacrifice multi-millions of lives to satisfy their swollen egos.

The devil stood in awe of the stupidity of a few human terrifying decisions. Innocent, they threw up their hands and looked toward the heavens, claiming, "We had no say in this mess."

Those who survived would wonder why they hadn't been taken. Their sorrow could never abate. Each day was unfamiliar. The radioactive threat was very real, tearing away the flesh of innocent survivors. Compared to the familiar bombing of Hiroshima, each strike in 1962 was three thousand times stronger. Death, after excruciating suffering, surrounded every living person.

Was the fall of Russia and the United States, the former most powerful country in the world, enough to coax the second coming? No one knew.

xxxxxxxxxx

Startled, she sat up, looking into the eyes of her brother and sister staring at Emma at the foot of her bed.

"Quick, run for momma. The earth is coming to an end!" shouted Emma. Her eyes fought the light filtering through the Venetian blinds, sweat beading on her forehead. Her senses did not fully comprehend why Mia and Dario were LOOKING at her.

Emma bit her lip, blood crawling down her chin. "Hold on, Mia and Dario, it's coming. Pray!" She bowed her head and sobbed. "Both of you need to get Lucky. Get him now!" Her face flooded with tears.

"Who's Lucky?" answered her brother.

"Yes, you gotta get Lucky, we're late."

"I wish I could. I keep getting crummy players."

Mia noticed her sister was placing her sneakers over her bare feet while still dressed in her pajamas.

"Are you okay, Emma?" asked Mia, worried about her sister.

"You two, the world is going to end, and Dario and I haven't got in our run. I'm going to ask you one last time to get Lucky!"

Tears appeared in Dario's eyes as he shouted, "Mom! Emma is still having one of her stupid fever dreams!" He continued to cry, frightened as he was last night.

"Don't call Emma stupid, Dario; she's not feeling well. And you should talk. Guess who had to change your sheets and soak your puddle pad in the tub yesterday. Was that stupid? No! And why? Because Mama says you sleep soundly, and it's too late when you wake in the morning.

"So is Emma 'stupid' when she gets a bad fever and it affects her mind, causing nightmares? No! And don't you forget! Now, little man, move to your room and get yourself dressed for school."

Mia's correction appeared to soothe the small boy. Dario hung his head while Mrs. Sacatti walked into the girls' room. He left to put on his school uniform, his eyes glistening while talking under his breath, "I'm never going to get a Sandy Koufax now."

"Oh, my goodness. God help us! Kids, your sister is suffering from a high fever. I need to help her out of her pajamas. Mia go to the restroom, soap up a hot face cloth, and wring it out. Bring a towel with you." Mia dashed out of the room

"Momma, Emma… Emma's delirious again. I'm worried about her," replied Mia, now helping her mother remove her sister's sweaty pajama top while Palmira washed her daughter's underarms and back. Get her other warm pajamas out of her drawer."

Palmira now placed her palm on Emma's forehead. "Dear God, you're still burning up, sweetheart. Mia, run again to the bathroom and get me a thermometer."

Mia returned in seconds as Mrs. Sacatti placed the thermometer in Emma's mouth. After waiting a minute, she looked at it and gasped, "One hundred and five decrees! I'm rushing Emma to my work to see Dr. Bishop. Mia, get another ice wrap out of the freezer and bring it to me." Mia did as told, returning in seconds. "Now honey, please do me a big favor and get your brother in the car while I dress Emma. I made each of you half an egg salad sandwich for breakfast. You'll have to eat them in the car."

First calling her husband at work she then placed the sandwiches in the car with Emma and Mia sitting in the front seat. Dario dug into one of the sandwiches sitting in the back of the Plymouth station wagon.

"Do you have to make noise when you eat, Dario?" said Emma, appearing semi-lucid with a frozen wrap covering her forehead.

Dario stuck out his tongue, half filled with soggy bread and eggs. His mother stared in the rearview mirror. "You behave yourself, Dario; you don't want me to pull this car over!"

"Mom, can I eat Emma's sandwich?" wondered Dario.

"Leave it alone, Dario; you've had enough. Pass the rest up front."

Don't push it, young man. That baseball card you want is beginning to fade. Dario sat up straight, listening to his mother.

Mia took small bites out of her egg salad sandwich as she watched Emma finish her sandwich remarkably fast. "Are you feeling better, Emma?"

"I'm getting better. Everything is fine, Mother. Could I go run now with Lucky?"

Who in the hell is Lucky? "Not dressed like that. I'm taking you to see Dr. Bishop and kids your father will drive you two to school from my work." Mrs. Sacatti slid her right hand over Emma's forehead. "You're still burning up, sweetheart. Dr. Bishop will give you a strong Tylenol to bring down that fever."

Dario asked, "Why does she keep saying, Lucky?"

Palmira pulled into her work at Dr. Howard Bishop's medical clinic, helped Emma out of the car, and brought her inside to see Dr. Bishop. Her other two children remained patiently in the clinic waiting room for their father with their school books on their lap.

Dr. Bishop, a Monday through Friday working general practitioner at eighty-two years old, employed only Palmira who learned not only to act as Bishop's secretary but emergency nurse as well.

In the meantime Howard Bishop sat with Palmira while asking Emma a few questions. He reassured Mrs. Sacatti that her daughter hadn't lost her mind. "As I said before, high fevers can bring on delirium and even hallucinations. Hopefully, this spray will bring the fever down, and she'll be fine. You need rest young lady, plenty of it if you're going to recover."

"Could she sleep in the backroom, doctor, so that I could keep an eye on her?"

"Of course. Emma I'm also going to spray some Midazolam up your nose. It'll help you sleep tight, dear."

After Mrs. Sacatti brought the medication Dr. Bishop sprayed the Midazolam into Emma's nostrils and then let her mother set up the bed and blankets in the backroom.

"Doctor Bishop, my husband is on his way to take my other children to school."

Eugenio soon arrived and dropped Dario and Mia off at school and returned to work. Emma slipped into a deep sleep in the backroom.

Palmira thought as she worked at her desk, typing, *Friday, only one more day until the weekend. Please stay with me, Lord.*

Late that morning at 10:30 a.m. Pacific Coast Time on Friday, November 22nd, 1963, Emma woke from her sleep her high fever still holding. "MOM! MOM!" she shouted.

Palmira tore away from her desk and rushed to the backroom.

Emma's chest heaved between each sob, her breath catching in ragged gasps. A rivulet streamed down her cheeks unchecked and relentless. Palmira held her daughter tight in her arms while covering a tissue over Emma's nose and chin.

"It happened, Mother!"

"What happened, dear?!"

"I don't know! Mother, I don't know!" Emma's throat tightened, a lump forming, making speech impossible for the thirteen-year-old to go on.

Palmira felt Emma's forehead and then placed a thermometer under her daughter's tongue, reading it within an appropriate amount of seconds. It read one hundred and four degrees.

———————

Televisions were turned on all over the world, and people in almost every country prayed for the recovery of the United States president.

At 1:00 p.m. central time, Walter Cronkite announced John Fitzgerald Kennedy had died.

Clued to their television much of the weekend, the 3rd, 7th, and 8th grade children of Eugenio and Palmira Sacatti sat closer together as one grieving family.

However, Dario, since Friday evening, kept insisting his mother and father allow him to open one of his three packs of baseball cards.

"Not during this crisis, Dario. You need to learn to show respect first," his mother said sternly, taking away any thoughts of her changing her mind.

On Saturday and into Sunday morning, the 3rd-grade boy, away from the ears of his mother, manipulated his father, convincing his father that ONE pack of cards couldn't hurt his "respect."

Officers marched Lee Harvey Oswald threw the basement hallway of the Dallas Police Department as the world looked on through universal media coverage. What looked like a gentleman dressed in a dark suit, a white shirt, a striped tie, and a distinctive grey fedora hat pulled out a .38 caliber Colt Cobra pistol and shot Oswald in the abdomen at close range. Lee Harvey died within a couple of hours.

There it lay, protected from the stain of inserted bubblegum resting between cards three and five, a based red card perfectly centered with a full picture of the coveted Dodger Sanford Braun Koufax.

Dario couldn't shout out any pleasure, not at a time when his sisters covered their faces, screaming at the live horror on the television, their hands draped over their eyes, protecting them from the outrage.

Shattering shrieks took away any discovered look from the broad smile underneath Dario's concealed mouth. *Thank you, God! Thank you! Wait 'til David Edwards knows I now got a Sandy Koufax. And Lonnie Price, I know how he'll be real happy.*

And, with much of the world stricken, one boy in the town of Long Beach, California, perhaps in the entire world, sat tickled that his prayers had been finally answered. In contrast, others prayed for the healing of an appalling disaster for a higher power to end this knawing sense of impending doom and insecurity.

Like the Sacattis, much of America and surrounding countries lived in a pervasive fear of violence and unexpected tragedy, coupled with a feeling of powerlessness to control their circumstances.

In time, the world traded their fear into a sincere heart of compassion, the world shrinking into more of a caring neighborhood. Politics and egos were set aside, and countries embraced the pillars of dignity and respect, similar to the stable values of Eugenia and Palmira Sacatti.

Requiring the utmost in patience, hope would return to America as it had to Dario Sacatti, and the world would dance once again as if nobody was watching.

Made in the USA
Las Vegas, NV
12 March 2025